Praise for
Little Beach Street Bakery

"I loved *Little Beach Street Bakery*.
Losing myself in Jenny Colgan's beautiful
pages is the most delicious, comforting,
satisfying treat I have had in ages."
—Jane Green

Praise for
Christmas at the
Cupcake Café

"Jenny Colgan's *Christmas at the Cupcake
Café* is an evocative sweet treat."
—Jojo Moyes, *New York Times* bestselling
author of *Me Before You* and *One Plus One*

"Like all of Jenny Colgan's books,
Christmas at the Cupcake Café is sheer
indulgence from start to finish."
—Sophie Kinsella, #1 *New York Times*
bestselling author of *Shopaholic to the Stars*

Also by Jenny Colgan

SUNRISE BY THE SEA
CHRISTMAS AT THE ISLAND HOTEL
500 MILES FROM YOU
THE BOOKSHOP ON THE SHORE
THE ENDLESS BEACH
CHRISTMAS AT LITTLE BEACH STREET BAKERY
THE BOOKSHOP ON THE CORNER
LITTLE BEACH STREET BAKERY
THE LOVELIEST CHOCOLATE SHOP IN PARIS
MEET ME AT THE CUPCAKE CAFÉ
THE GOOD, THE BAD, AND THE DUMPED
DIAMONDS ARE A GIRL'S BEST FRIEND
WEST END GIRLS
WHERE HAVE ALL THE BOYS GONE?
MY VERY '90S ROMANCE
AMANDA'S WEDDING

Summer AT Little Beach Street
BAKERY

A NOVEL

JENNY COLGAN

WILLIAM MORROW
An Imprint of HarperCollinsPublishers

SUMMER AT LITTLE BEACH STREET BAKERY. Copyright © 2016 by Jenny Colgan. All rights reserved. Printed in the United States of America. No part of this book may be used or reproduced in any manner whatsoever without written permission except in the case of brief quotations embodied in critical articles and reviews. For information, address HarperCollins Publishers, 195 Broadway, New York, NY 10007.

Originally published in Great Britain in 2015 by Sphere.

First William Morrow mass market printing: August 2021
First William Morrow paperback printing: March 2016
First William Morrow hardcover printing: March 2016

Print Edition ISBN: 978-0-06-307373-9
Digital Edition ISBN: 978-0-06-237125-6

Cover design by Amy Halperin
Cover photographs © Paul Boyes/Alamy Stock Photo (bakery); © Getty Images

Images of pastries and bird copyright © Ioza via Shutterstock, Inc.
Image of awning copyright © Lareen via Shutterstock, Inc.

William Morrow and HarperCollins are registered trademarks of HarperCollins Publishers in the United States of America and other countries.

21 22 23 24 25 CPI 10 9 8 7 6 5 4 3 2 1

To my darling Auntie Maura and Uncle Mike.
Please cancel the snake delivery now.
Thanks.

Summer AT Little Beach Street
BAKERY

A Word from Jenny

Hello! And welcome to the Little Beach Street Bakery ... if you've been here before, lovely to see you again! If it's your first time, well, you are so welcome, and I hope you are hungry. Let me give you a quick catch-up before we get started. (Neil fans: don't worry. He's back.)

Okay, so Polly lost her business in Plymouth and had to start all over again. She moved to a coastal town in Cornwall, where the tide comes in twice a day and covers the causeway. When she couldn't find a job, she started baking bread, because that's what she loves to do, and soon incurred the wrath of Mrs. Manse, who ran the town bakery (very badly).

Anyway, eventually Polly won her around and started working there. Meanwhile, she had a brief affair with one of the fishermen, Tarnie, then found out to her utter horror that he was married. He later died in a terrible storm, and it took—and is still taking—everyone a very long time to get over it.

Polly fell in love, finally, with Huckle, a big American chap who makes his own honey. She also inadvertently adopted a puffin and has, probably against her better judgment, just decided to buy a lighthouse.

Right, I think we're up to date! I do hope you enjoy *Summer at Little Beach Street Bakery;* I so loved writing it.

A Quick Word about the Setting

Cornwall to me is a place of the imagination as much as a real home to lots of people because I spent so much time there as a child. To me, it is like a version of Narnia or any of the other imaginary lands I liked to visit—I was absolutely obsessed with *Over Sea, Under Stone,* and of course the Famous Five and Malory Towers.

We used to stay in old tin-miners' cottages near Polperro. My mother was a great Daphne du Maurier fan, and she used to put me and my two brothers to sleep in the little narrow beds and tell us bloodcurdling stories of shipwrecks and pirates and gold and wreckers, and we would be utterly thrilled and chilled and one of us, probably my littlest brother—although he would probably say me—would be up half the night with nightmares.

Compared to chilly Scotland, sunny Cornwall was like paradise to me. Every year, we were bought those big foam body surfboards as a special treat, and we would get into the water first thing in the morning and body surf, body surf, body surf until physically hauled out, sunburnt along the crossed strap lines of my swimming costume, to eat a gritty sandwich wrapped in cling film.

Later my dad would barbecue fish over the little home-built barbie he constructed every year from bricks and a grill, and I would sit in the high sweet grass, read books and get bitten by insects.

And after that (because you get to stay up very late on your holidays), we'd drive down to Mousehole or St. Ives and eat ice cream while strolling along the harbor looking at the art galleries. Or we'd eat hot salty fried potatoes, or fudge, the flavors of which I was constantly obsessed with, even though fudge invariably makes me feel sick.

They were blissful times, and it was such a joy to revisit them when I started writing my Mount Polbearne series. We went on a day trip—as required by law, I think, of anyone visiting Cornwall—to St. Michael's Mount, and I remember being gripped and fascinated by the old stone road disappearing under the waves. It was the most romantic and magical thing I could possibly imagine, and it has been such a joy setting my books there. If I can convey through my books even a fraction of the happiness Cornwall has brought me in my life . . . well, I'll be absolutely delighted.

Jenny xxx

Prologue

When I sleep, which I can't, I can't ever sleep, I dream about him. I dream about him being totally stupid. Like, he's in a washing machine or something and I'm saying, get out of the washing machine, you prat. But he won't get out of the washing machine, he's all tiny and in the washing machine, and he gets smaller and smaller until he disappears."

"That's totally normal," said the calm, educated West Country voice.

"You say everything's totally normal," said Selina, pushing back her short hair crossly. "I could come in here and say, "I ran over two hedgehogs on the way here because they reminded me of his hair. One by accident, one on purpose," and you'd say, "That's totally normal."

"Did you do that?"

"No, but I might have. You'd probably still say it was normal."

"There is nothing normal about grief, Selina. It is common. But it is never normal."

Selina let out a long sigh.

"Why can't I . . . why can't I get over it? Start getting over it? Everyone else wants me to have got over it bloody ages ago. I can see it in their faces. It's embarrassing for them. I want to get over it. I want to get to sleep without drinking too much wine, and wake up without seeing the face of my bloody dead husband in the washing machine and stop bumming everyone out all the time."

"Where are you living now?" said the voice smoothly, as if Selina's outburst hadn't happened.

Selina shrugged.

"Don't know. I think I'm going to give up the Manchester lease. It's getting more expensive, and I don't feel any more settled there than I did anywhere else."

"Maybe it's time to think of going . . . home? Your home, or Tarnie's home?"

"I'm never going back to that place," said Selina, shivering. "I never want to go back there."

Chapter One

"Stop it," Polly said in a warning voice. "It's not funny." Neil ignored her and continued to beat on the little high window with his beak until she could be persuaded to go over and give him a snack.

He was outside the lighthouse they had moved into the previous month, all three of them together, Polly, Neil the puffin, and Huckle, Polly's American boyfriend, who had parked his motorbike and sidecar at the bottom of the tower. It was their only mode of transport.

The lighthouse hadn't been lived in for a long time, not since the lamps were electrified in the late seventies. It had four floors and a circular staircase that ran around the sides, thus making it, as Huckle had pointed out more than once, the single draftiest place in human history. They were both getting very fit running up and down it. One floor held the heavy machinery that had once turned the workings, which couldn't be removed. On the top floor, just below the light itself, was their sitting room, which had views right across the bay and, on the other side, back toward Mount Polbearne, the tidal island where they lived and worked, with its causeway to the mainland that covered and uncovered itself with the tides.

From these windows you could see the Little Beach Street Bakery, the ruined shop that Polly had revitalized when she had moved to the village just over two years ago, getting over a failed business and a failed relationship back on the mainland.

She hadn't originally expected to do much in Mount Polbearne except sit and lick her wounds until she was ready to head back into the fray again, back to working a corporate lifestyle; hadn't for a moment thought that in the tumbledown flat above the shop she would come back to life by practicing her favorite hobby—baking bread—and that this would turn into a career when she reopened the old closed-down bakery.

It wasn't the most lucrative of careers, and the hours were long, but the setting was so wonderful, and her work so appreciated, by both the townspeople and the tourists, that she had found something much more satisfying than money: she had found what she was meant to be doing with her life. Well, most of the time she thought that. Sometimes she looked around at the very basic kitchen she had installed (her old flat in Plymouth had sold, and she'd managed to get the lighthouse at a knockdown price mostly, as Lance the estate agent had pointed out, because only an absolutely crazy person could possibly want to live in a drafty, inaccessible tower with a punishing light shining out of it) and wondered if she'd ever manage to fix the window frames, the window frames being number one on a list of about four thousand things that urgently needed doing.

Huckle had offered to buy the place with her, but she had resisted. She had worked too hard to be independent. Once before she had shared everything, been entirely enmeshed financially with someone. It had not worked out, and she was in no mood to repeat the experience.

Right now, she wanted to sit in her eyrie of a sitting room at the very top of the house, drink tea, eat a cheese twist and simply relax and enjoy the view: the sea, ever changing; clouds scudding past so close she could touch them; the little fishing boats bobbing out across the water in faded greens and browns, their winches and nets heavy behind them, looking tiny and fragile against the vast expanse of the sea. She just needed five minutes' peace and quiet before heading down to the bakery to relieve her colleague Jayden for the lunchtime shift.

Neil, the little puffin who had crashed into her life one night in a storm and remained there ever since, did not agree. He found the activity of flying outside, high up, and still being able to see her through the window utterly amazing, and liked to do it again and again, sometimes taking off to fly all the way around the lighthouse and come back in the other side, sometimes pecking at the glass because Huckle thought it was funny to feed him tidbits out of the window even though Polly had told him not to.

Polly put down her book and moved over to the window, struck as she never ceased to be—she wondered if she would ever grow tired of it—by the amazing cast of the sun silvering in and out behind the clouds over the waves, the gentle cawk of the seagulls, and the whistling wind, which could turn thunderous on winter days. She still couldn't quite believe she lived here. She opened the old-fashioned, single-glazed window with its heavy latch.

"Come in then," she said, but Neil fluttered excitedly and tried to peck in between her fingers in case she had a tasty treat for him.

"No!" she said. "You are a fat puffin and no mistake. Come inside and stop tapping."

Neil thought this was a brilliant game and shot off around the lighthouse once more to show her what he could do. When he landed back on the windowsill, his big black eyes were expectant.

"Oh for goodness' sake," said Polly, then—and she would never have done this if Huckle had been there— she leaned over and gave him a scrap of the cheese twist, which the little bird wolfed down happily, pecking up the few remaining crumbs. He pecked so hard he ended up hopping backward and slipping off the window ledge.

"Neil!" shouted Polly, then felt a complete idiot as he flapped his wings and fluttered back up to window level.

"You are scaring the life out of me," she said. "Come in or go out, not both."

Neil chose to come in. He landed on the floor, then waddled across the room, inspecting the rough-hewn wooden floor carefully just in case there were any crumbs that Polly had missed.

"Right," said Polly. "I'm going back to work. Behave yourself."

She took a glance around the sitting room, making sure she had everything. Once you got to the bottom of the lighthouse, you very much didn't want to find you'd forgotten something and have to go all the way back up again. Huckle wanted them to get a fireman's pole, but Polly was highly resistant.

The little round room didn't contain much furniture apart from her absolutely lovely old posh sofa that she'd brought with her from Plymouth, and that had had to be completely unscrewed and taken apart to get it up the stairs. It had taken most of the day, but it was worth it, Polly thought.

On the floor below was a bedroom with a tiny bathroom hollowed out next to it; then came the machinery floor, then the ground floor with its basic kitchen, a bathroom and another sitting room. There was also a separate low building, an ugly pebble-dashed flat-roofed space with a couple of rooms, but they didn't quite know what to do with that. A little garden led down through the rocks; Huckle was going to take a shot at it, although he wasn't confident they'd manage to grow much more than mussels and seaweed. Someone had put little rows of seashells following the steps down from the lighthouse and across to the main path, and they made a pretty sight as Polly jumped down onto the cobbles, around the harbor wall and into Mount Polbearne proper.

It wasn't far, but at high tide and on stormy days you could get pretty wet going from one to the other as the waves smashed over the top of the sea wall and the spray filled the air with salt.

Today, however, was breezy but clear, a few small clouds scudding past the high lighthouse windows, a hint of sun threatening to come out but never quite managing it. The tide was out, which meant the road to the mainland was open, its brown cobbles glistening with water, and the fresh scent of the sea was heavy on the passing wind.

The little town of Mount Polbearne was perched impractically on the slope of the island, with everything leading up higgledy-piggledy to the ruined roofless church at the very top of the village.

The roads were cobbled and steep and winding; it was possible to bring your car into the town, but not advisable. Most people used the mainland car park and walked the few hundred meters. Some of the fishermen ran a taxi boat for anyone who got really stuck, but the majority of the locals knew the ebbing and flowing of the tides as well as they did the rhythm of the sunrise and sunset and adjusted their plans accordingly.

And life was simpler here on the island. It couldn't not be, when there was no such thing as Wi-Fi here (several people had suggested to Polly that she get it put in, but the telephone company had politely explained that they'd need to run an underwater cable and it would cost about £100,000 and would she like to contribute, so that had rather put the kibosh on that), or Internet shopping, or nightclubs or hen parties or airport flight paths or free newspapers.

Instead there were the rows of little gray stone houses, meandering ever upward, some with flashy new glass extensions and roof terraces and balconies made out of wire, courtesy of intrepid second-homers who came for the weekend and put up with much ribbing and overcharging from the locals. There was the old pub, the Red Lion, which was based around an old courtyard, and still had tie-up rings and troughs for the horses from long ago. There was Andy's fish and chip shop, with its picture of a huge fish and all the fishermen lined up grinning cheerily, which did the best herring and the freshest, crispiest chips—with extra bits—that would burn your fingers, then sting them with salt and vinegar. He sold Fanta and Tizer and dandelion and burdock, and it was a short hop over the cobbled Beach Street to

sit and eat on the harbor wall, watching the water and
fending off the seagulls.

There was Muriel's minimart, which sold absolutely
everything, and Patrick the vet, who shared his consulting office with a young GP called Callie, who only came
in twice a week; and the old bakery that used to be run
by Mrs. Manse, who had been Polly's landlady when
she first arrived in Mount Polbearne and had made her
life incredibly difficult by refusing to let her bake any
bread. Now she had retired and lived with her equally
bad-tempered sister in Truro, leaving Polly free to run
her own bakery as she wished.

The last place on the quay was a flashy new restaurant, too expensive for the original dwellers, but very
popular with visitors. It specialized in the fresh fish the
men unloaded from their boats every morning. At this
early hour nets were being mended, catches being tal-
lied up, and a couple of the fishermen waved to Polly as
she went past, asking what flavor of michette (a type of
small loaf very popular with the working men) she was
making that day. Then they all shouted a hello to Neil,
who, Polly realized crossly, was following her to work
again. It wasn't good for him to come to the bakery: customers gave him too many tidbits, and despite the fact
that her kitchen was utterly spotless—thanks to Jayden,
her assistant—if a health inspector ever came past and
caught so much as a whiff of seabird, she'd be in trouble.
The fact that nobody could possibly arrive on Mount
Polbearne without absolutely everybody noticing was
not, she had told Jayden sternly, the point.

It had been almost a year since the great storm, a
massive hooley that had blown up from nearly nowhere,
wrecked the fleet, and cost the loss of Cornelius "Tarnie"
Tarnforth, captain of the *Trochilus,* and, briefly, Polly's

lover. The day had not yet come when Polly could walk along the stretch of boats without remembering him. It had taken the town a long time to heal.

Polly dinged the bell of the Little Beach Street Bakery, with its pretty pale gray facade—painted by her ex, Chris—and its lovely italic writing: *Proprietor, Ms. P. Waterford.* She rarely looked at that without feeling a wave of pride. There was a small queue of people already waiting, and Jayden was dishing up the warm morning loaves. Today there was a choice of bread, and the heavy sourdough that was a harder sell but that made, in Polly's opinion, wonderful toast.

"Hey!" said Jayden. "Yes, everything came up very nicely. Except, uh, the chorizo michette. I had to . . . um, I had to . . . It was over-baked."

Polly looked at him sternly.

"Was it really, Jayden?"

She pulled off her coat and hung it on a hook, then went around the other side of the counter to get scrubbed up. Looking back, she saw Neil waiting patiently outside the door, occasionally hopping from foot to foot. He would do this until a customer came and let him in, which they always did. Not for the first time, she wondered about the availability of puffin obedience classes.

"Yes," said Jayden, his round cheeks going suspiciously pink. The customers waited patiently, scanning the heavy old-fashioned glass cabinets to choose their cream buns for later.

Polly raised an eyebrow.

"They were really good," said Jayden in a low voice. "I'm sorry. I tried to only eat one."

The problem was, Jayden was a wonderful member of staff. Prompt, polite, kind, efficient, and he cleaned like a demon; years working on the fishing boats had made him precise and immaculate. He wasn't at all handsome, but he was very sweet and charming, and everybody liked him.

He was also incredibly grateful not to be out with the fleet anymore, which he had hated. He loved having an indoor job with regular hours. He was honest with the money and nice with the customers (at least the local customers; he was getting slightly better with the incomers and holidaymakers, with whom he was either brusque or tongue-tied).

But he did have a terrible, terrible habit of chomping on the stock.

"It's not like I don't know you're doing it," said Polly, indicating his belly, growing ever stouter underneath his gray apron.

"I know. I'm sorry."

He really was sorry too, his face bright pink. He had grown a mustache last year for Movember, and everyone said it suited him—it rather did—so he had kept it, and now he flushed to the tips of it.

"I don't mind you eating a bit," said Polly. "But you know, that was meat. It's expensive."

Despite the mustache, Jayden looked about seven years old as he stared at the floor.

"You're not being cross with that nice young man," said Mrs. Corning, the reverend's widow. "He's a blessing, so he is."

The other ladies in the queue agreed. For some of them, Polly suspected, having a flirt and a chat with Jayden was the highlight of their days.

"He's a very hungry blessing," grumbled Polly.

"And she's left that bird of hers outside," said another lady disapprovingly. They all muttered among themselves. Polly felt like rolling her eyes but didn't. To some people she would always be the new girl, she knew. She moved along to the next person in the queue.

"What can I get you?" she asked politely.

"Have you got any of those yummy loaves with the little bits of sausage in them? I love them."

"No," said Polly, with a last glare at Jayden, who pretended she wasn't there and suddenly looked very busy. "We don't."

The shop bell dinged.

"Hey, Poll, you left Neil outside!" said a big booming American voice.

The shop, very small to begin with, suddenly felt smaller still as the shadow of Huckle fell over the counter. He was very tall, long-legged, broad in the shoulders, with a thick head of yellow hair that made him look larger still. Even now Polly was sometimes amazed that he was her boyfriend; he looked like he'd stepped out of an advert that would have lots of desert and cacti and cowboy hats in it.

"Seriously, man," said Huckle. Neil was sitting on Huckle's jacket sleeve—he didn't normally do this—gazing at Polly with a wounded expression.

"I didn't leave him anywhere," said Polly, exasperated. "Birds aren't meant to be in the workplace. He should be hopping over to the rocks and trying to pick up a lady puffin."

"Or another boy puffin," said Huckle. "I don't think you should be prejudiced."

Polly looked straight at him.

"Are you calling me a bird homophobe?"

"I'm just saying we need to be open to all of Neil's choices."

"Except the one about letting him in the shop!"

Huckle sighed. The old ladies gathered around to

examine Neil (or, Polly reckoned mischievously, to get their hands on Huckle's bicep). When they'd finally cleared, she leaned over to kiss her boyfriend.

"Hey," she said, breathing in his lovely warm scent, slightly tinged with the oil from the motorbike he rode everywhere. "Not out and about this morning?"

Huckle shook his head. "Sure am! I just popped in to tell you: Dubose is coming."

Polly bit her lip.

"Seriously?"

Her heart started to beat a little faster. She'd never met Dubose. She'd never met any of Huckle's family. Dubose was his younger brother, and something of a black sheep.

"What's he up to?"

Huckle rolled his eyes.

"Don't let me start. Apparently he needed a break."

Polly looked confused.

"Isn't he a farmer?"

"Yes," said Huckle. "Exactly. Farmers don't get breaks!"

"Like bakers," said Polly.

"Except tougher," said Huckle.

"Oh yeah."

Huckle shook his head.

"He's left Clemmie in charge." Clemmie was Dubose's girlfriend.

"Isn't she any good?"

"She's great! She's fine. But running a farm . . . it takes a lot of effort."

Huckle's brows drew together. It wasn't often that he looked cross. Polly thought it was cute.

"When is he showing up?"

"A couple of weeks, I think. He's 'bumming about.'"

Huckle gave a resigned smile. "He doesn't like making plans or being tied down by anything like notice. It's okay if he stays, right?"

"Well of course, but oh wow. Do you think he's going to like me?"

Huckle rolled his eyes.

"Dubose likes everyone," he said. Polly looked at him.

"Is that a note of jealousy in your voice?" she asked slyly.

"Is there a new young man coming?" said Mrs. Corning. "Oh, it's all excitement around here these days."

When Polly and Huckle had first met, he had been a beekeeper nearby, and she had sold his honey through the shop. After their first attempt at romance hadn't worked out, he'd gone home to his native Savannah and worked in an office job there. But he hadn't been able to readapt to an indoor, air-conditioned, corporate life after six months in the fresh open air of Cornwall, and he had come back again—his father had been born in the UK, which helped a lot with the passport situation.

Now, with so many people downsizing and moving to the country, where they had perhaps a couple of goats, some chickens and a hive or two, he'd become a traveling apiarist, consulting and helping people concerned about maintaining bee stocks and reversing the trend of the declining bee population. He also still had an interest in his original cottage, which was now occupied by an elderly couple who happily enjoyed the flowers and let Huckle manage the hives in return for a couple of jars of honey every month or so. It was a very cheerful arrangement. He wasn't making a lot of money, but then apart from a bit of diesel for the bike, and a big veggie box once a week from a local farmer, they lived pretty simply, him and Poll. They didn't need much. Well, he thought occasionally, actually, to do up the lighthouse and buy out Polly's business properly—she was still under license to Mrs. Manse, the original owner, and had to funnel a great deal of the profits that way—they would need a ton of money. But they didn't have it, and that was absolutely fine, he told himself, because what they did have was more than enough.

Chapter Two

"Okay," said Jayden. "I'm off to the other shop. Check on the mainlander."

Polly rolled her eyes.

"Jayden, everyone on the entire earth is a mainlander. There are seven billion mainlanders and seven hundred Polbearnites. You just can't separate the world out like that."

Jayden was busy with his broom, but she could tell from the cast of his forehead that he disagreed with her.

"Let me go and see her," said Polly. "I can walk Huckle to his bike."

"That means she wants to be rid of me," said Huckle, twinkling at the old ladies.

"I don't want to be rid of you," said Polly. "I want to be rid of Neil. I'm just hoping he'll follow you."

Sure enough, as they left together, Neil hopped happily into the sidecar. There was no doubt he enjoyed the ride.

Huckle grinned back at Polly.

"Do you want to cook?" she asked.

Huckle shrugged. "How about you cook and I run and get all the condiments and things you've forgotten from four stories below."

"Deal," said Polly, kissing him again. Huckle glanced at his watch, then hopped on the big bike. Neil stuck his head to the side to enjoy the slipstream.

"I don't know what that bird thinks he is," grumbled Polly, but she enjoyed watching them zoom off at high speed—accompanied by an infernal noise—toward the causeway, which was still uncovered from the morning tide.

She took a breath of fresh salty air deep into her lungs as the clouds danced like clean laundry across the sky, and wondered what Huckle's brother would be like. She'd never had a brother of her own; maybe it could be like that.

She made her way down Beach Street. Even though the island was so small, it supported two bakeries. The Polbearne bakery, the original one, still sold sandwiches, toasties and more traditional fare—iced biscuits, sponge cake and fancies—whereas Polly had been allowed to make her own way in her little bakery, with artisan breads, interesting olive loaves and savory tarts. Now that Mrs. Manse had retired, Polly was technically in charge of both shops.

It was the clearest of spring days. In the springtime, Polly really couldn't imagine living anywhere except in Mount Polbearne. Mind you, she felt like that in the summertime too, with the clatter of buckets and spades and the smell of suncream, and ice cream, and little lost sunglasses in pink and blue plastic left carefully on the harbor wall in case their owners returned to pick them up. And she liked the autumn, when the surfers came to make the most of the waves off Breakwater Point in their black costumes like seals, and turned up at her bakery freezing and absolutely starving. She served coffee and hot soup then, when they were quieter after the summer holidays were over and the children were back at school. And she liked the winter, when it was absolutely windy and freezing and pointless going anywhere, and she and Huckle would snuggle up together and watch box sets of American television shows and eat hot buttered toast and drink gallons of tea in their little eyrie as the storms raged outside. It was impossible to avoid the changing seasons on an island; impossible to insulate yourself from the world like you could in the city, in climate-controlled offices, under fluorescent lighting, with the occasional scrub of a park square covered in cigarette ends.

Here, she liked it all.

Polly had never imagined two years ago, when her entire life was in ruins, a blackened husk on the floor, that she could ever reach a state of such contentment, so in tune with the seasons and the days of her life. Even on the most freezing of mornings, or after a backbreaking stint with the oven, on days that didn't end until she'd done all the cashing-up late into the night, or the long hours sweating over VAT returns and deciding what was a cake and what was a biscuit; even when it rained for days and days on end while the rest of the country had bright sunshine, or when she wanted something new to wear and realized that nobody would deliver anything and it was too far to drive and she couldn't afford anything anyway; even then, she never regretted changing her life so radically, couldn't truly believe her luck. She also reckoned that she had had her share of bad luck, and that nothing more was likely to go wrong.

The universe, in general, has absolutely no truck with this kind of thinking.

Chapter Three

Flora Larson, who worked in the old bakery, always had the look of someone expecting to be in trouble at any moment. She was thin and stooped, with a hang-dog stance, and had a way of peeking up through an overlong fringe that simply looked guilty, even though there was a pretty face hiding in there somewhere.

But she could bake, which was a huge help to Polly. Jayden could do simpler things, but Flora had a touch with the dough, even though she had a tendency to mumble at customers, which Polly had asked her not to do, and she fiddled with her hair constantly, which made Polly worry about hygiene. Mrs. Manse would have eaten her for breakfast. Also, Flora's timekeeping was atrocious. Polly didn't want to make a fuss, but she thought it was very bad form when customers at one bakery had to pop into the other because they couldn't get hold of a sandwich.

This morning Flora was standing in the middle of a very untidy shop, with crumbs from yesterday not swept up, a disenchanted look on her face.

"Hi, Flora!" said Polly, trying not to sound exasperated. Jobs were hard to come by in this part of the world, particularly out of season. Polly had always sworn not to be a horrible mean old boss, but Flora did wind her up. Huckle thought she was hilarious.

"My ankles is soaking," Flora was saying crossly, staring at the floor. Sure enough, when Polly looked closer, she could see that Flora was standing in what was almost a puddle, her shoes and socks soaking wet and dripping on the floor.

"Did you mistime the tides again?" said Polly.

"They don't print it right on them almanacs," said Flora. "They just gets it wrong."

"It always seems all right to me," said Polly mildly.

"That's because you've got a posh watch and that," said Flora pertly. It was a new experience to Polly that somebody thought that because she was the boss she was rich and powerful.

"Well, shall we get on with setting up?" said Polly, as Patrick the vet strolled in for his morning scone.

"Hello, Polly," he said. "How's that ridiculous bird of yours?"

Polly had been about to say that she was thinking of giving Neil a job in the bakery, but managed to bite her tongue in front of Flora.

"You know, daft as a brush," she said.

"I have never known anyone keep a seabird as a pet," he said, shaking his head. "Never known anything like it."

Polly smiled. She liked hearing compliments about Neil.

"But don't let any of those cats near him," Patrick added, shivering. "Nasty creatures."

Patrick's dislike of cats had never held back his veterinary career, and he rarely bothered to hide it.

"I got a nice cat," said Flora, still standing there as Polly wrapped up a fresh scone still warm from the oven.

"This smells amazing," she said. "You know, Flora, you should go on *Bake Off*."

Flora giggled, her wet feet forgotten.

"My ma says that!" she said. "Reckon it would be nice being on television."

"*You* should do it," said Patrick to Polly.

"You are joking," said Polly. "I can't think of anything more horrifying. Plus, I think if being a baker is actually your job, you can't enter it. Otherwise Paul Hollywood would just win every year, don't you think?"

Patrick glanced at Flora.

"You should get out of those socks and shoes," he said. "You'll catch a chill."

Flora scowled. "I don't know why you can't just have your shop on the mainland, like normal people."

Polly picked up a tray of scones and sandwiches and gave Flora the loaves and savory twists she had brought with her. Division of labor was the most efficient way to run things, although she was under no illusions that it was particularly efficient at all.

"Can you tidy and clean up in here, please? You'll have the lunchtime crowd in soon enough, and there's a few day trippers. And can you prep for tomorrow as well?"

It was Friday. Saturday was a big day for day trippers.

Sunday they were traditionally closed. Polly was trying to figure out a way to open on a Sunday for the massive throughput but then take Mondays off. Having thought about this a lot, she had settled on the fact that nobody who lived on Mount Polbearne wanted that to happen and therefore they had better stay exactly as they were if she was to get a day off at all. Some things you didn't mess with. She was considering getting an extra member of staff to cover the summer season, and maybe even a café license to extend the Little Beach Street Bakery . . .

She smiled wryly at her own ridiculous ambitions. At the moment she couldn't get the two members of staff she did have to either stop eating the profits or avoid getting drowned on their way in to work. Possibly best not to leap ahead too soon.

As it was a fine day, Polly headed straight back to the Little Beach Street Bakery. On good days, it had queues out the door at lunchtime, because everyone wanted to eat their lunch sitting on the harbor wall in the sunshine. The fishermen had a kind of kitty situation going on, and all ate whatever sandwiches Polly had made for them.

"Hey," she said. "Today I have warm giant sausage rolls with ketchup and mustard on the side, plus a little pot of beans."

Archie, the fishing boat skipper, tried to smile.

"That sounds absolutely champion," he said.

"You tired?"

The fishermen were always tired. They had to land their catches early in the morning to make sure the freshest of fish were available for the restaurants that day. They worked extraordinarily long hours and still had to live their lives in the daytime. There were EU regulations on how much they could catch, but none on how long they could work, and it showed.

Archie had taken over *Trochilus II,* the boat that had replaced the original one that Tarnie had captained. He also had a baby boy, his fourth, called William. He looked knackered.

"Oh, you know," he said, handing over a pile of coins. "William's a lively one. Then the others have got to that age . . . they've got sports days and outings, and you know the schools are always on holiday, right? Children at school *never actually go to school.* When I was a kid I remember being at school the entire time. But now they don't ever go. It's called inset days, and it means, can you arrange some extra childcare, please."

Jayden served the rest of the queue while Polly got Archie a coffee from her beloved espresso machine. He obviously needed it. She passed it over with four sachets of sugar, and he emptied in all of them.

"And then the wife wants to go out to dinner and says I'm no fun, and . . . "

This was a long speech from Archie, who was normally a taciturn man, and he trailed off before it was finished and turned slightly pink.

Polly nodded. "I understand," she said. "You guys work so hard. Can't you sleep on the boat?" Sometimes Tarnie used to snatch a quick half hour as they headed out to the fishing fields, before the real work began.

Archie winced. "Maybe after I've been in the job a while," he said. "Right now, it's taking all my energy just to stay afloat. Me *and* the boat."

Polly nodded and patted him gently on the shoulder.

"I know," she said. "It's a tough living."

Archie looked out of the window. The fishing boats

made such a pretty sight, all pitched up in a row, their masts jangling in the faint breeze.

"I didn't . . . Until we started getting all these tourists," he said, "I didn't realize how soft other people had it."

Fishing, Polly knew, was in your blood or it wasn't. It was a vocation you were born to; otherwise, it was just too tough.

"It's not like that really, you know," she said. "You see people coming here in big cars and relaxing and walking along the beach and eating ice cream and you think that's what they do, but it isn't. It's their holidays, that's all, like when you went to Cyprus that time."

"Four years ago," grunted Archie.

"They all have their troubles too. Working really long hours in horrible offices for horrible bosses. Moving paper around all day and hating it. Commuting an hour there and an hour home every single day to do a job they hate that means they never see their own children."

"I see too much of the buggers," said Archie.

Polly grinned. "That's because you're a good dad," she said. "Now, I'll take the sausage rolls down. You go sit on the bench over there and have a snooze, and I'll wake you up in an hour."

Archie looked at her.

"I don't want the lads to think I'm slacking."

He was trying so hard to live up to the memory of Tarnie, and it was taking its toll.

"I'll tell them you're helping me shift something in the shop. Something really large and dirty and heavy," said Polly. "Covered in spiders. Okay?"

Archie nodded thankfully, and Polly walked him around the corner to an out-of-the-way bench between the old town cross and an empty stone horse trough. It was a sunny spot, and Polly noticed that his eyes closed almost immediately.

Down by the harbor wall, the wind was gustier. The rest of the crew were on the boat. Dave had started out as a beekeeper, sent by an agency last year, but his terrible fear of bees had meant he had ended up on the sea instead. He had turned out to be born to the job; a genuine fisherman who loved the water and, as they said, could sniff out fish. Then there was little Kendall, the youngest, who grinned endearingly at Polly, his eyes fixed on her paper bag, and Sten, who was new, a big Scandinavian chap Polly barely knew.

"Hey," she said. "Archie's just helping me with something."

Kendall grabbed at the bag and inhaled it.

"Oh, that smells good good good!" he said. "Did you bring us sweets for afters?"

"I don't sell sweets," Polly told him for the millionth time.

"Is Archie having a rest?" said Dave.

"No, he's—"

"Because he needs a rest."

The others nodded their agreement.

"He keeps trying to do everything," said Kendall. "It's okay. He's fine. He just gets a bit panicky. Tarnie wasn't panicky."

"He wasn't," said Polly, and they were silent for a second.

"He was a bit shouty, though," said Kendall. "Archie isn't shouty."

"Well, there you go," said Polly. "When he gets back, tell him you knew he was working; otherwise he'll never take ten seconds off ever again."

"He has to," said Sten, speaking for the first time.

His accent was slow and deliberate. "It is dangerous to run a boat on not enough sleep, *ja*? He needs to make himself relax."

Polly smiled. "I've never understood how anyone's meant to make themselves do that," she said. "But yes, I agree."

She went back and zipped through the rest of the lunchtime rush with Jayden, people cheerfully queuing halfway up the quay. This made her happy every time she saw it. The fact that people were there, day after day, handing over money for something she'd made with her own hands! Sometimes it didn't quite seem real; she wanted to rush up to someone eating a bun and say, "I made that, you know!"

She managed to avoid the temptation.

Once they'd cleaned up after lunch, if everything had gone—and it usually had—they'd close. Very early starts to get everything ready on time meant that by 2 p.m. Polly had normally already been on her feet for nine hours, and there was still cashing-up to do. Huckle tried to schedule his appointments so that he could sometimes nip back for an hour or two and, for the only time all day, they could relax, laze in bed for an hour, chat and laugh. Then he would be out again and Polly would cash up, start setting the dough for the next day, make supper and begin all over again in the morning.

Today, as she walked back into the empty lighthouse—it felt even emptier when Neil wasn't there—she could hear the home phone ringing. She furrowed her brow. She did use the home phone from time to time— the mobile signal could be a little erratic—but not that often, and certainly not in the daytime. She'd spoken to her mum yesterday, and everything was fine there. It must be Huckle; he must have been held up somewhere.

Polly mounted the stairs two at a time, wondering how long the phone would ring for. There was no point in rushing, she thought as she rounded the first landing. Getting up took as long as getting up took, and if she tried to rush, she wouldn't have enough puff to speak when she did make it up there.

The phone stopped, then instantly started again moments later. Polly swallowed and carried on. This wasn't a good sign. Unless it was a particularly committed salesperson.

She swung around the balustrade into the very top room, below the lamp itself. The phone had been there when they'd moved in and they hadn't changed it. Polly rather liked it. It was obviously old coastguard issue, in a bureaucratic gray color with stubby white buttons, many of which had mysterious functions she didn't understand. It also had a stern *brring brring* that reminded her of black-and-white war films.

She picked it up.

"Hello?"

The voice on the other end was quavering but strong.

"Is that Miss Waterford?" it demanded formally.

"Uh, yes."

"This is Janet Lange. Gillian Manse's sister."

"Of course," said Polly, steadying herself against the sofa, a chill entering her heart. "Is everything okay?"

"Only," the voice went on, as if it hadn't heard her, "only we've had a bit of trouble, you see."

"What's happened?"

Polly looked out of the window at the seagulls circling peacefully, at the tiny crests on some of the waves. Everything was as tranquil and peaceful as it always was.

"Well, I'm afraid Gillian has . . . passed on," said her sister.

There was a silence.

Even though Mrs. Manse had been old, and somewhat irascible, she'd still seemed a very strong figure to Polly. Certainly not somebody who could simply pass away or cease to be: she was solid, formidably so.

"But there was nothing wrong with her," said Polly. She found her hand at her face. "Oh dear. Oh dear me."

"I did tell her to lose weight," said Janet. She had some of her sister's brusqueness, but Polly could tell it was genuine shock. "I told her, I told her, but she was so stubborn! Her doctor told her a million times, and I told her too. You're too fat, Gillian. You eat too many cakes. That's what we told her. Sell the cakes, don't eat them. But she would never listen to anyone, never . . . " Her voice dissolved in sobs.

"Was it . . . was it sudden?"

Polly's voice appeared to be wobbling of its own accord. Mrs. Manse had had such a sad life, working all hours in the bakery after the loss of her only child at sea, a child she had never stopped mourning. She often went out after dark to watch for boats coming in, just in case her boy was on one of them. This had gone on for years and years and years, as her shop got more and more grubby and downtrodden and she retreated further into bitterness and regret.

"Aye," said Janet. "Reckon. Heart attack."

Her voice went quiet.

"We bickered, you know."

"I do know," said Polly, who had spent a lot of time listening to Mrs. Manse complaining about her new retired life and how annoying her sister was.

"But I loved her really!"

"I know," said Polly. "And she loved you too."

There was silence on the other end of the line.

"Well, that is so sad," said Polly quietly, and she meant it. She hoped that a bit of company, someone to eat with and watch telly with and play bridge with, had made a real difference to Mrs. Manse in her retirement.

"Aye," said Janet Lange, sounding as if she'd pulled herself together. She sounded more like her sister again too. "It's a right kerfuffle, though. Wants to be buried on the island and all sorts. Don't know how she expects me to manage that."

"Well, of course we must help," said Polly. "Let us manage all that."

Janet sniffed. "Aye, well don't go thinking she's left you those shops or anything like that. There'll be nowt in it for you."

It hadn't even crossed Polly's mind.

Chapter Four

"Or," said Huckle, "it will all work out fine and everything will be totally okay."

He lounged back on the sofa looking, as usual, so relaxed it was difficult to tell whether he was awake or asleep. Normally Polly found this an endearing and comforting characteristic. It was hard to get anxious or worry too much when you were around Huckle. He always had total confidence that everything was going to be all right, and occasionally it could rub off.

This was not one of those times, though. Polly was pacing anxiously around the lighthouse tower, gazing out at the darkening sea. Neil hopped up and down worriedly.

"I mean . . . it's all the houses . . . all that space. I mean, Mount Polbearne is trendy now . . . "

"Yes, thanks to you," said Huckle sleepily.

". . . and you know how nutty house prices are getting. I mean, what if her sister just decided to flog the bakeries off?"

"And who's going to buy a house in a village where you can't get a loaf of sliced white?"

Polly shrugged. "Muriel could stock a bit of bread. Honestly, with your American businessman's hat on, what would you do?"

"With my American businessman's hat?"

"Yes."

"What's that like? I mean, is it a massive JR stetson? Does it have a badge on it? Can I have a sheriff's badge? I think I would like that. Yes, I definitely would."

"You're not being as helpful as perhaps you think you're being."

"An American businessman would have bought this entire place decades ago and turned it into a gift mall; I think you're all nuts for struggling on. AND he'd have sensibly built a bridge."

Huckle looked over. It was rarely wise to get Polly started on the bridge, and he wished he hadn't mentioned it. He wasn't getting out of this conversation anytime soon.

"Well," he said, sighing. "Just call Janet back and ask her what's going to happen. Or ask her at the funeral."

"She just told me not to think I'll be getting any of it," said Polly. "She sounded scary."

"Interesting note of surprise in your voice," pointed out Huckle, who'd been at the sharp end of Mrs. Manse's tongue and hadn't enjoyed it in the slightest.

"But if she kicks me out . . . what are we going to do? I mean, I've worked and worked to build all this up, and it could just disappear to nothing . . . I mean, we wouldn't be able to pay the mortgage on this place and we'd have to move and I'd have to . . . Well, I don't know. Get a job at a pie shop!"

Huckle smiled. "Ooh, that'd be great!"

"I don't want to get a job at a pie shop!"

"You could be Reuben's personal pastry chef," said Huckle. Reuben was their extremely rich friend.

"I'll stick to the pie shop, thank you."

"Look at it this way," said Huckle. "Human beings are pretty lazy, right? Most of them. They're not all nutters that get up in the middle of the night like you."

"What's your point?"

"And she's an old lady. So what's more likely? That she's going to supervise some expensive development pulling out ovens and putting in swanky kitchens to sell a yuppie weekend lifestyle to idiots, and make you homeless, or just leave things as they are and rake in our vast riches?"

Polly smiled. "Well, when you put it like that . . ."

"And you had a contract, right?"

"No," scowled Polly. Then her face softened. "Also, this is making me think about stupid, selfish stuff. Rather than thinking about Mrs. Manse."

"Yes, and all the happy times you spent together."

"An old woman who had a very sad life is dead," said Polly, still staring out of the window. "That is really awful."

Huckle nodded, then got up and came over to the window. He put his arms around her waist and held her to him and they both gazed out at the moon. He kissed her gently on the neck.

"I know," he said. "I know. It is sad."

Neil waddled up crossly and stood between their legs in case they'd forgotten him.

"It is sad," Huckle said again. "And it would be even

sadder if her sister messed with what you've done here. But I'm sure she won't. She'll realize what a great job you're doing and let you carry on. I'm sure she will."

Polly rested her head back on his shoulder and followed the beam of the light above them as it glimmered over and across the waves. She wasn't sure at all.

Polly threw herself into organizing the funeral, as much as she was able. Janet was not inclined to be helpful: when Polly asked for a list of Gillian's friends, she merely sniffed and made an unpleasant noise and said Polly would know that better than her, so Polly just told everyone in the village who came in and hoped for the best. She also baked up a storm. Mrs. Manse would have liked that, probably.

There was a little graveyard up behind the old church, still consecrated ground, and they received the complicated permissions to bury Gillian there, as she had been born on the island and lived her whole life there. Amazing, really, Polly reflected: to stay within a square mile, to consider traveling to Devon a great adventure. She asked the fishermen if they ever remembered Gillian taking a holiday or going overseas, and they all looked at her strangely. Not a lot of people on Mount Polbearne took holidays.

The following Monday morning was gray and dreary, proper funeral weather.

It was not, Polly thought regretfully, the kind of sendoff she would like for herself; nor the magnificent party Reuben had thrown last year for Tarnie's funeral. It was a small service in the village meeting hall, presided over by the female vicar from the mainland, of whom

Mrs. Manse had loudly and publicly disapproved, and the eulogy was short and impersonal.

On the plus side, it was well attended. Everyone from the village was there, from the eldest to a row of squalling babies—there'd been a mini baby boom earlier in the year—who had never even gotten to be scowled at by Mrs. Manse for not having the right change for a Bath bun.

All the fishermen, Polly noticed, lined up manfully to pay their respects to someone who, despite her demeanor, had been one of their own.

Muriel, Polly's friend who ran the little supermarket, shut the shop for an hour and joined them.

"I've never before," she whispered to Polly, "been to the funeral of someone who only ever shouted at me."

"She did shout a lot," said Polly. "But she was all right really. Well. She was just very, very sad. Which makes this sad."

She had asked everyone if they wanted to say a few words, and nobody had particularly—they had all shuffled and looked at the floor. It had really made her miss Tarnie; he would have been perfect for the job, would have done it properly and respectfully, without nerves or fuss. But unfortunately it looked like she was the only person left after Janet declined to speak about her own sister.

After the ceremonial bit was over, Polly got up and stood at the pulpit, feeling incredibly shaky and nervous. She looked out over the entire town's population, telling herself crossly that it was just everyone she saw every day, people she knew . . . Actually, that made it worse. She coughed and tried to stop her hands from shaking as she unfolded her piece of paper.

"Gillian Manse was a daughter of Mount Polbearne,"

she started, her voice sounding incredibly quiet in the room. Huckle, standing at the back so that his big head didn't get in anybody's way, gave her a massive thumbs-up, which gave her the courage to go on.

"Um," she said, feeling slightly braver. "She devoted her life to this town, to feeding it, and to her family . . ."

Polly spoke about the hundred thousand loaves of bread Mrs. Manse must have baked in her lifetime, and about her devotion to her son, Jimmy—and when Polly mentioned him, and some of his scampish ways she'd heard about from the fishermen who'd known him as a young boy, there were smiles of recognition in the congregation—as well as mentioning her late husband, Alf, who had been well liked in the town. She even risked a joke about Mrs. Manse's fierce reputation, pointing out that it was all in defense of the town where she lived. When she stepped down, delighted to have finished, there was a small round of applause. But of course what meant the most was Huckle holding her close when she joined him and squeezing her hand.

Afterward, Polly had arranged for Jayden and Flora to appear with fresh sandwiches, little cheese curls, vol au vents and miniature flans, light as air. There was tea and coffee in the urns normally used by the Women's Institute, and at the last minute Andy, who ran the Red Lion pub and the chip shop, had sidled up sheepishly— he was known as being a tight operator—and said that Mrs. Manse had been good to him when he was a lad when she'd caught him stealing a hot cross bun, and could he donate two crates of beer, which perked the fishermen right up. So it wasn't as grim as Polly had feared it would be.

Mrs. Manse's family were huddled to one side, look-ing at the townspeople suspiciously. Some of the older ones remembered Janet, who'd left the island when she got married, a very long time ago. She was looking large and stolid in a long black dress that gave her a slightly Victorian air, her hair, unusually long for a woman her age, piled on top of her head.

Her two sons were also there. Polly was surprised. Gillian had never mentioned them, not once. Had it really been so hard for her, Polly wondered sadly, after she had lost her own son, that she could never have her sister's boys to stay, never pour some of that thwarted love into her nephews? People were so strange sometimes.

They were large, pasty men, soft around the middle, well upholstered, although apart from that they were not very alike. One was wearing a smart suit and was balding; the other had pale messy hair worn long or in dire need of a trim, and bad skin. He looked sullen.

Polly introduced herself, hoping that they would say that her speech about Gillian had been nice. They didn't.

"Aye," said Janet. "Hello." She was exactly like her sister, Polly thought. Janet and Gillian: peas in a pod.

"I'm so sorry for your loss," said Polly. "Especially after you'd just moved in together."

"Yes, I've got all her stuff cluttering up my place now," said Janet ungraciously. "Saves cleaning out the flat, I suppose."

"Right," said Polly. "Good." She looked at the two men. The older of the pair was busy with his phone. He gave Polly a quick glance, as if checking to see if she was of interest and finding she wasn't.

"This is Jeremy," said Janet, perking up for the first time. "And this is Malcolm."

"Hi," said Polly.

"Hi there," said Malcolm, looking around. "Wow, this place is a bit of a dump. Is there anything to eat?"

"It's coming," said Polly, flustered and looking around for Flora handing around the food. "Did you never come to Mount Polbearne to visit?"

"Yeah, when we were little," said Malcolm. "Didn't think much of it, to be honest. Not much going on around here, is there?"

"Oh, that's a . . . shame," said Polly. She tried to catch Flora's eye; she was meant to be circulating with the sandwiches, but instead she was standing gormlessly at the door and people were swarming around her to help themselves. Polly suspected that the fisher boys would eat everything in two seconds flat. Flora was holding the tray at an angle with one hand and twirling her hair with the other, and didn't see Polly at all. Not for the first time, Polly wondered if she was really cut out to be a boss.

"Ridiculous business living on an island," sniffed Janet. "Honestly, I told her a hundred times to move in with me before . . ."

Suddenly the tough, weather-beaten face started to crumple, and the teacup she was holding began to slip. Polly caught it and saw, all at once, the vulnerability behind the crabbiness. She put her hand on Janet's arm.

"I *told* her," said Janet. "After Jimmy died. I *told* her. It's no good shutting yourself away in the back of bloody beyond. She could have picked herself up on the mainland. Got another life. She wasn't that old. She wasn't too old."

Polly looked at Janet's two sons, but one was still on his phone, and the other one, Malcolm, was staring straight ahead as if this all had nothing to do with him. Tears ran down the old lady's face, and Polly put an arm around her shoulder.

"I know," she said.

"I never wanted to come back here, you know," said Janet. "I never wanted to. She turned it into a bloody . . . mausoleum."

Polly nodded.

"She was always so bloody stubborn," said Janet as Polly passed her a tissue.

"I think you two were a bit alike, maybe?" said Polly. Janet nodded. "Aye, mebbe."

She wiped away her tears crossly, as if embarrassed at showing so much emotion.

"I think," said Polly, "those months she got to spend with you were some of the happiest she ever had."

Polly believed this: the cheerful complaining Mrs. Manse had done, particularly about Janet, every time they'd had cause to discuss the running of the bakery, had indicated a woman definitely perked up. The fact that she hadn't had longer to enjoy it was very sad.

Janet almost smiled.

"Aye, mebbe you're right."

"CHEESE CURL?"

Flora had obviously recovered herself a little and plunged into the heart of the group, staring straight at Polly to make sure her boss knew she was doing what she'd been asked.

"Oh hi, Flora," said Polly.

"No, no thank you," said Janet, her mouth pursing and her face taking on a strict expression. Malcolm helped himself to four, pushing them into his mouth one after another.

"Who's paying for this?" observed Jeremy, lifting his head briefly from his smartphone. "God, the reception in this place is a disgrace."

Polly thought that Jeremy not comforting his crying mother was a bit of a disgrace, but wasn't going to mention it.

"Yeah, Mum . . . " said Malcolm, grabbing another couple of cheese curls before Flora could make a getaway, and looking businesslike.

Polly's heart started to beat faster. They must have discussed it. They must have an idea what they were going to do with the bakery. She wanted to turn her head to look for Huckle. Knowing where he was in a room was the best thing, she had found, in almost every situation. Janet had shaken off her arm and had wiped the tears from her cheeks with a real cotton handkerchief.

"Yes," she repeated. "Who's paying for this?"

"Well, we just did it in the bakery, you know. Out of respect."

Janet coughed and looked very formal.

"As you know, I'm my sister's executor. I take the role very seriously, obviously, and would want to stick exactly to the rules."

"Of course," said Polly, suddenly feeling sick to her stomach. "Of course. Whatever Gillian would have wanted."

Malcolm was looking around for more food. When he spotted Flora, he summoned her back with a brusque movement of his fingers.

"And, of course, my two wonderful boys," said Janet, looking at the unprepossessing specimens with beaming motherly pride and the closest thing to a smile Polly had yet seen from her. "They're the businessmen of the family. Malcolm's going to run all of Gillian's concerns until we work out the most profitable, and best, way to deal with her legacy. I think that's fairest for everyone, don't you?"

Polly didn't know what to say. This was so sudden. She'd gotten used to running her own business, making all the decisions and facing almost no interference from above.

"Now Jeremy's terribly busy doing important work in the city . . . He's quite the big noise in Poole, you know!"

"Okay," said Polly.

"But Malcolm is going to move out here, keep a close eye on things. You know, you can't be too careful with staff! And you did burrow your way in pretty close, hmm? Got your feet under the table? So we'll be taking a look at that."

Malcolm grunted. Polly stepped backward and just nodded dumbly. She caught hold of the side of the table.

"So you're moving to Mount Polbearne?" she said, trying to keep her voice light and pleasant. Malcolm rolled his eyes.

"Well, I'll be in and out, yeah. Till I get things ship-shape, know what I mean? No more slacking, huh? But I'm pretty busy. And I don't want to get buried alive in this hole."

This seemed an awkward thing to say at his aunt's funeral, but Polly didn't mention it.

"So are you leaving a job to come, or . . ."

Malcolm looked bullish.

"Uh, no, I'm kind of between things right now. I'm like a consultant? On lots of different stuff?"

"Okay," said Polly. But she didn't feel like it was okay at all.

The old bell that still hung precariously in the ruined tower at the top of Mount Polbearne began to toll solemnly, and the fishermen doffed their caps as they left the building and followed the coffin. A hearse couldn't fit through the narrow winding streets, so the coffin was carried by Janet's two sons, Archie, Jayden, Huckle and Patrick. Once again, Tarnie was conspicuous by his absence. No one at this funeral was not thinking of the last time they'd been together when somebody had died.

There was a glowering sky outside; it wasn't raining, but it was certainly threatening it. A few disconsolate day trippers at the harbor wall were looking about confusedly, unsure as to why everything was closed up. The entire town trudged slowly up around the winding cobbles, heads down against the wind, which whipped high this close to the sea and this far off the ground. Polly wished she had Huckle's hand to hold, or that her best friend Kerensa was back from whichever ridiculous holiday she was taking right now, but no such luck. She stayed close to Muriel, who ran the village shop.

"This is awful," Muriel was saying. Her baby, Marina, popped her head out of her sling and looked around with a worried expression on her face. "I know. It's okay, baby. She should be having her morning nap in the storeroom," she confided. "She can only get to sleep to the smell of cumin and aniseed."

"Is there anything you *don't* stock?" said Polly. "Apart from bread, obviously."

"Well, that frees up a lot of space," pointed out Muriel.

The old churchyard was beautiful in a strange way. The graves were very old and overgrown, the ancient stone crosses tilted on their sides, nearly all the writing eroded by the years and the wind and the sea. A few names repeated again and again: Perranmor; Tarnforth; Kirrin. It was mostly women and children. In Mount

Polbearne, the men died at sea, and the sea held their bones and their histories and their stories forevermore.

The freshly dug grave looked grim in the shadow of the ruined church. This was not a place for new burials; it seemed strange and odd, as if all the ancient skeletons were bunching up to make room.

"Then shall the dust return to the earth as it was," said the vicar quietly as the men, with the help of the sturdy undertaker from the mainland, tried not to fumble lowering the large coffin into the ground. Gillian had, Polly thought, always been big.

"And the spirit shall return unto God who gave it." And she made the sign of the cross over the grave.

At this, Polly stepped up with the bag she had brought specially, and everyone took a handful of flour from the sack and threw it onto the top of the coffin, as Mrs. Manse began that long journey from which there is no return. And everybody there hoped with all their hearts that her husband and her son would be waiting to greet her at the end of it.

Chapter Five

Polly was staring out of the window expectantly while trying to pretend that wasn't at all what she was doing, even though she knew it didn't matter as they were so ridiculously high up anyway: no one could see in. She'd changed her clothes, put on a nice flowery shirt. She was slightly out of the habit of getting dressed up, didn't really know what to wear for meeting a member of Huckle's family. She'd spoken to his parents on the phone, of course, but this was something different.

She knew Dubose was younger than Huckle, and that they got on, but he'd never really held down a job or stuck to anything in the same way as his big brother, and now he was working on a farm in between traveling stints. But he sounded like fun. Polly couldn't believe how important it was to her that he like her. Both her sister and her mum had fallen in love with Huckle in about ten seconds flat. She hoped it worked both ways.

"And don't poo."

Neil was sulking because Huckle hadn't taken him to the bus station. Polly had tried to cheer him up by bringing home his very favorite thing in all the world, a box full of polystyrene packing pieces. When he thought she wasn't watching, or when she left the room, she could hear him jumping into the box and stomping up and down, kicking at the pieces with his little webbed feet. When she came back in, he'd immediately flutter out of the box and stand facing away from her, staring out of the window.

The sky was pink-tinged when she saw the causeway gradually emerge, and soon after that she heard the roar of the motorbike banging up the cobbled streets. It was the noisiest thing on the island by far, but Polly could never hear it without smiling in anticipation. She nervously touched up the lipstick she didn't normally bother with, and descended the stairs.

A tall, slim figure stepped out of the sidecar and took off the spare helmet, shaking his head to reveal a mop of blond hair very like his brother's. His face was narrower than Huckle's, with a pointed chin, and he had pale blue eyes that looked absolutely primed to laugh.

"WHOA!" he said, looking up at the lighthouse. "NO WAY! You live here?"

"Way," said Huckle, lifting out a stained suitcase. He came around to stand next to Polly. "And this is—"

"Whoa! Yeah! Holly!" said Dubose, coming over and kissing her excitedly on both cheeks.

"Polly," said Polly.

"Even better," said Dubose, twinkling at her. "In fact that's exactly what I said, it's just my strange exotic accent made it difficult to understand."

Polly couldn't help but smile, even as Huckle was rolling his eyes.

"Come in," she said. Dubose let Huckle carry his bag.

"Where's Neil?" said Huckle, as they tramped around and around up the steps, Dubose exclaiming every five seconds.

"He's in a bad mood because you didn't take him to the bus station."

"He does like buses," said Huckle.

"This is your bird, right? Cool," said Dubose.

They entered the sitting room at the top of the tower, which Polly had spent a long time making as nice as she could. Neil had spread packing peanuts all over the room, everywhere, in a huge mess. He had pooed in the box for good measure.

"Neil!" said Polly in exasperation. Dubose burst out laughing.

Dubose regaled them over dinner with his traveling tales, most of them involving accidentally ending up at VIP parties or backstage at gigs. There were also a good few where he completely ran out of money or found himself upside down in a bin. He told a good story against himself.

"And those girls!" he sighed. "Oh Huckle, you gotta see those blondes up in Reykjavik."

Huckle gave a slightly tight smile.

"Isn't Clemmie missing you? Isn't it calving time?"

Dubose nodded. "She's an amazing girl. And she

knows that sometimes I just have to break free, follow my dreams, man, you know?"

"Do all your dreams end up with you sleeping in a bin?"

Dubose turned away.

"Polly, this quiche is absolutely sensational. I think you might be a genius. Are you a genius?"

"No," said Polly, smiling, even though she couldn't help watching the dynamic. It was strange to hear Huckle sounding fed up; it so rarely happened.

"She is a genius, Huckle. You should buy her a bakery."

There was a slight awkward silence. After a moment, Huckle started clearing away. Dubose glanced at his watch.

"So, where are we going now?"

It was 9:30.

"Um," said Polly. "Actually we normally just . . . go to bed."

Dubose looked aghast. "Seriously? But it's Friday night!"

"I know," said Polly. "But we've got people coming over on Sunday. Hopefully you'll like them."

"Well, that's a pile of bullcrap," Dubose shouted, wavering unsteadily on top of the gantry.

They were recovering from the rabbit pie Polly had made for Sunday lunch. It had been a sensational pie, but actually it was hard to remember now, as Huckle had also brought a couple of liters of his honey mead, which was guaranteed to remove all nerve endings from the waist down, as well as ensuring that the next day someone followed you around the room hitting you repeatedly on the head with a sharp-edged brick.

But today, Polly had been thinking dreamily, that didn't matter.

Above their sitting room in the lighthouse was the light itself. It worked automatically—every so often, as part of their complicated property deeds, a man would zip up the stairs and give it a polish and a checkover— and around the outside was a metal walkway, reached by a narrow staircase that allowed access for cleaning and maintenance. They had been told repeatedly, and in no uncertain terms, when they bought the property, that this walkway did not belong to them, that it was dangerous and to be used only by clipped-in, safety-harness-and-vest-and-helmet-wearing qualified lighthouse operatives.

So naturally every sunny day they went up there with giant bean bags and sprawled out around the little platform. It was best if you didn't look down between the metal slats, and not a great idea in high winds, but on a beautiful day it was absolutely stunning: you felt as if you were floating through the clouds. Today, Polly and her best friend Kerensa were on the sunny sheltered ledge at the top of the little staircase that led back into the main body of the lighthouse; Reuben was sprawled fearlessly across the metal walkway getting a suntan, and Huckle was perched on top of it with his back against the lighthouse itself, long legs stretched out to the other side, gazing out to sea. Dubose was sitting nearby and Neil was stomping about looking for more pastry scraps. His claws made a clicking sound on the walkway as he went around so often Polly thought he might get dizzy. When he got to Reuben, he just hopped up on his leg and walked over the top of him.

Meanwhile, Reuben and Dubose had got into a ridiculous barney about grain subsidies, which had made Dubose all pink in the face but which Reuben was patently enjoying.

"Poo on him!" hissed Kerensa. "Do it, Neil, I mean it! I'm sick of this argument."

"NO MORE POO!" said Polly loftily, just as Neil did in fact poo straight through the metal slats and all the way down to the rocks, where some children with fishing nets were pottering around looking for tiddlers and prizing off shellfish. The five at the top of the lighthouse peered down and held their breath, then let out a collective sigh of relief as the poo splashed harmlessly into a nearby rock pool.

"All I want is for my puffin to learn to use a human toilet," said Polly. "Is that really too much to ask?"

"And the other reason grain subsidies are great—"

"So anyway," said Reuben, ignoring Dubose and turning to Polly, "why don't you let me buy you the bakery?"

Polly gasped.

Reuben was quite relentless when he got on to a topic. He was an old friend of Huckle's who'd made a lot of money selling some kind of Internet thing in San Francisco—he often tried to explain it, but Polly could never quite get to the bottom of it. Anyway, now he owned a private surfing beach and stunning modernist house in north Cornwall. Kerensa was Polly's best friend from Plymouth. Initially she'd thought Polly moving to a tidal island was the stupidest idea she'd ever heard of. Then she'd started visiting. She absolutely couldn't bear Huckle's loud friend Reuben, until she accidentally got off with him one night, and since then they'd been utterly inseparable, and were now married.

"I mean it. This woman sounds worse than Mrs. Manse. And this Malcolm . . . what does he do?"

"Um, consultant?" said Polly.

"Um, grain subsidies?" said Dubose, who was still standing up and beginning to feel a bit foolish.

"What kind of consultant? Hospital consultant? Insolvency consultant? Would You Like Fries With That consultant?"

"I don't know."

"He sounds rubbish," said Reuben. "Let me buy him out. I'll tell him I'm a major bakery consultant—which by the way I totally could be—and then I'll buy both of them and then we're done."

"Well, we're not done, are we?" said Polly crossly. "I don't want you to buy me out of trouble."

"Why not?" said Reuben. "Buying people out of trouble is totally one of the things I'm amazing at."

"Is he always like this?" grumbled Dubose.

"You should probably sit down, Dubose," said Huckle. "We're pretty high up."

"You'd be a worse boss than this Malcolm guy," mumbled Polly. "Anyway, no. Don't. We're friends. We'd only fall out. Please."

"But I always buy everyone," said Reuben, puzzled.

Polly couldn't explain to him, couldn't make him see—in fact he would think it utterly ridiculous—how insulting his suggestion was to her. It was partly because she did think working with your friends was a bad idea, even if Reuben completely ignored the bakery after he bought it. But that would be bad too: it just showed how unimportant he thought what she did was. And also, although Reuben would find this concept hilarious, she thought she was like him. She was an entrepreneur, she worked for herself; she hoped one day to work her way up the ladder, to be the owner, not just the manager of her business.

One thing Mrs. Manse had been great about was leaving her alone—when she wasn't complaining—and letting her run things her way, and she had really loved it, really gotten a taste for it. She enjoyed making decisions and seeing how things turned out. She didn't want Reuben swanning in with his friends telling her she was doing it wrong. She didn't want a helping hand she hadn't earned. She wanted to do it herself.

"Well, not me," she said.

"And not me either," said Kerensa, drinking more mead.

"Apart from that bracelet that was so heavy you strained your wrist," pointed out Polly.

"Oh yes," said Kerensa, grinning. "I forgot about that."

Polly smiled at her.

"How's being back at work?"

Kerensa scowled. "Oh God, it's rubbish. I wish my staff behaved like flunkies. Everyone Reuben works with behaves like terrified flunkies."

"Maybe you should be more frightening."

"I'm not sure that's possible."

"Don't work!" said Reuben. "Anyway, it means I get less sex."

"Yes, just twice a day," whispered Polly, and Kerensa giggled and blushed. She had insisted on going back to work after months of honeymooning, touring the globe and staying in fancy hotels, eating in the best restaurants and, as she pointed out herself, getting fat.

"The worst thing is," she said, "the other women are all SO THIN. There's every imaginable fabulous thing you could eat in the world, ever, all the time, and it's all amazing and gorgeous, and they don't eat ANY OF IT. They just go and have spa treatments!" She scowled. "Before we got married, I thought I was really brilliant at being thin and not eating much. But man, they take it to an entirely new level."

"You look fantastic," said Polly, loyally but also honestly. Before, when Kerensa had been ferociously slim and fit, she had had a hard look about her. Now she was a little rounder and softer and looked a lot younger in the face, and it suited her.

"All those jumped-up Barbie dolls talking about suntans," shivered Reuben. "God. You're the best of them all, Kay, because I always choose the best kinds of things. Always. Which is why I chose you . . ."

He was about to start on a long diatribe again. Polly lay back in the sun and smiled to see her friend so happy.

"I did need to go back to work, though," whispered Kerensa. "It felt wrong just lying around spending money. I mean, it was fun for about five minutes. But after that it was all a bit WAGtastic."

"I agree with you," Polly said, mildly. "Obviously. Because I'm about to start working for Malcolm the Consultant."

"Unless you let me—" piped up Reuben.

"No!"

"Wow, man, your friends are very uncool," said Dubose.

"Well, he works for his money," pointed out Huckle mildly. "He's allowed to do what he wants with it."

Dubose scowled. "I do too."

Huckle nodded. "When you're not gallivanting off at spring planting season."

"If you wanna go work on a farm, GO WORK ON A FARM," said Dubose in exasperation. "It's not like you're doing anything useful here, hanging around fiddling with honey and eating pie. At least when you were in the city, Mom was proud of you."

Polly slipped into the bedroom where Huckle was getting ready for bed. He had left Dubose to it.

"What's up with you two?" she said.

"Oh, just brother stuff. I shouldn't let him get to me," said Huckle, but he looked sad. Polly reached up and cuddled him.

"If you ask me," she said, "I think he seems a little lost. Do you think things are okay with Clemmie?"

Huckle sighed. "She's VERY long suffering. It's not a bad farm they work, you know? But every time they make a bit of money, he hotfoots it away to find himself and leaves her there alone. I love him, but he's always had a problem with the really hard work."

"But he works on a farm!" said Polly. "That's about as hard as work gets, that and fishing."

"I know," said Huckle. "That's why he has to let off steam every now and again."

"Shouting about grain subsidies."

"He always kind of wears this big bravado thing on him."

"Classic little brother," said Polly. "He probably worships you."

Huckle frowned. "Funny way of showing it."

"Maybe he says the same about you."

Huckle put his faded blue chambray shirt in the laundry basket and changed the subject.

"What do you think about Reuben's offer?"

Polly made a face.

"I know how you feel," said Huckle.

"You do?"

"Oh, totally. He tried to set me up in the honey business. Can you imagine? 'This honey isn't right, Huckle! I'd do it much better! I have six international honey trophies.'"

"He probably does."

"But I'm still worried, you know. Worried about this new guy. And worried about money."

"Well, don't be," said Polly, coming up and kissing him. "What's the worst that can happen? Apart from me getting fired and us losing everything?"

There was a pause.

"Then we go crawling to Reuben," said Huckle, and they both grinned in the dim light.

"Yes, obviously," said Polly. Then she turned toward him.

"No," she said. "This is OUR life, remember. Not Reuben's, not Dubose's. Nobody else's."

"I remember it every day," said Huckle simply. "When I wake up in the morning and realize you're lying beside me."

"I think I need to kiss you again," said Polly.

She woke even before her early alarm, checking her head for mead damage. It wasn't too bad.

It was still dark outside. She could hear Neil trundling about in the sitting room above them, doing busy bird things. Downstairs in the second bedroom, Dubose wasn't stirring. At first she didn't quite understand why her stomach felt so hollow, then she remembered. Malcolm was 'popping in' that morning to 'get a handle on' the business. She felt incredibly nervous all of a sudden.

Since she'd started in Polbearne she'd had to learn plenty of new things, and doubted herself a lot—but not her baking ability. The one thing she knew, the one thing she turned to in times of nervousness and stress, was pounding and kneading and folding the dough, making it rise, warm and light in the oven, turning simple flour and water and yeast, salt and sugar into all sorts of things.

She got up now, shuffling quietly around the bedroom so she didn't wake Huckle, which was unnecessary as almost nothing did. He slept like he had an on/off switch.

They didn't have curtains in the bedroom, partly because the circular walls made finding and fitting them an expensive, time-consuming task, partly because nobody could ever see in, four stories off the ground, and partly because Polly liked the sun waking her in the summertime, given that she had to get up then anyway, and Huckle never minded. But there wasn't even a glimmer of dawn on the horizon as she splashed water on her hands and face, brushed her teeth, pulled on faded boyfriend jeans, Converses and a striped T-shirt, threw a jacket over the top and slipped out of the door.

She ran lightly across the cobbles and let herself into the Little Beach Street Bakery. The first thing she always did in the morning was switch on the coffee machine and grind up some fresh beans. The ritual was incredibly important to her day: she didn't feel properly awake until she'd had a strong cup of espresso, standing up against the kitchen cupboards, looking out at the dark.

Next she checked the great wood-burning oven. It had been a gift from Reuben and never really went out; they simply damped it at night. When it got really hot, it produced smoky focaccia, michette, pizza bases and pies that tasted better than anyone else's, particularly when eaten outside, ideally in the sunshine, with a little bit of sand for flavor. The other ovens too warmed up—no matter how chilly the dawn, the bakery was never cold—as Polly got working on the great batches of dough that had risen overnight, expertly molding the white and the brown into the tins that were lined up, clean but black with age and use, a patina that added, she was entirely convinced, to the flavor, along with the fine sea salt she insisted on, the best flour, and a few herbs snipped into the wholemeal loaf that brought out the sweet nuttiness of its crust. Yes, loaves cost more here than they did in the big supermarket on the mainland. She couldn't compete with that. She just had to hope that it was worth paying the difference for something she believed was so much tastier than mass-produced bread that you simply would never go back to it. Their daily repeat business would seem to suggest it was definitely a feeling that was shared in the town.

She made up smaller batches of their specialty bread, which went to Mount's, the smart restaurant, during the season—it wasn't quite the season yet, and they were shut on Mondays, so she made very little today. It was a wonderfully intense sun-dried-tomato focaccia, deep and sunny and rich, garnished with rosemary and olive oil. The whole thing tasted of summer in a bite; of lazy afternoons in Italian courtyard gardens (not that Polly had ever sat in an Italian courtyard garden, but she liked to think that was what it would be like).

She also made a raisin and cinnamon soda bread, which was dense and spicy; you wouldn't eat too much of it, but a slice toasted and spread with butter was basically afternoon tea on a plate. She took out some of the first batch to slice up as a tester on a little plate by the till. Few people could resist a taste now and then, and it helped convince those of her customers who were slightly put off by foreign-sounding names or anything more unusual than pizza.

By 7:30, everything was buzzing, warm and beautifully scented. Jayden whirled in full of energy, sweeping and mopping, slipping the bread out of its tins, something he could now do with relative ease without burning himself, which he had done repeatedly for the first two months.

Looking at him now, Polly was proud of how proficient he'd become, lining up the buns perfectly in their sparklingly clean case; packing away the white bread to take over to the old bakery for Flora to use to put sandwiches together. Everything seemed—touch wood—to be running like a well-oiled machine at the moment. She unlocked the safe and counted out the cashbox change, thinking, as she did every day—though she would never tell him this—that Huckle would be waking up about now, turning and stretching in the morning glow, his broad chest bare and golden . . .

She smiled happily to herself, relocked the safe, and turned toward the counter. She could hear the clatter and burr of the fishing boats coming home from their long night on the water, and glanced at her watch. Ten minutes to eight. Might as well do it now; people loved it when you opened slightly early, and although the day looked blowy, there were already dog-walkers up and about, marching over the rocks and down to Breakwater Cove. They would often come in for a warm roll, and occasionally, if she wasn't too busy, she'd make them a coffee too, served in a little paper cup. This was the lovely thing about April, she was thinking: lighter mornings. Dark winter mornings were tough. She'd tried changing the opening time to 8:30, but the fishermen had gotten very upset about it, so she'd reverted to the original arrangement.

She tied on a fresh apron, made sure her strawberry-blond hair was properly pinned back, prepared her welcoming smile, stepped up to the door—and got the shock of her life.

Right in front of the glass, staring in at her, was the large man with the messily cut hair from Gillian Manse's funeral: Malcolm, of course. She didn't know why, but she hadn't expected him till later, and even though she'd lain awake worrying about it, once she'd gotten into the everyday rhythm of work that morning, she had completely stopped thinking about him. She'd certainly not expected him to be standing sinisterly, peering in through her door window.

Once she'd jumped back a little, she calmed down and managed to plaster her smile back on, and unlocked the heavy glass door that had been replaced after Neil had rolled through the old glass and into her life one stormy night two years ago.

"Hello!" she said, as jauntily as she was able. "I wasn't expecting you!"

Malcolm stared crossly at his watch.

"I know. God, it's SO early. How on earth do people get up at this time?"

Polly didn't want to point out to him that she'd been at work for three hours already.

"Would you like a coffee?"

"Yes. Three sugars," said Malcolm brusquely. He

marched into the shop. Like last time, he was dressed like an unmade bed, a creased shirt half hanging out of a crushed old pair of chinos. He hadn't done up the bottom button, so a portion of soft, squishy tummy was plainly visible over the top of his trousers.

"Are you married?" asked Polly politely.

Malcolm sniffed. "Not going to get caught like that, no chance," he said, derisively. "Ha, won't get me tied down. Not a chance."

The fishermen trudged in, looking bone weary.

"Good morning!" said Jayden. This was the absolute high point of his day. "Cold out there? Freezing, I'll bet. Pretty tough, huh? Catch much, or were they too fast for you? Cor, wouldn't like to be in your shoes."

"Shut up, Jayden," they all said, as they did every morning, and Polly set the coffee machine to work yet again.

"Are you licensed to sell this?" grunted Malcolm.

"Uh, hmm," said Polly, suddenly wishing she was a bit better prepared. "Not exactly, but Mrs. Manse—"

"Whatever Mrs. Manse did and didn't tolerate," said Malcolm, raising his unpleasantly nasal voice, "and however much advantage you took of her good nature, she's not here now. Things are going to change around here, right?"

The fishermen looked at Malcolm, who, compared to them, seemed incredibly soft and lily-handed. Archie glanced at Polly with concern, but she didn't catch his eye.

Jayden was scooping pastries into a bag and didn't seem to notice the awkward undercurrents in the little shop, for which Polly was grateful. She was slightly worried that if she went to take the money, her hand might tremble a little bit.

The boys had departed, as well as Patrick and his old dog Pen, who still trotted faithfully across the lighthouse rocks every day, even though his limbs were arthritic. Polly always kept a bit of leftover bun for him. She normally didn't allow animals in the shop, but Pen was different. Malcolm was leaning nonchalantly on the glass window at the front, watching her beadily with his arms folded. His eyes were very pale, almost colorless, and his skin was doughy. He looked like he spent a lot of time indoors.

"What are you interested in looking at first?" asked Polly carefully.

Malcolm picked up one of the largest loaves, an unsliced white—not everyone liked it sliced. The big slicer in the back clattered away early in the morning, then they left it up to individuals. Polly watched him, wondering what he was going to do with it. To her amazement, he brought up the other large, soft-looking paw and pulled a great chunk off the top, just ripped into it, then put it into his maw before she could offer him butter or anything else. He chewed slowly and contemplatively, crumbs falling onto his already messy shirt. Jayden busied himself with washing up the tins while Polly simply waited.

She made herself smile again.

"Well?"

Malcolm shrugged, his mouth still full.

"Hmm, yeah, well."

He put the rest of the loaf back on top of the counter, spreading crumbs everywhere, but not before ripping off another bit and sticking it into his masticating mouth.

"Back," he grunted, and indicated the ovens at the rear of the bakery.

Polly led him through.

"So, this is where the magic happens!" she said, still trying to sound light and unconcerned. Malcolm took out a pen and pad and started jotting things down. He inspected the flour she used—00 grade; the salt. He looked at the sourdough yeast she had growing in the fridge; the milk, and the many bags and boxes of produce—local, almost all of it, from around and about: herbs and fruit and nuts and honey—and everything else she used to flavor and differentiate her various types of bread.

"What's all this rubbish?" he said. "You're not running a bloody restaurant."

"Yes, but we make different types of bread," explained Polly carefully. "All sorts of flavors. As well as pies, sometimes, and flatbread and things. Different savories and a few sweets, so it takes a lot of ingredients. Flora does most of the sweets in the other shop."

Indeed, Flora's way with a cream horn was one of her main weapons against her ever losing her job. She had an astonishingly light hand with pastry and a neatness of touch that Polly envied massively.

"Well, as a businessman," said Malcolm, which he'd offered absolutely no evidence of, but Polly wasn't in any position to query his credentials, "this all seems a total mess and incredibly inefficient and wasteful."

Polly tried to keep her voice calm.

"It seems to work all right with the customers."

Malcolm sniffed. "What, those brain-dead yokels? Yeah, they'll take any old crap. But I don't want to be . . . I don't want my mum to be cheated out of what these shops are worth."

"I would never do that," said Polly.

"Yeah, well . . ." He picked up a pot of fleur de sel.

"I mean, what's this? Salt?"

"Uh, yeah. Most bread has a little salt, and there are bagels, which have a little more, and—'

"Is this the cheapest you can buy? It's not even ground."

"I know," said Polly timidly. "But it's the best you can get. It's got a real fullness of flavor and a delicate . . . It's not too salty."

"Not too salty?" sneered Malcolm. "You're buying expensive salt that isn't too salty?"

He marked something in his little book.

"And this flour. Why are you buying Italian flour?"

"It's the best," said Polly again, feeling more and more worried. Jayden was in the shop, chatting to the early-morning customers and making the old ladies laugh. She had, she realized now, overconfidently expected that Malcolm would pop in, have a cup of coffee and a bun, say, "Wow, this place is fantastic, keep up the good work," and that would be that.

"Yes, but punters don't notice, do they?"

"I think they do."

"No," said Malcolm. "I don't think so. If I'm hungry, I'll just buy a pasty in a motorway service station. I don't care if it's got poncey flour in it, or super salt that they magic out of not too salty land. I just want something to eat."

Polly stared at the floor.

"I've got all the accounts," said Malcolm, obviously thinking he was sounding really tough. "I'm going to be going through them with a fine-tooth comb. This place is barely scraping a living, and I want to know why."

"Because we're a low-cost, high-volume business in a seasonal location with year-round fixed costs," Polly could have told him, had he looked like the listening type. Which he didn't. You didn't run a bakery for the money—well, maybe if you had a high-end cupcake shop in London or something, she imagined. Otherwise, you only did it because you loved it; because it was a good solid way to make a good honest living, whatever this guy seemed to be implying. It certainly wouldn't make you rich.

"Also, I'm renting out the upstairs flat again." Malcolm sniffed. "It's ridiculous it's been sitting empty all this time. So you may have to be quieter in the mornings."

"We can't," said Polly. "That's when we start business for the day. You'll have to find a tenant who doesn't mind."

"We'll see about that," said Malcolm.

"You'll lose money if you make us open later," Polly said, which seemed to have a slightly calming effect. "A lot of money. Most people want to buy bread first thing in the morning."

There was another burst of feminine laughter from the front of the shop.

"Does he just stand around chatting all day?" asked Malcolm, nodding his head toward Jayden.

"No," said Polly. "He works really hard, and it's good for repeat business that the customers like him so much."

Malcolm and Polly looked at one another for a moment. Polly knew she was being scrutinized, and she hated it, absolutely hated it: the implied criticism in his words, the suggestion that she was being at best profligate with her stock, and at worst criminal. It was all going much, much worse than she'd imagined.

"Well, like I say, there's going to be some changes,"

said Malcolm. "I'll be having a look at the books and letting you know."

"Okay," said Polly, relieved that he was at least leaving. "Would you like to take anything for lunch? And we can go and look at the other bakery if you like."

Malcolm shook his head. "I've seen enough," he said, obviously reveling in sounding like a bit of a hard man. He waddled back into the shop and headed for the door. Polly's gaze followed him, and her heart sank.

Not now, she thought. Not now.

Neil was standing outside the door, hopping from foot to foot in a manner that he had learned generally got people's attention, waiting for someone to let him in. Polly groaned internally. Couldn't Huckle have shut him in the house for once? Well, obviously he couldn't; she couldn't either. One, it was cruel, and two, he would go and revenge-poo in her shoes. But still, now, of all times. A billion puffins in the world who were flock animals, she thought crossly, and she got the one with a mind of his own.

Old Mrs. Hackett was making her slow way up the harbor, pulling a shopping trolley. She came in every day about this time for half a loaf of brown, because she lived alone and liked a tin of vegetable soup and toast for her supper, so every morning Polly sold her half a loaf of bread at half price and threw the rest away. She had no doubt Malcolm wouldn't approve of this strategy either.

Malcolm had got halfway to the door, trying to look dignified, but he was obviously fighting a losing battle with himself. He turned back.

"Actually," he said, "I will take two . . . I mean four of those doughnuts. And that little loaf with the bits in it. And a slice of that stuff with the cheese. I mean two slices. I just need to do . . . quality control."

Jayden wrapped them all up efficiently, without a word.

"And two buns."

Polly's heart sank. The Little Beach Street Bakery made the same amount of money every day, more or less, because they stayed open until they'd sold all their stock, then they shut. If you wanted something specific, you knew you had to come early. But if Malcolm was simply taking it all away, they were going to lose quite a bit of money. And she had absolutely no doubt he would have something to say about it if their takings were noticeably down, without necessarily connecting it to him walking out with his pockets overflowing with doughnuts.

Mrs. Hackett was at the door now.

"Hello there, Neil me lover," Polly heard her say from behind the heavy glass. She'd have to open the door for her too, she knew. Mrs. Hackett had arthritis in her hands and wasn't as strong as she'd once been. But she was a lovely old woman who'd taught at the school when it had still been open and was known by everyone in town. Meanwhile, Malcolm was juggling the packages Jayden was giving him one on top of the other.

With a sigh, and a warning look at her puffin, Polly pushed open the door.

"Hello, Mrs. Hackett," she said. She tried to be quick, but you couldn't hurry Mrs. Hackett, who in any case was pulling her trolley over the cobblestones and also wearing a floppy hat that would get stuck if Polly didn't open the door a bit wider.

Neil eeped loudly and jubilantly and hopped into the shop, to a chorus of hellos from everybody there. Malcolm watched, clearly incredulous.

"What's this bird doing in here?" he said. "We've

already had a dog in, and dogs aren't allowed in food shops. I'd have expected you to know that, Pauline."

"I do know that," said Polly, who didn't want to tell him that he'd got her name wrong. "It was just Pen. He's so old, it's hard for him to stand outside."

"But BIRDS! You can't have birds flying about a shop! What next, a bunch of seagulls coming in? It's disgusting. Out! Shoo! Shoo!"

There was a sharp intake of breath from one of the old ladies. Nobody ever talked to Neil like that. Polly felt awful but she didn't say anything. It was horribly disloyal, but maybe Neil would hop back out of the shop instead of getting them shut down for health and safety and losing her her livelihood forever.

He regarded the newcomer with his black eyes, then—and if he hadn't been a bird, Polly would have sworn he'd done it on purpose—he hopped up onto Polly's shoulder and tilted his head so that he was nuzzling her ear.

"Get down, Neil," Polly murmured, but to no avail. He was making happy little eeps. One of the old ladies gave him a piece of her bun, which he bit into happily, his beak scattering crumbs across the floor.

Malcolm had gone absolutely puce.

"This is *your* bird?" he said. "You can't have a *bird* in here! You can't . . . you can't . . ."

"He doesn't come to work with me," mumbled Polly. Malcolm did kind of have a point: she shouldn't have Neil in the bakery, but nobody ever seemed to mind. "I think he was just . . . passing."

Malcolm stood back, shaking his head, as if he'd never seen anything so disgusting in his entire life.

"I think *you* have to decide whether you want to run

a food preparation service or a bird sanctuary," he said. "And decide soon."

Still balancing his parcels, he marched crossly out of the shop.

"He seems nice," ventured one of the old ladies.

"Mabel, he's horrible," said Mrs. Hoskings.

"Really?" said Mabel. "Ah, I'm wearing my peepers, not my lookers." She fumbled with her spectacles. "Still, nice to have a bit of new young blood around the place, hmm?"

"I wouldn't be too sure about that," said Polly, putting Neil out through the door crossly. He checked to make sure she wasn't kidding, then waddled across the road to pester the fishermen for scraps.

"And fly, you lazy bird!" Polly shouted at him, but yelling at Neil certainly wasn't going to make her feel any better.

"Yes, well," said Mabel, packing away her sausage rolls in her capacious handbag. "Last time we had some new young blood around the place, you snaffled it up. Leave some for the rest of us this time, would you?"

Polly gave a half-hearted grin.

"You," she said, "are welcome to him."

Polly didn't head back for a quick break that morning after the early rush: she was too anxious and keyed up about Malcolm's visit.

She tried to put a spin on the meeting whereby it hadn't gone too badly, but she could tell that it had. She imagined him marching back to Janet with a long list of her sins, announcing that the bakery had to be closed down immediately. As usual thinking up good things to say long after the moment had passed, she wished she'd pointed out to Malcolm that actually her predecessor had kept costs down and made everything as cheap as possible, and it had led to the closure of the Little Beach Street Bakery and the near collapse of the old Polbearne bakery, because everyone just went to the mainland to get their nice bread and avoided the horrible cheap stuff at all costs. She vowed to say this to him. Definitely. Next time she saw him . . .

The rest of the day passed in a blur of the usual cheery people, many of them asking why she looked so gloomy—which is absolutely the last thing to say to someone who looks gloomy and is always unlikely to improve matters—until she was quite fed up. They sold the last cream horn, and Polly stomped outside with a cup of coffee on her own.

It was still cold and windy; the sun had not burned through the cloud as it sometimes did, and not many people were about. It was much easier on days like this, Polly thought, to remember Mount Polbearne as it had been when she had first arrived: shuttered, closed down, tatty everywhere, in stark contrast to the slightly social-climbing aspirations of grandeur it had now.

It was nice this way too, though. Bleak. Choppy. The tide was in, the waves right up to the harbor wall. One or two people were braving the windy high street, though it could hardly be called that, consisting as it did of the chippy and pub at the bottom end, Muriel's shop, the post office, a gift shop of mysterious means, the vet/doctor's and a tiny ironmonger's, which wasn't much more than a hole in the wall. Otherwise, apart from a couple of lonely dog-walkers almost out of view, and the ever-circling gulls, Polly had the harbor to herself. She pulled her big sweater down over her hands and warmed them around her coffee mug, which, inevitably, had a puffin on it. Huckle had gotten into the habit of buying her anything he ever came across with a puffin on it, so she now had puffin pajamas, tea towels, oven gloves and all sorts of nonsense. At first she'd told him to stop, it was tacky, but she'd gotten used to it now. Plus all the pictures around the house were company for Neil as an only puffin.

She stared out at the choppy gray water, then back at the mainland. The causeway was covered over and Mount Polbearne was isolated, a great island citadel standing all alone. For once, it suited her mood. She understood now why people became so protective of their turf, why they feared incomers. Mount Polbearne had had its own way of life for hundreds of years. It suited them just fine. They didn't need some mainlander coming in and telling them more efficient ways to get their daily bread. At that precise moment, Polly chose to ignore the fact that she had been born and raised in Plymouth.

A car was standing in the island car park. She squinted at it; it seemed vaguely familiar. Whoever it was, they had only just got ahead of the water, and might have to stay a while. She looked at the two figures leaning against the car. A portly young man, and a slender young woman. Not local, but not strangers either. She tried not to stare as they made their way carefully up the harbor walk, bent against the wind, the spray in their faces. She recognized the local estate agent, Lance. He'd gone to work in another office, she'd heard. Well, he must be back. But who was that with him?

Lance saw her and came up to her.

"Thank God," he said. "Have you got a couple of

buns for us? We're starving. Traffic out of Looe was bloody terrible, then we had to go like stink not to miss the tide. My car's got so much salt damage it's basically held together by rust."

Polly smiled. "It's nice to see you again, Lance."

Lance looked over his large stomach to stare at his shoes.

"Yeah, well. After I lost them SO much money on that bloody lighthouse."

Polly tried to hide her smirk, but couldn't. At one stage there had been a plan to build a bridge from Mount Polbearne to the mainland, and Lance had confidently expected to make a fortune selling properties on the island, particularly the lighthouse. In the end, the council had listened to the islanders and voted against the bridge, after which Polly had promptly managed to pick up the lighthouse for a song. Lance had not forgiven her.

"They sent me off to the north! Bloody Derbyshire!"

"I've heard it's beautiful up there."

"I'll tell you this: it snows all the bloody time."

Polly smiled again. "But you're back."

"Yeah, no one else wanted this beat . . . I mean . . ."

The woman he was with had been standing looking the other way, staring out to sea, but now she turned around, and at once Polly realized she knew her. She could only gasp.

"Selina."

Chapter Six

So, you've decided to go back?"

"Well, I can't seem to go forward."

"What are you hoping to find there?"

"I'm hoping to understand."

"And what if you can't understand?"

Selina twisted her wedding ring around and around her finger.

"I don't know."

Polly was completely shocked to see Tarnie's wife. Or rather, of course, his widow. She had only met Selina twice before, once in Polbearne, and once at the funeral. Since then she hadn't seen her at all, had heard she'd gone back to her parents and hadn't been the least bit surprised that she hadn't wanted to see hide nor hair of Mount Polbearne again.

"Hi," said Selina, but she clearly didn't really remember Polly. Well, why would she? thought Polly. She was only the woman who'd secretly slept with her husband (she hadn't realized Tarnie was married; he didn't wear a ring) then met her briefly just after her husband had died at sea.

"Hi," said Polly. "Um, I run the bakery."

"Right," said Selina without interest.

"It's the best bakery in the southwest," said Lance. "And I should know. I've tried them all."

He patted his stomach cheerfully.

"Can you get us a couple of fruit slices? And a loaf of that olive bread to take away? I love that stuff."

"Sorry," said Polly, indicating Jayden mopping up inside. "We're done for the day. We're shut."

"Yes, but you're not shut to *me*," said Lance. "I let you steal a lighthouse off me."

Polly smiled. "I know that. But when we're out of food, we're out of food."

Lance looked crestfallen. Polly thought of the little olive loaf she'd been keeping back for Huckle's supper.

"Oh, all right then," she said. "What are you doing here?"

"Funny you should ask," grunted Lance. "Selina . . ." He struggled for her surname for a second.

"Tarnforth," said Polly, without thinking. Selina gave her a surprised look.

"Uh, aye," said Lance. "Selina's looking at the flat above your bakery."

Polly made them all a cup of tea—it really was getting chilly outside, nothing like the lovely weekend—and rustled up the olive loaf, which she served with the incredibly expensive French salted butter she got sent over occasionally as a very special treat. Poor old Huckle would have to make do with the chippy.

She tried to keep her tone light.

"So, you're thinking of moving here?" she said.

Selina was still pretty, but very thin and drawn, and there were hollows under her eyes. She nodded.

"My parents thought I should have a fresh start, you know? Well, lots of people did. So I moved away, got a new job, gave up teaching—not much use when you're bursting into tears in front of your class every ten minutes. They were very generous with compassionate leave, but there came a point when even they were just like "Come on.'"

Polly tutted sympathetically. It must be bloody awful to have something so bad happen to you, then everyone whispering about it all the time afterward.

"And I was SO sick of being the tragic widow of the town. Everywhere I went, everyone lowered their voices and put on their best kind, speaking-to-an-idiot-child tone and tilted their heads and were so, so nice to me." She grimaced. "Drove me nuts."

"So you moved somewhere new?"

"Yup," said Selina. "Went up to Manchester. Great town."

"You liked it?"

Selina gave Lance a look that suggested he should be somewhere else. Being a terrible estate agent but a pretty decent human being, Lance took the hint and took out his smartphone and started fiddling with it.

Selina shrugged. "Went out a lot. Hung out with people too young for me. Who didn't know anything about me. Did the city thing. Casual sex, you know."

Lance was still looking at his phone, but his ears went bright pink.

"Mmm," said Polly, pouring more tea. "Did it help?"

"Not as much as you'd think," said Selina, frowning. "And I had my doubts from the outset, to be honest."

Polly nodded. Selina let out a great sigh.

"And I have to . . . my therapist thinks this too. Because I have a therapist now. How wonderful is that? I always hoped I'd have a therapist."

"Lots of people have therapy," said Polly mildly.

"Lots of people have scabies," said Selina. "Didn't want that either."

Lance stiffened. "You have scabies? Only, the lease . . ."

"It's a figure of speech," said Selina. She was sharper, more brittle, thought Polly, than the last time she'd seen her.

"So, my *therapist* . . ."

Polly had a sudden flashback to the couples' therapist she had insisted Chris go with her to at one dark stage toward the end of their relationship. It had been incredibly painful. Chris had sneered at the expensive cars parked outside the practice, its smart reception, the well-dressed therapist with her trendy glasses. He'd sneered at Polly too, for wanting the therapist to like her, for answering questions helpfully.

"Oh yes, you win that one," he'd say, in a tone of voice so nasty she simply couldn't recognize the sweet, shy art student she'd once known. And then she'd hear herself, placatory, soothing, talking like an annoying nagging mother to a recalcitrant child, and she couldn't recognize herself either.

The counselor had done her best, but had started quite early on to talk about debt mediation services to "get to the root of the problem." At the time Polly had taken this at face value and thought it would be helpful (which it would have been if Chris had ever agreed to go). Now she saw it starkly for what it had been: a counselor who could clearly see that what had once been between them had gone, and who was trying to ease them apart in the most practical way possible.

It made her sad to think of it, even as she consoled herself with the fact that Chris had a new girlfriend, and she was happier than she'd ever been. But all those years . . . all those years, she told herself, got you where you are now. All those years were necessary. If you were just happy from the day you were born, how would you ever know? How would you appreciate how good life could be if it had never been crap?

But of course it was worse for Selina; so much worse. She'd been perfectly happy, more or less—things hadn't been perfect between her and Tarnie, but that hardly mattered now—and it had been torn out of her hand, like a wave smashing a bottle against a rock.

". . . my therapist thinks it won't be a bad thing to come home. Reconnect with Tarnie's world, feel close to him instead of blocking it all out with sex and getting drunk. Well, I think that's what she thinks. That's therapists for you: you suggest something and they just say 'mmmm' and you have to figure it out from there."

Polly nodded. "Well, it seems like it might make sense. But you never liked it here, did you?"

Selina shrugged. "My husband disappeared for weeks on end, worked all night and came home knackered and stinking of fish, with no money in his pocket. That's what this place did for him. And I begged him and nagged him not to, and he wouldn't listen to me for a bloody second. Just as well he died, we'd only have ended up divorced."

The pain in her words was so stark, Polly couldn't help putting her arm around her.

"Oh, fucking hell," said Selina. "When does it stop, this? When do I stop feeling like this, being like this, all the time? Is this the answer, or just another dead end?"

"I don't know," said Polly honestly. "I really don't know."

Polly hadn't been up in the flat for a long time. Jayden occasionally stored flour there if they needed to, and sometimes Neil forgot and flew back to the wrong house, but otherwise she hadn't had much call to go up there in the last year. It reminded her too much of the pain of moving, alone, to a strange place; of the long, cold months of the winter after Tarnie had died, when Huckle had gone back to America and she had waited for him, not knowing what to do, missing him so desperately that all she could do was bake bread and stare out to sea and wonder if this was the rest of her life.

"Can you show me it?" Selina asked, when Polly revealed it had once been her flat. "Only Lance will just give me the spiel."

"I won't," protested Lance. "I'll probably forget it."

Polly's instinct was to decline, but she couldn't, of course. She put on a smile, cleared away the tea things and said that of course she would.

"Polly knows what an excellent piece of—"

Polly gave Lance a warning look.

"Obviously when it's had some modifications done,"

said Lance, coughing. Polly gave him an even more meaningful look.

"Oh, just come on then," said Lance crossly, and Polly let them through the side door of the bakery so they wouldn't have to go outside into the crashing wind.

The stairs were as vertiginous as ever, the little bulb taking a strong pull to make it work, and there was a lot of noise as they clattered upward. Lance had the Yale key; Polly had a spare in case of emergencies. With the bakery shut downstairs, the building was ominously silent.

But as they stepped into the flat, even on such a gray day, the light flooded through the huge front windows that looked straight out to sea, as if you were flying over it.

"Wow," said Selina, moving forward. "That's quite a view."

Polly thought of the nights she'd fallen asleep in front of that view. Her old armchair was still stationed by the window, but the rugs and the pictures and the lovely sofa had of course all gone across to the lighthouse, on a day of hard work that had caused more swearing among the fishermen than she'd ever heard before, and she heard them swear a lot.

The bare scrubbed boards still inclined gently toward the front of the room, meaning you couldn't leave an orange on the floor safely, but the roof tiles were mostly watertight now, and the bathroom and the kitchen, though the most basic of units (and avocado in the case of the bathroom), were at least now clean and safe to use. The basic bed in the back room was still there. Polly had a very quick and uncomfortable flashback to a sun-drenched afternoon she had once spent there with Selina's dead husband, but she suppressed it immediately.

"This really is a dump, right?" Selina was saying, looking distastefully at the kitchen. Polly felt slightly offended. Okay, it was a dump, but it had been *her* dump. "Does it get cold in the winter?"

"The bakery heats it up?" said Lance hopefully.

Selina looked confused.

"But we've just been in the bakery, and it's freezing up here," she said.

"Yeah, but we're shut now," said Polly. "It's probably really warm at . . . five a.m."

Selina sighed, then went and looked out of the window again. Her face grew thoughtful. It was a look Polly recognized.

"It's a lovely view," said Polly. "It's very restful."

Selina frowned at the lighthouse.

"Does that thing light up?"

"It's a lighthouse," said Polly.

"Does it shine in here?"

"You see, I never thought to ask that question before I moved in," said Polly. "But you can buy really good blackout blinds these days."

Selina looked at the lighthouse again.

"Do you really live there?"

"Yup," said Polly.

"By yourself?"

"No . . . with my boyfriend," said Polly. "And my . . . my pet."

Selina's face dropped.

"You're so lucky," she said.

Polly didn't know what to say. She knew she was.

"Are pets allowed here?" Selina said to Lance.

"Um, dunno." He looked at his papers. "No snakes."

"Do I look like I keep snakes?"

"Nobody looks like they keep snakes," said Lance

wisely. "But you find the buggers all over the place. Take it from an estate agent. Worst bit of my job."

"The worst bit of your job is *all the snakes*?" said Polly.

"Yes," said Lance stoutly.

"I would not have guessed that."

"Me neither," said Selina. "Anyway, no. It's a cat."

"Snakes with fur," said Lance, sniffing, then remembered he was meant to be showing a flat. "And also, wonderful. I love them."

"He's beautiful," said Selina.

"It's nice to have a pet," said Polly, stopping herself when she realized she was about to add "when you're all alone."

"What have you got?" said Selina. "We could have a play date."

"I've . . . it's a bird," said Polly. There was no point in explaining Neil to people who didn't already know. They either thought she was a total weirdo, or cruel, or a cruel weirdo.

"Oh. Like a canary?"

"A bit like a canary," lied Polly.

"Although I do think it's cruel to keep birds in cages."

"Oh no, this one is totally free-range," said Polly. "So probably no play dates."

"Oh, Lucas is very gentle," said Selina.

"So you're taking it?" interjected Lance cheerfully. If the client was already booking social occasions, the deal was probably in the bag.

Selina glanced back at the flat and sighed, then looked ahead at the horizon.

"Yes," she said. "I guess I am."

Chapter Seven

"I can't believe I'm doing this."

Kerensa was getting dressed in Polly's bedroom. Polly was trying not to send covetous glances via the mirror at Kerensa's patently very expensive matching underwear. She couldn't remember the last time she'd worn matching underwear. Come to think of it, Huckle had also mentioned mildly in passing that if it wasn't too much to ask, could she possibly stick to the traditional number of holes in her underpants, i.e., three.

"Are you eyeing me up?" said Kerensa, expertly applying layers of serum, moisturizer, primer, CC cream and bronzer in the manner of somebody painting a house. "Only, I'm totally married."

Her enormous engagement ring caught the light of the evening sun.

"Yes," said Polly. "It's been a really tough secret to

carry around all this time. But I feel like I'm there now. Actually, no, I just like your posh bra."

Kerensa smiled. "I know. I spend a lot of time with not much on . . ."

"Can we not go into this again?"

Kerensa glanced at where Polly was sitting on the bed, haphazardly trying to paint her nails.

"How do you guys sleep on such a tiny bed?"

Kerensa's bed was bigger than king-size. It was in fact called emperor-size. It was basically about four beds stuck together, in Polly's opinion. The sheets were changed every single day. This would have horrified Polly if she hadn't been so desperately envious. There wasn't much of Kerensa's life that she was envious of— she was too busy to travel, she couldn't imagine wanting to kiss Reuben, she didn't really have a lot of interest in handbags, and there was nowhere she'd rather live than the lighthouse.

But the bed was really very, very nice.

In the lighthouse, by way of contrast, they hadn't been able to get a full double mattress up the stairs, never mind a bedstead, and there wasn't a flat wall to stand it against anyway. They could have conceded defeat and moved into the little dank room at the bottom of the tower, but Polly was having none of that. So instead they slept upstairs in a three-quarter-sized double bed. Huckle's feet stuck straight out the bottom, as if he were in "Goldilocks and the Three Bears." Kerensa thought it was appalling. Polly didn't know how Kerensa could find Reuben so far away in their acres and acres of white linen. She herself vanished inside Huckle every evening, curled up underneath his arm, a tangle of limbs until it was impossible to know where one of them ended and the other began, their hearts beating in unison, their breathing slowing together. On the rare nights when he was away from home, she had found herself propped up in front of the window, looking out to sea again, completely unable to sleep without him. Even though she wouldn't mind a proper bed, Polly knew she would never again sleep as soundly as she did on those nights in their tiny rolled-together space.

"We manage," she said defiantly.

"I suppose you're so knackered from running up and down those ridiculous stairs . . ."

"You're right," said Polly. "If only I were wealthy, I could hire someone to carry me up on their shoulders."

Kerensa grinned. "Or put a lift in."

"If you put a lift in," pointed out Polly, "there'd be nothing left but lift."

Kerensa pulled on a pair of tights, brand new, an expensive make, straight from the packet. She never wore her tights twice. Polly couldn't get her head around that fact.

"You're making best friends with the widow of the guy you banged. Are you *sure* this is a good idea?"

"It's just a night out," said Polly, glancing at her watch. "It seemed mean to go out with everyone and not invite her. I remember what it was like when I first moved here and didn't know anyone."

"Yeah," said Kerensa. "You had to go out and shag the first married fisherman you saw."

Polly gave her a look.

"Oh, come on," said Kerensa. "Isn't it better this way? Better out than in? So I don't accidentally sploof it up after my third glass of wine?"

"No," said Polly. "Seriously, I don't want it mentioned at all. It's embarrassing to me, and it could be devastating to her. She's in a bad state. This could make things worse."

"Or maybe the truth would help?"

"Sometimes the truth helps," said Polly. "Other times it makes everything a million times worse, especially when the other person isn't there to shout at. I thought he was single, remember? If he'd even bothered to mention her, I wouldn't have gone anywhere near him. It was all his fault. So why make her feel worse? Plus, she needs friends right now, and I think we can be that."

"Well, as long as you manage not to sleep with her brother or anything . . . Where's the Huck?"

"At a honey conference in Devon, would you believe," said Polly. "It's like three hundred apiarists. They all get together to discuss floral patenting and hive conservation and drink mead. But Dubose is coming."

"He's cute," said Kerensa.

"Yes," said Polly. "He's slightly less cute when he leaves his laundry all over the stairs and spends a lot of time complaining that there's not much to do here."

"There *isn't* much to do here."

"See, I get enough of it from you. I don't need it from anyone else."

"Okay," said Kerensa. "Tell me about Huckle's conference. Tell me they get dressed up."

"Well, there's a dinner . . ."

"No, I mean tell me they get dressed up as bees."

"They do not get dressed up as bees."

"That is so disappointing."

"Well," said Polly, "I *might* have bought Huckle a black and yellow striped sweater."

"No way!" said Kerensa, grinning. "Are you making him wear it?"

"Are you joking? He fills this house head to toe with puffin shiz. I need to get my revenge somehow."

"Ha," said Kerensa. "Do you think they listen to a lot of old Police songs?"

" 'Don't Buzz So Close to Me'?"

" 'Da Bee Bee Bee, Da Ba Ba Ba.' "

The two girls burst out laughing.

"Okay, we're obviously pissed already," said Kerensa, looking at her glass. "I think we need to go out before we're too pissed to get down the stairs. Down is harder than up when you're pissed."

"I know, like horses."

"What do you mean, like horses?"

"Horses can walk up stairs but not down. If you find a horse at the top of a lighthouse, it's really terrible news."

"I do not know how I functioned in the world without knowing that."

Kerensa slid a long-sleeved, very plain but clearly insanely expensive dress over her head.

"Cor, that looks like it was made for you," said Polly cheerfully.

"Um, yes," said Kerensa. "That's because it was."

"Seriously?"

"Seriously," said Kerensa. "Someone stuck a pin in me at the fitting and Reuben threatened to sue them."

"Your life is weird now," said Polly.

"You're the one whose most pressing future purchase is a FIREMAN'S POLE."

Dubose joined them as they left the lighthouse. He was wearing a pale gray shirt that Polly knew for a fact was Huckle's, but she didn't mention it.

The air was warm and stiller than it had been recently as they walked companionably down across the rocks, Kerensa as usual in ridiculous shoes. Neil came fluttering up from the rock pool he'd been splashing in—his outdoor swimming pool, as Huckle called it. Kerensa bent down.

"Hey, small bird," she said. Neil eeped at her. Kerensa was not his favorite. She never carried snacks and she didn't like getting bird footprints on her expensive clothes.

"You know, I saw a million puffins coming down here today. And do you know what they were doing? They were playing with their mates, right? Flocking and shagging and making noise and bouncing about all over the place. Have you got no mates? You haven't got any mates, have you?"

Kerensa straightened up.

"Your bird's weird. You need to sort him out with some friends or a girlfriend or something."

Polly stiffened.

"He seems perfectly happy to me."

Neil hopped toward her feet and rubbed his head affectionately on her tights. His beak caught and he accidentally started a ladder in one of them. Kerensa rolled her eyes, but Polly just scratched him behind the ears, which he loved.

"I'm just saying. He's not a baby anymore. Shouldn't he be out and about more?"

"Yeah," said Dubose. "That bird needs to get laid."

"Well, I'm not stopping him," said Polly in an injured tone. She got very defensive about Neil. "If he wants to meet a lady puffin, he can do that whenever he likes."

"How's he going to meet one if you don't take him to any flocking areas?" said Kerensa. "Do they have Tinder for puffins? They could call it Flounder. Heh heh heh."

Polly sighed. She did wonder sometimes, in her heart of hearts, if she should have been stricter about taking Neil back to the sanctuary once he'd escaped and come back to her. She did worry about thwarting his natural development by making him so dependent on them—he couldn't hunt if his life depended on it, could barely fly and even by puffin standards had a distinctly rounded tummy. Plus if this new guy Malcolm was going to be absolutely determined that birds wouldn't be allowed in the shop . . .

"Did you just come down from your castle tonight to give me grief?" she said to Kerensa.

"Always," said Kerensa. "Did you come down from your tower tonight to give me a drink? Because I have to say, I'm feeling rather thirsty."

"Partaay!" said Dubose.

The Red Lion was already buzzing when they got there. It wasn't the holiday season yet, but early and un-expected sunshine had meant extra day trippers, which meant happy workers, so nearly every table in the cob-bled courtyard was full.

Andy had a band playing, a bunch of fishermen from down the coast at Looe. There was a fiddler, an accordion player wearing a flat cap, a singer and a percussionist.

"Fuck me, it's the Mumfords," said Kerensa gloomily, but Polly enjoyed listening to the traditional shanties on a starry spring night within sight and sound of the sea. They did "Sir Patrick Spens" and "The Poorest Company" while Kerensa went to the bar. She started shout-ing before she even got there, until the scared-looking bartender remembered her from last time and went to the back of the fridge where he kept her secret stock of decent Chablis, as opposed to the warm horse piss that made up their wine list the rest of the time.

Polly went over and said hi to the Polbearne fishermen, including Jayden but not Archie, who had obviously gone home to his long-suffering wife and family, something for which she was extremely grateful.

"How are things?" she said.

"Oh," said Sten, the tall Scandinavian. "New quotas are coming. The boat needs expensive work. The price of fish goes up and nobody wants it anymore."

"But apart from that, fine?" said Polly. The others nodded.

Patrick the vet was at the next table.

"Hey," said Polly, smiling. "Can I ask you a question?"

Patrick looked at his whisky and soda with some apprehension. "Is this one of those ones where you pretend you're asking about an animal the same size and weight as you but then it turns out it is you and you didn't want to call the doctor?"

The doctor was based on the mainland and only came to the island once a week or so, grumbling madly about access all the time, whereas Patrick lived here and often found himself approached for human advice. He couldn't blame them, but he was terrified of accidentally giving advice that led to serious problems, so it wasn't his favorite part of the job. He was semi-retired in any case, only saw the local animals from time to time.

"Um, no," said Polly. "Does that happen a lot?"

Patrick shrugged. "It's been known. What is it? It's not that bird of yours, is it?"

Patrick had a fondness for Neil. The little puffin had tickled his fancy, even though he thought it was wrong of Polly to keep him as a pet.

"I think he's having social problems," began Polly. Patrick raised his eyebrows.

"Actually, I'm not really a bird psychologist . . ."

"He doesn't have any bird friends. The seagulls are just big bullies, and the other puffins . . . I think they're laughing at him."

"Well, stop making him wear a jacket."

"It was only that one time, when it was cold," said Polly.

"And I still don't think those wellingtons . . ."

"No," admitted Polly. "Those wellingtons were a mistake, on balance."

Patrick let out a sigh.

"Look," he said. "I did warn you this would happen."

"I know," said Polly, hanging her head.

"You domesticated an animal that isn't designed to be domesticated."

"I know that."

"It's probably not too late to re-wild it, you know."

"Maybe I should domesticate another one to be his friend."

Patrick eyed her. "You will not!"

"No. I won't."

Polly sighed. "I just want him to have what's best. And for the other birds to accept him."

Patrick nodded. "I know, Polly. But you know what you'd have to do."

Polly was still deep in thought when Kerensa came back, having finally gotten the barman to clean the glasses, plus dig out an ice bucket, plus let the wine breathe. She was pretty much all yelled out.

"What?"

"Oh, nothing. Apparently re-wilding Neil would be difficult but not impossible."

"I'm sure he's fine. Playing all by himself in his rock pool. Maybe he'll think his reflection is a friend . . . Oh Polly, your face!"

"Whoa," said Dubose suddenly, putting down his beer bottle. "Now who is THAT?"

Polly and Kerensa turned around.

At first Polly couldn't make her out in the dark of the pub courtyard, lit only by strings of fairy lights that could make this bit of Mount Polbearne, the fishermen said, look like a cruise ship when you were out at sea.

Then her mouth fell open. A young girl was walking toward them, wearing a soft Lycra dress that clung lightly to her slim figure. Her black hair was combed back and fell like a waterfall onto her shoulders; her eyelashes were so long they cast shadows on her cheeks, her dark eyes huge. The entire pub fell silent.

"That's . . . that's Flora!" said Polly in astonishment.

Flora approached them. She looked like some beautiful witch girl.

"Can I sit with youse?" she said. "Only I missed the tide again."

"You may!" said Dubose, jumping up and pulling out a chair for her. "I'm Dubose."

Flora looked at him without interest.

"You look beautiful," said Polly. She couldn't help it: the transformation from dowdy, greasy-haired Flora, always staring at the floor and giving wrong change, into this goddess was overwhelming.

"Oh, I know," said Flora in a flat voice. "People keep saying. It's boring."

The girls exchanged looks of disbelief.

"So are you from around here?" said Dubose. "I'm from America!"

He said this with a flourish. Flora looked up at him mournfully under her big lashes.

"Oh," she said.

"You're fascinating," said Dubose, heading to the bar to get her a drink. As he did so, Polly noticed out of the corner of her eye the fishermen all gazing open-mouthed. Jayden was so pink she thought he was going to burst.

"Does this . . . does this happen to you often?" asked Polly.

Flora nodded. "Yeah."

"But don't you want to go and make it as a model or something?" said Kerensa. "I mean, I could introduce you to some people . . ."

Flora shook her head.

"I just want to bake," she said. "That's all I've ever wanted to do. And people just want to take stupid photos. It's rubbish."

Polly grinned. "I can't believe I've wasted my life like this," she said, "when all I had to do was to be born unbelievably beautiful."

"It's rubbish," said Flora. "People just bug you all the time."

"Is that why you never wash your hair?" said Polly.

"Yeah," said Flora. "Oh, also, I forget."

Suddenly, Jayden was at the table. He'd obviously had a couple of jars and plucked up the courage.

"Hello, young ladies!" His mustache was thicker than ever, his cheeks round and unusually pink.

"Hello, Jayden!"

"Hello, Miss Polly! Hello, Kerensa! Hello . . ."

Jayden had completely lost the power of speech.

"Did you want something?" said Polly gently. Jayden,

so incredibly charming and sweet with the older women of the town, was generally terribly unsuccessful with the opposite sex if they were younger than fifty. Turning red was something of a giveaway, although Jayden also turned red if he was warm, cold, excited, cross, tired or perturbed, so you couldn't exactly rely on it.

"I just . . . I couldn't help hearing . . ."

Jayden's table was three noisy tables and a fiddle band away.

"I couldn't help overhearing that Miss Flora . . . might need a place to stay."

"That's some pretty good bionic ears you've got going on there," said Kerensa.

"Because, you know . . ."

"Jayden, you live at your mum's," said Polly.

"Uh, *thanks*," said Jayden crossly. "We've got a spare room, you know. I'm only trying to be polite. I don't know why everyone's making such a big deal about it or getting so worked up about it, honestly. I didn't even hear what was going on and even if I did I don't even care, so there. And I don't live at my mum's. I lodge with an older woman. I pay rent. So actually I'm a young single man renting. It's just coincidence that it's my mum's."

He stalked off.

"Uh, yes please?" said Flora quietly.

Jayden froze. Then he turned around incredibly slowly.

"SERIOUSLY?" he said.

"Uh, yeah?" said Flora.

Jayden looked like he was going to faint. He flushed a brighter pink than ever, and his face was a mixture of delight and terror.

"I'll just tell my mum . . . I mean, my landlady. She can make up the spare bed."

He looked shyly at Flora and then back at the floor.

"You can come and sit with us if you like."

"No thanks," said Flora, staring at the floor too.

"Oh," said Jayden. There was a moment's silence. "Okay. Phoning my mum."

As he sidled away from them, Polly burst out laughing.

"Flora, I think you've pulled."

Flora looked unhappy.

"I've always pulled," she said.

"Well, I really feel sorry for your terrible, terrible problems," said Polly, smiling.

"Did I go to the bar for ten seconds and miss out?" said Dubose, smiling his nice white smile. His eyes were drawn to the entrance to the courtyard. "Oh well," he said, perking up.

A slender figure was standing nervously underneath the eaves, scanning the busy tables. Polly glanced over, then waved heartily.

"Aha," said Kerensa, taking another large gulp of her wine. "It's the Merry Widow."

"Be. Nice," hissed Polly, composing her face.

"Hey, I'm not the one who—"

"Shut up."

Selina came over looking apprehensive.

"I wasn't going to come out," she said. "But I was sitting in there all alone . . . It's quite spooky, isn't it?"

Polly nodded. "A little bit, but only at first. It's quite useful knowing that nobody can get across from the mainland. Keeps all the baddies out."

"Or in," said Selina, glancing about. "I think I was half asleep. Then I heard the music and thought I would come down."

"Well, you're here now," said Polly. Even compared to Kerensa, who was very slim, Selina was punishingly skinny, in a tight black top that emphasized her knobbly collarbones, and jeans that were falling off her.

"Hi," said Selina directly to Kerensa.

"Hello," said Kerensa, slightly standoffishly, Polly thought. She really wanted them to get on; it would be much more fun. Plus it would be nice to have a new friend in the village. Kerensa was always heading off to the Monaco Grand Prix or Coachella; Muriel, between working in the grocer's and looking after her new baby, couldn't keep her eyes open for more than half an hour, and conversation with Flora had its limitations.

"Can I have some of that wine?" asked Selina. "Possibly quite a lot?"

Kerensa softened a bit.

"Are you going to screw up your face like Flora does?" she said.

"No," said Selina. "I'm going to neck it, then buy us some more."

Kerensa smiled. "Welcome."

Dubose leaned in and joined in the conversation.

"How on earth did you end up married to a fisherman?" he asked in genuine puzzlement.

"Sorry," said Polly gently, sitting beside Selina. "We don't have to talk about him if you don't want to."

Selina shook her head.

"No," she said. "Everyone pussyfoots around me all the time. I really, really want to talk about him."

Polly nodded.

"Well," said Selina. "I was on holiday down here, staying in one of those really posh houses."

Flora suddenly brightened.

"Are you one of the posh girls?" she asked.

"Not any more," smiled Selina. "Why?"

"Oh yes, you should do that," said Polly to Flora. "Looking like that, you could marry Prince Harry or something."

Selina laughed so hard at this, Polly was worried she was going to choke. She also, Polly thought, had the look of a person who hadn't laughed enough for a very long time, and wasn't always entirely sure when it was appropriate.

"Um, okay, do NOT marry a posh boy," said Selina. "Unless you like, you know, being their mummy, dealing with drug abuse, never ever knowing how they feel and having to stick things up their bottoms."

Flora looked horrified.

"Seriously? All of them?" asked Polly, fascinated. She didn't know any posh people.

"All of them," said Selina. "Every single one."

Flora bit her lip.

"Are you joking?"

"No," said Selina. "I would never joke about that."

"So you married Tarnie because . . . what, because you didn't have to do any of that?" said Kerensa, getting borderline hysterical.

"Kerensa!" said Polly. "Seriously, watch it!"

Selina shook her head.

"Oh, I'm meant to talk about him," she said, rolling her eyes. "Therapist says so, and it's costing me enough . . ."

"Well, you can't have everything," said Kerensa.

"He was going back and forth between here and Looe back then," said Selina, taking on a slightly dreamy look. "Oh my, he was so handsome. It was before the beard. I was very against the beard. I think he only did it to annoy me."

"Oh, I quite liked it," said Polly without thinking, earning herself a warning kick under the table from Kerensa. "What? Oh."

But Selina went on, lost in her reverie.

"He was gorgeous. Every other idiot I'd met was such a prannet, going on and on about the City, or oil speculating, or what their daddy did or whatever."

"While requiring insertion," added Kerensa.

"Quite," said Selina, lighting up a cigarette and waving it around. Polly and Kerensa didn't mind, but Flora looked horrified.

"Get used to smoking if you want a posh boy," said Selina. "Their parents abandoned them to boarding school. They all have to smoke to stop themselves from crying."

"Maybe I shouldn't marry a posh boy," said Flora. She glanced over at Jayden, who hadn't taken his eyes off her, and who waved furiously.

"I sure am learning a lot tonight," said Dubose.

"And he was real," Selina went on. "He didn't speak unless he had something he needed to say. He didn't turn on the charm . . . I hate charm. Such a bloody overindulged characteristic. As if it means anything. Charm is just a way of fuckers getting you to do what they wanted you to do all along. They might as well hold a gun to your head. They're both shortcuts."

"Hear, hear," said Kerensa. Reuben was so abrasive and uncharming that Polly found it came all the way around the back and ended up charming again.

"He just said it like it was . . . of course at first I found that really attractive. Later on it made me want to kill him every time I attempted to start a conversation about our relationship."

The women nodded.

"And he was just . . . he was just so different from all the nobbers that I'd known before. So straight. So honest."

Polly gazed at the table, her ears burning.

"So," said Selina, "I gave up everything. Oh my lord, my parents went mental. I felt like one of those sixteen-year-olds in the newspapers every summer who goes on holiday to Turkey and accidentally marries a waiter. Seriously, you'd think that's what I'd done. My stepmum was the worst. She's a vicious character to begin with, but she'd fought her way up from nothing to marry my dad, who had a bit, and she was all like 'You don't know what it's like being poor, Selina. You think it's romantic, but it's not the least bit romantic when the boiler breaks down in the middle of the winter, and he's off on the high seas.'" She mimicked a high-pitched estuary voice. "'Also, you know, all sailors have venereal disease.'"

There was a silence.

"Of course the worst of it is, she was right."

"About the venereal disease?" Polly had suddenly sat up straighter.

"No, for God's sake. You knew him. You know what a brilliant bloke he was. No, about the having no money. It sucked. I couldn't get a teaching job anywhere. All there was on offer was hotel cleaning or bar work. Both of which I tried, by the way."

She shook her head. Andy had silently come over and left another bottle with them, and Kerensa refilled their glasses. Selina was less animated now.

"That's why . . . that's why going back to town was so awful. It was full of people who never knew him. Didn't know how decent and kind and right he was, who only saw my off-brand fucking trainers and us fighting all the time. After he died I tried somewhere new, and that was awful too. I always ended up having two glasses of wine too many and ruining everyone else's night out."

"Is that why you came back here?"

"That," said Selina heavily. "And because I didn't know where else to go."

The boys, Polly noticed, had started dancing a hornpipe, and she pretended to watch them, all the while hugging her knees to her chest, her heart going out to Selina, who had finally announced, "Let's change the subject! I can't do the miserable widow act for very long. PLEASE. I really can't."

And they had chatted of other things, but carefully. Dubose took on the job of trying to make Selina laugh and was reasonably successful, and Polly chatted to Archie who had just come in, stopped by the table, done a massive double take at Flora, then smiled tiredly.

"How's she doing?" he asked Polly quietly, a little away from the group, nodding at Selina.

"I think . . . I think she's making some progress," said Polly, then looked at him more closely. The lines were still deep around his eyes, and Polly remembered how close he and Tarnie had been, sailing together for so many years. A lot of people were worried about Selina, but Archie had been right there and was trying to carry on without him, and the pain showed on his face. The ripples from the sinking, Polly thought, had spread out like a stone cast in a pond and made their presence felt in all directions.

"How are you?" she asked.

Archie shrugged. "Nights like tonight," he said, looking around at half the town out under the fairy lights, drinking, talking, laughing, "I really miss him. And sometimes I'll be throwing a line and I half think to look around for him, but he's gone. And I keep thinking, am I doing it how he would have done it? Would he have been happy with me?"

"Of course he would," said Polly encouragingly.

"I hope so," said Archie. "I really, really do."

Polly patted his hand. "Get more rest," she said. "The job is knackering enough on its own without you having to worry all the time about everyone else. You're doing well. You really are. The lads are happy, and the fish are coming in."

The boys finally stopped dancing and bowed to a scattering of applause, then, out of breath and pinker than ever, Jayden came over to their table and stood in front of Flora.

"Did you like me dancing?" he asked.

"You were dancing?" said Flora, in an uninterested voice.

Polly stood up.

"Come on, let's go home."

"Flora is coming with me!" yelled Jayden loudly to the rest of the bar, who raised their heads only briefly. Flora rolled her eyes.

"To your mum's," she said, getting up with some reluctance.

"Do you need a spare T-shirt?" said Polly.

"It's all right," said Jayden. "My mum's got lots of nighties."

They all looked at one another.

"Probably," said Jayden. "Or you can borrow one of my T-shirts."

"As a sleeping bag," said Flora.

Jayden and Flora headed up the winding hill to Jayden's mother's tiny two-up two-down fisherman's cottage, which clung to the hillside like a child clinging to its mother.

Polly and Kerensa walked side by side, trying not to sneak glances back at Selina and Dubose, who were very close together, slightly tipsy, behind them.

They walked past the Little Beach Street Bakery, its windows crumb-free and empty, apart from a wedding cake Polly had made for a family on the mainland, which she was displaying in the window until it was ready to go. Polly turned around to say good night to Selina.

"I think you did a good thing coming back here," she said. She couldn't bear the look of misery in Selina's eyes. "Tarnie . . . your husband . . . he's in every stone of this place. Every brick. You can talk about him all day if you like. Nobody didn't know him, and nobody didn't like him. This was his place, he came from here, and you can be here too."

Selina paused for a moment.

"Thanks," she said. "Sorry. Arriving has been a bit overwhelming. Thanks for letting me unload on you lot."

"No problem," said Polly. She watched, slightly concerned, as Dubose squeezed Selina's hand and leaned over and kissed her hard on the cheek. But then he rejoined Polly and Kerensa.

Later, after they'd had a cup of tea back at the house, and Kerensa had gone to bed in the real, big proper bed in the annex downstairs, Polly went up to look at the sea and text Huckle, hoping it wasn't too late. It wasn't too late, he explained laboriously when he phoned, rather drunk, but the mead had come out again and had made it completely impossible to form co . . . co . . . co . . . understandable words, but did she know that he . . . he . . . no, listen, this was important, no, don't hang up, okay, because he loved her more than everything in the world, did she understand that? Because it was vitally important that she understood that, okay?

And Polly laughed and said she did understand, and let him talk on while she got ready for bed, until he told her once more that he loved her.

Then she gave Neil a big cuddle and remembered her slightly worrying conversation with Patrick, but decided to put it out of her head for now, as the little puffin fluttered about getting comfortable in his bed, made from an old tea box. (She had bought him an expensive dog basket but he hated it. He liked the rustling of the cardboard. Also, when he had one of his invariable accidents, she could just throw the box out and get another one. Neil had never quite become house-trained, although he had gotten a lot better).

Finally, going to the window, she looked out over the little town. She could see the fairy lights at the pub being switched off, and the street lamps going out; only the beam from the lighthouse continued to swing around in the thick of the evening; and down in the town, just where she used to sit, a low light shone, and a small shape sat in front of the window, sleepless, alone, in the tiny flat above the Little Beach Street Bakery.

Chapter Eight

After a lazy Sunday, during which Huckle was frankly good for nothing except eating bacon sandwiches and groaning, and Dubose disappeared completely, Polly wasn't looking forward to Monday morning. She had a strong suspicion that Malcolm was going to show up again. Unfortunately, she was right.

Ironically, the shop had never looked better. It was a beautiful day. The cobbles seemed freshly scrubbed under a clear blue sky. The pale gray frontage was fresh and clean; the windows, thanks to Jayden's hard work, shone. Regardless of what other problems she might have, thought Polly, it was just a wonderful morning to be alive. The warm scent of the first batch of newly baked bread was already rising on the air. Hopping down the steps from the lighthouse (Neil, who had wanted to leave with her, was tucked under Huckle's sleeping arm), carrying two extra trays of proved dough to make cinnamon rolls, she was in an exceptionally good mood.

"Hey, Jayden," she sang out as she came through the door. "Nice job."

Jayden looked up from where he was scrubbing out a drawer, pink as ever.

"Well?" said Polly, washing her hands and rolling out the cinnamon dough with the butter cinnamon mix, then expertly rolling them up again into spirals and chopping them into neat slices.

"Well what?" said Jayden gruffly.

"How did it go with Flora?"

Jayden stopped and sighed.

"She looks like an angel," he said, his eyes dazed. "She looks like a star. I can't even look at her, she's so beautiful."

"But did you talk to her?"

Jayden shook his head.

"How could I talk to her? It's like she's out of a film or something. She's too beautiful. I couldn't say anything to her at all." He sighed. "I can only worship her till the end of my days."

"I don't think she'll like that," said Polly. "Can't you talk to her about baking, or something else she likes?"

Jayden looked taken aback.

"But she's so beautiful!" he said.

"Okay," said Polly. "I'm starting to see Flora's problem."

"She doesn't have any problems," said Jayden. "She's perfect."

Malcolm stumbled in at about ten o'clock. He did not look well. His peaky face was gray and lumpy, and his hair was dirty. He was wearing the same rumpled trousers as he had the week before, but they looked even more wrinkled and stained, and he smelled a little stale.

"Hello, Malcolm," said Polly brightly. "We're bird free today, as I hope you can see. Cinnamon roll?"

If he could resist her cinnamon rolls, Polly thought, then he was a stronger man than she gave him credit for. The lightly melting sweet buttery inside; the soft, yielding doughy exterior . . .

He polished it off in two bites.

"Not bad," he said. "You can get 'em from the services in packs of three."

He put out a paw to reach for another one. Polly resisted the urge to slap him down.

"So, did you have a good weekend?"

She passed him a coffee with three sugars, which he gulped down.

"Heavy one," said Malcolm, sounding pleased with himself. "Down the Sugar House. Out with the lads. Bit of footie, few pints, nightclub. There were some right slags in there, though, know what I mean?"

This was directed at Jayden, who looked confused. Polly knew his mother would have boxed his ears if that word had even crossed his brain.

"Yeah, they all think they're just so great in their little short skirts."

He took another slurp of his coffee and shook his head.

"Little . . ."

He seemed to recollect where he was and didn't finish the sentence, smiling instead, showing gray teeth.

"So, yeah, great weekend, yeah."

He sniffed.

"Right, I've been poring over these figures, right? Okay? So I think I've got us a plan together."

Polly wiped her hands, washed them again, then she and Jayden started pounding out the lunchtime bread together.

"See," said Malcolm, "you doing this. It's inefficient, is what it is. You making all this bread every day."

"I know," said Polly. "If I wanted it to be efficient, I'd probably just go and work in a factory or something."

"ZACTLY," said Malcolm, looking pleased. "Doesn't make any sense you doing this every day. I bet you'd rather not."

Polly looked at him, astonished.

"But I love doing it," she said.

"Bit much like hard work, innit?" said Malcolm.

Polly shook her head.

"No," she said. "Well, yes. But it's good work. Good, honest work that people like."

Malcolm sniffed again.

"That's all very nineteenth century," he said. "Nice and everything, but cahm on. Centralized distribution, bulk discounting . . . that's how things work these days. In the business world. Cost, that's all anyone cares about. Why do you think everyone shops in Lidl?"

"Nothing wrong with Lidl," said Jayden.

"Zactly."

"I didn't say there was anything wrong with Lidl," said Polly, exasperated. "But there's more than one way of doing things. There's no reason you can't get some things cheaply and pay a bit more for other, special things. It's the difference between a plastic bag and a Hermès bag."

Polly had never seen a Hermès bag in her entire life,

but she'd read about them in the kind of magazines she pretended fervently to Huckle she didn't really enjoy.

"Both work, but you don't necessarily want them to do the same thing."

"Yeah," said Malcolm. "You pick the one that makes financial sense."

Polly's mobile rang. This was unusual, partly because coverage here was patchy at the best of times, partly because her mother was terrified of mobiles and never phoned them in case they were accidentally one thousand pounds a call. Polly kept in touch with her old friends via Facebook, and everybody else she knew would just drop in to see her; it was never a mystery where she was going to be.

"Excuse me," she said, heading out the back to take the call.

"Hello?"

The voice on the other end of the line was posh, sharp and quick.

"Hi? Is that Polly Waterford?"

"Yes, um, hi," said Polly, helplessly watching through the door as Malcolm ate another cinnamon roll, then another. Those things retailed at £1.50; he was chomping through the day's profits at the speed of light.

"I'm Kate Lacey. I write for the *Bugle on Sunday,* but I'm based down in this neck of the woods. We're doing a pullout for our food section entitled 'Best Artisan Food Shops in the West Country,' and your name came up."

"Really!" said Polly, totally delighted and thrilled. "Who from?"

"All sorts of people," said Kate, sounding amused.

"We set up an Internet forum and your name kept appearing."

Polly couldn't help the massive beam spreading across her face.

"Well, that's . . . that's lovely news."

"So we're going to come down, maybe take a couple of photographs, would that be okay? We're going to make it kind of a lifestyle piece."

Polly bit her lip and immediately wondered if there was a way to get Neil in the pictures.

"Of course."

"Lovely, how about the first Tuesday in June? It'll go in our big summer issue. Maybe a Saturday, get a bit of a bustle, local color."

"Perfect," said Polly.

"Okay then, give me your email and we'll be in touch."

Polly came back into the shop absolutely beaming, as Jayden served a line of customers. Thankfully they seemed to be buying all the cinnamon rolls, thus getting them out of Malcolm's line of sight.

"A newspaper is coming to do a feature on us!" she said. "A proper big Sunday newspaper! With pictures and everything! As one of the West Country's best artisan shops."

Malcolm looked unimpressed.

"A *newspaper*?" he said. "Who reads sodding newspapers?"

"Lots of people," said Polly.

"Neh," said Malcolm. "Everyone gets their news on their phone these days. Look at this."

He showed her his news feed. It was almost exclusively stories about Formula 1.

"Who actually goes out and buys a boring old newspaper?"

"I do," said Polly.

"This won't be something lots of people read, though, will it?" said Malcolm. "It'll be some posh nonsense for five idiots in London. It'll be no use to us at all."

"But we can put it in the window," said Polly. "And people will see it and come down and visit . . ."

She lost herself in a reverie of foodies from far and wide exclaiming over her olive loaf, begging for the secrets of her cultivated yeast. Poilâne, she knew, the famous Parisian bakery, had people who sent their private jets for loaves. Obviously that wouldn't happen to her. But how incredibly exciting to be in the paper.

"I think it will be amazing for us," she said, undaunted. "It will be . . . um, won't it be like really good marketing? Marketing is very important, isn't it?"

Malcolm snorted. "Yeah, fine. They can come and take all the pictures they like. Maybe you could glam up a bit, actually? Wouldn't hurt to put a bit of lippy on, would it, darling, when they come to take the shots? Maybe a short skirt."

Polly furrowed her brow.

"I haven't got any short skirts."

"No," said Malcolm pensively, giving her a quick up and down. "Well, maybe that's for the best."

Polly served another customer wordlessly, clenching her nails into her palms.

"So anyway, that's settled," said Malcolm, dumping a large pile of slightly stained paperwork on her desk.

"What's settled?" said Polly, pinging the till and turning around.

"From next Monday," said Malcolm, "everything will get delivered centrally. One delivery a week. From a factory, like you said. You sell that, put some lippy on, we'll have this place making money in no time. I'll just take a couple more of those roll things on my way out."

Huckle wished he knew how to stop Polly crying. Every time she managed to control herself, another wave would come over her and she'd lose it again.

"And . . . and the newspaper is going to come and see me . . . and I'll be serving up some fricking ham and pineapple sandwich on WHITE PLASTIC BREAD! And everyone will laugh at me."

"Hush," said Huckle. "Nobody reads papers."

"Don't YOU start."

She snivelled again.

"And once a week! How can you have a bread delivery ONCE A WEEK? What's it going to be like? It's going to be worse than Mrs. Manse's!"

"Hush," said Huckle. "You can just sell the contraband on the side, like you did when I met you."

"I can't," said Polly, sobbing. "I can't, because then I didn't have the mortgage, did I? I didn't have to have a job; I didn't have much, but I could just about survive. But I can't do it again. I'm a discharged bankrupt, it's been hard enough as it is. If we lose the lighthouse . . ."

Huckle rubbed her back.

"We won't lose the lighthouse. I can get a job again in a minute."

"Yes, but not a job where you'll be home every night to cook and play with Neil!" said Polly. "It'll be a job that needs you to wear a tie and not live on an island, won't it?"

Huckle shrugged, acknowledging the difficulty.

"Maybe," he said.

"Oh God, it might be a job in America."

"No," said Huckle. "It will be a job wherever you are."

"But I want to be here," said Polly. "I want to be here with my bakery. But I can't start over again! I just can't."

"You can," said Huckle, although they both knew how impossible it would be.

"I can't!" said Polly. "Malcolm and Janet would run me out of town. They would. They'd probably apply to some town hall about having me shut down; they'd make sure I couldn't rent premises. And I couldn't do it anyway. Can you imagine me trying to get a business loan? I want to open a bakery in a town of eight hundred people that already has two bakeries. Oh, and it's on an island and I'm a discharged bankrupt with a ridiculous overpriced mortgage because I live in a stupid lighthouse."

"I feel you're focusing very much on the negative," said Huckle carefully. Neil waddled over from where he'd been biting the tea towels and rubbed himself on her ankle.

"Tell me what the positives are, Huckle. Please tell me and I'll try and focus on them."

Polly sank to the ground and buried her face in her hands. She was such a picture of misery, Huckle felt his heart ache for her; she looked like an inconsolable child.

"Ssh," he said. "The positives are . . . maybe there'll be a sudden retro fashion for white-bread sandwiches? You could call it . . . I don't know. Mother's Pride."

Polly didn't raise her head.

"Or maybe," he said, "you won't mind not having to get up and bake every day."

She looked at him then, aghast.

"But that's what I *do*," she said. "That's all I want to do. I love it."

Huckle put his arm around her.

"We can find somewhere else to do it," he said. "There's always somewhere else."

"I don't want to be anywhere else."

"Don't be daft," said Huckle. "You and me together, wherever we want to be: what can possibly go wrong?"

"Eep," said Neil.

"Oh yeah," said Huckle.

He sat down beside them both as the evening light shone golden through the lighthouse windows.

"Well, this is what you English call a pickle."

Polly took a walk the next morning after she'd prepared the day's dough. She wanted to get some exercise, shake off the cobwebs and the crossness; she'd found, too, that a walk often cleared something up in her head, helped her see the way a little more clearly, and she hoped it would today, because she'd lain awake half the night feeling totally helpless, until Huckle, fed up with her wriggling, had turned her toward him and said, "Now stop it, this is ridiculous. Go to sleep right now."

And strangely, something about the power of his words had relaxed her body, and she had finally fallen fast asleep.

It was a bright, windy day with a hint of gray cloud above the scudding white, but the rain would probably hold off. Polly never bothered with the weather forecast.

It simply didn't apply to them, out on this little rocky outcrop between Cornwall and France. It was certainly chillier out in the water, and windier. But they often escaped the heavy rain that sometimes sat low over Cornwall's rolling green hills and fields; the mainland could be completely smothered in thick cloud while Polbearne gleamed in fresh sunlight, and it felt like their little semi-island wasn't actually connected to the real world at all.

Polly set off in the direction of the beach. The causeway was open, but it would be covered over again in a couple of hours, so she would just have to get by with marching in a circle, possibly doing a couple of circuits if she needed to. But the cliff above the beach was quite steep, so at least she'd get some exercise.

Neil came with her, hopping cheerfully from stone to stone, fluttering a little, then coming down to settle; occasionally, if they hit a flat bit, he perched on her shoulder.

"You are such a lazy boy," said Polly, rubbing his feathers affectionately.

What to do? What to do? The idea of not lighting her amazing wood-burning oven every morning made her so sad. Of course she could stay in bed longer, but that was scant consolation to someone about to lose the only job she'd ever loved. The town would no longer smell, early in the morning, of heavenly fresh-baked bread, bread with a crunch you could feel on the outside giving way to a soft and yielding inside.

When the fishermen came in early in the morning, their fingers stiff and red from gutting fish in ice on the quayside, she took real delight in pressing warm rolls and hot cups of coffee into their hands, seeing the gratitude on their faces. Would it be the same when fresh, expensive salted butter didn't melt into the delicate crumb? When the plastic bread brought in en masse, filled with preservatives, emulsifiers, coloring and all the rest, flopped lifelessly and congealed into a flavorless gray mush that stuck to the roof of your mouth? Would that be the same?

Maybe she should call Janet, she thought. But she remembered how Janet had looked at her sons at Gillian's funeral; the pride with which she had referred to Malcolm as a "businessman"; the fact that she had never once come to visit her sister in Mount Polbearne, never once returned to the town of her birth in all the time Polly had been there; clearly didn't have the faintest interest in what the bakery did or how it functioned as long as it supplemented as efficiently as possible her meager pension. And, Polly suspected, gave Malcolm something useful to do.

She clambered over the rocks and onto the beach. The skeleton of the tanker that had been wrecked last year—in the same storm that had claimed Tarnie's life and destroyed most of the fishing fleet—was still there, a rusting carcass. Some people said it was an eyesore, that it ought to be cut into pieces and taken away (every bit of its cargo, including 15,000 rubber ducks, had already been removed). But it was also an odd kind of tourist attraction—people traveled from a long way away to have a look at it, and many amateur divers came up on the weekend to wreck-dive, even though this was considered to be an extremely dangerous and foolhardy enterprize.

Polly sat down, took out her flask of coffee and paper bag containing a cream puff and looked out at the wreck with a shiver. She rather liked it, in a creepy kind of way. She knew it was a bit ugly, dumped in the bay like a leftover piece of Meccano, but something about its rusting hulk and pathetic angle in the water made her contemplative and a little melancholy. It had started to feel part of Mount Polbearne: the tip of the iceberg among the many wrecks that lay beneath the surface of the water, seduced and then led horribly astray by her rocky shores and deadly coves.

Neil hopped over to look into the paper bag with interest. Polly watched him nudge it with his beak, practically an expert, pushing at it to get at the goodies inside.

"Neil!" she said, affectionate but still exasperated. "You are SO greedy."

Neil looked at her inquiringly, then picked up the bag with his beak and brought it over to her.

"Seriously?" said Polly. "Seriously? You do this now? You *fetch*?" She looked at him. "I'm not sure whether you're some kind of a bird genius, or whether I should be getting really worried about you."

She fished about in the bag.

"Here," she said, breaking him off a little of the cream puff. The pastry was lighter than air and utterly delicious. Polly finished hers in a millisecond, then gave Neil the bag with the crumbs in it. He immediately turned it upside down on his head and started staggering about blindly on the rocks.

"Neil!" said Polly. "Neil, get back here."

His wings were fluttering wildly inside the little bag, and he knocked over her flask with all her coffee in it. Polly swore and finally caught up with him, plucking the bag off. Neil shook his head sharply and fluttered up and down in the air to make sure his wings still worked.

"Don't put bags on your head," said Polly. "Don't talk to strangers, don't let anyone touch your special area, and ESPECIALLY don't put bags on your head. How many times have we been through this? And fly over the road, don't walk."

There was a laugh from somewhere right behind her. Nobody was normally about this early; Polly whirled around. Selina was just behind her, dressed in workout gear. She waved.

"God, you gave me a fright," said Polly.

"Sorry," said Selina. "But the little guy . . . it was pretty funny."

"Oh, I've told him and told him," said Polly. "Whenever I can't find that puffin, he's inside a bag somewhere."

Selina smiled and moved forward.

"Don't worry," she said. "I appreciate anything that makes me laugh. Sorry if it's a suffocating bird."

"What are you doing?" said Polly.

Selina rolled her eyes.

"If I tell you, promise not to tell anyone?"

"Totally."

"Well, my therapist thinks I should do yoga. And get lots of fresh air. So I'm trying to combine the two, even though it makes me feel like a total idiot when I do. I creep out before anyone's awake."

"Oh no, I think that's good," said Polly. "You can't do it in the flat?"

Selina shook her head.

"God, no, there's . . . well, lots of reasons. And the floor makes me do a roly-poly."

"Yes, it would," said Polly, thinking of the wobbly old incline. "Well, I'd offer you some cream puff, but I think we're kind of out."

"And your coffee's gone," said Selina, looking at the knocked-over flask. "You can come and have some of mine if you like."

"I would like," said Polly, pleased. "I've just been sitting here mired in my own thoughts, which are all rubbish."

"That *never* happens to me," said Selina, winking, and they walked off together, a slightly chastened Neil hopping behind them.

Polly explained the bakery situation to Selina as they clambered back over the rocks, feeling even in the telling that a little bit of the weight was lifting off, even if no immediate solutions were presenting themselves.

"For fuck's sake," said Selina, which was actually very helpful under the circumstances. "They're total morons. They'll run the place into the ground."

"I don't think *they* think so," said Polly. "I think they think they can get all our profits without any actual expenditure."

"In that case," said Selina, "I think I have some magic beans they might be interested in."

Polly gave a weak smile.

"Look," said Selina. "As soon as they see it's not working, they'll change back to doing it your way, won't they?"

"I'd like to think that," said Polly. "But they'll probably just figure I sabotaged it, and sack me instead."

"Hmm," said Selina. "Tricky one. Can't you start up what you did before? Sell the illicit stuff?"

Polly shrugged. "I didn't own a lighthouse before. And I think the bottom is probably going to drop out of the lighthouse market any day now, so . . . we're a bit stuck."

"Does your other half not work?"

"He does, but . . ." Polly scuffed her shoe. "It sounds stupid, but all my life I've dreamed of being able to go it alone, know what I mean? I started up my own business with my old partner when I left college, and, well, that failed, but it was so amazing when the bakery started to take off. I know it wasn't wholly mine, but it was my baby really. The idea of failing *again* and having to start over . . . God, it doesn't bear thinking about."

"Can't you buy them out?"

"No," said Polly. "Janet probably only wants ridiculous offers, like she's some kind of multimillionaire magnate selling a house of solid gold. Nobody would be stupid enough to pay what she's asking. Well, one of my friends would, but I'm absolutely not asking him. I don't want to be a hobby baker."

"Hmm," said Selina. "Well, you know, I only ever wanted to marry rich, and look how that turned out."

There was a short silence. They both stumped up the tiny hill toward Beach Street, the lighthouse looming on their right-hand side.

Jayden had turned the lights on in the bakery, and Polly gave him a wave.

"Have you got time for that coffee?" said Selina. "I've got a new cappuccino machine. It does instant froth."

"Ooh," said Polly, glancing at her watch. She really ought to go and help Jayden, but it was so ridiculous that in a few days' time all this food she'd so lovingly prepared would be reduced to plastic trays of pre-packaged sandwiches, and tightly sealed factory bags of sliced white that would never go off or get hard. She sighed.

"Why not," she said.

"Watch the fourth step . . ."

"It's all right," smiled Polly in the dark stairwell. "I know."

Neil, as usual, had taken the short way up, simply flying to the windows of the flat. He seemed very at home, probably because he had found it tricky in his little head to really come to terms with the fact that they'd moved.

Polly looked around the flat, both so familiar and so unfamiliar. She felt nostalgic for a period that had barely passed, and had to remind herself that however bad things were at the moment, they had been much, much worse on the cold, blustery morning she'd first arrived.

"Oh, it's nice," she said admiringly, and it was. There were none of the cozy rugs and cushions she had furnished the place with when she had lived there; instead it was stark and white, like an art gallery, with huge arty black-and-white photographs hung on the walls. There was an uncomfortable-looking square black leather sofa with two square armchairs, and a glass coffee table, and no blinds on the windows.

"How are you dealing with . . . um, the light pollution issue?" Polly asked carefully.

"You are totally the worst neighbors ever," said Selina, firing up a huge and frightening-looking coffee machine, filled with pipes and gauges, which hissed and spat. "I wear an airline mask."

"Oh, yeah," said Polly, glancing about. "Where's your cat?"

"Lucas? Oh, he'll be snoozing somewhere on the bed. He's the laziest animal you can imagine," said Selina.

"Cool," said Polly, and went over to the window to let Neil in as Selina busied herself with tiny square coffee mugs.

It all happened extremely fast.

Polly undid the old-fashioned brass clasp on the window. Overjoyed, Neil flew into what he considered his own rightful home, and looked around cheerfully, wondering where the snacks were.

A voice came from the little kitchen.

"Also, I have to tell you, there's somebody . . ."

Polly went to pick up Neil, aware of the fact that there was a cat somewhere in the house, but was suddenly completely and utterly distracted by a man walking out of the bedroom dressed only in a towel—a man, moreover, whom she recognized. It was Dubose, of all people, emerging from the bedroom she used to sleep in. She gasped. And in that instant a flash of tortoiseshell fur bolted into the sitting room. It burst into the air in a huge eruption of sharp white teeth and whiskers, jumping astonishingly high as Polly watched open-mouthed in shock.

Selina's cat brought Neil down with one paw, slamming him to the floor. Its claws raked down his stomach as the puffin fluttered and eeped hysterically, screaming, actually screaming out loud, just as he had done the night the storm had thrown him through the door downstairs.

"Oh my God!" Polly said, trying to pull the cat off him. Lucas, who already had a mouthful of feathers, fought back, his needle-sharp claws raking bloody lines down her arm.

"Oh my goodness," said Selina, rushing over. "Lucas, baby. Lucas, darling, get off the nice bird, please."

Dubose rushed over to help, his face a mixture of guilt and boldness.

As Neil opened his mouth to screech once more, Polly summoned all her strength and yanked the yowling cat off him. Sweat was pouring off her as she tried to separate the two animals. Neil attempted to take off, but he was bleeding and didn't seem to understand why he couldn't fly. Watching him wobble down to earth like a plane landing in a cross-wind broke Polly's heart. She fought the base instinct to hurl the cat away with full force; instead, she marched him up to Selina and placed him none too carefully in her arms.

"Can you . . ." her voice was coming out high-pitched and hysterical, she knew, "can you put your cat away for a moment, please?"

She realized she was shaking. Selina took Lucas, stroking him.

"There, there, baby," she was saying. "Calm down."

Lucas was spitting fury and trying to wriggle out of her arms to get back to Neil and finish what he'd started.

"I can't believe you let that bird in here," said Selina in an accusing tone.

"What are you talking about? You told me you had the gentlest fricking cat on earth," said Polly, her voice tight with panic as she collapsed next to Neil. "And why the hell is HE . . ."

But any thought of Dubose left her mind immediately as she knelt next to the little puffin. Neil was bleeding; his thick black feathers were torn. She could feel his heart beating incredibly quickly through his chest.

"God," she said. "I have to get to Patrick. Sssh. Sssh."

She took off her cardigan and wrapped it carefully around the little bird, who was whimpering; a horrible noise. Then she got up slowly from the floor. Selina was attempting to hold a still maniacal Lucas in her arms, Dubose standing silently beside her. Polly was forever glad later that she was too upset to speak, because anything she would have said she would never have been able to take back. She simply pushed past them both and ran down the stairs with Neil in her arms.

"Hey," said Jayden, coming out to polish the door handles as she shot past. "What's up?"

But Polly was running faster than she'd ever run in her life, straight along Beach Street, past the fishermen, who hailed her too, Archie standing up when he saw the look on her face, and past Muriel's shop. This early in the morning, before the causeway opened and the day trippers arrived, Mount Polbearne was quiet and sleepy, and it was extremely unusual to see someone run.

Patrick was in early checking out a dog for worms— not exactly a difficult diagnosis, he had concluded, from the way the animal had dragged itself into the surgery on its bum. He'd need to disinfect the entire area again later. It was tricky being a single-handed practice sometimes.

His door was flung open with surprising violence, banging against the far wall. Old Mr. Arnold jumped in alarm. Mifty saw his chance and wriggled his bum on the table again.

"Stop it, Mifty," said Patrick, looking up. He froze when he saw Polly's face.

"What is it?" he said, but he hardly had to ask. "Is it Neil?"

Polly nodded, trembling and wordless, offering the bloodstained cardigan. Neil's breaths were shallow and his eyes were closed.

"Oh my," said Patrick. He turned to the old man.

"Can I just move Mifty for now?" he said. "I'll fix his prescription later."

"Is that that little bird from the bakery?" said Mr. Arnold. "Oh dearie me now."

Patrick hastily scrubbed down the table and washed his hands.

"Put him here," he said.

Polly couldn't bear to place him down; she was numb

with shock. Patrick had to move forward and gently prize Neil out of her stiff hands.

The little bird looked tiny on the large table. There was a long rip in his side, and his head was nodding in and out.

"Oh dear me, dear me," Mr. Arnold was still muttering in the corner.

Polly found her voice, although it came out as a high-pitched squeak.

"Fix him," she managed. "Fix him, please. Fix him now."

Patrick rubbed the top of his bald head.

"That's fine. I'll need you to hold him."

He took down a book from the shelf.

"Why are you reading?" said Polly, her face completely white. "Don't read now. Fix him." She went to pick Neil up again.

"Hush," said Patrick, quite sternly. "Don't touch him, please. I'm double-checking the dosage. I don't anesthetize birds very often; I don't want to get it wrong. If you wouldn't mind standing to one side for now, that will be quite the best way to help Neil."

Polly swallowed, her hands gripping the chair in front of her—the nearest thing she could find—so hard her knuckles went white.

"It's very dangerous to anesthetize a bird," he went on. "Especially when they're in shock. If it wasn't Neil, I would say let him go."

Polly swallowed hard.

"Has he eaten in the last two hours? Well, that's a stupid question. Of course he has."

Patrick rummaged about in a drawer and took out a large plastic-wrapped contraption that looked like a toilet plunger.

"We usually use these on very large dogs," he said, glancing at Neil nervously. "That beak of his gets in the way a little. Okay."

He attached the tube that ran from the gas mask to a canister marked *Isoflurane in Oxygen,* and very carefully attached the mask over Neil's head. The little bird panicked at first, then, as Polly went forward and rubbed his neck, gradually relaxed and closed his eyes.

"Fine," said Patrick. "Stand back, please."

He looked at her.

"Was it a cat?"

She nodded.

"Those damned things," Patrick muttered to himself. "They're a bloody hazard. I did warn you."

His face was serious as he bent down to take a closer look at Neil's injuries. Polly stood back.

"Is there anyone you'd like me to call, love?" said Mr. Arnold. Polly immediately wanted Huckle's arms around her, but she couldn't speak, not yet. She shook her head numbly. No. She couldn't bear it; couldn't speak to anyone until she knew. Neil had been knocked out by the anesthetic, but all Polly could think was that he looked like he was dead.

Mr. Arnold (and Mifty, squirming frantically) stayed by Polly's side throughout the operation, the old man's hand gentle on her shoulder. Patrick donned a pair of huge magnifying glasses that made his eyes look very strange, and bent to his work.

He plucked away all the feathers over the main site of the wound and gently swabbed away the blood. There seemed an awful lot of it for such a tiny creature. There were three great raked tears through Neil's stomach; one per claw, sharp as needles, which had slit through him like a knife through butter. Polly couldn't look and turned away.

Patrick felt around deftly.

"I think you've been lucky," he said. "It seems to have missed the vital organs."

Polly looked up, her eyes full of hope, but Patrick's face was still grave.

"I can stitch him, Polly, and put him on antibiotics . . . but with this kind of thing, it's not the injury, it's the shock. The anesthetic and the shock . . ."

He cleaned up some more, filled the wounds with powder, then started to stitch, his hands surprisingly nimble for a middle-aged man. Polly watched, holding her breath.

Time seemed to stretch on forever, shadows passing by the low window of the surgery, a door opening here and there, a particularly strong gust of wind making the ancient windowsill tremble a little. Polly stayed rooted to the spot, unable to move in case something she did or said made a difference.

Finally Patrick stood back. He gave Neil two injections of antibiotics under the skin of his stomach, then he stroked the little bird on the tummy and looked around.

"He needs to be kept warm," he said. "I need a blanket."

"I've got Mifty's outside," volunteered Mr. Arnold.

"I don't think worms are exactly what this little fellow needs right at the moment," said Patrick.

Polly handed over her bloodied cardigan and Patrick wrapped the still comatose Neil up in it. When he handed him to Polly, she let out a muffled sob. He felt so light and fragile in her arms.

"Thanks, Mr. Arnold," said Patrick. "I'll write up

Mifty's prescription and drop it off on the way home, okay?"

Mr. Arnold nodded. "Right enough," he said. Then he doffed his cap to Polly. "Good luck with Neil, miss. It's always nice seeing him about the place."

The old man and his wriggling dog left the surgery, and Patrick watched them go, then set about disinfecting the entire room. He glanced at her, and Polly saw to her horror that he was cross with her.

"I told you," he said quietly. "I told you not to keep him. He's a bird, he's not a pet. He's not domesticated."

"I sent him away," said Polly. "He came back."

"Well, he shouldn't have done," said Patrick, his anxiety for the little animal turning into anger as he spoke. "You've raised that bird to think that everyone in the world is his friend; that anything he ever meets is going to give him a snack. I had to stitch through an extra layer of fat, by the way, which is difficult to do."

Tears rolled down Polly's cheeks.

"So when he meets something like that bastard cat, he hasn't a clue what to do, has he? He's completely overwhelmed. Not a clue. Do you think that cat would attack a flock of puffins?"

"That cat is a fucking psycho," muttered Polly.

"No, it wouldn't," went on Patrick remorselessly. "Because flocking birds have excellent defense mechanisms against cats, which involve flying away from predators, not waddling over to see if they've got any treats."

Polly went bright red and stared at the floor.

Patrick realized his fear had made him sound gruff, and he stretched out a hand to the little bird.

"I suppose I don't have to tell you to nurse him carefully," he said, his tone conciliatory.

Polly shook her head.

"And I'll report the cat to the police," she said.

Patrick looked at her.

"The cat police?"

"Cats can't go around attacking whatever they like! It's . . . it's naughty!"

"Well, spoiled fat puffins shouldn't make themselves such delicious, tempting targets," pointed out Patrick, regretting it instantly when his words brought on a fierce storm of sobbing.

"Look," he said, "I didn't mean to be so hard on you there. I realize Neil . . . I realize *the puffin* you insist on keeping gave you a terrible fright. But it was entirely preventable."

"I know," said Polly, taking the Kleenex he passed her from the box on his desk. "I know. I know."

She hugged Neil a little tighter, lifting his tiny body up so she could hear him breathe.

"We'll keep him here until he comes around," said Patrick. "Would you like a cup of tea?"

Polly nodded.

"And I have to phone Huckle," she whispered.

The motorbike was noisier than ever on the cobbles as Huckle made it back from the old honey cottage in double-quick time. Thankfully the causeway was open, or he'd have swum across. He left the bike in the middle of the cobbled street and charged in.

"Is he all right?" His normally tanned face was white.

Polly held up the little bundle.

"We're just waiting for him to come around."

Huckle moved across the room, as ever looking slightly too big for the furniture.

"Hey, Neil, hey, little buddy. What happened to you, hey?"

Suddenly the little bird's eyes fluttered very briefly, and his beak moved from side to side.

"He can hear me!" said Huckle joyfully. "Hey, buddy! You need to get well so you can go in the sidecar again. He loves the sidecar," he added to Patrick. "He sticks his head out so he can feel the wind in his hair. Feathers."

Patrick gave Polly a meaningful look.

"Is he all right?" she said, as the little bird stirred in her arms. "Is he okay? Is he in pain?"

As if in answer to her questions, Neil threw up all over her trousers.

"Yay!" said Huckle. "Neil is great at being sick! That's my boy."

"Could you stop being so American for just a second?" said Patrick, moving Neil swiftly back to the consulting table and listening to his heartbeat with a very small stethoscope. Huckle stood behind Polly and draped his huge arms around her, resting his great blond head on her little one. She held on to his arms tightly, trembling as she watched Patrick.

"Hmm," said Patrick.

"You smell amazing," whispered Huckle in her ear, to try and make her laugh, though right at this moment it wasn't working.

All three of them watched as Neil blinked once . . . twice, then opened his eyes and tried to wobble up.

"Neil!" breathed Polly. She broke the circle of Huckle's arms and knelt down beside the operating table. "Neil. Are you okay?"

Neil tried a very faint attempt at an eep. To Polly it was the sweetest sound she had ever heard. She stretched out a finger to scratch the feathers behind his ear and, just like he always did, he tried to move his neck to rub himself against her.

Polly's eyes filled with tears again.

"Oh my God. Oh my God, he's going to be all right."

She turned to Patrick, who was filling in a form.

"Thank you!" she said. "Thank you!" She gave him a huge hug.

"Um," said Patrick. "Have you got puffin sick on your trousers?"

"Uh, yeah," said Polly.

"Now it's on my trousers."

"It is," said Polly. "Sorry about that. Can I hug you instead?" she asked Huckle.

"Not a chance," said Huckle. He bent down next to where Neil was lying, still a little confused, on the table.

"Hey, little fella," he said. "Hey, you. Good to have you back."

Neil eeped again, more strongly this time.

"Yeah, he knows his daddy," said Huckle.

"You're not his daddy," said Patrick, shortly.

"Can we take him home?" said Polly.

Patrick nodded.

"I'll write out your prescription for antibiotics . . . two drops, three times a day. I assume you have no trouble getting him to eat?"

Polly shook her head.

"And you absolutely have to keep him warm. But after that . . . I seriously think that the right thing to do is try the sanctuary again. Puffins live for thirty-five years, Polly. Thirty-five years to fly and hunt and flock and reproduce and do everything puffins are meant to do. It's not too late for Neil."

"Jeez, he was serious, wasn't he?"

Polly was stunned that it was only lunchtime. She felt like a month had passed. Holding Neil in a shoebox Patrick had rustled up for her, she walked carefully down the street to the bakery. She wanted to sleep for a million years, but she couldn't, of course. She had work to do. Lots of work; she'd missed the entire morning.

"I saw you run past!" said Jayden, standing in consternation behind the empty counter. "All I've had this morning are three dozen standard loaves and about fifty people yelling at me because they're hungry."

"Sorry," said Polly. "There was an accident."

Jayden's eyes bulged.

"Who? What happened?"

"Neil got attacked," said Polly. Jayden's hand flew to his mouth. "By a cat," she added. "A cat who lives upstairs from the bakery."

"She'll have to get rid of it," said Huckle, looking worried.

"I don't think you can just tell people with cats to get rid of them," said Polly.

Huckle shook his head.

"I know, but I'm not comfortable with you down here and that thing upstairs."

"He needs to be by the oven," pointed out Polly, who still hadn't put Neil down. She hadn't told Huckle about Selina and Dubose either. "And he needs to be near me. We'll protect him."

"We will," said Jayden, holding up a rolling pin and looking fierce.

Huckle looked at them and sighed.

"All right," he said reluctantly. "But be careful."

Polly nodded.

"Don't you have to be somewhere?"

"Not if you need me."

"No, don't worry about it," said Polly. "I'll be okay. I'll see you tonight. Go. The bees will be getting cross. And that's no good. Cross bees."

"They *were* looking pretty annoyed," mused Huckle.

"Well, definitely go then. I'll see you later."

"Are you sure? You look incredibly pale."

"That's because I am a strawberry blonde," said Polly valiantly.

Huckle looked at her for a long moment, then caressed her cheek.

"Okay, darling. Take it easy. I'll see you later."

"Are you all right?" said Jayden when Huckle had gone. "Let me make you some tea."

"Thanks," said Polly, as he disappeared into the back of the shop. "Also, can you get those spare kitchen trousers out? I think I need to change."

She looked down at Neil, who was eeping piteously to himself.

"Oh, what am I going to do with you?" she said, popping the box on top of the oven, which was pleasingly toasty to the touch but not too hot through its great ancient cast-iron walls.

The bell tinged. She looked up, for a moment not really focused on who was coming through the door. There was a pause, and a loud sniff.

"What the fuck is that stink?" came a loud, grating voice. "Jesus."

Polly blinked.

"Bloody hell, this place reeks."

Polly's heart plummeted.

"Hello, Malcolm," she said glumly.

"Seriously, what the hell *is* that smell?"

"Um. A bird threw up on me," said Polly quietly.

Malcolm was so horrified he just stared straight ahead.

"A what?"

Polly prayed that Neil would stay quiet.

"A bird," she said. "I was just about to change."

"You came into a place where you handle and prepare food with vomit on you?" said Malcolm. As if in answer to his question, Neil coughed and vomited again.

Malcolm was not a handsome man, and anger made a deep purple flush spread right over his face, from his thick creased neck upward. As Polly stared at him, helpless, he took out his phone.

"Hello, Mum. Look. That girl. The one who's running the bakery . . . No, not that one, the snotty one."

There was a pause.

"Yeah, well I've found the place completely empty, no bread, no cakes or nothing, AND she's brought that damned bird in again . . . Yes, I did tell her. Yes, she's had a warning. And wait till you hear this."

Polly stood dully waiting for it to end as Malcolm told his mother about the spew. There was another long silence, but she could hear Janet chattering away in horrified tones on the other end. She wasn't the least bit surprised when Malcolm finally hung up and turned to her, full of righteous aggression.

"My mother agrees with me, obviously," he said.

He drew himself up to his full height, which was about five foot six, and made the most of his Alan Sugar moment.

"I am sure you will understand that we have absolutely no choice but to let you go."

Chapter Nine

As if she were sleepwalking, Polly left it all behind. Carrying the box, she walked through the shelves filled with flour; past the fridge, where her ugly-looking but delicious-tasting sourdough was moldering and bubbling over in its pot. Past the fresh sea salt, and the cardamom pods and caraway seeds; the vast sack of raisins, and the fresh and powdered yeast. Past the recipe book Polly had started putting together so Jayden could bake sometimes; past the stupid puffin postcards Huckle had sent her every time he came across one, pinned up on the noticeboard along with the rota; past the government inspection she'd passed with flying colors eight months before; past the freshly laundered and starched white aprons and chef's trousers.

Past Jayden standing open-mouthed, a pot of tea brewing carefully next to him on the countertop. Polly's world crashed around her as she mutely followed Malcolm to the back door.

"Now, you could consider taking me to an industrial tribunal," said Malcolm, so excited by this that spittle came out of his mouth. "But I can tell you now, you won't win. I've been in four industrial tribunals, and I've never won. You never win. I can tell you that for nothing."

Polly didn't even look at him. She concentrated on holding Neil, who had started to flutter and was obviously distressed by her distress. She couldn't allow this to happen; couldn't upset him after his operation.

"Sssh," she crooned to the little bird. "Sssh."

Malcolm shook his head.

"Unbelievable," he said. "Honestly, I think you're crazy. I really think you are."

They got to the door.

"I'll pay you to the end of the week," said Malcolm. "Out of the goodness of my heart. But I don't want to see you here again."

"Oh lord," said Polly, barely realizing she was talking out loud. "You are *such* a pig."

As Malcolm spluttered and prepared to retaliate, Polly walked numbly on, past the beautiful gray-painted frontage with its looped italic writing:

The Little Beach Street Bakery
Proprietor, Ms. P. Waterford
Established 2014

That didn't last long, she found herself thinking. It had all crumbled to dust.

They had a little gas heater in the cupboard, and Polly found it and switched it on. It wasn't just Neil who was cold. She fed him the crumbs of some rolls she had sealed up in plastic, and gave him some salt water to drink. He lapped at it dispiritedly, and—she was prepared this time—threw up again, but she rubbed his feathers and there was definitely a spark back in his eye as he started hopping around the room a little bit.

"You're amazing," she said. "Fabulous recovery."

Huckle came in and saw her face.

"What's wrong? Isn't he better?"

"It's not that," said Polly, dissolving. "He's going to be all right, but . . . I've lost everything." She burst into tears.

Huckle took her in his arms.

"Well, you've still got me and Neil."

Polly shook her head.

"Patrick was really cross with me. He says I have to let him live wild, otherwise something else is just going to eat him."

Huckle blinked.

"I mean, I can't be with him every second of the day," said Polly. "Although I will now, seeing as I have nothing else to do."

Huckle stared at her.

"Don't worry about it now. Everything will be okay."

"But I'm going to be thirty-three years old! And I have nothing!"

"That's totally not true. You have lots of things."

"And it's all being taken away from me. It's a disaster."

"Hey, sweetie. This isn't how you are. It won't last, I promise. You don't do this."

"What don't I do?" sniffed Polly as Huckle opened a bottle of wine, poured her a glass, looked carefully at it, then poured in some more.

"You don't moan. You just roll up your sleeves and get on with things. That's what you did when you came here. That's what you did when I went back to the States. You just keep going and everything works out. Because you are magnificent," said Huckle.

"But I work and I work and I work, and it just doesn't. What if this is the end of the road for me, Huckle? I can't stay here now. What am I going to do? Before I got that job, I was starving to death."

"Well, *I'll* take a job," said Huckle.

"Yes, in London or New York or Savannah," said Polly.

"All the hell holes," said Huckle gravely.

He put his arms around her.

"Trust yourself," he said. "Trust that you are talented, and that people like that. Put the hours in. And it will all come good."

"And then some prick who would eat a deep-fried towel turns up and ruins it all," said Polly.

"There's no point being bitter that there are wankers in the world," said Huckle. He sounded funny saying "wanker" in his thick Southern accent. "If there weren't any wankers, you wouldn't know how to spot the nice people."

He paused for a few seconds.

"Also, you know, you did walk into a catering area covered in bird sick."

"I was in a state of heavy emotional distress," said Polly. "But God, I know. I know."

She stared out across the sea. The sky was turning

a deep purple on the horizon, fading upward to a light pink. It was utterly beautiful.

"Okay," she said to the little puffin, glancing at her watch, trying to be the capable woman Huckle seemed to think she was; trying to do whatever she could. "Come on, you, you need to take your antibiotics."

She squeezed the right number of drops onto some toast and watched as he cheerfully pecked away at it.

"He's going to be okay," said Huckle. "Thank God. Have you heard from that woman and her cat?"

Polly shook her head.

"No. I think she should keep out of my way. She nearly killed my bird, and she lost me my job."

"Well, I don't think that's entirely fair," said Huckle.

"And Huckle . . ." Polly took a deep breath. "Dubose was there."

"What do you mean, he was there?"

"He was there. In her bed."

Huckle's face turned stony.

"He went after a vulnerable woman?"

"Oh, I'm sure it wasn't like that."

They heard feet ascending the lighthouse steps. Polly stared at Huckle.

"Please don't," she said. "Please don't let us have any more trouble today."

Huckle looked back at her.

"But he's got a girlfriend at home!"

The steps continued upward. The tread was measured, careful, defeated-sounding.

"Did he . . . did he cause this?"

"No," said Polly. "That cat was a menace. I was just a bit . . . surprised to see him there, that's all."

Huckle looked as close to furious as Polly had ever seen him. Slowly, tentatively, the door handle turned.

There was silence in the room.

"Is he . . . is he okay?" said Dubose. He genuinely did look completely and utterly distraught.

Huckle shrugged. "No thanks to you," he said. "And Polly lost her job."

"Oh God, man," said Dubose. "I had no idea. I am so, so . . ."

Huckle shook his head. "You never do, do you?"

"Why?" said Polly quietly. "Why were you with Selina? You know she's gone through something awful."

"Yeah," said Dubose. "She said to me, 'I've been through something awful, and I need to do something nice.' That's all it was."

"Would Clemmie think that?" said Huckle, his face still stony.

"Oh, here we go again," said Dubose. "Perfect Huckle with his perfect life and perfect girlfriend, life all sorted."

Polly and Huckle shared astonished glances.

"And Dubose the total failure dropout as usual. Selina invited me over, and the fact that she had you in too means she obviously wasn't as ashamed of me or as bothered by me as you guys are. She was happy to see me, by the way. She didn't bother asking blah blah Dubose how's your four-thousand-miles-away girlfriend or yadda yadda Dubose how's that farm you're on holiday from? We're two grown adults."

"Who nearly killed our puffin."

"That's . . ." Dubose lifted his hands in consternation. "That's CAT business."

He turned on his heel.

"Right, fine. You got me. I'm going."

"Dubose," yelled Huckle down the steps after him. "Don't go. We'll sort it out."

But there was just the noise of Dubose banging around in his bedroom.

"It's okay," he shouted up. "I'm out of your hair now! No need to keep letting you down."

Huckle ran downstairs.

"Bosey," he said. "Bosey, please."

But Dubose had gone.

It had been a long day. Polly and Huckle sat in silence, Huckle trying to contain his anger.

"He always does this," he said at last. "Rushes out when the going gets tough."

Polly was kneeling by the tea box, looking at a snoozing Neil.

"Will he come back?"

Huckle shook his head.

"I don't know. Maybe he'll go home. He must be needed at home." He yawned. "Oh God, what a crappy day. Come on, let's go to bed."

Polly took a longing look at Neil.

"No," said Huckle. "He's not getting in the bed. That is where I absolutely draw the line. Bed is for you and me. In fact, that is the only thing that might take our minds off everything right now."

"I don't think so," said Polly, shaking her head. There was a pause.

"Ah," said Huckle. "A challenge."

He drew her closer to him, and pulled down her T-shirt, gently kissing the top of her freckled shoulder. Polly opened her mouth to say something, but he shushed her.

"Come and look at the sunset. Forget everything else. I am going to do things to you, and they are going to take a long time, because you are sad and have had a terrible day, and I am sad and have had a terrible day, but fortunately there are two things in my favor: one, shock makes people slightly horny, it's a well-known fact. And two, I am an extremely patient man and I have nowhere to go and nothing else to do but make you happy."

Chapter Ten

"Did you feel that it helped?"

"Sleeping with an American who was only passing through, and breaking up the one friendship I'd made since I arrived?"

Pause.

"Well, I've had better evenings."

"Do you think you can be a little gentler on yourself?"

"I'm not sure I deserve to be."

Polly woke the following morning feeling much more optimistic. By the time she and Huckle had fallen into a contented, exhausted sleep, it still hadn't been that late, and she had, of course, no bakery to wake for and slept all the way to eight o'clock, which in her terms was the equivalent of about noon.

The sun was shining straight through the bedroom window, glistening across the waves, which were bouncing merrily. One or two thready clouds danced across the turquoise sky, but otherwise it was a perfect, perfect day. She threw open the funny little curved window and took in great breaths of fresh salty air.

She turned around. Huckle was still fast asleep, his huge arms flung out across the tiny bed. A ray of sunlight landed on his hair, brightening it to gold, and caught the fine curls on his chest. He was quite, quite beautiful, and it did her heart good just to look at him for a little while. She loved him so much it scared her sometimes: scared her into worrying that one day things would change and she wouldn't love him, or he wouldn't love her, or some other catastrophe.

That wouldn't happen to them, she vowed. Yes, it was going to be tough—really tough. But she'd had tough times before and come through them, hadn't she? He was there for her. It would be fine. It would be all right.

She padded upstairs. To her intense joy, Neil was up on his feet. He was waddling about, tentatively but independently, and eeped happily to see her. She mixed him up some tuna with his antibiotics, and examined his stitches, but they were clean and dry, she was delighted to see.

"Well, you are a sight for sore eyes," she said, kissing his head. Then, not knowing quite what to do with herself when she didn't have huge batches of loaves to make up, she pottered around the sitting room, tidying up the plates and glasses she hadn't had time to put away last night before . . . She smiled at the memory.

She switched on the coffee machine. There was some

cheese bread left over from yesterday: she would toast it for Huckle. She didn't really feel like baking today. Or ever again, she thought glumly. Huckle had declared the night before that they would take the day off and have a wonderful time and go up and have lunch at Reuben's, but she didn't really feel like it. Also, she was slightly terrified that she might have a couple of glasses of wine, then Reuben would offer to buy her the bakery or hire a hit man or something, and she wouldn't be able to resist. Plus she needed to nurse Neil. But Huckle had been very persistent.

Huckle lumbered into view, completely naked and yawning. She watched with pleasure as he stumbled around the room, hair sticking up in a thatch.

"You know," she said, "if we have to move to a normal house, you won't be able to just march past the windows in the scuddy like that."

Huckle rubbed his eyes.

"Free country," he snuffled. "Give me some of that cawfee."

Polly handed him a cup.

"How are you feeling?" he asked, smiling his sleepy grin.

"A bit better," said Polly. "Well, I'm not having a massive meltdown. Have you heard from Dubose?"

Huckle shook his head.

"He probably stayed at Selina's last night and is catching the tide this morning."

"You really don't think we'll see him again?"

"We will," said Huckle. "The next time. There's always a next time. He's forever getting himself into scrapes."

"Well, he's missed the cheddar bread," said Polly, handing him a plate of toast.

"I see that," said Huckle, tearing into it. "God, this is amazing. Hey. I was thinking."

"What?"

"Would you like your birthday present early?"

"It isn't my birthday for four months."

"Four months early or eight months late, it's all the same. I just thought you might need cheering up. I got it for you and I can't wait to give it to you."

It gave Polly a warm feeling inside to think that he'd been planning that far ahead. They hadn't been together very long.

Huckle took out a box and smiled, and she smiled back.

"Won't I be sad when I don't get a present on my real birthday?"

"I think you'll be okay, I have a terrible memory for this kind of thing. Don't mention it again, and I'll forget I ever gave it to you."

Tentatively she put her hand out and opened the box.

Inside was a charm bracelet, pre-loaded with charms. It was exquisite. A sterling silver chain with a P, an H, an N, a lighthouse, a loaf of bread, a motorbike and a puffin. She gasped.

"You got me a puffin charm? How on earth did you find that?"

"It was pretty tricky," said Huckle. "Mostly involving googling the words 'puffin,' 'bracelet,' and 'charm.' Was good he didn't die yesterday, though. That would have pretty much ruined it."

Polly fastened it on carefully.

"It's gorgeous," she said. "I absolutely love it." She did. It was perfect. "Also, can I pawn it?"

Huckle didn't catch on at once that she was only joking, then he did and held her to him for a long time. He wished as he did so that he could shower her with gifts; that he could buy her beautiful things every day, not just cheap charms. He loved making her happy so much.

"You seem better," he said tentatively. She nodded vigorously. Then she grimaced.

"I was thinking," she said, "that not phoning Jayden, and going into the shop with sick on me, might on some level be construed as . . . possibly my fault."

"Mmmm," said Huckle noncommittally. "I mean, it doesn't stop that guy being a total jerk."

"TOTAL jerk," said Polly. "I couldn't have worked with him."

"It would only have been a matter of time," said Huckle.

"I mean, the spew probably didn't help . . ."

"Probably not."

Huckle held her face.

"You look so much better than yesterday."

"I *feel* a lot better than yesterday."

"Have you come up with a Perfect Polly Plan?"

"Shut up."

"Okay then, shall we just go and get drunk at Reuben's?"

"That's as far as I'd gotten."

They packed an overnight bag, anticipating a long lunch, and put plenty of straw in Neil's box to keep him cozy and warm. He was so much better already, it lifted Polly's heart to see it, and she tried to put all the awful stuff to the back of her mind.

It was an absolutely beautiful day, the roads still quiet, tiny clouds scudding across the sky, and the heavy smells of early-season flowers descending from the hedgerows. Cows were munching buttercups in the meadows, the new grass growing fresh and pale green on the hillside, the huge yellow fields of rape glowing in the morning light. Early wild briar roses cascaded from hedges; lavender banked the untrimmed roads. It was impossible that the heart could not be lifted and cheered by the fresh air and the scented lanes and byways of central Cornwall.

"Don't mention any of this to Reuben," Polly had told Huckle before they set out. "I don't want him trying to buy me out of trouble."

"Roger," said Huckle, vowing to ignore this completely. Anything that would help Polly he would do, and he wasn't too proud to take the cash, even if she was. Plus he knew she'd have one glass of wine and tell everybody anyway, so he wasn't terribly worried about his culpability.

Reuben owned a house above a beach on the north coast of Cornwall, where the best surfing was. He also owned the beach. It was quite the most spectacular place Polly had ever visited. He had a large bar and professional kitchen down there, and a beach café for himself and his friends, of whom he had hundreds, all beautiful, all talented, mostly transient. When it came to actual real friends, he had Kerensa, Polly and Huckle. Which was still, as Huckle pointed out, not bad going.

The surf was quiet this morning, but there were still a couple of men out in the far distance hitting the waves. Kerensa had mostly banned the girls who came down from London to stand around looking like they were in a swimsuit commercial and make cow eyes at Reuben even though Reuben had never given them a second glance anyway—not before, and certainly not now. He could be a bit annoying, but you couldn't fault his devotion to his wife.

Reuben was already tinkering around the kitchen barking orders to a sous chef, who was looking at a lobster tank.

"Ooh," said Polly. There was a large silver half-shell bucket sitting in the shade, filled with champagne, pink and white. "You know, I think I will do my best to forget my worries."

"Okay, well try not to forget absolutely everything." Reuben was a notoriously generous host.

"Where's that guy who thinks he understands grain subsidies?"

"Long story," said Huckle, "I think I'll let Poll tell it."

Huckle kissed her as he held his hand out for her to dismount from the sidecar, an act it was absolutely impossible to accomplish with grace. They picked up Neil, looking for somewhere nice and sunny to put him down for a restorative snooze, and grabbed their bathing costumes. It would be a bit nippy, but Reuben had installed heated towel rails in the little beach hut changing rooms, with personalized robes, so you ran out of the sea all chilly and wrapped yourself up in the fluffiest, coziest bathrobes you could imagine, until you were warmed enough by the sun to take them off again.

Kerensa came down to meet them, nut brown from the sun, teeth standard-issue rich-person white these days, eyebrows arched expensively. As she got closer, Polly noticed that her teeth weren't smiling, they were gritted.

"How are you?" said Polly. "I am so glad to see you, I have had the worst—"

"Awful," said Kerensa.

Polly looked up, startled. This conversation seemed to be the wrong way around.

"Yay!" said Reuben. "I'm making lobster salad, and lobster thermidor. Basically, if you're a lobster, you don't want to be within five miles of us today. Except you do totally want to be within five miles of us, because I am only serving the best sustainable local lobster, because that is the kind of brilliant guy I am. Also, everything is fucked."

Polly and Huckle looked at each other. Polly gave Neil his antibiotics on the last piece of cheese toast and tucked him up in a little yellow blanket under a tree.

"Seriously, where did you get the blanket?" said Huckle.

"Muriel gave it to me as a present," said Polly. "It was her baby's."

Huckle shook his head. "All right."

"What's wrong with Neil?" said Kerensa. "Did someone tell him he wasn't a person?"

Reuben busied himself opening the champagne.

"Pink first," he announced.

"No, he just . . . he had an accident," said Polly, taking a glass. "Can I explain later? It's a bit emotionally exhausting. Anyway, I think we should make a toast."

"Happy un-birthday!" chorused everyone, and Polly showed off her bracelet for Kerensa and Reuben to admire.

Kerensa looked at Reuben, then he brought out a bag from behind the champagne bucket.

"What?" said Polly.

"Well, Reuben got you a birthday present too."

"It's not my birthday!"

"I told him not to," said Kerensa. "I am staking my

claim here and now and saying that I have a separate gift for you. That you can have IN SEPTEMBER."

Polly looked inside the bag. It was pale blue, from Tiffany's.

"He's such a show-off," hissed Kerensa. "I am totally embarrassed by him and everything he stands for."

"But the shame turns you on, totally, a little bit," said Reuben.

Polly had never seen a real Tiffany's box before, although she recognized the iconic wrapping, of course.

"My goodness," she said. There was a bag tied with a ribbon, then a box done up with the same dark blue ribbon. Inside there was another, smaller blue velvet bag with a drawstring, and inside that something wrapped in tissue. Polly was laughing now. "This is like pass the parcel," she said. "I ought to be handing it around."

She opened it and gasped.

This charm bracelet was solid platinum. Apart from that, it was absolutely identical in every single way to the one Huckle had given her.

"Reuben, you PUTZ!" said Huckle. "Man, what is WRONG with you? Why did I even tell you? This was my big thing! You knew this was a big deal for me."

Polly just stared at it, completely confused.

"It was a great big deal," said Reuben, nodding happily. "Huckle buying you a really nice present. I figure you like Huckle's one—and who isn't going to like it, it's a great idea—so I reckon you like mine too. And you know, one day you wanna wear silver, one day you wanna wear platinum, right? So you got the option. Just like one day girls wear blue things, one day they wear black things."

"Thank you for summing up the history of fashion so well," said Kerensa.

"One day you have your lovely bracelet from Huck, next day lovely and much more expensive bracelet from your friends Reuben and Kerensa. I am basically a genius."

"You doof!" Huck was saying. "You knew this was a totally special thing for me!"

"I told him it was a stupid idea," said Kerensa.

"Hey, man," Reuben looked the closest he could to wounded, which on his perpetually cheerful, entirely freckled face wasn't very. "I just thought you had such a good idea, man. For once in your life. So sue me."

Polly came over and kissed him on the cheek.

"I love it," she said. "You were right about how much I'd love it. And having two is absolutely brilliant. So it was a genius idea, thank you very, very, very much."

"Seriously, you like it?" said Kerensa. Polly kissed her too.

"I love it. But give me my other present as well, on my real birthday."

"I suppose it can be backup for when you lose the first one," conceded Huck.

"I'm not going to lose the first one!" said Polly. "All I'm losing this year is jobs."

She told them the whole story, to sympathetic noises from Kerensa. Somehow, telling it while sitting outside in the sunshine, wearing two beautiful bracelets, one on each wrist, with Huckle and her friends there, Neil happily asleep and recovering, the sun on her back and a second glass of pink champagne in her hand, it didn't feel quite so bad. Until she got to the end.

"So now I am basically, not to put too fine a point on it, screwed. Hey ho!"

She took another slug of pink wine.

"I am quite tempted to stay here for the rest of my life drinking this. Would that be all right?"

There was a long silence, long enough that Polly lifted her head and looked around.

"What? I was only kidding, you know. Mostly kidding."

Kerensa shook her head. She was looking at Reuben.

"You want to tell them?"

"No," said Reuben.

"You want me to tell them?"

"No," said Reuben, pouting out his bottom lip.

"Someone has to tell them."

"It's been in the papers," growled Reuben, getting up to go and poke at his lobsters.

"What's been in the papers?" said Polly. The papers came late to Mount Polbearne—on windy days not at all—and between that and how hard she worked, and the slowness of their Internet connection, Polly had gotten out of the habit of reading anything other than the *Western Mail* or, if she was being entirely honest with herself, sometimes looking at pictures of celebrities on tabloid sites.

"I'm going to tell them," hollered Kerensa.

Reuben shrugged. "I don't care, you know."

"I know."

"I don't care if you want to leave me now."

"Fuck off!"

"What?" said Polly, jerked out of her reverie into wakefulness. "What's going on?"

Kerensa looked at Reuben.

"I'm not leaving you, so tough shit."

"Why are you not leaving him?"

"Well, because I'm just not."

Huckle leaned forward.

"Guys, could you tell us now what's up? Or otherwise leave us a trail of sinister clues that end at the Louvre or something? Either way."

"I'm hungry," said Reuben.

Polly was suddenly terrified that there was something wrong with one of them. Surely not. There couldn't be. Not when they'd just gotten married and were starting their life together. Her heart was in her throat.

"What is it?"

Kerensa rolled her eyes.

"Well, enjoy the champagne," she said. "Because we really need to get through this cellar."

"You're moving?" said Huckle.

"Oh yes," said Kerensa.

Reuben was expertly popping a lobster into the pot.

"How? Why?" said Polly.

Kerensa glanced over.

"Well, as it turns out, we also have news," she said. "Because SOMEBODY—and you may decide for yourselves which one of us you think it was—has decided to invest all of their money. All of it, please note. Not some of it in spread investments and some of it in government bonds and some of it under the bed and some of it in beautiful property. Nooo. All of it."

Polly watched Kerensa and Reuben carefully.

"Every last penny . . . in a series of Star Wars sequels."

"Oh, they're coming out!" said Huckle. "I've heard about them."

"No," said Kerensa in measured tones. "Those are the licensed ones you've heard about, the ones that George Lucas is doing. You haven't heard about our ones. The Jar Jar Binks spin-off trilogy."

Everyone fell silent.

"You're not serious," said Polly.

"Oh, very serious," said Kerensa. "And the Jar Jar Binks musical—opening directly on Broadway, by the way, none of this touring and building up a show from scratch, oh no . . ."

She downed her wine and refilled her glass again.

"Oh, and the line of Jar Jar themed restaurants in capital cities across the world."

Huckle turned to look at Reuben.

"THIS is what you've been away doing?"

"Hey," said Reuben, crossly. "They say you'll only ever make money doing something you love."

"Yes, something you love that other people love too," said Huckle. "Like Polly making a loaf of bread. Or Kerensa making a . . . conference organizational strategy."

"That was nice of you to pretend to include me," said Kerensa.

"Thank GOD," said Polly.

Everyone else looked at her.

"What are you talking about?" said Kerensa. "This is a horrendous disaster."

Polly shook her head.

"I thought . . . I thought somebody was sick, or somebody was going to die, for God's sake, after last year . . . I mean, seriously, it's only money."

"So speaks someone who's never had any," said Huckle wryly.

"Reuben can just go invent something brilliant like he did the last time. You'll get it back."

"It's not just money," said Kerensa. "It's actually negative money. It's actually more money than we really have."

"But I thought you had all the money."

"That was before somebody tried to mount a two-hundred-and-forty-strong-cast Broadway production," said Kerensa. "Was it me? I can't remember."

"What are you going to do?" gasped Polly.

"Well, I'm already back at work, which, frankly, I'm extremely relieved about, as there's only so much swanning about the world on room service one can take."

Reuben looked a little gloomy. Kerensa's expression became a little cheerier.

"And I shall take Reuben as my fuck toy."

Reuben perked up.

"Kerensa!" said Polly.

"What? What? Would you rather I threw myself off a bridge shouting 'No, no, I shall kill myself just because I married a total idiot'?"

"No," said Polly.

"I've still got my flat. He can sit in the corner of it doing computer things. And sex things. And apologizing to me every ten minutes."

"Seriously, man, it's all gone?" said Huckle gently.

"I've sold this place to a Russian oligarch with a nine-strong security detail, Kalashnikovs and an army-issue helicopter," said Reuben, waving his arms. "Actually, I liked him."

Polly looked around. She was suddenly sad. They'd had so much fun here in this crazy place. It was where she and Huckle had shared their first kiss. Where they'd celebrated Tarnie's life; where she had come after she'd taken Neil to the puffin shelter. She would miss it. Huckle, sensing what she was thinking, came over and rubbed her neck.

"God," she said. "It's . . . it's really hard luck."

"Still," said Kerensa, "I'm slightly less frightened about my sister killing me for her inheritance."

"Yeah, but Dahlia is psychotic, though," pointed out Polly, who had met Dahlia previously. "She was trying to kill you way before you met Reuben."

"Oh yeah," said Kerensa. "I thought she said it was an accident, those stairs."

Polly shook her head.

"Nothing is ever an accident with Dahlia."

"True."

"So," said Reuben, indicating to the sous chef, who brought over four perfect plates of fresh lobster ceviche, "let us eat, drink, be merry and forget our troubles."

Huckle looked slightly embarrassed.

"Okay, or let's drink to Huckle, who doesn't have any troubles."

"Meanwhile," said Kerensa, "I have to go out to work and stop buying handbags while having a sex toy trapped in the sitting room who doesn't know how to use a bus pass."

"I will totally invent a better bus pass," said Reuben darkly.

Polly raised her glass.

"Oh lord. To all of us."

Polly had never eaten ceviche before. It was kind of raw lobster with lime and chilies and some sort of salad cream stuff, and it was the most incredibly delicious thing she thought she'd ever tasted. The sous chef rushed to top up their glasses with an ice-cold Chablis, and Polly felt herself getting slightly fuzzy in the hot sun.

It really didn't feel like anything could ever go wrong, even though things were patently going horribly wrong. They toasted one another again, and when Kerensa asked what she was going to do about the bakery, Polly just shrugged and took another slug of wine. As the afternoon grew hotter, they all tore into the sea, its delicious freshness an absolute balm. Polly lay in the bouncy, salty water and stared at the sky. As usual there were some pesky seagulls circling overhead; even being rich couldn't keep them out. Although of course Reuben wasn't rich any more. Nobody was.

Reuben and Kerensa already appeared to be getting slightly amorous in the water, which Polly absolutely had no interest in witnessing. Instead she let the waves take her where they would, drifting down to the edge of the bay, just underneath the house, which was a big futuristic cube with a round balcony at the front, designed to make you think of the Starship *Enterprise*. Or, as Reuben had said, Tony Stark's house, seeing as he and Tony Stark had so much in common.

She was a long way away from the others now. Huckle liked to go for it when he was swimming. It seemed like a natural element for him; he could move his powerful shoulders and cut through the water with ease. Generally Polly didn't really like putting her head under the water, and she was always a bit worried that something would bite her toes. But today, hazily bobbing up and down, she felt like it didn't matter quite so much anymore; that she was perfectly content as she was, at one with the water, happy and free. Getting lots of sleep had helped. A couple of glasses of fizz, too. She reflected on her friends' terrible news. It would, she knew, be a shock for them. But on the other hand, Kerensa had always done well at her job and was used to working for whatever she had.

And Reuben had started out doing computer things in his garage; there was no reason why he couldn't go back to that. He liked showing off his money, but he wasn't obsessed with it. And they genuinely did love each other, she knew. Thank God Reuben hadn't married one of the beautiful popsies that used to hang around trying to catch his eye and his credit card. Chances were she'd have disappeared faster than the ice in the champagne bucket. Or, Polly thought, maybe just hung around for the oligarch. Perhaps popsies came with the territory, like built-in washing machines and centralized vacuum cleaner systems and surround-sound stereos.

She looked up at the house, squinting in the sun. There were vans and lorries parked up there, and men were carrying stuff out of the house. Even from down here she could make out a full-sized sculpture of a naked Reuben and Kerensa who were . . . Oh God. Giggling, Polly realized she was slightly more drunk than she'd thought, and quickly checked that she could touch the seabed with her foot. She could. Good.

It felt nosy watching the removal men, and sad, too, to see them bundling up all the fun that Reuben and Kerensa had had. And confusing: how on earth where they going to sell all those hideous naked portraits of Kerensa?

Suddenly Huckle was right behind her; he'd swum up quickly, under the water, his powerful arms grabbing her so she squealed. He didn't pull her under, though; he drew her close to him and gave her a cuddle.

"Hey," he said. "Whatcha doin'?"

"Being nosy," said Polly, indicating up the hill. "Look at all that stuff they have."

"Ah, it's only stuff," said Huckle. "They're practically having sex with each other over there."

"They really are disgusting," grumbled Polly. "Well,

I'll have to keep watching the removals men. Only place I can put my eyes."

"You know what I see?" said Huckle, floating gently behind her.

"What?" said Polly, looking at him. "Wow. You look like an aftershave advert. And a classy one too, not one of those tacky Mark Wright ones."

Huckle pointed.

"What am I looking at?"

"You're looking at a nine-foot standard lamp with a picture of a dog on it," said Polly. "It's gross. All of their stuff is gross. I just didn't notice before because the view was so nice."

Huckle shook his head.

"No."

"You're looking at a ninety-six-inch cinema-size curved 3D television screen, the one in the upstairs lounge that Reuben can never find the remote for and Kerensa only watches *Homes Under the Hammer* on."

"Not that either."

Polly squinted.

"Okay. I give up."

"What are they putting all that hideous tat into?"

"Hideous *expensive* tat, I think you meant to say."

Huckle smiled. "I know. Amazing, all that money and they . . . What's the British term?"

"I believe it's spunked," said Polly gravely.

"They spunked it all on that."

"Well, and lots of charity. And extraordinary hospitality for their friends," pointed out Polly.

"Yeah," said Huckle.

They watched as two men brought out what appeared to be a solid gold grandfather clock in the shape of a dragon, with two flashing rubies for eyes.

"Anyway, never mind about that now. One last time."

He took her head between his great hands, and pointed it in the direction of the clifftop.

"What are you looking at? Lots and lots of?"

Polly blinked.

"I don't know. Removal vans?"

"Yes!" said Huckle, who was also slightly drunk. "Don't you see?"

"We set up a removals business? Because I have to tell you, these guys seem pretty good."

"NO!" roared Huckle, laughing. "Polly, I love you so much, stop being thick."

"I'm not being thick, you're being NEEDLESSLY MYSTERIOUS."

Both of them were laughing now as Huckle shook his head.

"Van!"

"I don't get it. Like the shoes?"

"Like a BREAD VAN!"

Polly laughed. Then she stopped. Then she laughed again.

"What do you mean, a bread van?"

"Well, you know, like a pizza van. A van with an oven in it and they make pizza."

"Yes," said Polly.

"Well, you could get one for bread. And drive it around Polbearne."

Polly turned to face him. The water splashed in her face.

"Not just like that."

"No, not just like that," said Huckle. "You'd need permits and stuff. But the council know you."

"The council hate me," said Polly. "We helped stop them getting that expensive bridge they wanted."

"Oh yes," said Huckle. "Okay, so we put a false mustache on you."

"But they won't let me take a bread van into Polbearne."

"No," said Huckle. "But they might let you take one into the car park on the other side, where the fish man goes. So Polbearne people . . . They might have to cross the causeway to get to you." He blinked. "But you know, I have an idea they would. And the day trippers—they'd hit you first."

"I don't want to work in a van," said Polly. "I want my lovely ovens and my lovely shop."

"You should have thought of that before Barfgate. And I tell you what, if you don't have a plan soon, you might be sleeping in a van too."

Polly sighed. "Where would we even get one? How would we pay for it?"

Huckle's eyes strayed to where the charm bracelet had been, before she had taken it off and zipped it into her bag for safekeeping so she could go swimming.

"No way," said Polly. "No way, that thing is mine."

"Not my one, doof," he said. "Reuben must have bought you the platinum one before all this shit went down."

"They won't take it back, though," said Polly. "It's personalized and everything."

"They might melt it down for you."

Polly shook her head.

"I couldn't do that."

"Mine's the sentimental value one, you know?"

"I do know."

"I mean, mine's totally the best one."

"Now you're sounding like Reuben."

"Well, that's useful," said Huck. "Because I am attempting some entrepreneurial brilliance. Is it working?"

Polly put her arms around his neck.

"I wonder," she said. "I wonder if we could."

Huckle kissed her full on the mouth.

"We can do anything."

"Hey, you guys, stop with all the sexy stuff," came Reuben's whining voice across the waves. "Honestly, you're disgusting. And come and eat this pavlova before they take the oven away."

Chapter Eleven

Polly woke the next morning in one of Reuben's sumptuous, ridiculous guest suites. It had a circular bed and automatic curtains, which, drunk the night before—after they had finished eating on the beach, they had come in and watched *Star Wars* episode 3 one last time in the big cinema—she had insisted on opening and closing until Huckle begged for mercy. Neil was on the floor beside them, still sleeping soundly.

At first Polly wasn't sure what had woken her, until she realized it was a removals man, carting off a sink from the capacious en suite. She blinked.

"Actually," she said, "could you leave the loo for a bit?"

Huckle was still out for the count, gently snoring. Polly felt rather rough as she stumbled to the bathroom, but the view—the bathroom had a huge window over the bath, straight out to sea, nothing in your eyeline but sharp, sharp blue—woke her up.

"I will MISS this place," she said, as Huckle started to stir. "I can't believe some Russian guy is going to come here and ruin it."

"Ruin it how?" said Huckle, groaning and running his fingers through his thick hair. "I don't know how it could actually be more tacky."

"I am thinking, gold everywhere and more animal skins?" said Polly.

"Oh yes, that would do it," said Huckle. "You seem suspiciously perky for a morning after at Reuben's."

"The swim helped," said Polly. "Oh, and also I slept through the film. He's shown it about nine million times, and it's been shit boring every single time. So actually I feel pretty good."

Huckle smiled and glanced at his watch.

"I think he said something about his housekeeper going today."

"So sad," said Polly vehemently. She had always liked the idea of a housekeeper.

She took one last glance around at their stunning surroundings.

"Shall we lock the door and bid it farewell?" she grinned.

"I believe under the circumstances that's the respectful thing to do," said Huckle, rolling over in the bed.

Back in Mount Polbearne, having taken their leave of Reuben and Kerensa, bravely holding hands in what was left of their grand entrance hall, Polly and Huckle looked at the finances together, up in the sitting room.

Outside, it was a wild night. The gray clouds had come over and torn themselves up and now there was a storm brewing. Polly had, as she always did, gone down and forbidden the fishermen to go out in bad weather, and they had, as they always did, pretended to listen to her then turned around and gone anyway. Actually this was unfair: since the previous year, Archie had been much more conscientious and careful around weather forecasts and had occasionally held back the fleet. But he did not think this would be worse than a bit of wind and rain, and they were behind on their quotas, and so, with a weary look on his face, he cast off the lines, and they chugged bravely into the hungry waves, Polly watching them go, anxious as ever.

The wind had blown out the power temporarily. The lighthouse itself had back-up generators, but the building wasn't connected to those, so Huckle went searching for candles. Normally Polly didn't mind a power cut: they snuggled up together and had an early night. But tonight they were looking at paperwork, which was torturous but essential and unavoidable, so they lit as many candles as they could find and worked off the laptop's battery, peering at the piles of bills on the table. They did live cheaply—Mount Polbearne didn't offer that much in the way of shopping unless you wanted a bucket and spade, chips, or a piece of driftwood with "LOVE" spelled out on it in white paint, and Polly cooked most things they ate from scratch—but there was the mortgage, and taxes, and electricity and water and just the usual flotsam and jetsam of everyday life. Polly had poured all her meager savings into the lighthouse, and now they had a vastly reduced income. Almost nothing, in fact. She shook her head in disbelief.

"Oh goodness, it's worse than I thought," she said. "Seriously, it is awful."

Huckle nodded gravely.

"Mind you, Reuben's will look just like this, minus several million extra dollars."

"I know," said Polly. "But somehow I can't help thinking that they'll be absolutely okay."

"Well, sure," said Huckle. "They're probably thinking exactly the same thing about us."

The candles flickered, and their shadows glowed high up against the rough whitewashed wall, a pin of light in the thick darkness of the sea, with the great swooping lamp above them. Polly looked at their silhouettes, their heads close together against the dark, and leaned in even closer.

"What are we going to do?"

They'd looked into buying a van, and it was possible—entirely possible—but expensive. Well, everything was expensive when you had no money, that was an absolute fact, but to buy a van, and get it clean and ready to work and certified, would take time. And they didn't have time. Polly needed to work. She had to.

She'd met up that morning with Jayden, who'd texted her in a panic.

"That weird man," said Jayden. "Flora doesn't like him either."

"Flora doesn't like anyone."

"That's true," said Jayden, going slightly pink.

"So," prompted Polly. She couldn't deny it: it made her feel slightly better to hear someone saying she was really missed, and she hoped Jayden would.

"He's brought in all this kind of garbage pre-packed stuff," said Jayden. "I don't think it's actually much cheaper than you doing it. I think it's much more expensive actually."

"But he doesn't need to pay me to do it," said Polly.

"Oh yeah," said Jayden. "I never thought about that."

"You just pour it out in front of the display case."

Jayden nodded.

"It's not as nice as yours," he said sadly.

"Well, that's good," said Polly. "Maybe you'll eat less of it."

"He counts the stock," said Jayden gloomily. "It's all plastic-wrapped. A plastic-wrapped eclair isn't very nice."

"A *plastic-wrapped eclair*?"

Polly genuinely couldn't believe it. She couldn't believe that anyone would do that. What kind of a fiend would plastic-wrap an eclair?

"But everyone is so conscious of their weight these days, and what they should and shouldn't put in their bodies . . . and if they're going to have a treat, something as lovely and gorgeous and delicious as an eclair, why wouldn't they have the best, made with proper cream and icing, and fluffy flour that's been raised that morning, and all chilled deliciously so it's absolutely gorgeous and fresh in your mouth, and one, two, three bites and you're happy for the rest of the day, because it's lighter than air, and nothing so light and lovely can really be bad for you, not when it's made with love from good stuff." Her mouth took on a defiant line.

"I know," said Jayden.

Polly wrapped her arms around her knees and stared out to sea.

"I hate him so much."

"Me too," said Jayden, quickly glancing behind him to make sure Malcolm wasn't stalking about.

"Um . . ." Jayden was bright red and staring at the ground. "Um, would you like me to quit for you? Because you know I would."

Polly's hand flew to her mouth.

"Oh no, Jayden, NO! Definitely not. No. Not at all. Honestly, I would not want you to do that for me. In fact, as your ex-boss, I order you NOT to do it. Seriously."

Jayden had hated being a fisherman, and he loved working in a bakery. Jobs in the region tended to be seasonal and hard to come by, and Polly couldn't bear the idea of him giving up the first job he'd ever had that he actually liked. She put her hand on his arm.

"Thank you," she said. "Thank you for that, it means a lot. I'm very touched. But no, you don't have to give up your job for me. You just need to do it properly, hang on in there, then when Malcolm gets bored with it and goes to do something else . . ."

She tried to think of precisely how this would happen, but she couldn't, quite. She made sure her voice didn't choke up too much.

"Just don't . . . don't clean it as well as you did for me. No, hang on, what am I saying, you'll make everyone sick. That's a terrible thing to say, ignore me. Just do what you always do, Jayden. You're great at it."

Jayden beamed. "Thanks," he said. Then added, "Nobody ever said I was good at anything before."

"Well, you are very, very good in a bakery," said Polly. "Far better than that ratfink deserves."

Jayden looked up at her.

"You'll be all right, Polly," he said. "I know you will. Whatever you do."

But now that the numbers were in front of their eyes, Polly had lost the optimism that seeing Jayden had given her.

They simply didn't, couldn't, add up, even if they could borrow money to buy a van, which they couldn't because Polly was a discharged bankrupt and Huckle was an American. Even then it would still take time to get it up to scratch, sort out the paperwork. Time they didn't have. The repayments on the lighthouse were very high, and that was before you even got near all the work it needed.

Huckle looked at the soft candlelight playing on Polly's features as she bit her lip anxiously. She looked absolutely lovely, but he hated seeing her so worried and sad. In fact, he felt his only job was to keep her from being worried and sad, and to make her laugh and keep her happy, like she'd been yesterday splashing in the water of Reuben's cove, even now Reuben no longer had a cove; even when their splashing days were over.

"Well," he said, in that slow way of his. He wasn't looking forward to this, but it had to be said. "Well, Polly, there is something."

Polly blinked. "I know, I know. We move. We move, we go and get office jobs again, we drive through traffic every day for the rest of our lives, we work nine to five, we never see the sun go down over the sea or have a picnic in the middle of a Tuesday afternoon. I know that's life, Huckle. I know that's how it is for most people, and I know I'm not special, or different, that I don't deserve to be doing something else. It just took me longer to figure it out than everybody else. It's time to grow up. Get rid of this millstone lighthouse and go do something else."

There was a long silence. Then Huckle drew her to him and gently kissed her neck.

"Actually, I was going to say exactly the opposite," he said, drawing her up to sit on his lap. "You belong here. You belong here doing what you love. You should stay here. Build it up again. Heck, fail again if you like. It doesn't matter. It will work out in the end, what you do. Keep doing the right thing, and do it right and it will come right. That's my promise to you."

Polly looked at him, not comprehending.

"And meanwhile, for a little while . . ."

There was a pause.

"Clemmie rang. Dubose's girlfriend. She rang me, looking for him."

They hadn't seen or heard from Dubose; Polly assumed that if he was at Selina's, she'd have seen him, even though she was steering clear of the bakery, but she hadn't. It was like he'd vanished into thin air.

"He hasn't even gotten in touch?" she said, shocked.

"That's not unusual."

"Oh my God, what if he left us that night and drowned on the causeway!"

"I think we'd know," said Huckle. "Anyway, I called Mom. He sent them an email . . . asking for money."

"Oh," said Polly. "Your brother is the WORST chancer."

"I know," said Huckle. "But anyway. I've been thinking."

Polly felt an anxious feeling deep in her stomach.

"I can go back," said Huckle.

"No," said Polly instantaneously.

"Shush," said Huckle. "I can go back. I can make money on the farm. Gaw, making money is all I used to be good at, till I got into the honey trade. I haven't worked on a farm for a while, but I can do it. And it pays reasonably well. Clemmie will put me up."

"You can't go!"

"Are you going to listen to me or are you just going to talk yourself into a gigantic panic?" said Huckle kindly but firmly. "Listen to me. I'd been thinking about this anyway, even before what happened, otherwise I can't see how on earth we'll ever make the lighthouse into anything other than a death trap."

"It's not a death trap!"

"What about that stair moss?"

"I can't believe you're bringing the stair moss up again."

"I just think most people live in houses that don't have moss."

"Well, hooray for them."

Polly's face looked cross. Huckle rubbed her back and arms.

"Look," he said, his voice low and soothing, "I go back to the States, work for a few months, make some money. Clemmie needs help. And I'll save Dubose his job for when he gets home. Not that he deserves it. I'll send you the money. I will trust you not to spunk it all on shoes and getting your nails done."

Polly managed a tiny grin. She couldn't remember the last time she'd had her nails done.

"When you've got your van up and running, I'll come back again. Get back into my highly demanding career of being occasional honey-collector and bee-keeper and hanging-out-with-Polly-and-Neil-er."

Polly looked at him.

"But you can't go. I'll miss you!"

Huckle nodded. "Well, good. I would find it very difficult if you didn't notice or remotely care."

"Can't we get through this together?"

"This *is* getting through this together," said Huckle. "All of us together. Sorry, Poll. I apologize for my family baggage."

Polly's eyes were wide. She thought of Selina sending Tarnie off for weeks on end, his dangerous work miles away from home. She thought of sailors' wives everywhere who waited months for their men to come home; of men who raised families while their wives did night shifts and collapsed, exhausted, to try and grab a few hours' sleep in the noisy day; of the men who worked on oil rigs; of divers, and soldiers, and women who left their children behind in other countries to earn a crust. And poor abandoned Clemmie, in love with the handsome, carefree Dubose.

Huckle grabbed her and held her tight.

"Don't think I won't miss you," he said. "Every second of the day."

"All those American girls will want to eat you up," grumbled Polly, trying to stop a tear coming to her eye.

"Yeah, fortunately I can only get turned on by an English accent these days," said Huckle. "Seriously, anything else just puts me right off."

Polly laughed.

"You are surrre, monsieurrr?"

"What's that?" said Huckle. "Lebanese?"

"Shut up! It's French!"

"Oh," said Huckle. "Well, actually, you know, that one appears to be working too."

"Disproves your theory," said Polly. Huckle shook his head and pulled her closer to him.

"Proves it," he said. "The only person in the entire world for me is you. We need this for us."

"You promise it won't be for long?"

They blew out the candles one by one, except for one each, which they took downstairs to their bedroom and placed on either side of the bed. Outside there was nothing except, every so often, the waves, and then Mount Polbearne, lit by the light from above their heads.

"This is kind of romantic," Polly said.

"Whoop! Sorry, it's hard to pee in the dark," yelled Huckle from the bathroom. "Sorry!"

"Okay, so there *was* a romantic mood going on," said Polly, smiling. She went and looked out of the window. Could she manage? Could she cope with Huckle gone? He was her rock, her everything. But also, she felt inside herself, also there was something else.

Because she'd been alone before. Because she'd started over before. Because, Kerensa's help aside, she had had to deal with Tarnie's death alone too. And that had changed her. She wasn't as needy as she had once been. Even though she had failed, she knew somewhere deep inside that when you were tested with the worst that could happen and you didn't fall apart, then more things were possible than you imagined. Everyone was stronger than they thought they could be when the worst came to the worst. It was one of the very few good things about confronting the worst.

Huckle came out of the loo looking slightly shamefaced and cuddled up to her.

"What are you thinking?"

"I am thinking," said Polly, "that as long as you come back . . ."

"I have a gorgeous naked woman who bakes, a friendly local pub, a motorbike and a lighthouse," said

Huckle. "I am fascinated to know just exactly what you think this world holds that is better than what I have going on right now. Apart from, you know. A fireman's pole."

She smiled and cuddled up to him.

"Don't take this the wrong way," she said.

"Uh-oh," said Huckle. "Are you going to watch *Game of Thrones* without me?"

"No!" said Polly, horrified. "God, I would never do that to you! The betrayal! No, we can watch it together every night. I'll stay up late and you can watch it on the farm."

Huckle nodded. "Okay," he said. "Employers almost never mind that."

"No, it's not that," she said. "But you know I don't mean this the way it's going to sound . . ."

"I'll take your word for it," said Huckle.

"I can do without you," said Polly. "For a little bit, you know. Just a little bit. In fact, you offering to fund my van . . . it's amazing. It's wonderful. I'm completely thrilled and incredibly grateful."

"Excellent," said Huckle. "I have plans to exploit this for years."

"But it's not just doing without you," said Polly. She sat up in bed and wrapped her arms around her knees. "There's someone else I'm going to have to do without too, and that's really going to make it hard."

Huckle looked at her.

"Are you sure?"

She nodded, a massive lump in her throat.

"It's time. It is time, while everything else is changing. I have to do without you . . . and Neil has to learn to do without us."

Chapter Twelve

It was a windy, bright morning with a chill in the air. The tide was in and the spray was high as they took a long, meandering walk around the headland and up and down the town, occasionally chucking Neil off things to see how he could manage. He fluttered and bounced cheerfully and seemed, in every respect, totally recovered. Which meant only one thing.

Polly had one hand in Huckle's pocket, to keep out the chill. He looked at her. She had a bit of a set to her jaw, but apart from that she seemed all right.

"You seem calmer than I thought you were going to be," said Huckle gently.

Polly nodded. "I know."

Neil perched on her shoulder.

"That's because, I don't care what Patrick says, Neil

won't want to go. He'll come back. He'll find his way home. He knows where we live. He knows where his home is. I'm going to do the right thing and take him to the sanctuary, but it won't make any difference, you know."

Huckle made a noncommittal sound. He thought Polly was in denial. He would miss the little bird too, but Patrick was right: Neil had to go and find his place in the world, and his place was with puffins, not humans. Huckle would be heartbroken to see the little fellow go. But he understood Polly was clinging onto something else, some belief that Neil wouldn't leave, and he didn't think it was very helpful.

"So," she said defiantly, "I've decided not to be that sad."

"Okay," said Huckle, grasping her hand more tightly in his pocket. "Wow, it is fresh today."

He looked at her.

"Are you sure you don't just want to come to Georgia with me? It's wonderful this time of year. Big bougain-villea everywhere; all the houses dripping with ivy; warm, fragrant evenings . . ."

She looked at him.

"That does sound nice," she said. "Are you sure you'll want to come back?"

"Yes, ma'am," said Huckle. "But couldn't I take you anyway?"

"We've been through this," said Polly. "The more flights you have to pay for, the longer it will take to save up the money. Plus I have to be here to talk to the council and do all that stuff."

As they were talking, Archie stepped out in front of them.

"What?" he shouted. "What the hell is this?" He held up a plastic-wrapped white-bread ham sandwich. "Taste it," he said, proffering it to Polly. "Taste this!"

"No thank you," said Polly.

"It's disgusting," he said, his face all red. "It's bloody horrible. It's a disgrace! Two pounds fifty! Two pounds fifty for this! That's more than one of your pricey old loaves with seeds and stuff in it."

"That you didn't like."

"I didn't always like them," said Archie. "But I liked them a hell of a lot better than what we've got now."

He looked haggard and tired.

"Archie, are you getting enough sleep?" said Polly.

"No," said Archie. "But at least I was eating properly before. This. This is a *travesty*."

"I know," said Polly. "I don't like it either."

"You have to do something about it," said Archie. "You have to. Everyone will just stop going."

"But where are you going to eat?" said Huckle.

"I know," said Archie. "Hunger strike is quite a difficult sell, to be honest."

He looked sad.

"Their sausage rolls taste of poo," he said. "You know, I am trying and trying and trying in this town. We're all trying to adapt, to move on, to adjust. And now this happens. I can't run a good fishing boat on poo rolls! I can't inspire and lead my men on this!"

"I'll try my best," said Polly. Huckle shot her a warning look. The plan was not to tell anyone what they wanted to do. They didn't put it past Malcolm to block it in some way.

"Well, try harder," said Archie.

Polly watched him go.

"I worry about him," she said.

"You worry about everyone," pointed out Huckle accurately.

They wandered up the little main street.

"I'll just . . ."

"You shouldn't," said Huckle. "It'll make you upset."

"I just want to see."

She popped her head around the door of the old Polbearne bakery. Flora was standing there looking as sullen as ever. She was back in slouchy, greasy mode, her shoulders bent, her hair in her eyes, her bottom lip sticking out ferociously. Polly had to squint to see the stark, angular beauty that was there underneath; it was a good disguise.

Flora was dressed up in a ridiculous maid's outfit— black dress, white apron, frilly mob cap—which made her look like a cross between an underhousemaid and a strip-o-gram. She was standing in front of packets of pallid pastries, looking thoroughly bored.

"Hi, Flora."

"Oh, hello, madam," mumbled Flora.

"It's just me," said Polly. "Polly."

"I have to call everyone madam now," said Flora.

"Oh well, that will definitely make up for the terrible food," murmured Huckle.

"How are things?" said Polly.

Flora shrugged. "Everyone keeps coming in going blah blah blah, where's Polly, this is horrible, I think I've been poisoned," she said. "Then they don't come in any more. Malcolm is very cross."

Polly tried not to be pleased about this. She glanced back at Huckle.

"Do you think he might give me my job back?"

"I think he might have done," said Huckle, "if you hadn't told him he was a pig."

"Everyone wants to call their boss a pig," said Polly. "Come on, if you can't make a big fuss when you're being sacked and storm out going 'You're a pig!' you're not really a human being."

"What are you? A pig?" said Huckle.

"No! It's emotional distress! It's good to let it out! He'll understand."

"He thinks this is all your fault," said Flora. "He thinks you've turned the town against him."

"I think he did that the first time he said 'This town is total shit,' " said Polly. "And started selling people plasticine masquerading as food."

Flora offered Neil a little piece of plastic bun. He sniffed at it, pecked at it briefly, then backed away.

The bell tinged behind them, and Polly and Huckle turned guiltily. Malcolm was standing there. At the sight of them his face went purplish around the jowls. It wasn't a good look on him.

"WHAT HAVE I SAID ABOUT BIRDS IN THE SHOP?" he hollered. He turned to face Polly. "And you've got a cheek, turning up here again."

Polly flushed bright red. She hated confrontation of any sort.

"I was checking up on Flora," she said.

"Don't you worry about Flora," said Malcolm. "And stop bloody poisoning the town against me."

"Actually I think you're the one who—"

Huckle put his hand on her arm.

"We haven't said a thing, sir," he said politely. "Polly feels awful that she brought mucky stuff into a food preparation area, don't you, Poll?"

Polly swallowed hard.

"Um, yeah," she mumbled. "Sorry about that."

"In fact," said Huckle, "I think she'd probably come back and work for you. Buck things up again, if you wanted that."

Polly blushed bright red to the tips of her ears. She was furious with Huckle. On the other hand, if there was just the tiniest chance that he didn't have to go away, they had to take it, no matter how humiliating it was for her.

Malcolm smiled, relishing the fact that they'd come back to beg. He'd hoped for this.

"Ha! Not a chance," he said. "Run my business into the ground with her messing around the place? Not bloody likely. Ha! Oh no, when the summer season starts up, that cash will be all mine, and I'm not risking that. SO sorry, but you must understand. Health and safety is health and safety! Political correctness gone mad, I call it, but you must understand, my hands are totally tied."

Polly felt her own hands clench into fists.

Malcolm, thoroughly overexcited, turned to Flora with a lascivious look on his face.

"You're looking quite lovely today, my dear. I do like that new uniform."

"Thank you, sir," said Flora sullenly.

"Can you do the curtsey?"

Flora bobbed reluctantly, to Polly and Huckle's amazement.

"Piiiiggggg!" whispered Polly under her breath, and Huckle uncharacteristically gave her a small pinch.

"Hush," he said.

"Okay, bye," he said loudly, as Polly clearly didn't trust herself to speak. He shepherded her out the door.

"That man is such a PIG!" shouted Polly at the top of

her voice. "All he does is RUIN things. Horrible, horrible man! He's starving the fishermen to death and he's enslaved Flora and he's racist!"

"How do you figure he's racist?" said Huckle.

"Oh, everyone knows that anyone who says 'political correctness gone mad' is just itching to be allowed to say something racist."

Huckle wisely ignored this.

"To be fair, Flora doesn't seem massively less happy than she did before," he pointed out.

"I wish you hadn't asked for my old job back," said Polly, kicking at a stone in the road. "It was humiliating."

"I know," said Huckle. "I'm sorry. I just wanted to be a hundred percent absolutely sure and positive that it was going to play out that way."

He turned her around to him. A little weak sunlight played off the waves uncovering the shiny ancient stones of the causeway.

"Because otherwise, my darling, how on earth could I bear to go?"

Polly held Neil close to her in the sidecar. Patrick had signed him off and approved very much of her decision to take him back to the sanctuary. Get a puppy, he had advised. Something bred by evolution for thousands of years to make a good pet. Polly had looked at him with narrowed eyes until he looked away first. He had also begged her to make him some bread for his freezer in return for the outstanding operation bill, which Polly had explained she couldn't pay for a little while.

"It has genuinely done terrible things to my quality of life," said Patrick. "We took you for granted, Polly."

Polly shrugged. "Life changes," she said. "These things happen."

Patrick looked at her. The spark had gone right out of her.

"It doesn't always seem fair, though."

"That's because it isn't," said Polly dully. "It's not meant to be. No one promised anything."

She glanced down at Neil, who was absentmindedly trying to eat some gauze he'd found on Patrick's desk. It had unrolled, and he was chasing it.

"He'll be okay," said Patrick, reading her thoughts. "He'll be fine. It will be fine."

"How many times does he have to fly back before I can keep him?" asked Polly suddenly.

Patrick sighed. "Polly . . ."

"I mean it. How many times?"

"It doesn't work like that," said Patrick. "You have to let him go. The more time he spends with other puffins, the more his natural instincts will come to the fore. He's not a cuddly toy. You're not in a Disney film."

"I am, actually," said Polly. "I'm in that bit in *Fantasia* where it all goes horribly wrong for Mickey Mouse and he starts to drown and all those mops keep hitting him."

"Now don't think like that," said Patrick. "Animals are only ever our guests. We are absolutely so lucky to have them, and they stay with us for a time and make our lives better, and then it's over."

Polly nodded. But she didn't believe him.

The same cheery Kiwi girl they'd met before was still working at the puffin sanctuary up on the north coast, standing square in her khaki shorts, curly hair pulled back in an unflattering pigtail.

"Hello," she said cheerfully. "Did you find *another* one?"

"No, it's the same one," said Polly stiffly. She'd been worried that Neil would get anxious being back here again, but he was dozing peacefully in his box.

"Oh yeah!" said the girl. "I remember you now! Homing puffin. Amazing."

She picked Neil up out of his box. He regarded her sleepily.

"You've been in the wars, young man," she said, looking at his scars. "What happened?"

"Attacked by a cat," said Polly.

The girl nodded.

"Yeah, you have to watch for that. That's why he'll be best back at sea."

Polly nodded numbly. It's not forever, she told herself. It's not forever.

"Hey, you," she said to the little bird, bringing her nose up close to his beak. "It's time to go on your holidays, okay?"

Neil eeped and looked around him with interest. There were very few puffins on Mount Polbearne; the seagulls had pretty much staked out their territory. He glanced back at Polly with a puzzled look.

I will see him again, thought Polly. She had to think this. I will see him again. Because otherwise I cannot cope.

She kissed him very briefly, and then the Kiwi girl put him down on the rocks, next to some little pools where puffins were already congregating. The noise of the birds filled the air; there was guano spattered over the rocks. They seemed, undeniably, to be having the most wonderful time together. Nearby, excited children in windbreakers had gathered to watch them being fed a huge meal of fish. Other flocks tore across the sky in groups, tumbling and wheeling in their freedom, dancing on the gusts of wind.

It was Huckle who bent down quickly, checking that Neil still had his Huckle Honey tag from a long time ago, and buried his face in the little bird's feathers.

It was Huckle who watched him on his way, taking one tentative, slightly wobbly step, then another, then standing on the side of the rock pool like a child on his first day of school, shooting sideways glances at the other puffins, inching steadily closer to them while attempting to appear nonchalant. It was Huckle who, completely without embarrassment, blew him a kiss.

"Go, sweet baby," he said. "On you go."

Polly, by contrast, felt frozen. She couldn't move. She flashed back to Neil playing all by himself, so lonely by the rock pool outside the lighthouse, and damped the feeling down immediately. He would come back. She gripped onto Huckle's hand so tightly he almost yelped. But instead, he just squeezed back.

"Well, if we're going to do it, we should do it all at once," Huckle had said, which had made a ton of sense when they were discussing it in the lighthouse by candlelight, all cozy and cuddling and getting ready for bed, but absolutely bloody none when they were actually standing at the railway station three days later.

Polly had insisted on getting the cab to the station with him; there was a bus that would take her back. Well, there was one bus a day. She didn't know when it was, but she really didn't care. As long as Huckle was on Cornish soil, she had to be with him.

"What are you doing to my phone?" he protested, as she fiddled with the buttons.

"I'm putting in a Google alert for Mount Polbearne," she said. "So you can see what we're up to."

He laughed. "But nothing is what we're up to," he said. "That's why we like it here."

Polly looked at him.

"It's just a reminder," she said. "The last time you went, I really did think I would never see you again."

"I know," said Huckle, taking back his phone and tossing his kitbag over his shoulder. It had been his father's in Vietnam, and he had never used anything else. "But this time you know you will. It's just a job. A hard, boring job, and then I will be back again with big bunches of cash and be a kept man who dabbles in honey."

"And me," pointed out Polly. "I want you to dabble in me."

Huckle smiled. "Oh well, obviously. But you know, you are much more than just a hobby to me, Polly Waterford."

They stood, both very still. The railway station—a branch line, with hardly any services; Huckle would have to change to even get to the London train—was utterly deserted. Birds of all sorts could be heard singing in the hedgerows. Bushes grew over the platform edges, and the long-abandoned tearoom had dandelions and daisies bursting through every crack in the concrete. The hum of the electric lines emphasized the heavy stillness of the morning. It felt like a storm was on the way.

Polly blinked.

"You know what I reckon?" Kerensa had said a couple of nights earlier, as they had gloomily shared a bottle of Mount Polbearne's cheapest white wine (from the grapes of several former Soviet bloc territories, according to the label).

"What do you reckon?" Polly had said.

"I reckon all this hardship's going to be good for you. I reckon he's going to propose."

"Don't be stupid!" Polly had said vehemently. "How would we pay for a wedding? Sell a kidney?"

"It's not about the wedding," said Kerensa.

"Says you," said Polly. Kerensa's wedding had been a Kardashian-style extravaganza that had left everyone broken, tearful and exhausted, which Polly still doubted had been Kerensa's original intention.

"Don't ask me what kind of house we could have had back in Plymouth for the price of that wedding," growled Kerensa. "I have decided not to think like that for the sake of inner peace."

She took a large slug of the tongue-stripping wine.

"This also helps toward inner peace."

Polly nodded. "Anyway. God, no, with everything else going on, it's way, way not on the agenda. We haven't even discussed it."

Kerensa raised an eyebrow.

"Yes, but before he goes . . . he'll want to do something, won't he?"

Polly had shaken her head. She hadn't ever felt that she and Huckle . . . Well, she certainly hadn't envisaged a big white wedding day—Polly was always happier in the kitchen, behind the scenes. Having to be a bridesmaid at Kerensa's wedding had been quite enough fuss for one lifetime. But she did, sometimes, in her quieter moments, think of a blond, golden-skinned chubby baby boy (and a lot of stair gates).

But she had never brought it up, and Huckle had certainly never mentioned it, and the timing couldn't possibly be worse, so she had put it out of her mind completely.

"Neh," she said, feigning a nonchalance she didn't really feel. It had taken Huckle a long time to get over his last girlfriend, Candice, and a long time to get ready to commit. She didn't want to push things. "I am not in the least bit fussed about all that. At least, not compared to the two million other things I have to fuss about right now."

Kerensa knocked back a bit more of the wine.

"Quite right," she said tipsily. "For richer for poorer is a right fricking pain in the arse."

Not a breath of wind stirred the heavy foliage, the wild thyme that grew unconstrained up the rusting fence of the old branch line, the vast field of daisies that made up the bank. Polly and Huckle looked at one another. It was as if there were nobody else in the entire universe; as if, like in *Where the Wild Things Are,* the vines had claimed the world all around.

Huckle took a step toward her and lifted her chin with his strong hand. His eyes were amused, as always, that clear blue that looked out on a world he expected to be good to him and, as a result, generally was. But today there was sadness in them too, and concern.

Polly swallowed and tried not to think of her conversation with Kerensa. She suddenly wished she weren't wearing her faded old rolled-up dungarees with a floral shirt. She couldn't possibly have known that Huckle thought she looked lovelier than she would in the priciest ballgown imaginable; he would carry this image of her in his heart. The sun was glinting on her hair, and he pulled her close and gently kissed the freckles on her nose, and realized, suddenly, that there was so much he wanted to say, but if he started, if he even tried to get the words out, then he would start to cry, and he wouldn't get on the train, and they would be in an even worse situation than they were in already.

So even though he saw Polly's eyes on him, wide and slightly confused, he still couldn't speak, right up to the second when there was a faint push of wind, then a whistle, then a roar, and the train with its out-of-date rolling stock with the hand-operated doors slowly pulled up.

"Huckle . . ." Polly was saying, when suddenly out of the carriages spilled a huge party, a massive group of young men and women, all giggling and carrying champagne; the men in morning dress, the women in colorful dresses and hats and fascinators, all laughing and shouting at the tops of their voices, as behind them at the front of the station drew up, seemingly out of nowhere, a fleet of smart black cars with blue and pink ribbons tied to them.

"A wedding," murmured Polly. It must be taking place in one of the grand hotels down on the coast—a very smart thing by the looks of it. The train nearly totally emptied, and, amid the noise and color of the huge gang, Huckle climbed aboard, carefully hauled up his kitbag, then leaned his big shaggy head out of the pull-down window.

"Polly," he said. She looked at him hopefully, eyes wide, holding onto his hand. But he was too far up to kiss, and neither of them could believe it when the guard blew the whistle and the train started to move slowly with so much left unsaid between them and so much left unkissed, and Polly started to speed up with the train, but that was silly of course, and all she could say was "Goodbye!" and all he could do was lean out, shouting, "I'm coming back! I'm coming back!" in a way that sounded to Polly like he was trying to convince someone, possibly her, possibly himself. And then, in a breath on the falling wind: "I love you."

And then the train was a dot on the green horizon, and Polly turned away, into the great, happy, celebrating throng who were chattering excitedly and loading themselves into cars, which swept off gaily down the little railway lane, to whoops and cheers and a cork popping out of a bottle. Polly watched them go, then trudged in the same direction, to sit and wait for a bus that would never come, to go home to a lighthouse where everything that was light had been extinguished.

Chapter Thirteen

I'm still so lonely."

"Can't you put yourself out there a little more?"

"I tried that. Then he vanished completely from the town, so I learned my lesson about that. I don't know. I think they all hate me because of my cat. And because I nobbed Huckle's brother or something. They all talk about me all the time."

"Is that the reality, do you think, or something you're projecting?"

"What's the difference?"

Two weeks later, Polly had more or less given up on trying to sleep. It wasn't as if she had anything to get up for. In the kitchen, her pans, her loaf tins and baguette brick and living yeast went ignored and unused.

All the pleasures she had taken so seriously—feeding herself and her friends, enjoying the merits of good food and good company, doing things slowly and getting them right—all of this had gone by the wayside. She had lost it. She felt so sorry for herself. Malcolm had got Jayden to paint over her name, which he had done, feeling like a war-time collaborator, he'd explained later, even though Polly said it was fine, it didn't matter. Except he hadn't got quite the right pale gray color that Chris, Polly's ex, had used, so all you could see were big brown chunky paintbrush marks.

Every night Polly sat by the window pretending she wasn't watching out for Neil. Huckle would call, but he was worried by how down she sounded, how unlike herself. He was very concerned about her.

Huckle himself was frenziedly busy. He had turned up tired and dusty, astonished anew by the heat in the great flat plains of Georgia, with the corn high, to find Clemmie in a state of nervous collapse trying to deal with suppliers, creditors, field workers, unseasonal rainstorms and generalized chaos. When she saw him, she burst into tears.

"I thought you were Dubose coming home."

"Won't I do?"

Clemmie sobbed. "You'll be . . . you'll be much better."

As soon as Huckle pulled out the farm accounts, he understood why. Everything was a terrible mess. He couldn't figure out what Dubose had been doing all this time. With a sigh, tired and jet-lagged, he let Clemmie make him some iced tea—he'd missed it terribly—and sat down in the tiny dark office in the old wooden farmhouse. It was going to be a long couple of months.

Two weeks later he was just about starting to get a handle on it. He spoke to the merchants, timed out a proper schedule for the laborers, and started to get everything gradually moving into line. The accounts had involved night after night of painful reworking of columns of figures; it reminded him of his old city job, and why he'd left it behind. His days started early—the farm had a dairy herd as well as crops—and carried on well into the evening. Clemmie fed him grits and bacon in the morning; waffles; proper fried chicken at night, but he barely stopped, even to eat, which meant he wasn't nearly as attentive to Polly as he knew he ought to be. But right here in front of him, as the golden heat poured down on the vast acres of land, there were jobs and livelihoods that Dubose had been in severe danger of simply dribbling away, and he had to get his head down and sort it out. He couldn't remember ever working so hard.

Even though Huckle had set up a bank account for her and started sending little bits of money as he gradually turned the farm around, Polly hadn't used a penny of it. She hadn't gone to see any vans, hadn't started thinking about what would be good and easy to make in very enclosed conditions, and summer was coming in fast. The season was short, and she would really have to make the most of it before people decided that coming to Mount

Polbearne for a good lunch was such a waste of time they just wouldn't bother.

The time difference was five hours, which was tricky, as late at night Polly sounded sleepy and a little despondent. And she talked about that puffin a lot. Huckle wanted to tell her to get back into the kitchen and bake, for heaven's sake, but he didn't know a way to say it without sounding cruel. He decided he needed to get Reuben to give her a kick up the arse. But finding more time in his day was tricky at the moment.

Back in Cornwall, the weather had stayed as heavy and unsettled as Polly's mood, and she had given up on sleep altogether. She threw on one of Huckle's heavy plaid winter shirts, put on her sandals and clop-clopped down the circular stairs of the lighthouse, slipping out of the door into a warm, starry evening and an almost-full moon.

She pulled the shirt around her and wandered down over the rocks. The pub and the chippy were closed; the fishermen long gone off to the hunting grounds, where radars beeped to tell them of the fathomless unsuspecting shoals beneath their feet where they could drop their nets. It would not, she thought, looking up at the jewelled sky, be a bad night to be a fisherman. Some nights were very bad. But not tonight.

She walked slowly across the low-tide shingle beyond the harbor wall, between the groins. It was almost a beach when the tide was out and the old road to the mainland was revealed in all its glory. She picked up a stone and hurled it with all her might into the water. Then another, then another.

"Oi!" came a voice. "Careful now, you'll have someone's eye out."

Polly jumped.

"Oh goodness," she said, turning around and forgetting to be cross. "You startled me."

Selina stood there.

"Sorry," she said. "I saw you down there and . . . well. I wanted . . . I wanted to apologize."

Polly swallowed hard.

"You nearly killed my bird," she said before she could help herself. "He nearly died."

"I didn't know it was your bird," said Selina. "He just hopped into the room. I had no idea. I'm so sorry."

"Cats shouldn't kill birds."

"Can I tell you that I've already had that vet on and on and on at me about this?" said Selina. "He also threatened to de-claw Lucas, which let me tell you I think is illegal."

Polly was pleased to hear about Patrick sticking up for her.

"But I am so, so sorry. I didn't realize he meant so much to you. Lucas was just doing what cats do."

"I know," said Polly. "I do know. Neil shouldn't have been hopping about in a house; he should have been flying around outside."

"Well, that is what most birds do, isn't it?"

Polly's eyes were shining with tears.

"We had to send him away."

"No way," said Selina, genuinely shocked. "That is so harsh. Not because of Lucas?"

"No," said Polly. "Well, yes. And no. No. Just because."

Selina came and put her arm around her.

"I am so sorry," she said. "I am so, so sorry." She

paused. "I cannot tell you how weird it is for me to be saying that to somebody else for a change."

Polly managed a weak smile.

"I can imagine."

She swallowed the lump in her throat.

"I miss him," she said. "I miss them both, I miss them so much. Huckle's gone too."

"I know about that," said Selina. "I haven't heard that mad bike for ages. I overheard someone in Muriel's saying he'd gone away for work. Then they all looked at me like that was my fault too. After . . ."

"Where did Dubose go?"

"I don't know," said Selina. "It's kind of my hobby, making men disappear at short notice."

Polly looked at her.

"Why . . ."

"Because," said Selina. "Because I was unbelievably lonely and because he was nice to me."

Polly got a massive flashback to the previous year, and to Tarnie. She shook her head.

"I understand. And people aren't blaming you."

"Really?" said Selina. "They all think you're mad for buying that lighthouse, by the way."

"Thank you for that totally surprising piece of news," said Polly drily.

Selina looked down and kicked a rock with her foot.

"So apparently I've managed to completely screw things up for everyone. That's the message I've been getting. Everywhere I go, everyone falls totally silent. Apparently I keep a tiger in my house who brutally attacked the mayor or something."

She looked up, her mouth still twisted.

"I had no idea Neil was the most popular person in this town."

"Yeah," said Polly sadly. "Yeah, he is."

"And I'm the psycho bitch who tried to get him killed."

"I'm sure they're not saying *that*."

"Might as well be," said Selina. "You know, even the vet doesn't like Lucas."

Polly kept a prudent silence.

"How's the shop doing downstairs?"

"What, since I lost you your job too?"

"Just asking," said Polly.

"They put a pile of unsold tuna sandwiches outside, and it stank the place out for a week. Lucas went berserk, ripped open all the bin bags."

"Oh God, poor Jayden."

Suddenly Selina sank down onto a rock and crossly hurled a stone out to sea.

"Poor Jayden! Poor Polly! Poor Neil! Poor everyone else. You know, this was the last place; the last place I could come. This is pretty much the end of the road for me. No job, nothing to do, the compensation is basically gone. And now I'm here and everybody hates me. I mess it up and I mess it up and I mess it up, and even when I don't bloody mean to mess it up, it's my bloody fault for owning a bloody cat, as if I'm the only person ever to own one of the damn things! I didn't realize. I thought it was just some bird."

Polly shook her head.

"Sorry. It was my fault. I've learned. He shouldn't . . . I shouldn't have had him as a pet. Seabirds aren't pets. He shouldn't have been following me about."

Polly's voice caught in her throat.

"It's right that he's gone."

Selina was still staring out to sea.

"Everything I touch turns to shit."

Polly took off Huckle's big warm shirt and wrapped it around Selina's shoulders.

"Sssh," she said. "It's okay. It's not your fault. None of it was your fault."

All the animosity Polly had been harboring toward Selina and her cat melted away when she saw how fragile and sad Selina was; instead, she felt guilty for having avoided her, being too caught up in her own problems and too upset over what had happened to Neil to want to spend any time with her.

Dawn was a little way off, but not far; it was the very coldest, bleakest hour of the morning, the time when absolutely everything feels at its worst.

Polly knew only one way out of this. It was the first time she had felt like this in a while. Maybe it was being with someone else sad. Maybe it was the morning itself, or the truce that comes when you realize that, in fact, the rest of the world isn't out to cause you pain and trip you up. That most people's intentions are the same: just to get by the best they can, which sometimes succeeds and sometimes does not. That Selina wasn't plotting to harm her bird and make her lose her job. That we are, in the end, just fallible human beings and we all make mistakes, and if you can forgive other people, then that is almost exactly the same as forgiving yourself and feels just about as good.

"Hey," she said. "Um. I was thinking."

Selina scrubbed her face crossly with the cuff of Huckle's shirt, which made Polly a little sad as she would have to wash it and it wouldn't smell of him any more.

"What?" Selina said.

"You know," said Polly. "When I feel awful, there's only one thing that makes me feel any better."

"I don't really want a drink," said Selina.

"It isn't that, actually," said Polly.

Selina looked at her.

"What, then?"

"Come with me," said Polly, and she held out her hand.

In the lighthouse kitchen, Polly turned on all the lights, which were horribly bright as they hadn't gotten around to replacing the humming overhead fluorescent tubes. They both winced.

"Okay," said Polly, noticing that Selina was still shivering. She really was most frightfully thin. "First things first. And first thing is coffee. Black."

"Does it have to be black?"

"Yes," said Polly. "I forgot to buy milk again."

She turned on the coffee machine, instinctively glancing around for Neil, who was fascinated by the noise it made and liked to advance on it bravely. Then she remembered that of course he wasn't there. He'll be back soon, she told herself sternly.

She filled two little cups with thick, creamy coffee and added sugar against Selina's protestations.

"Sssh. We have work ahead. Right."

She fetched the living yeast from the fridge, where it had been growing for weeks, uncared for.

"What is that?"

"Be quiet and drink your coffee," said Polly, running her hand under the mixer tap until the water was warm. She added the warm water carefully to the yeast and mixed them together.

"That looks even worse," said Selina. "And it smells."

"Shut up," said Polly. She tied on the ridiculous puffin apron Huckle had gotten her, and gave the much prettier Cath Kidston one to Selina.

"What's this for?"

Polly took the flour down from the top shelf—the good stuff—and shook the entire kilo bag into a large mixing bowl. She added a sprinkling of finest sea salt, a pinch of sugar, and a little water, stirring all the time until with her expert eye she judged the consistency to be exactly right. Then she poured it into the bread mixer and adjusted the speed.

After that, she covered two of the surfaces in the kitchen with plenty of soft flour, and divided the mixture in half.

"Right," she said.

Selina eyed it carefully.

"I don't cook," she said.

"Well, that's useful," said Polly. "Because this isn't cooking, it's baking."

She turned on the radio. Local radio was good this time of the morning, as the DJ, Rob Harrison, played lots of loud getting-up songs for the early-morning farmers and fishermen and surfers and fruit-pickers: it was as if he knew they needed a hand.

"This'll do," she said, as Pharrell blasted across the room. "Let's go." She started to punch and pull at the mass of sticky dough. "Just do what I do."

Selina stared at her, then glanced at her very nice manicure.

"Take your rings off," said Polly. "Come on."

Selina looked down at her fingers, her hands trembling.

"Oh," said Polly, stopping her kneading for a second. "Sorry. Don't take your rings off."

Selina's slim wedding and engagement rings sat on her right hand, not her left; on her widow's finger. Polly hadn't noticed before. Selina looked at them for a long moment.

"No," she said. "No, I will. I shall. They're chains to me."

Polly didn't say anything for a long moment as Selina looked at her hands again. Then slowly, gladly, she drew both the rings off over her finger and, with one swift movement, plunged her hands into her big sticky ball of dough.

"Argh!" she said, smiling for the first time.

Polly nudged the radio up with her nose, a talent well developed in almost all bakers, then they really got down to it: punching, hurling, throwing the dough about, beating it and taking out on it everything they had against the world. Polly knew it was almost impossible to overknead dough by hand—it was the mixer you had to watch out for—so happily got into it, realizing as she did so how much she had missed this; how much she had missed the sore feeling, the workout in her arms as they whacked and threw the dough. She felt the knot in her shoulders gradually begin to relax and work itself out; her shoulders themselves descended, and she realized they must have been sitting somewhere up around her ears, as if carrying all the troubles of the world on them, or holding up the sky on their own.

The radio changed to another fantastic high-energy song, exactly what they needed, and Polly felt she was hearing music for the first time in a long while; enjoying it as she hadn't for months. She even felt her hips start to move, and a smile spread across her face as she noticed that Selina was so engrossed in what she was doing, so involved in hitting and pulling and punching the dough—or Tarnie, or her troubles, or whatever it was—that she too was twitching involuntarily in time to the music.

"That's it," said Polly encouragingly, as the dough began to change, to become smooth and malleable as the gluten became more elastic.

"Wow," said Selina, slightly pink in the face and out of breath. "This is like boxercise."

"Tastes a lot better than boxercise," promised Polly.

Behind them, the first fingers of pink were beginning to cross the sea.

"Right," said Polly. "Let's get them to the warm spot . . . Curses!"

"What?"

"My oven has been off for so long. Normally it's never off," she said sadly. "And I always have a warm spot. Oh well."

She turned the oven on anyway, and set the dough inside bowls covered in clean tea towels to rise. Then she deftly washed up and cleaned the surfaces. When she turned to offer more coffee, she found Selina sprawled across the table sleeping as deeply and contentedly as a child.

Polly fetched a blanket from upstairs, gently moved Selina to the armchair by the doorway and covered her up, then wandered outside with her coffee. The dew was lying heavily on the scrubby grass between the rocks, the sky lightening by the second. She needed to check the dough; the fishermen would be back soon, and it would be nice to have something warm to give them. She would crack open one of Huckle's last batches of honey, the orange flower, with the faint citrusy flavor she loved so very much.

She found herself humming happily, putting the

dough into tins and leaving it to rise again. Her fingers itched, used to doing ten times this much work in the morning, and she suddenly realized how much she had missed it. She really had. Not getting up at the crack of dawn might at first have seemed a bit of a luxury, but work was her; it defined her. Not working was making her sad and stressed. She needed to start getting things organized, she thought, putting the bread tins into the oven and deciding to quickly make some flaky pastry for croissants. Couldn't hurt.

The smell of baking bread woke Selina from where she was curled up like a cat on the armchair. Even though she had only slept a couple of hours, she stretched luxuriously.

"Oh," she said, blinking her long cat's eyes open. "What is that? It smells divine. I feel hungry." She looked puzzled. "I never feel hungry," she said in confusion. "Why am I hungry?"

"Hey," said Polly. "I think you're hungry because you helped make your own breakfast."

"I did?" said Selina. She frowned. "God, I thought I dreamed that." She looked around her. "But here I am, in a lighthouse."

"Quite," said Polly. "Here."

She served the fresh bread at the rough wooden table, spread with melting butter over its light-crumbed soft center, the well-kneaded crust crispy and nutty. A spoonful of honey over the top and a huge mug of tea (Polly disliked tea mugs that held less than about a pint) completed the simple repast. The early-morning sun shone in through the windows.

"Oh my God," said Selina. "Oh my God, this is absolutely perfect."

She tore into the bread with her little very white teeth. Polly smiled. It felt undeniably good to be feeding people again.

"Well, it should be," she pointed out. "You made it."

"Oh my," said Selina. "Well, I am brilliant."

Polly smiled again.

"Eat as much as you like," she said, holding up a large tray piled with thick honey sandwiches and an empty mug. "I'm just going to see the fishermen."

She could see their boats chugging across the horizon. She hoped they had had a good night.

"What's the cup for?"

"Fishermen make the best tea on earth," said Polly. "I always fill up from their urn."

The boys were cold, hungry, exhausted and entirely delighted to see Polly again.

"I thought you'd gone forever," said Kendall. "I thought you might go and live with your bird."

Archie snorted. "Don't be ridiculous, Kendall. You mean with Huckle."

Kendall looked at Archie.

"Could have been either, I say."

"Good God," said Polly. "What kind of a crazy lady do you think I am? Don't answer that."

Fortunately they were all busy chewing.

"How's business?" she asked Archie, who just shook his head. He still looked so unhappy.

"I'm doing my best," he said, then drew closer to her. "I just . . . I just wish . . ."

"What?" said Polly.

"Nothing," said Archie miserably.

"Tell me."

He looked at her.

"Can I?"

"Of course."

"Well last night . . . you know it was a little choppy?"

"Uh-huh."

"I'm just . . . I just get so scared." He looked away. "I'm . . . I'm terrified, Polly. I really am. I feel I have no business being in charge of the boat or the men or anything like that."

"But you're doing a great job! Everyone thinks you're brilliant!"

"That's because I've never been tested," said Archie, with feeling. "They haven't found me out."

"Hush," said Polly. "Anyway, everyone feels like that."

Archie held up a sandwich.

"Easy for you to say," he said. "When you can make stuff like this."

Now that Polly was feeling more in the swing of things, she headed to the mainland—where they had a decent Internet connection—to meet Reuben, who had been drafted to help with Operation Van.

They met in a little café in Looe, where all the men had beards and wore lumberjack shirts and the drinks were served in jam jars. Polly found this very peculiar.

Reuben turned up forty minutes late, which was all right, as it gave her time to go through all the vans that were on offer. Almost all of them were old burger vans that looked heavily engrimed with the grease of a thousand late-night drunks stumbling out of nightclubs, but Polly wasn't afraid of a little hard work. They ranged a lot in price, from two and a half thousand upward, but Huckle had been adamant that they use his money to get exactly what they needed.

"If you're going to do this," he said, "you have to do it right."

She also had a file open to list the things she needed to do. The actual baking economics she could do in her sleep; she had worked long enough to know exactly what she needed and how much she needed to charge. In fact, with fewer staff, no rent and few fixed costs, she could get away with less than the bakery.

And as she had no regular clientele to service, she could concentrate on the stuff with the slightly bigger profit margin—sandwiches and pizza as well as the loaves—and leave the cakes and buns to Malcolm's plastic patrol. She would, in any case, need to make a very clear case to the town hall that she was not doing the same as the existing businesses; she was going to try and license it as a snack bar.

She scrolled through the list of bedraggled-looking second-hand vans, her heart sinking slightly as she did so. Each one, she thought, represented someone's hopes and dreams come to nothing; their brilliant catering idea turned to dust. Who did she think she was to suddenly start something up in the middle of nowhere and expect it to work? Was she mad?

She couldn't think like this, however. She couldn't. This was their best option at this point—her only option as far as she could tell—and Huckle was busting a gut thousands of miles away just so she could have this opportunity. She scrolled through page after page of trucks that sold pasties and dirty white converted caravans . . . and then she saw it.

She looked at it. Then she looked away. Then she looked at it again, her negativity forgotten.

Piaggio Porter 2010, it said.

It was markedly more expensive than all the other trucks there. But . . .

It was a converted VW-style camper van, in a two-tone color scheme of dark red and white. One side slid open to reveal rails of baking trays, just like in the bakery. Behind them was a professional wood-burning oven. On the other side was a window that opened out to sell through, with a canopy over it. It looked to be in absolutely perfect nick; the description announced that it had been kitted out to sell pasties two years before, at a cost of £30,000. Whether this was true or not Polly couldn't say, but it looked absolutely perfect. Which was probably, she reflected, why it was twice as expensive as everything else for sale in the category.

She was still looking at it when Reuben came in. She had been worried about him; worried that he'd have lost his swagger, his chippy requirement to tell everyone how well he was doing. But she needn't have been; as she was ordering her second, shamefully expensive elderflower and ginger beer drink, he bounced in on his ridiculous limited edition Kanye West trainers—Polly only knew this because he'd mentioned the fact so repeatedly she was surprised the insolvency people hadn't taken them away—his wide, freckled Norman Rockwell face as cheery as ever.

"Hey!" said Polly, delighted to see him. "How are you?"

"I am fantastic," said Reuben. "Cheerfully triumphing over minor setbacks!"

"I see that," said Polly. She glanced out onto the street. "How did you get here?"

He grimaced slightly at that.

"Can you believe they took my Segway? How am I meant to get around now?"

He waved his hand at a member of staff who was peering at his phone.

"Flat white."

"Um," said Polly, as the waiter carried right on looking at his phone. "He doesn't work for you."

"He does right now," said Reuben. "While I'm sitting in his coffee shop."

"Yes, but he won't see it like that," said Polly. "You have to say please."

"Why do I have to say please? I'm giving him money for it. And if he was actually getting it for me, I'd be giving him extra money for that too."

Reuben said this loudly—he said everything loudly—which appeared to have the required effect, as the bearded waiter pushed himself off the counter slowly.

Reuben took his flat white with some satisfaction, but without saying thank you.

"So you don't mind being semiretired?" said Polly.

Reuben shook his head.

"Don't be ridiculous," he said. "I'm working more than ever. And I'm finally getting enough sex."

The rest of the coffee shop pretended not to be earwigging. This wasn't very much like a business meeting, thought Polly. And also: how could Reuben and Kerensa possibly be having *more* sex? Then she thought about how much she missed Huckle and blushed.

"Anyway," she said. She showed him the van she'd found on the Internet.

"Oh yes," said Reuben. "I like it."

"So what do I do?" said Polly. "I mean, how do I put this kind of thing together?"

Reuben turned her laptop toward him.

"What is this computer? How old is this? It's rubbish. How can you even carry it around with you? Mine is made out of NASA titanium. It weighs four ounces."

"I don't know what that is," said Polly patiently.

"You can spin it on one finger," said Reuben. "This is a terrible computer. I want to buy you a new one."

"Didn't your computer get taken away?" said Polly.

"Hmm," grumbled Reuben.

He started a new spreadsheet. He typed unbelievably quickly.

"Okay," he said. "Business plan 101."

"What's 101?"

Reuben looked at her and grinned.

"Stop looking so nervous, kid."

Polly glanced at the picture of the van again.

"I have run a business," she said. "I do know a bit. It's just . . . So many things seem to fail. Everything seems to fall apart."

"Don't be stupid," said Reuben. "Of course they do. That's how it works."

He smiled at her encouragingly.

"Do you know how many failed start-ups I ran before we hit it big?"

Polly shook her head and shrugged.

"Nine! Nine of the fuckers. But I didn't care because I knew I could make it. Then I did make it. Then it all went to shit again."

He raised his spoon and his voice.

"But you carry on! You get it back! All you have to believe is that you are awesome."

"I'm kind of average," said Polly, tentatively.

"You live in a freaking lighthouse! You. Are. AWE-SOME!" said Reuben. "Not as awesome as me, since you never owned a helicopter. But apart from that . . ."

Polly looked at him.

"Say it!"

"I'm not going to say it! I'm British!"

"SAY IT!" Reuben turned around to the waiter, who was now leaning against the wall. "You say it too; get yourself out of this coffee shop and into doing whatever it is you and your beard really want to do for a job."

The nonchalant waiter perked up suddenly.

"I want to be a film editor, man."

"Awesome," said Reuben. "That's an awesome thing to want to be. Go do it!"

"Reuben!" said Polly. "This isn't *The Wolf of Wall Street*."

"Everything is," said Reuben, who thought that film was both the best film ever made, and completely aspirational.

"Do you want this or not? Do you want to succeed or not? Do you want your life to get better or not?"

"Yes."

"Then say it."

Polly sighed.

"SAY IT!"

"I am awesome," she said, quietly.

"Louder," said Reuben.

"I am awesome," she said at a normal volume.

"LOUDER!"

"I. AM. AWESOME!" screamed the bearded waiter suddenly. Then he tore off his apron, threw it on the floor and marched out the door.

Reuben and Polly watched him go in surprise.

"Aha, free drinks," said Reuben. "Awesome."

They stayed in the café, heads together, for two hours, and hammered out the basics and structure of a solid yet flexible business plan.

Polly had learned a lot from running the graphic design business with her ex, even if it had ultimately failed. She had also picked up plenty from watching Gillian Manse deal with the books—she had been very efficient; too efficient, in fact. The old bakery had managed to hang on by virtue of good solid money management far longer than it ought to have done. Polly wondered if an earlier retirement might have led to a happier, longer life for Mrs. Manse.

But she wasn't distracted for long: she was soon pulled back into the world of profit-and-loss accounts and offset capital expenditure. This was as close as she had ever seen Reuben to working. He was completely and utterly engrossed, and his fierce concentration didn't let up for a second. For the first time she could absolutely see why this short geek had taken over the world, and why you wouldn't ever bet against him doing exactly the same again one day.

"Do this," he said. "Use Huckle's money; the bank can't help you, although you can open a small business account, which lets you bank free for six months. Make sure you get that."

Polly nodded.

"I'll come and look at the van with you. But your job now is to charm City Hall into granting you that trading license. Print out pictures of the van. Even if you don't get it, I think the fact that it looks so pretty will help you a lot. And you're only asking to set it up in a car park after all. I can't see that it will be that much of a problem; they let ice cream vans come past, don't they?"

"Not up to town," said Polly, thinking of the terrible blow it would be to both Muriel's shop and the chippy if their precious Wall's concessions were challenged. Cornetto money from the hot days of summer kept them going right through the deep storms of winter. And she was trying to do this to someone else's business.

"Well, speak to them anyway. Then they'll probably need to inspect the van."

"You know a lot about this," said Polly.

"No," said Reuben. "I'm just assuming they might like to check from time to time to make sure you're not selling rat juice. Were you planning on selling rat juice?"

Polly shook her head. Reuben got up, then carefully shook out his wallet and left enough money to cover his own coffee. Polly did the same with her cordials.

"Gotta respect the small businesses, man," said Reuben, patting the door frame of the café as they left. "Gotta respect 'em all."

He gave Polly a light kiss on the cheek.

"Right. I'm off home. Talking about business plans always makes me feel sexy."

Polly rolled her eyes and followed his gaze. Parked behind the café was a tiny, glittering, incredibly expensive-looking micro-scooter.

"Seriously?" she said.

"Oh yeah," said Reuben. "Totally. I hid it in a hedge. Okay. What are you?"

Polly smiled at him. He'd been a proper tonic.

"Um, awesome?"

Reuben shook his head and got on his scooter.

"Nope."

Polly was confused.

"What then?"

"FUCKING AWESOME!" he screamed, scooting away in his ridiculous trainers, highly expensive three-quarter-length trousers and designer sunglasses. As he vanished down the vertiginous hill narrowly missing a woman struggling with a huge buggy, Polly heard a faint echo on the breeze.

"FUUUUUCKKKKKIIIINNNNGG AWWWWWEEEESSSOOOOMMME!"

Chapter Fourteen

In the event, once Polly had printed out all the forms at the library in Looe, it wasn't nearly as complicated as she'd expected. The lady at the council had looked at her briefly, run through her application and told her that they would have to have a proper council bin nearby, that any rubbish or extra seagull infestation would result in a review, that they would need a health and safety certificate publicly displayed and that it would be for a three-month trial period only. Her spot would be in the side entrance to the car park: no entry to Mount Polbearne itself, which was a World Heritage Site and needed to be treated like one. She could also have one picnic table, as long as it didn't protrude more than fifteen centimeters into the public roadway; she would be liable to spot inspections at any point, and she could operate between the hours of eight and four, seven days a week. All for thirty-five quid.

Polly nodded, unable to believe it could be quite so straightforward. Those weeks of lying around feeling sorry for herself seemed such a waste now; could this possibly work? Might it? She'd rung the sellers of the van, who, yes, still had it, and was steeling herself to go and negotiate. Reuben had offered to go with her, but Polly had figured that while she personally thought Reuben was ace, sometimes the first impression he gave wasn't entirely the best way to get a nice friendly deal out of people.

"Oh," said the council woman. "And you'll have to wear a hairnet."

Polly looked at her.

"Seriously?"

"I don't make the rules," said the woman. "Well, I do, obviously, make some of the rules." She smoothed down her cerise suit jacket, which looked too warm over her floral frock. "But in this instance, it comes from far higher up. Yes, higher up even than me!"

"A hairnet?" said Polly. Suddenly her image of a lovely scenic little van with gorgeous chic food and even a place to sit and eat while staring out at the sea took on a slightly dowdier perspective. A hairnet really hadn't been in it.

The woman looked at her sternly.

"Is a hairnet going to be a deal-breaker?"

"No," said Polly quickly. "But is it—"

"Yes."

"Okay," said Polly. "What about, like, really natty little baseball caps?"

"We're not in the business of giving out licenses to the uncommitted," said the woman, hanging back from handing over the forms.

"Yes. All right, all right. Thank you so much. I'll do absolutely everything."

"You certainly will!" said the woman. "Or we have instant authorization to shut you down. Good luck!"

Polly was on a train, en route to Penzance. She was speaking to Huckle on the phone. Jayden had given her a lift to the mainland in the taxi boat that morning while the causeway was underwater.

"Got nowt else to do," he had pointed out gloomily. Sales had absolutely fallen off in the bakery, and he wasn't allowed to chat to customers now, so he spent most of the day just staring out to sea. He was still pretty glad he wasn't out there, but it was becoming a close-run thing, particularly when he saw the lads coming in of a morning, laughing and joking and giving him a terrible slagging for his nasty sausage rolls.

Malcolm wasn't much better, complaining about how lazy and useless Jayden was, then disappearing for a couple of days, coming back smelling of old booze. And he spent much more time in the other bakery. Jayden suspected he was trying to chat up Flora. He himself had gotten absolutely nowhere with her, but he still felt she could do better than that sleazy jackass.

The cheery grin had gone from Jayden's features as he puttered Polly across to the mainland. It was a windy morning, sunny, but with a chill breeze that necessitated a warm cardigan for emergencies.

"Bring something good back," he said to Polly. "Sort it out."

He turned pink.

"If it . . . if it goes well . . . can I come and work with you again?"

"Of course," said Polly, who hadn't in the slightest

figured out how she could possibly manage to do everything herself, but equally couldn't see how there could be two full-time jobs in it either.

Jayden perked up.

"You'll do it, Polly. You've done it before."

Polly remembered his words as she gazed out of the window at the beautiful vista of cliff and sea. Tucked in among the green was an amazing old boarding school that looked like a castle. Muriel had told her it was there, but she'd never noticed it before. She watched dreamily as a posse of distant figures pranced around on a lacrosse court. It was very different from her own upbringing, she thought. And her present, when she considered it.

"Poll?" Huckle sounded uncharacteristically irritated. "Are you listening? You sound miles away."

"Sorry," said Polly. "Just got distracted. Maybe I should go and teach home economics."

"What?"

"Sorry. Ignore me. I'm talking rubbish. AND in a quiet carriage!"

Shocked with herself, she got up and went out to where the loos were. Now he was almost impossible to hear.

"Don't pay more than four K for it, Polly! Four K, okay! I know you don't like doing it, but you have to bargain. You're a businesswoman now. You're not trying to get these people to like you, you're doing a job. And it's the only job you have, so do it right. It's not all about making scones, you know."

Polly was disgruntled.

"I know that," she said.

But he was right, she knew. She hated bargaining, couldn't even bear to do it in a market, found the whole concept humiliating.

"Well, do it," said Huckle, sounding stern, and with a shiver she thought how much she missed him.

"Are you naked?" she said suddenly.

"Stop it! I mean it! Get to business!"

"I will get to business. What are you wearing, though?" She could hear the smile in his voice.

"I have a meeting with the bank, to sort out the farm."

"And?"

"So I can't stop and chat to you."

"Just tell me . . ."

"Suit, striped shirt. Blue tie."

"Ooh," said Polly. "I think I like that even more than you naked. Are you looking all buttoned up? I like that in a man, like you could burst out any second. I could undo the buttons very, very slowly . . ."

She reckoned she could hear him breathing slightly more heavily on the other end of the line.

"Shut up," he said eventually. "I have to get to my meeting."

"Don't be too long."

"The less of my money you spend on this truck, the sooner I'll be home," he said, and his voice held a heavy weight of longing.

It took Polly a while to find the address the man had given her on the phone. Eventually, though, she found him: a tall, skinny chap in his late twenties with a prominent Adam's apple and wearing a baseball cap.

"Hi, Evan, yeah, sorry," he said immediately, as if apologizing for his very existence.

"I'm sorry," said Polly. "It took a little longer to get over than I thought."

"Where do you live?"

"Mount Polbearne," said Polly, waiting for the customary intake of breath as people wanted to know how it was possible to live there. What did they do? How did they get to the shops? Didn't they get drowned all the time? But Evan barely raised an eyebrow.

"Huh," he said. "Right."

Polly would have liked a glass of water, but she wasn't sure whether she should ask, or whether the Huckle School of Business would say this made her look weak, so she didn't mention it.

"Uh, the van?" she said. Evan looked anxious.

"Oh yes," he said, fumbling with keys. They were outside a tumbledown row of little terraced houses, and she followed him through to the back garden, the thought briefly crossing her mind that statistically very few serial killers advertised catering vans, right?

"Have you had many people look at it?" she asked perkily, wondering if she should try to dial the first two 9s on her phone just in case.

"No, just you," came the dolorous voice.

The garden was larger than she'd expected. It was overgrown and messy, bits of cracked paving stone here and there, rampant weeds, stained plastic chairs and, at the bottom, a large garage. It took Evan a while to find the right key, but he managed to in the end.

"So," said Polly brightly. "You're out of the catering van business, huh?"

In answer to this, Evan just let out a shiver, and a low "hmm" noise. There was also something that might have been "Thank God."

The garage was dark, the dirty windows letting in hardly any of the bright light of the day outside. At first it was difficult to make out anything but the big looming shape. Polly blinked and moved forward. Evan hung back, as if reluctant to approach it.

"So . . ." said Polly, but Evan still didn't move. She looked back at him. He had a look of unabashed disgust on his face.

"Um," said Polly. "Are you all right?"

Evan's shoulders shook a little, and Polly wondered if he was going to cry.

"This damn van," he said finally.

"Oh," said Polly. The front of the garage was a normal up-and-over door. "Do you mind if we just open this so I can take a look?"

Evan shrugged, so Polly took hold of the handle and twisted it. The door rose with a groaning noise, and light flooded in.

The van was in even better nick than it had looked in the advert. There was no smell of old grease or decay, which she had feared. There were some scratches on the dark red bodywork, but this was easily handled, she reckoned. She went all around it and nervously kicked the tires. She had absolutely no idea why anyone would do this, but Huckle had told her to do it to look like she knew what she was about.

Evan showed no sign of moving to help her, so she pulled open the door by herself. Sure enough, inside were the rows of immaculate stainless-steel baking trays she'd seen in the advert, perfect for fresh loaves. The large oven wasn't a brand she was familiar with, but she could see immediately that it was well put in, with good ventilation and space for it to get very hot at minimum discomfort to the chef. The sink was plumbed in and looked nearly new. She didn't understand.

She stepped down from the little van. The canopy that extended out above the selling side was in a cheery red and white stripe. She walked around the van again and again but couldn't find a single thing wrong with it.

"Evan," she said. "What happened here?"

Evan hung his head. "Do you wanna cup of tea?"

Polly nodded.

They sat on stained deckchairs in the garden, sheltered from the wind. Polly stared at the van through the open door.

"It was me and my brother." Evan was staring at the floor as if confessing something. "We were going to work together. Make pasties, take them around the festivals, you know what I mean?"

Polly nodded. "Great!" she said.

"Sunk our life savings into doing the van up," said Evan. His skin was pale and unhealthy looking in the sunlight. Polly wondered if he spent a lot of time playing computer games.

"It was that summer, our first summer . . . Do you remember? Three years ago?"

"Was that the year all those people nearly drowned at Glastonbury?"

Evan nodded.

"Oh God, the rain. It rained and rained and rained and rained. Half of Devon fell down the cliffs. Everywhere we went, we just got besieged by people trying to shelter under the canopy. They didn't want pasties, they just wanted not to get any wetter. Everything covered in mud, everything. Wet. Cold. Up at the crack of dawn every day. Insane traffic. Stuck in the mud. Parked. Couldn't move. And the other concessions. It's a war zone out there, you know. A war zone. They stop at nothing. Tires down. Fire put out. Although that could have been the sideways rain."

He looked up at her, eyes burning.

"We were at one of the field parties. Stuck as usual. Nobody who wanted a pasty could get to us because everyone was trying to shelter under the canopy. We asked them to move. Do you know what they did? DO YOU KNOW WHAT THEY DID?"

Polly shook her head, clutching her tea.

"They overturned the van! Our Nancy! They overturned her in the mud and left us sprawled there, five hundred best pasties squashed in the muck, rain coming down, St. John's Ambulance and the Manic Street Preachers. It was like the Somme. Except worse, because of the Manic Street fucking Preachers."

He shivered again.

"I'm never going back."

"What do you do now?" asked Polly politely.

"I'm joining the army," said Evan unexpectedly. "I figure it can't be worse. And also, one day I can shoot those hippy bastards."

Polly wasn't quite sure what to say to this, so she sipped her tea in silence.

"And how long did you run this business?"

"Don't do it," said Evan fiercely. "You seem like a nice girl. Get out while you still can. Don't go up against the ice cream vans, whatever the hell you do. Most vicious bastards on the face of the earth."

"Ice cream vans?"

"Ice cream vans OF DEATH."

"Okay," said Polly. "Did it get damaged when it fell over?"

Evan shook his head.

"She's brilliantly engineered, Nancy. Couldn't put a

foot wrong. She was a loyal and faithful workhorse in a war we couldn't win."

Polly thought he was definitely spending too much time in his bedroom.

"Okay, well . . . Can I take her for a test drive? I'll leave my passport with you."

"I'm telling you, don't ruin your life."

"Ha," said Polly. "Honestly, it is far too late for that." She looked at him again.

"Have you got the keys?"

"They're in there," he said. "I can't watch. Honestly. I can't see her go again. I've got PTSD. My doctor said he might put me on medication and everything."

"I'll just take her around the block," said Polly patiently. "Also, are you sure you really want to join the army?"

"I'll wait at the corner," said Evan. "If you lose your nerve, we'll push her back together."

Polly had driven a van before, when she'd moved her furniture from her old apartment in Plymouth over to Mount Polbearne, and this was smaller than that one, although she could feel the weight of the oven at the back. But it was cleverly situated and balanced out by the engine, which had plenty of pull in it, so actually it wasn't that difficult at all. Stupidly, because she couldn't park in the car park overnight, she would have to move the van every day, but she could manage that if she got the tides right.

Inside, everything was in remarkable nick. There were less than 5,000 miles on the clock. Polly felt sorry for Evan because she thought this van might be worth a lot more than he was selling it for. On the other hand, she had Huckle's voice of business ringing in her ears, plus only a certain amount of money in her pocket.

She pressed the horn experimentally. It gave out a jolly tooting noise that made her smile. Then she stopped the van on the corner to see how easy it would be to set up. The canopy was wound out by a handle, and she propped it up on the two stands that slotted into the sides. The serving hatch was a nice size, and on the back of the sliding door on the other side of the van was a fold-down work surface on hinges. The trays for fresh produce were to her left, looking out of the hatch, and the big oven, a little fridge for drinks and a tiny sink were to her right, blocking the back of the van, which she guessed wasn't meant to open at all. She moved around. She didn't know where on earth they'd put a coffee machine. Regretfully she shelved, yet again, the idea of running a little coffee shop too. One day.

She looked over the serving hatch cheerfully, seeing in her mind's eye a whole line of people queuing up . . . She'd need lots of those little paper bags, quick twist over, hand them over, then the next one. She wondered if she could do a sail-in service for the fishermen and the pleasure boats, given that her pitch was at the back, next to the sea wall. She could throw them sandwiches and they could chuck fish back as payment . . . She smiled at the daftness of the idea, but she felt, deep down, that it could be done. Could it?

"'Ello!"

There was a small child there, not more than eight years old and covered in freckles. He screwed up his eyes.

"What you got? What you got in the van?"

"Uh, nothing yet," said Polly, smiling. "What were you after?"

"Dunno," said the boy. "But I like your van."

"I will take that as a good sign," said Polly. In fact, she did have some gingerbread she'd whipped up the day before, dense with treacle, rich and not too sweet so it could be spread with butter. But she thought better of giving treats to a strange child, so she winked instead.

"One day there will be food in this van," she promised. "And you can buy some."

"Cool," said the kid. "Will it be chips?"

"No."

"Aw. I like chips. Pizza?"

"It'll be bread," said Polly, smiling. The boy looked at her.

"What, toast and that?"

"Um, yes, or just fresh bread."

He looked at her skeptically.

"Seriously?"

"Yes! It's a good idea!"

"So people will come and want chips and you give them some plain boring old bread?"

"Yeah, all right, kid."

"I think they're going to be totally cross when there's no chips," said the boy. "What about ice cream?"

"I'm just driving off now."

The boy watched her all the way down the street, shaking his head sagely.

"Okay, thanks, Lord Sugar," Polly said to herself crossly, looking at him in the rearview mirror. Her happy mood had been punctured somewhat.

Evan hadn't moved from the corner when she returned.

"Oh," he said. "I slightly hoped I wouldn't have to see it again."

"I wasn't going to steal your van, Evan," said Polly.

He nodded. They went back into the garden. She wasn't quite sure how to do this.

"Okay," she said. "I'd like to buy, um, Nancy."

Evan looked at her.

"But it's cursed, I told you. You seem nice. You shouldn't buy it."

"I'm sure it isn't cursed," said Polly.

"What, you're saying it was our fault?"

"No!" said Polly.

There was a silence. Evan let out a great crushing sigh. Polly was worried about him. She also wasn't sure who should speak first. In the end, they both did.

"Well," said Polly, just as Evan said, "So."

She let him go first, but he was letting her go first, so they fell into silence again. Finally Evan sighed again and sat up a bit.

"She's brand new," he said. "You know, we did all the fitting-out ourselves. The oven, the sink, the fridge. It's all absolutely new."

"I realize that," said Polly, getting worried.

"I mean, nobody had touched that stuff before us. Before those damn festival bastards got their paws on it. Now it's contaminated."

"Mmm," said Polly. What had Huckle said? Act calm and unconcerned; stare into the middle distance; pretend this wasn't really bothering you and that you could easily walk away at any point. That was what to do.

She looked over at the long grass waving in the gentle summer breeze and tried not to stare at Nancy, the unfortunate red van, parked neatly back in the garage. She couldn't stop nervously fiddling with her bag, though, which held all the cash she had withdrawn. She had never seen so much money before, not in real life.

There was another long silence. Polly felt her heart

thumping. What if he wanted a return on his investment? Maybe if she offered him another couple of hundred . . . No, she told herself. Huckle had said she should get the price down, not up. She had to bargain down from £5,500 to £4,000. But if she could get it for £5,000, she could always say she had argued and debated the issue for ages but he simply wouldn't budge. Obviously Huckle wouldn't really believe this, but it was her plan nonetheless.

"So," said Evan, "I'm not letting it go for less than two thousand pounds."

"What?" said Polly, thinking she'd misheard. "Two thousand?"

"Eighteen hundred and that's my final offer," said Evan. "Just get that thing out of my sight."

"But you can't sell it for that!!"

"Okay, sixteen hundred if you've got cash and the paperwork."

"No, no, I mean, that's far too cheap."

"To pass on a curse," said Evan, sombrely. "I think you will end up paying far more than money."

"Yes, but even so," ordered Polly. "Two and a half grand. Otherwise I'm stealing off you."

"You are delivering me," said Evan. "Two two-fifty." Polly rolled her eyes.

"Two thousand four hundred," she said. "And that's my final offer."

"Done," said Evan glumly.

Polly leaned over to shake his hand.

"No, thank *you*," said Evan. "You carry the dark mark now."

"Let me just pay you," said Polly, suddenly quite anxious to get out of there. She had bought a cheap day return, but couldn't believe she wasn't actually going to have to use the other half of it. "You don't want a ticket to Looe as well, do you?"

Evan shuddered. "Oh God, we did the Looe Beach Festival," he said. "Someone threw up cider scrumpy all over our serving area. We ended up getting fined for putting down so much bleach we killed all the surrounding wildlife."

"I'm sorry to hear that." Polly reached for her bag and tried to get up without looking as if she was rushing out of there.

"Anyway, I have to go," said Evan. "I've got a World of Warcraft tournament."

"Right, fine, don't let me keep you," said Polly, trying to surreptitiously draw the right money out of her wallet without calling attention to the fact that she actually had much, much more in there.

Evan brought out the logbook—the van was indeed absolutely brand new, three years old, straight out of the factory, major services all up to date, MOT. Polly couldn't believe her luck. He looked at her as he went to sign it.

"This is your last chance," he said.

"I'm going to risk it," said Polly.

"You're brave," said Evan. "Really brave. I would say good luck, but that . . . that isn't possible. I just hope you don't die trying."

"Thanks," said Polly as they finished the transaction.

She looked for him out of the back window. He was watching her drive away, shaking his head mournfully at her foolish hubris.

"Come on, Nancy," said Polly, patting the wood-effect steering wheel. "Let's see if us girls can't make a better job of it."

Polly thought, going back to the lighthouse again, how lonely it'd be to turn up with something so fantastic—Nan the Van!—when Huckle wasn't there to exclaim how brilliant it was, nor Neil to hop around it and give it a good old explore. Maybe it would be tonight, she thought. Maybe tonight the little puffin would find his way home. Maybe he'd gone via Reuben's old place. He liked it there too. But he was coming back. She knew it.

When she finally got Huckle on the phone, he sounded absolutely exhausted, but very pleased.

"Did you really bargain him down to half price?" he said incredulously. "Polly, you didn't show him your legs, did you?"

"No!" said Polly. "It just turns out I am a naturally brilliant negotiator. Amazing, huh? You didn't think I had it in me."

"Hmm," said Huckle. "What does she look like under the bonnet?"

"Um, great," said Polly. It hadn't even occurred to her to look at the engine, and she wouldn't have known what to look for if she had.

"Poll," said Huckle. "You are lying to me! Are you sure you haven't actually brought home a packet of magic beans that you're going to plant in the garden and the man said a van would definitely grow out of them?"

"No!" said Polly. "I'd send you the photo if the Internet connection didn't mean it would take eight hours to arrive."

"Eight hours is fine," said Huckle. "I don't mind."

"It's not magic beans."

"Is it possibly two halves of two different vans, soldered together?"

"I can't believe you doubt my amazing powers of negotiation," said Polly. "Also, I wish I'd told you I got it for four grand and pocketed the difference."

"Adding theft to lying," mused Huckle. "You are a naughty girl."

Polly smiled.

"Will I be properly punished when you get home?"

"Oh yes," said Huckle, staring at the great big pile of government forms and paperwork he'd brought home from town, which should all have been completed months ago. "I expect so."

"Can't you come home now? Now we've got the van? I can get loads of supplies with the rest of the money, and Jayden says he doesn't see why I shouldn't have all the leftover herbs and spices from the bakery, seeing as they don't bake fresh any more—it wouldn't be stealing, they don't use them, they're just sitting there. So we could just start, and you could come home."

"Businesses don't just start," said Huckle. "You took over a going concern before. It doesn't normally work like that. You're going to have ages when you'll have quiet days and off days and nobody even turning up. It's not even the summer season yet. You'll need cash to keep you going through that. Council tax is due. And the TV license, even though, one, I have no idea why you Brits have to pay money for the TV, and two, you never watch it."

"Force of habit," mumbled Polly. "Also, if you don't pay it, they put you in prison."

"I am so glad I have committed my life to this place," said Huckle gravely. Polly heard doors opening and chatter in the background. "Okay, I have to go."

"Uh, totally," said Polly, as if she too were busy, rather than having absolutely nothing to do for the entire evening except rattle around an empty lighthouse, half-watching telly with dreadful reception, feeling alone, and fighting—and eventually giving in to—the desire to eat the rest of the gingerbread. "Bye, my love."

"And to you," said Huckle.

Huckle hung up the phone and headed back into the farmhouse kitchen. Clemmie was sitting there wearing an old linen dress, her stout boots by the door. She was looking tired and beaten down. She looked up at Huckle, her voice soft, and very Southern.

"Huckle, while he was over there . . . did he . . . I mean, was there another girl?"

Huckle put his hands up.

"You'd have to ask him," he said. He absolutely didn't want to get involved in this kind of thing. Clemmie's soft eyes grew even sadder as she passed him a huge plate of ribs with a baked potato. She sighed.

"You know, you could pass the farm on," said Huckle. "Once I've got it sorted out. Once it's on its feet again. You could sell the stewardship as a going concern, head back to the city."

Clemmie shook her head.

"No," she said. "This is ours."

Then she looked up at him and touched her stomach.

"And this is ours too."

She hadn't even been showing.

"Oh, Clem," said Huckle, his heart nearly breaking for her. He wanted to hunt down his brother and knock some sense into him.

"Does he know?"

She shook her head.

"I want to tell him face to face."

Huckle thought painfully of his promise to Polly: to sort things out, to make a little money, to come straight home. Suddenly he resented being stuck in the steamy humidity of Georgia while Polly was sitting on a rock enjoying the fresh sunshine and chill wind of his beloved Cornwall. He wanted to be there with her.

He cleared the table for Clemmie, who immediately fell asleep in an armchair. He put a blanket over her and went upstairs. But he couldn't sleep. There was no air conditioning in the tiny spare room.

He lay awake listening to the cicadas, worrying— what if Dubose didn't come back? What would he do then?—and listing all the work that had to be done the next day. Having grown up on a farm, Huckle was under no illusion as to how tough it was. Which was why his mother was so desperate for him to be out of the game, into an office job. But being indoors was no use to him either. Really he just wanted to be . . . He thought back to a day the previous year—in fact it must have been Polly's birthday, the real one, not a silly fake one. It had been the day he had finally gotten that fricking bath installed.

They couldn't afford the lovely claw-foot bath that Polly craved—the bathroom had a window out to sea, and she dreamed of lying and gazing out across the water. But then, a few days before her birthday, Huckle had been clearing out some old hives from a grand house that had been sold off for apartments. The builders had moved in, and he had seen it. It wasn't the fancy type that everyone wanted to pretend was reclaimed; it was a genuine, ancient, enormous old copper can, the type that at one time wouldn't even have been plumbed in. He regarded it with awe.

"I know, what a lot of old shit," said the builder, marching past him, carrying a length of copper piping. "Honestly, almost everything is reclaimable these days; you can sell any old tat for a fortune and those idiots think they're getting something bloody special. But that . . ."

"Um," said Huckle. "Actually . . ."

It had been bigger than the sidecar, so he had had to drive back incredibly carefully, with the enormous bath balanced upright like a giant, bound down with ropes. It was not safe. It was not even vaguely safe. Every driver passing him honked their horn and called him an utter fricking idiot. It fell off when he turned left around a corner. It took him twenty-four hours to plumb the bloody thing in without water going everywhere. Neil had adored the entire enterprise, never hiding his delighted surprise when yet another rivulet would drip and then gush from an unsoldered piece of pipe, and would waddle over and splash happily in it while Huckle cursed and swore and grabbed another piece of piping.

Finally, though, it was done. The brass, burnished up, shone beautifully in the pink early-evening light: it was autumn, and the sun set early, but that day it was unusually clear. Polly was yawning after a long day at the bakery. People seemed to crave carbs at this time of year; she got a lot of requests to heat things up, too, which she happily obliged with, but it all took time. Jayden had pointed out that she could probably make a fortune simply by selling toasted cheese and large mugs of tea, and at one point she was seriously considering it.

Huckle had greeted her at the door, taken her hand and led her to the bathroom (from which she'd been banned for the last three days, having to use the downstairs shower instead—although she was still getting used to the astonishing luxury of living in a house with two bathrooms, so hadn't minded).

"Are you saying I smell?" said Polly who did, as always, smell absolutely gorgeous, of warm bread and cherry jam and icing sugar.

Huckle pushed open the door. He'd finally lit the hundred obligatory IKEA tea lights they'd picked up last year when doing some rudimentary furnishing. Around them he had arranged, for want of a flower shop in Mount Polbearne, fronds of fragrant heather from the sand dunes. He'd used half a bottle of the expensive bath oil Polly's sister had sent her at Christmas, which Polly thought was too good to use, and had bought a bottle of the second cheapest Prosecco at Muriel's shop. He couldn't quite stretch to an ice bucket, but he'd popped out all the ice cubes they had into the sink and filled it up with cold water, which would have to do.

The copper bath tub, while very slightly resembling something out of Dr. Frankenstein's laboratory, nonetheless gleamed prettily in the candlelight, with the fragrant steam evaporating against the windows—curtainless, facing out onto the darkening sky. In the bath, despite the fact that the water was obviously far too hot for him, Neil was paddling cheerfully, making occasional bites at Polly's rubber duck, whom he had fallen in love with, but who seemed oblivious to his advances.

Polly turned to Huckle and flung her arms around his neck.

"That is the absolute best, best not-exactly-a-claw-foot-bath-more-of-a-tin birthday present I've ever had!"

"Truly?" said Huckle, looking down into her smiling face. "You wouldn't rather we'd just saved up for a new one?"

Polly shook her head.

"Is it watertight?"

"Um, more or less," said Huckle, glancing at the pipes with some trepidation.

"And you found it and put it together for me?"

He nodded. "Yup. Plumbing is hard."

Polly was already pulling off her top.

"I love it! I love it! I love it!"

Huckle picked up the Prosecco, then looked around.

"Bugger," he said. "I forgot the glasses."

"The glasses two stories down the freezing staircase?" said Polly.

Huckle nodded.

"We'll use the tooth mug," she ordered. "Wash the toothpaste out first."

"Oh, I don't know," said Huckle. "It might add a slight frisson to the flavor. Or improve it. It's not very expensive Prosecco."

Polly grinned.

"Suits me."

Naked, she was lovely in the candlelight, completely oblivious, Huckle thought, to the effect her naturalness achieved. She didn't look perfect, not like the women in magazines—or his ex-girlfriend, Candice, who did nothing but work on how she looked. But Candice hated being naked, would never look at herself in a mirror without criticizing all the imaginary flaws in her taut, relentlessly worked-out body. To Polly, being naked was just something you were when you didn't have any clothes on. The wide curve of her hips was a beautiful thing to see.

"Neil, out," she ordered.

Neil hopped onto the side of the bath, then eeped at her.

"What? Oh," she said.

"What is it?" said Huckle.

"He wants me to get rid of the duck too. Jealousy issues."

Polly hurled the rubber duck out of the bath, whereupon Neil went for it and started dragging it by the beak out of the bathroom. Huckle watched him go.

"Your bird is weird," he said.

Polly didn't answer.

"Have you washed the tooth mug?"

"Yes!" he said. "Shall I open . . ."

Polly slid into the water.

"Oh my God, this is amazing," she said. "Ow."

"What was that?"

"Rivet. Don't worry about it, I love it. I'll just avoid the rivets."

She closed her eyes in happiness, and sank right under the water.

"Oh GOD, a proper bath."

There hadn't been a proper one before, and her last flat had had a half bath in avocado, which was unpleasing in half a dozen different ways.

Huckle smiled at her as she gradually surfaced. She looked at him holding the bottle.

"Don't open it quite yet."

He raised an eyebrow.

"No?"

"No. I think we should christen our bath."

Huckle didn't need asking twice. He pulled off his T-shirt. Polly smiled appreciatively, as she always did. She genuinely didn't believe she'd met a more beautiful man in her entire life. He had a loose covering of golden hair on his chest, running down in a fine line across his flat stomach, and on down below his navel.

"Watch the rivets," he said somewhat hoarsely.

Later, Neil played for hours in the terrible soapy mess they left on the bathroom floor.

Huckle dozed, woke, glanced at his watch. It was early in England; she wouldn't be awake yet. He wanted time for a long chat; to tell her how much he missed her while also breaking it to her that he would be a little while yet. He wished he hadn't pushed her to take Neil to the sanctuary. He knew she thought the little puffin would come back any moment. Huckle didn't.

Last year Neil had been a baby, making his way home to the person he thought was his mummy. This year he was a teenager; he no longer had any of the soft, ticklish brown puffling feathers Polly had loved rubbing. Huckle reckoned that girl—or other boy—puffins were going to be a much more interesting proposition. He wished Polly had a little company, particularly now Kerensa had gone back to work full-time.

Hours later, with dawn slowly beginning to light the sky, and the men up and stirring in the yard, Huckle hauled himself painfully out of bed, washed his face in the little stand-alone sink, brushed his teeth, shrugged himself into his dungarees and padded downstairs in search of the strongest coffee available before he headed out to work. He had to leave all thoughts of Mount Polbearne far, far behind him. It would be a long time before he was going home.

Chapter Fifteen

It didn't take long for Nan the Van to become a massive source of interest to the local community. There were not many vehicles on Mount Polbearne, and even less for children to do. Someone had suggested putting a swing park in the grounds of the ruined church at the top of the town, but this had been vetoed on the grounds of the whole World Heritage Site thing getting in the way. It was disappointing, but they did, everyone realized, have a point, in terms of what a see-saw might look like on the ancient silhouette of the proud tidal island community.

So coming to see the van became quite the outing, and Polly found herself most days trying to prize a child off the terribly tempting metal step to the cab, and considering a "Do Not Climb" sign. Of course everyone being local and friends of hers, they didn't consider for a moment that she might not be in the mood to have their children climbing all over her van, and Polly couldn't possibly risk turning into Mrs. Manse and telling them not to. So she just tried not to wince too much when they scuffed it.

She got Reuben around the first time she attempted to fire up the oven. He was furious she hadn't taken him with her when she went to buy the van.

"I'd have got it down for you," he said crossly. "You know I am totally the best at business and all of that. You were very dumb, Polly. That cost you a lot of money."

Polly nodded.

"So what did you get it for?"

"Oh, better than half price," said Polly airily. Reuben was silent for two seconds, which was about the maximum time Polly had ever known him silent.

"Huh," he said. "Well, I could totally have done better than that."

He could have, too. Polly dreaded to think about poor Evan, left in his tatty little house, playing on his computer, with two pounds fifty from Reuben counted out in coppers in his pocket.

"I know," she said, then turned to him with her most appealing look. "But I thought you'd probably be best at lighting the oven."

She had borrowed the fire extinguisher—the really big one, for if the lighthouse got bombed by a foreign power or a plane crashed into it—just for safety. It had taken her half an hour to lug it down the stairs.

"Okay," she said. "I think I'm ready."

In fact she was more than ready. Selina had wandered over early that morning, pretending to be passing but actually hoping to be invited in, which she was, and found Polly, unable to help herself, making up a large batch of fresh salty ciabatta, and a dark round *campagnarde* loaf. And thirty-two buns. And a Swiss roll.

"Are you having a party?" asked Selina, who rolled up her sleeves happily and joined in.

"No," said Polly. "It's really just a rehearsal. A practice. I got slightly carried away, I think."

"You think?" said Selina. "Maybe if five thousand people turn up to hear Jesus speaking . . ."

Polly sighed. "I know. I've missed it."

Selina stayed and chatted until Reuben turned up and they went down with the fire extinguisher.

"Who are you?" said Reuben rudely.

"This is Selina," said Polly carefully. "She was married to Tarnie, the fisherman."

"You had a lovely party for him last year," added Selina. "It was really appreciated."

"Oh yes!" said Reuben. "I remember you! You look a bit hot for a fisherman's wife."

"REUBEN," said Polly. "Don't be Reuben-y."

"I'm making a perfectly reasonable observation. He looked like a hairy stick. She looks hot."

Polly's hand flew to her mouth. But to her utter amazement, Selina burst into giggles.

"He did!" she laughed. "He did look like a hairy stick."

Now Polly felt insulted on Tarnie's behalf.

"I thought he was nice-looking," she said. "Lovely blue eyes."

"Yes, but you know. Quite a lot of hair. On a stick." Selina was still laughing. "Oh God," she said. "Nobody has been rude about him for SO LONG."

"See!" said Reuben. "Polly thinks she knows what I should say."

"I don't!" said Polly. "I mean, on balance, yes, I

would probably err on the side of being polite about somebody who only died a year ago."

"It's okay," said Selina. "I'm not in the least bit offended. I'm cheered up, in fact. Are you going to light the oven in the van? I've made tons of stuff."

Selina's part in the process had in fact been confined to a bit of dough-rolling, but Polly didn't mention this.

"I certainly am," said Reuben. "Stand well back."

He stoked up the wood-burner, which was enhanced and superheated by gas flames at the back and sides. It really was a state-of-the-art piece of equipment: it heated quickly, but still gave a fantastic, wood-smoked flavor to everything. A chimney with a little point came out of the top of the van, and they kept the side counter propped open for extra ventilation.

Polly had scrubbed the van down the day before, even though it was in impressively good nick and had really been hardly used at all. She wondered if Evan and his brother had given up too easily. Now she watched with bated breath as Reuben leaned in with an extra-long match and fired up the oven with a very faint crumping noise. As he stood back, the flames of the gas caught and the wood started to crackle.

"I now pronounce this tiny weird cook van thing OPEN," he said. "For Polly and the hot widow."

"Reuben, if you don't stop calling Selina hot, I'm telling Kerensa."

"What? Why? She doesn't mind. I think loads and loads of women are hot, but there's only one I want to bone all the time. It's great."

Polly rolled her eyes at Selina, who was still smiling and apparently found Reuben quite charming. Then she stepped inside the van, leaned out of the window and waved. Selina and Reuben took the official first pictures, with the lighthouse in the background.

"So," Reuben was saying to Selina as he did so, "don't you think it's about time we found you a nice man?"

"Can he be taller than you?" Selina said.

"Yeah yeah yeah," said Reuben. "I got it. I totally got your hairy-stick tendencies down, baby."

"Um, me and Nan the Van would love a tiny bit of attention for ten seconds if that's at all possible?" Polly hollered cheerfully, putting in her very first loaves.

Polly woke that first bright summer morning at 4 a.m., before her alarm, bristling with excitement.

She called Huckle first off, but he was in a noisy bar with a clutch of the laborers, and she could barely hear him. There had been a fair amount of slacking off before Huckle had arrived, as the men had no direction and no motivation to do more than the absolute minimum. He'd had to come down pretty hard on all of them, and they'd complied and done their absolute best, turning the farm around in barely more than a month. He was utterly proud of how hard they'd worked and felt they needed a night off, so they had all set off to town in the back of a pickup truck and found the nearest sports bar. They sounded extremely exuberant.

Hearing all the noise around Huckle made Polly feel more isolated. Also, she couldn't remember the last time she was in a packed bar having a good time with a bunch of people. It sounded like fun.

"No, no, I'm listening," said Huckle, as several hundred men shouted at a baseball game that was going on on the TV screen over his head. He was drinking gassy bottled beer and wishing he were at home with Polly; in fact it hit him so hard, he very briefly wanted to cry. Polly, however, sounded a bit impatient.

"So!" she was saying.

"Um, uh-huh?"

"SO! It's TODAY!"

"I thought it was Monday."

"It's Tuesday, Huckle! It's Tuesday where I am."

Huckle blinked, confused. Another roar went up from the spectators.

"It's opening day! I'm starting today!"

"Oh yeah? Uh, cool."

"You sound busy," said Polly, thoroughly deflated. Out of the lighthouse window she couldn't see anything at all; it was like the rest of the world had simply cut its tethers and drifted off.

"Work stuff."

"YAY!" went the crowd, as their team scored a home run.

"I'll go outside," said Huckle hurriedly. Outside, everyone was dancing in the street and blowing horns.

"Sorry, it's kind of the World Series."

"Right," said Polly. "I hope the Blues win."

"Seriously? No way! The Blues are rubbish!"

Polly half-smiled.

"Well. Anyway. I just wanted to tell you. It's Tuesday. I'm starting today."

Huckle was about to wish her luck, but with a quick crackle and a hum, his phone conked out. He glanced at it. No battery at all, not even enough for a quick text. He cursed quietly and wondered if he could make a run for it.

"Huck! My man!"

It was Jackson, the chief stockman.

"Come in, come in! We all owe you one. You're going

to save all our jobs! Come in and lemme buy you a beer! This has been a great day."

Reluctantly, Huckle let himself be led back inside.

This was not shaping up to be Polly's great new day, she realized glumly. The clouds had rolled in and it was absolutely hosing it down outside. She wondered briefly if there was anything in Evan's curse, but put the thought out of her mind completely as she expertly and automatically rolled loaves into tins and laid out her neat rows of buns to half-bake before finishing them off as needed in the van so they arrived with the customers fresh and warm. She eyed up her ingredients carefully. How many people, she wondered, would queue up in the rain in a car park for a loaf of bread?

Well, it was too late to think about that now. They were committed. She was in. Huckle was in. Nan the Van was downstairs . . .

Polly trudged in and out of the lighthouse four times carrying the bread and buns and placing them carefully in the steel trays. Then she started up the van. She had timed everything to hit low tide, but in fact the rain was sheeting across the cobbles, making everything damp and slippery, and she found herself faintly concerned that the van might skitter and slide into the water . . .

No, of course it wouldn't, she told herself sternly, although she never drove across the causeway herself; she was always with Huckle in his sidecar.

Well. Huckle wasn't here. He hadn't been here for a while and he wasn't here now and there was no point in thinking about that, she told herself crossly, seeing as he was only off trying to help her out in the first place.

At 8 a.m. on a wet, filthy late May morning, clouds down around her ears, she parked up in the little municipal car park next to the causeway. On warm summer weekends it was mobbed, filled with people unpacking picnics and fishing rods; children with shrimping nets, excited about the thrill of a road that was sometimes exposed and sometimes underwater; red-foreheaded fathers bringing out windbreaks and suncream and water bottles, as if they were tracking through the Sahara.

But this morning, there was absolutely nobody here at all. Old Jim the angler passed by, his rod held upright by his side.

"Morning, Jim," said Polly.

"Morning, Polly," said Jim, but he didn't seem to be in the least bit inclined to ask what she was doing out here with a soggy hairnet on, erecting a canopy in a deserted gray car park first thing in the morning.

"Can I interest you in a bun?" asked Polly cheerfully.

Jim looked at her.

"My mum makes my sandwiches," he said mournfully. "On my fishing days, like."

"You wouldn't like to try something different?"

Jim shook his head emphatically.

"My mum knows how I like my sandwiches, you see," he said. "Cheese and pickle, with the cheese not touching the pickle."

"Okay," said Polly. "I don't have any like that. I have buns, though."

Jim shook his head again.

"Naw, you don't want a bun after a sandwich. You want a Kit Kat."

He sloshed on through the heavy rain, his oilskins well worn and a cheery yellow sou'wester on his grizzled head.

"Bye then!" said Polly. "Good luck with the fish!"

She got the canopy up; it wasn't easy, and she wasn't entirely sure it looked brilliant, but she got there in the end. Then she went back into the van—which was at least cozy from the oven. A little too cozy, in fact: she had to open the back door as the oven really heated up, which had the annoying result of letting in all the rain—and looked at her two hundred buns and wondered if perhaps she'd been a little bit optimistic for her first day.

She'd mentioned it a little bit around town, but not too much, given that she didn't really want word to get out that she was starting up some kind of alternative service. She didn't entirely trust Malcolm not to find a way to stop her, his loathing for her seemed so strong.

"That's your marketing plan?" Kerensa had asked her. "Adventurous."

And now she sat all alone in the cheery red van, wishing she'd brought a book, feeling like the only person for miles and miles around, the only person in Cornwall. She looked at the neat lines of buns and told herself not to eat them all.

At 9 a.m., a seagull marched right up the steps into the van—they had been getting bolder for a while—and Polly told him where to go with a swearword. The seagull was totally unfazed by this and cawed at her, fixing its beady eyes on the buns.

"I never kick birds," Polly told it seriously. "Never. Not in a million years. But what I am going to do here is *pretend* to kick you, and see if that works."

She threw her leg out in front of her. The seagull totally ignored it. She yelled at it again. It gave her a disdainful glance. Then she made a big lion roar. That worked, and it scuttered backward and flapped down the stairs, but she didn't know if she could do that all day.

She sighed and glanced at her phone.

How's it going? Kerensa had texted. That was a bit carly, Polly reckoned.

Brilliant, she typed back. *The Duchess of Cambridge just came in and ordered 190 cakes for Prince George.*

Then she thought better of that and deleted it and worked out what time it was in Savannah (4 a.m.), and sighed.

She was gazing out at the rain and telling herself not to worry, she'd gotten through worse than this, then crossly wondering precisely how many days she would have to say to herself, "Not to worry, you've got through worse than this," because as life philosophies went, it wasn't the one she'd have chosen, when a car drew up; some kind of aggressive-looking BMW that was a little tatty around the edges. Polly put her hairnet back on in case it was thc council, and also pasted on a cheery smile in case it was someone from the authorities. It was neither.

"WHAT THE BLOODY HELL DO YOU THINK YOU'RE DOING?"

Malcolm danced out of the car as if he were Rumpelstiltskin, puce with fury.

"What the hell is THIS?"

Polly flushed bright red. She knew she probably had to expect this at some point, but confrontation was so far away from how she usually engaged with people, and now it was here, it was torture.

She glanced to the side, wishing that Reuben were here. Reuben loved this kind of thing. He'd have gotten into a fight straightaway. And he'd have enjoyed it. Kerensa too, she'd have gotten stuck in. Even Huckle could probably have calmly defused the situation.

Instead, Polly felt absolutely horrible inside, frightened and panicky at the idea of dealing with somebody who was cross with her. Then she felt ridiculous for feeling that way: why must she take everything so personally? She was a grown-up, wasn't she? She ought to be able to handle it. How on earth could she call herself a businesswoman otherwise?

"It's just a van," she squeaked.

"It's not! It's a filthy plan to ruin my livelihood!" screamed Malcolm, even though it was ten o'clock in the morning, and his livelihood really ought to have been up and running for five hours.

"Are you trying to make my mother starve, is that your plan? Are you trying to ruin everything? Are you really such a bitch you would do that?"

Polly shook her head.

"No," she started. "Not at all. It's just . . ." She told herself not to cry. Huckle wouldn't cry. "It's just . . . this is the only thing I know how to do."

Malcolm stared at her.

"So you'd take food out of the mouth of its rightful owner?"

"What? No. Not on purpose! Well . . ."

He marched toward her, his red pimply face clashing unpleasantly with his mustard-colored mackintosh.

"You know," he spat, his eyes fierce, "I wanted to be a professional."

"What kind of professional?" Polly asked in a shaky voice.

"Trumpeter," replied Malcolm as if it were patently obvious. "And when I couldn't get a job—because the industry is totally stitched up, by the way, it's not what you know, it's who you know—when they locked me out of that, well, I didn't let it get me down, did I?"

"I don't know," said Polly, staring at the ground, realizing she wasn't really handling this very well and trying to remember all those assertiveness tips Kerensa had given her.

"I picked myself up and never looked back, and look at me now."

Jumping about in a wet car park at ten o'clock in the morning, Polly thought.

"Stupid bloody trumpet."

"Do you miss playing the trumpet?" Polly asked timidly.

Malcolm sighed for a moment, then looked cross again. His lips, Polly now noticed, did look about right for playing the trumpet: slightly splayed, and with a free run of spittle when he was exasperated, which he undoubtedly was now.

"No," he said crossly. "A bit. Anyway, that's not the point. The point is that YOU have to get wise to some life lessons now."

"It's perfectly legal for me to be here," said Polly, trembling. "I have a license."

"Yes," snarled Malcolm. "And that means it's perfectly legal for ME to be here too."

A car slowed down in the rain, windscreen wipers sloshing vehemently. Malcolm marched up and tapped on the window.

"I hope you weren't going to buy bread from here, mate," he said, unpleasantly chummy. "Because it's bloody awful."

Polly's hand flew to her mouth.

"But . . ." she said.

"You ruin my business," he said, standing upright and shouting through the rain, "and I'll ruin yours. And I reckon I'll hold out the longer."

Polly wanted to cry.

"Why don't you just go somewhere else?" he said. "I

don't care where. Go away. Go back to where you came from."

"*Plymouth?*"

"Yeah," said Malcolm. "I'm from an old Mount Polbearne family. We were here first."

But she had never even seen him here.

"Go take this rust bucket and try it out elsewhere."

Another car looked as if it were slowing down in the filthy driving rain, then the driver saw Malcolm waving his arms as if they were a couple having a massive domestic, and quickly thought better of it.

"You can't win here. You can't do it. You should just give up now. You failed in the bakery, you're failing here. It's all over."

Polly hiccupped a kind of snorting sob, then did the only thing she could think of: she brought down the little shutter in the van and slammed it hard, and the door too.

It was, she realized, absolutely no solution. On the other hand, she was now inside and warm and cozy, and Malcolm was still outside, pacing about in the rain. Which was a small mercy, after all. Plus now she could weep in peace.

Malcolm shouted a few more things, but, thankfully, with the wind and the rain outside, and the generator inside, she couldn't hear what they were. She waited for a while, until she had stopped crying, and tried to tell herself that he was just a horrible pathetic trumpet-playing moron, even though a bit of her knew deep down that it was a bit sneaky to open the van.

But it wasn't, she told herself. She was standing up against mediocrity; against lazy, horrible food sold to people who didn't know things could be better, that food could be better, and if food was better, life was better. Stood to reason. Yes.

She had to tell herself that what she was doing was worthwhile; that she wasn't providing just industrial mulch churned out by a factory that didn't care if something was good and nutritious and made of the very best stuff; that would fill everything with long-life chemicals, and spongifiers and E-numbers and salt and wood shavings, for all she knew, to bulk out something that was cheap and filling and easy, but wasn't good. What she did was good, and it was important, and she was going to tell the world a thing or two . . . just as soon as she could bear to unlock herself from this van.

She heard, faintly, over the rattle of the generator, the sound of Malcolm's car driving away. She pulled up the shutter to deliver her sermon, but the car park was once more windswept, damp and completely empty. And she did not feel as if she had scored a victory.

By 4 p.m., Polly was ready to drive the van into the sea and was giving considerably more weight to the concept that it was indeed cursed.

The rain had barely let up. A family with three squalling children in the back of their car had driven up, cheerfully hoping for fish and chips, talking about how the weather had ruined their holiday, so thank God they'd seen a fish and chip van, it was the only thing just about holding the kids together; never again, this would teach them to holiday at home; they'd wanted to go visit Mount Polbearne, but they couldn't risk it in this weather. The mother looked on the verge of tears.

"I've . . . I've got some cheesy ciabatta loaf," offered Polly.

"You've got what, love?" said the mother, glancing

nervously back at the car and pulling her windbreaker closer around her shoulders. The car windows were all steamed up, with the occasional ominous thud hitting the windows, like something out of *World War Z*.

"Just chips will be fine, you know. Absolutely fine."

"I don't do chips," said Polly apologetically. "This is a bread van."

The woman really did look as if she was going to burst into tears.

"A *bread* van?" she said. "At the seaside?" Her pink-lipsticked mouth sagged. "What . . . what on earth were you thinking?"

There was a cry coming from the dirty car that might have been "Chips! Chips! Chips!"

"A *bread* van?" said the woman again, as if Polly might suddenly pull back a curtain and say "Only kidding! Haddock or cod!"

"'Fraid so," said Polly. The woman shook her head.

"Well, do you know if we can get fish and chips near here?"

"There's a great chippy on Mount Polbearne," said Polly.

The two of them turned together and looked out at the great rocky outcrop, half hidden in the gray mist, its causeway completely obliterated by furious-looking gray waves; never more an island than today.

The woman took a step backward.

"Never again," she said. She glanced at the car as if dreading stepping inside it once more. She glanced again at Mount Polbearne. Then she retreated, and Polly felt absolutely awful.

At 5 p.m., as the causeway slowly uncovered, and just as she was wearily packing up, she spotted Muriel charging toward her. The relief of seeing a friendly face was enormous, and Polly waved expansively. Muriel waved back and made it over in double-quick time.

"What a day," she said. "Filthy. I hope it picks up soon, I haven't sold a single bucket and spade in four days."

"You've sold other stuff though, right?" said Polly.

"Oh lord, yes. Hot chocolate mostly. Hot chocolate and the *Puzzler*."

"I haven't sold anything," said Polly glumly, even though she hated to sound self-pitying.

"Well that's because you started trading in the middle of a storm," said Muriel sensibly. "You can't expect everything to come together at once. Anyway, *I* am here to save you, because I have the secret village orders."

Polly's face lit up. Here it was! The locals! This would save her! She knew the good people of Mount Polbearne wouldn't let her down. She could have kissed Muriel.

"Yay!" she said. "That is fantastic news! Great! What would you like! And I can drive you back over too!"

Muriel looked at the van doubtfully.

"I think I'd rather have the walk, to be honest."

"It's pissing down!"

"Yes, well, you know. Just till you get the hang of it."

Polly smiled. "All right. What are you after?"

Muriel took out a piece of paper.

"Okay. Campagne for Patrick. Sliced white for me. Half a dozen buns for Mrs. Cranford."

Polly waited expectantly.

"And?"

There was a slightly awkward pause.

"Um," said Muriel. "Um, that's it."

"That's it?" said Polly, thinking with some despair of the queues outside the bakery door, the appreciation she was so used to.

Muriel looked concerned.

"I know, Poll," she said. "I think . . . you know, you've been away for a while. I think maybe people are just kind of getting used to you not being there. I mean, they lived without the Beach Street Bakery for a long time . . ."

As she wrapped up the few orders in paper bags, Polly felt her heart grow heavy. Okay, so it wasn't that she'd expected to be hoisted on the villagers' shoulders and paraded around the town—okay, well maybe a tiny little bit, but not *really*. But she had hoped . . . she had hoped there would be enough day-to-day trade, enough people who missed her, to make it at least financially viable, particularly out of season.

"Well, we're just starting out," she said bravely, accepting the few meager coins Muriel passed over. "It's very early days."

"It is early days!" said Muriel, nodding fiercely. "It's day one! And look how cute your van is."

"Mmm," said Polly, who had spent all day staring at Nan the Van and was starting to go off her.

The rain had eased off and an experimental, watery ray of sunlight poked its way through one of the thick gray clouds. It lit up the causeway, its sodden cobbles winding their way home.

"Are you sure you don't want a lift?" Polly asked.

"It looks very slippery," said Muriel. "Do you know what, you drive on, and I'll be right behind you. Then I'll be well positioned to get help in case of, you know. Accidents."

"I'm perfectly competent!" said Polly.

And she was. She was perfectly competent. Was that going to be enough to keep her on the road, though?

Chapter Sixteen

The whole week continued gray and miserable. Every morning, Malcolm, showing much more gumption and energy than he had done hitherto, would turn up in front of the van, threatening Polly, mentioning lawyers' letters and laughing at her stock, which diminished every day as she ran lower on supplies—she hated throwing stock away or passing it on to the fishermen for free, which wasn't teaching them the right behavior either.

Huckle phoned, sounding so utterly knackered that Polly couldn't bear to tell him that they were sliding briskly into failure; she tried to be perky and upbeat, didn't mention Malcolm's bullying behavior at all, just in case Huckle got the next flight back and beat him to a bloody pulp. Instead she talked about building slowly, waiting to capitalize on the season; how all it would take was a spell of fine weather.

She had no idea that Polly sounding calm and measured was far more terrifying to Huckle than her usual state of either wild enthusiasm or deep despair. He was very worried.

By the second week, Polly was really starting to question herself. She'd sold a few things—some long-distance lorry drivers had somehow made their way to her and enjoyed the change from bacon rolls and greasy spoons, and she sent them on their way to Land's End and Penzance and Truro with as broad a smile as she could manage, hoping against hope that they'd be able to spread the news around their communities.

But it wasn't enough. It wasn't nearly enough. Muriel and Patrick buying loaves and the fishermen occasionally placing orders for sandwiches was all she was getting from the town. The holidaymakers would occasionally buy a loaf out of sheer desperation, because there was nothing else this side of Mount Polbearne and it was something to do while you were waiting for the waters to recede if you turned up too early or too late to make the crossing. But people missing the road was not, she knew, a business plan. She was not making a living. Nothing like it.

She sat in the van all day, scrubbing it, doing her best to cheer up for a few customers here and there, then staring at the sea, at the walls, trying not to panic as the time ticked by, endlessly slowly, until she would finally pack up for the final tide of the day, fall into bed in the lighthouse all alone, and start all over again the next morning. She didn't know how long she could keep this up.

It was a slightly more promising day, the first Tuesday in June. There was an early-morning mist across the water and into Beach Street, and looking down from the lighthouse you could hardly see a thing. But the sun soon burned it off, and it was going to be warm when the dawn had lifted, Polly could tell as she loaded the van with her morning's efforts: a particularly good and, she knew, soon to be wasted sun-dried tomato focaccia, which came with a little tub of olive oil to dip, the sweetness and saltiness blending to make the most delicious mouthful; some light iced raisin buns, the perfect mouthful for people waiting for the tide, so she was slightly more confident about those; and a michette studded with lardons and plenty of freshly ground black pepper, which was her concession to a bacon sandwich. If you wanted a bacon sandwich and you got one of these, she reckoned you would be pretty happy, all in all.

She drove carefully across the causeway. She knew the islanders regarded Nan with some amusement and not a little concern, but actually Polly was entirely confident about driving her. Selling things out of the side was where it all started to go wrong.

She parked up in her usual spot—the car park was getting a little busier day by day, not by much, but the season was revving itself up to get into gear. Please, she begged silently, yet again. Please let this pick up for me.

This morning, there was an unusually smart car already parked there; a sporty little white BMW with a soft top, the type of thing Kerensa used to drive before her vehicle options came down to a choice between a micro-scooter and walking.

Polly looked at it, wondering if it would be someone else wanting a holiday home. Although that tended to be families. This car did not belong to someone with a family, or if it did, they were a particularly daring one.

She got out of the van, propped up the canopy, arranged the still slightly steaming loaves, added the little chalkboard of prices, and tried her best to look cheerful.

An incredibly thin, elegant-looking woman, her hair pulled back in a shiny swinging ponytail, clambered out of the car. She didn't look local at all, Polly thought. Mount Polbearne wouldn't be right for her; she needed something a bit more developed, for sure, if she was after a second home. But Polly arranged a cheery smile anyway. A customer was a customer, after all.

The woman marched over, a broad smile showing well-looked-after teeth. She had a high stride, like a rather pretty horse, and Polly envied her, whoever she was.

"Hello!" the woman said, sticking out her hand with the easy confidence of someone other people were generally pleased to see, whether they knew it or not. "Kate Lacey?"

It took Polly a second to place the name.

"Oh my God," she said.

"Oh, you know who I am?" said Kate. "God, that's amazing. Call the papers. Hang on, I am the papers." She rolled her eyes.

"The newspaper," said Polly, frozen. "Oh my goodness, the newspaper."

"Yes, I was just going to ask you the way to Polly Waterford's bakery? On Mount Polbearne? I appear to have misjudged the tide."

"Yes, it's tricky," said Polly. "Um . . ."

She looked at Nan the Van, who had gotten very splashed around the bottom with mud and salt water as she trundled her way across the causeway every morning.

"You see, the thing is," she said, "I forgot to call you. Only, *I'm* Polly Waterford."

Kate looked confused.

"What, and this is how you get to work?"

"Not exactly," said Polly, her heart sinking. This was to have been her break, her amazing crack at the big time. But now, with her stupid van . . . This incredibly chic woman was just going to turn around and go home, she knew it. Or worse, write something scathing and awful. She heaved a great sigh.

"Um, I don't work for the bakery anymore."

She didn't want to elaborate, but Kate pounced at once.

"Why not?"

"Um, new owner," said Polly, doing a quick censorship job. "So it's a bit different. Sorry, I've been manic, I forgot to let you know, and I should have."

Kate narrowed her eyes.

"So basically you now have a burger van?"

"Um, it's not quite . . ."

Out of the corner of her eye, Polly caught sight of the tatty old BMW turning in to the car park. Oh no, she thought. Oh no, not now. No no no-no-no. Please. Anything but this.

Her wish was not to be granted. The car screeched to a halt, throwing up a spray of water that soaked their legs, and Malcolm jumped out, red-faced as ever.

"Don't eat here!" he shouted. "She's dirty."

Polly sighed and turned bright pink, her humiliation complete. This was what would be written up for the national press; any chance of any sort of a career in baking completely scuppered by people being able to read about this, which would be on the Internet, and therefore visible forevermore.

"Please, Malcolm," she said, in a low voice, but it was no use. Polly wanted to cry as the journalist listened politely to him without identifying herself—why would she, when she was already getting all the real dirt?

Finally he ran out of steam and stopped ranting, a satisfied look on his face.

"Right, well that's done for another one of your customers. Almost none left now, huh? Feeling sorry yet? Hmm? Got something else to go and do? Maybe something secretarial. Or bird management, huh? Ha! Good one, eh! Bird management!"

Polly couldn't think too much about Neil at the best of times, and this was emphatically not the best of times. A lone tear came to her eye. Malcolm slammed his car door and drove away across the causeway.

Kate watched him go.

"Do people drive off the causeway often?" she asked in clear tones.

Polly shook her head.

"No, never," she said.

"Shame," said Kate. She turned back to Polly, a smile playing on her lips. "I'm assuming that was the new boss."

Polly nodded.

"Wow," Kate said. "No wonder you don't work for him any more. He's *mental*."

Oddly, the simple fact of someone else saying that Malcolm was behaving strangely had a huge effect on Polly. She had, she realized, been thinking that on some level she deserved this kind of bullying and had had nobody around, not really, to convince her otherwise.

"I'd report him," said Kate. "That's harassment."

Polly swallowed. She didn't forget, though, that Kate was still a journalist. Making any comment at all probably wouldn't be that great an idea.

"Would you . . . would you like something to eat?" she offered shyly.

"Yes!" said Kate. "That's why I'm here, remember?"

They sat together on the car park wall and ate slices of the warm lardon michette underneath the heavy gray sky and chatted about their lives. Kate was very impressed that Polly lived in a lighthouse, and Polly was sympathetic as Kate told her at great length about her problems with the separated man she was seeing back in London, so it ended up being a rather mutually enjoyable conversation.

After an hour, Kate got up to leave. Polly had served one other person in that time, an old man who wanted two rolls. She had felt nervous doing so, not wanting Kate pitying her any more than she did already. She piled Kate up with goodies to take away with her.

"Are you not going on to the village?" she said.

Kate frowned. "What's that man's bakery like?"

"Gruesome," said Polly. "Well, unless you like your bread to last two months, in which case it's ideal."

"Hmm," said Kate. "Maybe not, then. Nice to meet you. I have to tell you, though, we don't normally review vans in our restaurant pages. I don't know what my editor will say."

"I realize that," said Polly.

"I'll give it a shot, okay?"

"Don't tell them about the shouting."

Kate frowned. "Can't promise."

"I know."

They smiled and shook hands, and Kate left, and Polly sat there in the car park for another four hours.

Chapter Seventeen

Huckle was sitting uncomfortably at an elaborately set table in his ex-girlfriend's house, which was as immaculate as a house could be. He wished he weren't. When Candice had heard he was back over, she'd insisted, and she was hard to say no to. It was odd, he thought. It had taken him so long to get over her, and now that he was—and she was engaged to a very fit man called Ron, who did triathlons—he could barely remember why.

Candice had invited a girl for him to sit opposite. She was blond and giggly and patently thought she was there for Huckle, as indeed she was.

Candice wanted Huckle back home and in her social circle again; she liked him, and thought he was throwing his life away burying himself in some other country. He wasn't engaged, he wasn't married, he'd chosen to leave the country—all was fair in love and war, wasn't it? And it would be quite the coup for her if she managed to matchmake her hot sexy ex (There were a lot of things Candice had not liked about Huckle—his lack of ambition, the way he absolutely didn't care about appearances or being socially acceptable. The bedroom, however, had never been a problem. She missed it more than she could ever have admitted, no matter how many triathlons Ron trained for.) and get him back his high-flying consulting job. Everyone would think she was amazingly cool, and she could throw such a lovely party.

"Polly *again*," sighed Candice, after he'd slipped out to take a phone call from Cornwall. "Goodness, she really is quite needy, isn't she?"

Huckle frowned. Polly had been a little down on the phone, it was true, but that was pretty normal these days. He was getting used to it.

"She's having it tough back there," he said. "It's taking a bit longer for her to get this thing off the ground than she thought. I don't know why it's making her so miserable, though." He put it down to her missing him and Neil, but was surprised at her lack of natural bounce. You normally couldn't keep her down for long.

"Well, that's no way to run a business," said Candice. "Did you consider coming back to your old firm? You'll make all the cash you need quite a lot quicker than at that stupid farm. Let your brother sink or swim, that's by far the best thing for him." She was always interested in Huckle's work and gave him lots of useful advice.

Huckle shook his head. He had promised Clemmie he wouldn't tell anyone about the baby, not even Polly. Truthfully, now that he'd gotten the farm working properly and turning a profit, he really ought to leave. But he couldn't. He wasn't sure how to break it to Polly, but if she was having trouble with this van, if she really couldn't make it work, then maybe he would just have to stay anyway, just to make a living. Goddam Dubose.

"I don't think so."

"Would you like me to put in a word?"

"Not yet," said Huckle. It wouldn't ever come to that—staying in the US full time to make a crust. Would it?

"Well, have you met Lily?"

Lily smiled broadly. Her teeth were absolutely perfect, her skin the color of honey. Huckle smiled back politely, although his thoughts were elsewhere.

"Hi!" said Lily. "I teach yoga! You look like you could do with some."

"Do I?" said Huckle.

These days there is a roaring trade in 'quaint'—a few distressed tables, wild flowers in a jam jar, some bunting, bits of driftwood here and there, and voilà, welcome to 2015. Very wearying, I'm sure you'll agree. So thank goodness for the lone pioneers out there determined to get a bit of proper old-fashioned grit and authenticity back into our eating.

Not for Polly Waterford the fake coziness of so-called traditional surroundings.

She hammers out her lonely trade in a brutal, windswept car park, maintaining the purity of her perfectly baked artisan bread—and for once the term is justified, rather than being as over-used as 'organic' was five years ago—for an incredibly select audience, if you can even find her. Regularly sworn at by tramps, and battered by weather, Polly makes bread only for herself, and if you are lucky enough to track her down and share in it, you can consider yourself a true gourmet.

She lives alone in a lighthouse,

"I don't live alone in a lighthouse," said Polly crossly in her kitchen, then realized she was speaking out loud to an empty lighthouse.

which gives her the absolute solitude and purity she requires to perfect her loaves. She is not interested in prettifying anything, not even herself, which makes the tough path she has chosen and the weather-beaten effects on her life all the more admirable and impressive.

Polly growled to herself. "If I'd remembered a journalist was coming, I'd have put some lipstick on. And probably washed the van."

However, if the outside is rough, inside is very special indeed, with some of the most astonishing campagne breads, wholemeal rolls—it seems there is absolutely nothing Polly can't tackle with her scrubbed raw hands.

The phone rang. It was Selina.

"Darling, is that you in the paper?"

"Yes," said Polly. "It makes me sound like a witch. A terrifyingly lonely witch."

"It's amazing!" said Selina.

"Being a witch," said Polly.

"She says you're the most amazing find."

"Yeah, if you want some new spells."

Polly's phone beeped with a waiting call. She apologized to Selina and switched over.

"You're a witch!" shouted Kerensa joyously. "Show us your spooky powers!"

"Shut up!" said Polly. "I'm not a witch!"

"She totally makes you sound like one."

"I know," said Polly.

"But, you know, it's really good!"

Polly heaved a sigh.

"Do you think so? It basically makes me out to be a cross between Maleficent and the A-Team."

"That is a stupendous thing to be," said Kerensa. "Remember, I'm a marketing guru. Also, all Reuben's friends can come now."

"What do you mean?" said Polly. "I thought Reuben lost all his friends when he lost his money."

Kerensa snorted loudly.

"Thank you for that huge vote of confidence in my life partner."

"Oh yeah, sorry," said Polly. Reuben had hung out with lots of cool dudes and model-type women. Polly just assumed they'd have passed on to the next multimillionaire.

"No, you're right," said Kerensa. "They are horrific fair-weather friends. But they keep their hand in with Reuben, just in case he does something genius again and all the parties are back on."

"Well, they do sound completely charming," said Polly. She paused. "Hang on," she said. "Why is he only sending them *now*?"

Reuben had obviously been listening on speakerphone and came on the line.

"In case you were garbage, of course," he said. "What if you'd moved and turned into total garbage? Sheesh, don't be nuts. Of course I had to wait and see."

"Oh," said Polly. "Well, thanks, I guess."

"Don't mention it!"

"You even look witchy in the photo," said Kerensa.

"Stop it," said Polly. "My mum's already had a panic attack."

They'd sent a photographer down later that day—which Kate hadn't mentioned would happen, so Polly still didn't have any bloody makeup on. The wind had really gotten up by then, and there wasn't a soul to be seen anywhere around. He had made her sit on the wall, the van slightly out of focus behind her, and behind that the great looming mass of Mount Polbearne. In the photo, her strawberry-blond hair was flicking behind her head as she stared out to sea, her face thoughtful—or, as Polly's mother's put it, miserable—as if you could see her thinking, oh lord, this is a mistake. The headline underneath read, *Purity in Polbearne*.

"Lonely Virgin Witch," Kerensa said cheerfully. "Even better!"

Huckle looked at the link online. He stared at it, his heart so full of longing he could hardly breathe. She looked so sad; he had never seen her so sad. And she had gotten so thin. Where was her full bosom, the gentle curves of her hips? This Polly was angular and thoughtful.

He felt unnervingly homesick for the life they had had: the quiet evenings listening to seagulls, teasing Neil, companionably reading, or cooking, or just being near one another, when neither ever left the room without a gentle caress, a quick passing kiss, a tender embrace. He wanted to reach out to her, but they seemed to be drifting further apart. He printed out the article, then folded it up and slipped it into his wallet.

Did you want me to talk about a new job for you? Candice's text message had said. Of course, trust Candice to still be working first thing on a Sunday morning. She'd probably already had her workout. She wanted Huckle to go to brunch with her and Lily—hemp smoothies and egg-white omelettes, and Ron talking about his share portfolio.

He didn't want to text her back quite yet. Didn't even want to admit to himself that he was stuck on this farm for the near future, and even if he wasn't, even if by some miracle Dubose did show up, that he still needed a job to carry them through the long Cornish winter, given what the article had made clear: that Polly was making absolutely no money. They were living in a place with no insulation that needed absolutely loads doing to it to even make it habitable. They needed money! They needed money, goddammit. He loved Polly, but could she pull this off? It didn't look like it. It really didn't. He gazed at the picture for a long time and wondered how on earth he could break it to her that he was not coming home anytime soon; that he felt like he was being torn in two.

Huckle couldn't get through on the phone for ages. He guessed everyone was chiming in with their thoughts. He hoped they were positive. Finally, it rang, tinny and so far away.

"Hey!" he said. "Who is that unbelievably hot woman in that magazine?"

"Seriously?" said Polly. "Because everyone else is sending me links to the Samaritans. Apart from two really strange guys who wrote on the newspaper website that they'd like to marry me because they liked bread and being by themselves."

"Hmm," said Huckle. "Well, you should have smiled."

"Really?"

"I like it when you're smiling."

"That's been quite tricky," said Polly.

"But it's a good piece."

"Is it?"

There was a slightly awkward silence between them. This was new.

"It doesn't matter," said Huckle. "Because you know, I'm . . . I mean, everything is going well here. I'm turning the farm around. Definitely."

Another pause.

"Well," said Polly. "That's great."

"And, you know, I'm sure this is the start of something for you . . ."

"I hope so," said Polly. They both did.

Chapter Eighteen

In fact, they didn't have to wait long. By Monday, there were a few more cars.

By Tuesday, there was a line.

"Oh my God," Polly had said that first morning. The people who came weren't like any she'd served before.

They were very intense and peppered her with lots and lots of questions about process and ingredients and provenance and methodology. They were, as Selina said when she came over later and stayed to help, foodies, people who only liked the rarest and newest of things. She was, it seemed, a discovery. Many of them tried some of the seeded loaf she put out for testing as if it were wine: holding it in their mouths, rolling it around and around, or pinching it between their fingers and making humming noises. All the men had beards.

She texted Kate to say an ecstatic thank you, and

Kate had texted back to say not at all, she deserved it, and she had looked like she needed it. Which was true.

The other odd thing was that many of the cars didn't then go on to Mount Polbearne, even though it was a clear day with low tides. Many just drove into the car park, bought some bread—for boasting rights, Selina informed her—and drove off again. There was also a healthy proportion of surfers who Polly semi-recognized as being friends of Reuben, all of whom bought warm loaves and little pots of butter to take to the beach with them but then started tearing it off as soon as they got the bag in their hands. Most people did that: it tasted better fresh from the oven, crammed greedily into your mouth, the little seeds getting caught in your teeth, the nutty, salty crunch of the crust spluttering into life, the soft insides squelching with delicious warmth and runny butter.

"This is AMAZEBALLS," said one of the surfers loudly, which was very gratifying.

The oddest thing, though, was that every car that drove past or came into the car park slowed down, opened its windows and had a look at what was going on, as if the very fact of a queue was enough to make people stop, and as soon as they smelled the scent of the fresh bread billowing across the car park, they found they did want some after all, and their children certainly did, and the crumbs scattered in the billowing wind, and Polly experienced something she hadn't felt for a long time: the sure and deep happiness of feeding people something homemade and natural and good; seeing their faces crinkle with happiness as they inhaled the smell of it, or cracked the crust and squeezed the soft innards together. Just for an instant, she saw in each of them the hungry child they once might have been, rushing home from school on a cold day, desperate for toast; or the older ones recalling a trip to Italy, before they were married and weighted heavily with responsibilities, and how for the first time they'd eaten bread like that in the sunlight, and how wondrous it had been.

Handing out the buns, wrapping with a flick of a wrist the big loaves in her paper bags, she was sold out by 11:30 and found herself, unexpectedly, shutting up the van. There was a big sigh from the people left behind in the queue who hadn't been lucky. Selina said this was clearly a good sign as they started to dissipate.

Malcolm drove into the car park just as they were about to leave. He smiled approvingly as he saw the shut-up van.

"That's right," he hollered out of the window. "Know when you're beaten."

Selina went to answer him, but Polly held her back.

"Don't," she said. "I don't want to make things worse."

"But he's an arsehole," explained Selina.

"I know that," said Polly. "But an arsehole who thinks I'm not a threat is much better for me, do you see?"

"Hmm," said Selina. "If you say so."

She looked around sadly.

"It's nice to see something go well," she said.

"Well, I can thank you for that," said Polly. "Us making up really helped me over my funk."

"Is that true?" said Selina.

"Yes," said Polly. "Also, have you gotten Lucas declawed yet?"

Over the next few days, exactly the same thing happened—people lining up, including, Polly was wildly gratified to see, some of the beards coming back as repeat custom. She upped her quantities every day and still emptied out before lunchtime. The weather was getting better too, which meant a fuller car park, and somehow word was getting around that you could basically pick up your picnic from there rather than lug it all the way, so she was doing a pretty good trade to families too. After a week when she barely slept at all and found herself constantly high on adrenaline, she finally called Huckle to tell him the amazing news: that they were starting to be successful at last.

She was sitting with the old-fashioned phone on a chair facing the sea. Some seagulls were circling, having a fight about something. She couldn't admit to herself how much she missed Neil; how jealous she was of those bloody seagulls. Nor how many nights she had sat bolt upright in bed, convinced he was going to come knocking at her window, that he would be back; nor how she would always look at Selina's flat as she passed, just in case he'd forgotten and gone there instead.

But there was no sign of him, and this was breeding season, and well, the weeks had passed, and . . . Polly swallowed hard. He would come back. He must. He was her puffin and that was that. Although if he remembered being sent away twice . . . maybe he had just gotten the hint that they didn't want him anymore.

No. She couldn't think like this, not when she had made such big strides. But it was almost as if the pressure easing slightly on Nan the Van had made the loss of Neil suddenly much more acute. She tried not to think how lovely it would be for him to be able to hop up and down on top of the van, and snarf up the crumbs in the car park, and say hello to everyone . . .

She told herself sternly that a car park was absolutely no place for a small bird who was not as speedy as he ought to be, and tried to put a smile on her face before she called Huckle. She would have liked to have left it later—it was the middle of the afternoon for him—but she really couldn't: she was exhausted, and she needed to be up at four to start on the loaves. She really missed Jayden for the scrubbing and the mopping parts; having to do all that herself was tiring her out, but she had absolutely no choice: the kitchen and the van had to be totally spotless at all times. She wouldn't be able to keep her eyes open another second, and she really wanted to call him now.

"Huck?"

Huckle was just heading into the dairy. He absolutely knew it wasn't Polly's fault that their time zones weren't compatible, but it sure did tend to come up at the most inconvenient moments.

"Hey," he said.

"Okay, are you ready for our accounts?"

He perked up a little to hear her voice sounding brighter, not in the dull register he'd gotten so used to over the last few weeks.

"Hey, Jackson," he shouted through the open door. "I'll be two minutes, okay?"

"Sure thing," said his colleague equably. Over the weeks they'd been working together, he'd come to assume that Huckle's girlfriend must be the most crazily high-maintenance woman out there, given the horrendously inconvenient times she called him. But the animals seemed to like him, and that was all that mattered.

"Go on," said Huckle.

Polly named a sum that wouldn't even cover his tractor fuel.

"Mmm," said Huckle.

"But!" said Polly. "You're missing something."

"I am?"

"Yes!"

She hadn't spoken to anyone else apart from, briefly and hurriedly, customers all day. She was loving talking to Huckle, even if it sounded like he had to get away.

"Go on, then," said Huckle. She told him the lame takings most days, even though it made them both sad. She'd actually stopped doing that this week; he'd just assumed it was because they were too depressing even for her.

Polly paused dramatically.

"That's . . . NET!"

"What do you mean? A fishing net?"

"Okay, well done, great big important farmer."

Huckle smiled.

"Well, I'm not sure you know what net means."

"Shut up and don't be insulting! Those are net figures after materials, fuel and . . . Are you ready?"

"I'm ready," said Huckle.

"Paying you back for the van."

There was a pause.

"What, all of it?"

"No, not all of it," said Polly, slightly deflated. "Don't be ridiculous. No, I mean, pro rata. For the week."

Huckle quickly did some sums in his head.

"But that's . . . that's incredibly good!"

"I know!" said Polly.

"Is that just from the article?"

"Well, let's say the article and also me being awesome," said Polly.

Huckle smiled with genuine pleasure.

"This is really starting to move. Are you upping volumes?"

"I am," said Polly. "And the weather forecast for the week is blue, blue skies ahead."

"Warm?"

"Well, what do you call warm?"

"Let's not get into that," said Huckle. It was 106 degrees Fahrenheit outside.

"Warm enough for buckets and spades and sweaters," said Polly. "And the first schools will be starting to break up soon—those posh private ones where they're all fancy and think holidaying in some decaying old British resort is really groovy."

Huckle shook his head.

"That is amazing," he said. "That's great. I can't believe you're turning it around."

"Can't you?"

"YES. Yes, of course I can!"

Now it was Polly's turn to smile.

"Well," she said, "I think someone could probably use that other half of their ticket soon."

Huckle blinked.

"It's early days," he said. "I mean, this might just be a blip."

"Life is a blip," said Polly. "You've kind of just got to get on with it anyway, haven't you?"

"Yes, but, you know. To be sure."

There was a long pause.

"Don't you want to come home?" said Polly finally.

"What? No, of course I do. That's not fair. But I can't leave Clemmie."

"Look," said Polly. "You have to realize Dubose isn't coming back. He thinks he's a student on a gap year.

He's bouncing about. Tell Clemmie it's over. She needs to just go back to . . . Well, I don't know where she's from. But she can't run a farm by herself, and she's taking too much of you."

"Yes," said Huckle. "But there's another thing."

And he told her.

Polly swore vociferously.

"Tell him," she said. "Just email him and tell him."

"I promised I wouldn't. She wants to tell him herself."

"But then you'll be there forever."

"I won't."

"It's not fair," said Polly. "It's just not fair."

She heard the petulant note in her voice and hated herself for sounding so selfish and horrible. Ugh. She knew it wasn't Huckle's fault; he was doing the right thing. She just missed him so much.

"It's a great farm," said Huckle. "It could work really well for them. Much better than Clemmie going back to her mom's in the city, raising a baby alone."

"Well, that's what's going to happen."

There was a long pause.

"Polly," said Huckle. "That's my niece or nephew we're talking about."

Polly bit her tongue in frustration and disappointment. She wanted to be better than this, not to let her anger come through.

"I know," she said. "I know. But you should just tell him."

"It's not my place to do that."

Polly heaved a great sigh.

"And," said Huckle, "you know, the money . . . I mean, I can make money here. Good money. So that will help . . ."

"*I'm* making money!"

"As of three days ago."

"WHAT?"

"Mr. Huckle?" Jackson's voice came through the barn door.

"Look, I didn't mean it like that," said Huckle. "I'll call you in the morning, okay? I really have to go."

Polly felt a lump in her throat. She wanted to beg him to come home, to go to the airport and come home, for crying out loud. But of course she couldn't. She wanted to be nice, she really did. But she was so very tired.

"Fine," she said. "Don't call me in the morning, though. I'm too busy."

Huckle blinked.

"I want to."

"Well, whatever," said Polly.

There was a pause.

"Oh," said Polly. "And you didn't ask me if Neil has come back yet."

"Did Neil come back?" asked Huckle in disbelief.

"No," said Polly. And she hung up the phone.

Chapter Nineteen

Y ou should be looking happier than you are," observed Kerensa, who had stopped off to see Polly between dashing from one meeting to another across the Cornish coast. She ate one of the sugar buns. It was delicious. She looked at another, then shook her head.

"You can have one," said Polly.

"I can't," said Kerensa. "If I grow too big for these clothes, I can't afford any others."

"Yes, and you shouldn't be looking as happy as you are," said Polly. "I am horribly jealous."

Kerensa smiled to herself.

"Oh well, you know. It's not so bad."

"What's Reuben doing?"

"Amazing things," said Kerensa. "We've worked our way through most of the Kama Sutra. Also, he's working on a dating website for people who . . . take a bit of time to get to know."

"You mean ugly people?"

"No!" said Kerensa. "No, just people most folk don't like when they meet them. He's trying to get Malcolm to sign up."

"I don't think Malcolm knows everybody hates him."

They were picnicking in the fine weather out on the seafront by the harbor wall. Archie was fixing nets, rocked on top of his boat by the gentle swell, helped by Sten the Scandinavian. It was painstaking work. The sun was blazing.

Polly's only problem now was capacity, in her own ovens and in the van itself. Whatever she made, she would sell. Holidaymakers were coming from far and wide: the local caravan park had let her put up a flyer, and now people would troop down with their flasks and sit outside the van on the rocks. Dog-walkers came past every day and made a morning collection, and the Mount Polbearne residents kept up their regular shopping lists via Muriel. It was all going incredibly well. Polly just needed somebody to share it with.

They both turned around. They weren't sitting next to the Little Beach Street Bakery; Polly didn't want to risk Malcolm coming out and shouting at her simply for existing in the same postcode, if Mount Polbearne even had a postcode. They were along the harbor a bit, but they could already hear the voice coming out of the shop, roaring.

It was Jayden, tearing off his apron, his round face totally red. He threw the apron back into the shop and marched out.

"I quit, you absolute utter bastard!"

"Uh-oh," said Polly. She had never seen Jayden cross in her entire life.

"I quit, and nobody is going to work for a bastard like you!"

Polly jumped up and went toward him.

"Are you all right, sweetie?"

"He's a bastard!" said Jayden, marching straight up to them, out of breath and beside himself with distress. "Oh. Is that a toasted teacake?"

"It is," said Kerensa. "And you can have it if you sit down and tell us every sordid detail."

But Malcolm had already appeared in the doorway and, looking back at him, Polly reckoned she could already see the source of the problem, and what had been going so very wrong.

Malcolm had his arm possessively around Flora's neck.

Polly gasped in astonishment. Flora looked as blank and unconcerned as she usually did, but Malcolm's blubbery lips were open in a smile of triumph, and he stroked the girl's shoulder smugly.

Polly shook her head in disbelief.

"No way," she said. "She prefers *Malcolm*? How dare he lay his filthy paws on that beautiful girl?"

Jayden looked very close to tears.

"What happened, Jayden? It's not just because he's her boss, is it? He didn't insist or anything?"

Jayden shook his head.

"No," he said. "It's because she said she was tired of all the poetry and the flowers and stuff. I thought girls liked poetry and flowers."

"Flora is not like other girls."

"No." Jayden sighed. "You know what HE did?"

Polly shook her head again.

"He bought her a mixer."

"She wants to bake," said Polly. "Is he going to let her? She could save the shop if he lets her bake."

"No, it's just for fun. She's not allowed to bake in the shop."

"THAT MAN!"

"Did you know he plays the trumpet?"

"I did know that," said Polly.

"He's been serenading her! Under her window!"

"With a trumpet?"

"All I can play is the spoons."

"Lots of people like the spoons," said Polly, trying to be reassuring.

"Flora said she thought the spoons were rubbish," said Jayden. "I don't think she liked the trumpet much either. But she liked the mixer. Also she said he talks to her, whereas everybody else just dribbles."

"Oh Jayden," said Polly. "That is bloody rotten news. I am so, so sorry."

Jayden sniffed loudly.

"I don't care," he said. "It's all crap what they sell anyway. Disgusting. It's making everyone constipated, all that terrible white stuff. It doesn't do anybody any good. Bungs up your insides. I hope it bungs up *his* insides," he said bitterly, glancing back at the Little Beach Street Bakery. He hung his head. "She was SO beautiful," he said mournfully.

Polly thought of the beautiful Flora. She had always kind of assumed that being beautiful would be a short cut to everything, not just a mixer.

"Why won't he let her bake in his shop?" said Kerensa, shaking her head.

"He said he didn't want her to mess up her beautiful

hands," said Jayden. "But you're going to keep taking all his business, aren't you?" he added hopefully.

"Well, I tell you what, I don't feel guilty about that any more," said Polly, who'd been the victim of too many bruising early-morning attacks. "But even more so now, knowing I won't be doing you out of a job."

"Can I come and work for you?" said Jayden. "Can I come to your van? I haven't been allowed to visit it. Malcolm banned everyone. Sorry about that."

"That's okay," said Polly, although she did think a little regretfully of those first few days without even the hint of a friendly face. "I understand. But Jayden, I don't have enough business yet to pay you properly . . . I can probably let you do a few mornings and a bit of cleaning, but that's about it. And I don't even know if it's going to keep up."

"Of course it is," said Kerensa. "All you needed was for people to discover how brilliant you are. Now that they have, you're away!"

Polly smiled. "Thanks, K." She touched her hand.

"I'll do it," said Jayden. "I'll shovel up all your mucky stuff. Then I'll dump it on his doorstep."

"You will not," said Polly. Even though it was no longer hers, she still loved the beautiful soft gray of the Little Beach Street Bakery frontage; it was quite lovely, even if she couldn't set foot over the threshold anymore.

"Okay," said Jayden. He added quietly to himself, "Maybe in his car."

"If you could do an early-morning shift," said Polly. "But it really isn't much. I'm so sorry."

"I don't mind," said Jayden. "Anything is better than working for that demon."

Kerensa smiled at Polly.

"When's Huckle coming back?"

Polly's slightly more buoyant mood deflated instantly.

"Oh lord," she said. "Don't ask."

"Ah," said Kerensa.

"I can't wait," said Polly. "I need him back! Soon! Now, in fact. I'm growing old up there on my own."

"Well, I'll be there at five," said Jayden stoically. "I'm going to go see if anyone else needs night work doing."

"Thanks, Jayden," said Polly. "You know, it's going to be all right, I promise."

They waited till he'd walked slowly off up the hill.

"Is it going to be all right?" said Kerensa in a low voice. "Of all the couples I never thought I needed to worry about, you two are top of the list."

"I don't know," said Polly, hugging her knees. "I really don't know."

She remembered last year, when Huckle had just assumed she'd want to stay in Savannah with him, live the easy, sunny life of an American girl, let him look after everything. And it was appealing, no doubt about it, the thought of not having to worry about money, or deal with absolute rotters like Malcolm . . . Even as she was thinking this, she suddenly heard the sound of a trumpet start up somewhere in the distance and heaved a sigh.

"Is it worth it just to stay here?" said Kerensa, putting into words Polly's darkest fears. "If Huckle doesn't want to come back?"

"It has to be," said Polly stoically.

"And it is lovely there," said Kerensa.

Polly looked around.

"But look at this!" she said. "Look at all of this! How is this not lovely?"

"Because it's freezing and we don't have any money?"

"No!" said Polly. "Because it's mine. It's something

I did and I built and it has its ups and downs, but it's all my own work, do you see?"

"But in America . . . that's his too," said Kerensa gently.

Polly swallowed.

"But when I met him, he was just a honey seller. He was a local guy working in local food, local sourcing, creativity, just like me. Just like what I wanted to do."

"Yes, but back then, he was getting over an unhappy love affair, burying himself away. It wasn't . . . it wasn't necessarily who he truly was."

There was a long silence after that.

"Oh, K, do you really think so?" said Polly.

"I don't know," said Kerensa. "But he's not here. And I think it's time you found out."

Polly stared out to sea.

"But I couldn't . . . I couldn't leave here."

"Why not?" said Kerensa softly. "There are lots of places you could be happy in, but at the moment Mount Polbearne is not one. It's stressing you out like a mad thing. There are lots of places to be happy, but only one bloke I have ever seen you happy with, Polly Waterford."

Polly bowed her head.

"But the van is picking up."

"That's true."

"And . . ."

"And?" Kerensa looked at her.

"And I need to wait for Neil to come back."

"POLLY!"

"I know, I know. But he will, I know it. And if I'm not there . . ."

"Neil. Is. A. BIRD."

"He's a very special bird."

"He's off somewhere right now having an amazing time, doing whatever birds do. Okay? He has a little brain and is having the absolute time of his life being free. Like he has to be. You have to understand that."

Polly nodded.

"And if you let Neil get in the way of you and Huckle having a proper grown-up relationship, where from time to time you compromise on each other's careers and let each other come and go and do whatever you need to do and support one another unconditionally—and by the way, Huckle has always supported you, even when you're moaning about him taking on a major responsibility that must be a massive pain in the arse for him too—then you will be very, very sorry indeed. And I don't think it's what Neil would have wanted for you either."

"I know," said Polly.

She looked up, feeling rather hangdog, only to see Malcolm and Flora walking arm in arm along the seafront. Malcolm was gesturing expansively.

"Oh yes, my family have been pretty important around here for a long time," he was saying in a loud voice. "Yes, we pretty much ran this town for hundreds of years. Go back a long way. It's a great responsibility, of course."

"Wow," Flora was saying. "That's amazing."

She looked at her watch.

"Ooh, I've missed the tide again."

"Not to worry," said Malcolm. "I've got a flat here too, of course."

Flora spied Polly.

"Oh, hello, Miss Waterford! Were you in the paper? My mam says you were in the paper. Not one of the ones we read, but still, in the paper! That's good. They came and asked if they could take my photo too, but I said not likely."

"If they'd taken your photo, you'd have been whisked straight to London," said Polly. "Still not tempted?"

Flora shook her head.

"Noooo. Full of disgusting old men trying to touch me up all the time, like always."

Polly looked pointedly at Malcolm, but he stared impassively out to sea, ignoring her.

Flora stepped closer to Polly as Malcolm walked on.

"I know what you think," she said quietly. "But I never meet anyone who's just interested in me."

"Are you sure he's not just pretending?" said Polly.

Flora shrugged her shoulders.

"Nobody else even tries," she said. "That cute bloke Jayden who worked for you. He doesn't even say hello."

"Ah," said Polly.

Flora looked at the ground and scuffed her long, elegant foot across it.

"I am sorry, you know," she said. "I did like it more in the bakery when you were doing stuff."

"Thanks," said Polly.

"And your bird was amazing," she mumbled.

Polly looked up at her, surprised and touched.

"That means a lot," she said. "Thank you. And don't feel you have to—"

"Flora!" shouted Malcolm from further up the cobbled hill. "Come and show me that thing you do with the whirly machine."

"He wants me to bake for him!" said Flora, turning pink. She set off after him, and Kerensa and Polly watched her go.

"Cor," said Polly. "That 'treat 'em mean keep 'em keen' thing works in strange ways."

She stared out over the horizon. A great storm appeared to be blowing up, black clouds pushing hither and thither. She frowned at it.

"That doesn't look very nice."

"I know," said Kerensa glumly.

"Want to stay over? You've missed the tide."

"No, I'll wait for the next one. I wish Reuben still had that damn boat and could just come and pick me up. That is the one thing I miss. And the helicopter."

"It'll take him a while on the micro-scooter."

"Don't diss the micro-scooter," said Kerensa. "He's lost about nine pounds on that thing."

"What, through shame?"

Kerensa smiled. "You should know by now that Reuben doesn't do shame."

She linked arms with Polly.

"Come on, let's go halves on a small glass of cider."

Later on, Polly waved Kerensa off across the causeway. The tide was going out, but the waves were still splashing over the top of the cobbles. Kerensa was a good and unfazed driver, though, and pushed the little Datsun she'd been reduced to through without incident.

Polly frowned at the sky and kept her fingers crossed that the power would stay on if there was a big storm. It was the time of year for it: they'd had a couple of very hot days now, but there was still a lot of cold air circling around in the system. The lighthouse itself never went out, of course—it had a back-up generator—but the rooms were on the mains, and sitting in the dark above the sea frankly wasn't a lot of fun, unless Huckle was there, in which case it was a ton of fun.

The clouds kept gathering, and there was a strong feeling of electricity and static in the air without anything actually happening. It was getting warmer, and the clouds had a purply mustard streak that Polly didn't like at all. She decided to ring Huckle quickly.

"Hey," she said before he could get a word in. "Sorry about yesterday."

"Nobody said this was going to be easy," said Huckle straightaway. "That's okay. You're allowed to feel like you're alone. But you know, you're not."

"I know," said Polly. "Kerensa told me that. And Jayden, too. Then Selina rang, and—"

"See!" said Huckle. "You are totally surrounded by all your mates at all times. I don't have a friend in the world out here! Except for . . ." His voice trailed off.

"Except for who?"

"Well, I see Candice a bit, you know. Only a friendly kind of thing."

Polly felt a sudden clutch of nerves. She'd never met Candice, but she knew that a) she was incredibly fit and blond and beautiful, from a photograph she'd come across, and b) she had broken Huckle's heart completely and utterly before Polly had met him, so much so that he'd had to move to another continent to get away from her. He said he was totally over it, but men say a lot of things.

"Well, obviously," said Polly, her heart thumping in her chest. There was a pause. "Do you see her a lot?"

"I see her AND HER FIANCÉ RON from time to time, yes."

"And what does she think you should do?"

It was then that Huckle made his fatal mistake.

"Well, you know, she's a businesswoman . . ."

Polly went completely silent. There was a very long pause.

"And what am I?" she said finally. "A hobbyist?"

Huckle felt exasperated and guilty.

"Polly," he said. "You have to stop this."

"Stop what? Running a shop?"

"No! Trying to catch me out! Ever since I left, you've been trying to find hidden meanings in what I'm saying. Blaming me for stuff we both agreed to do."

"I'm not doing that!"

"That's exactly what you're doing."

"Well, I'm very tired."

The exhaustion showed in Huckle's voice.

"We're all tired, Poll. You have to try a little harder."

"You're not the one sat here all alone in—"

"In a lighthouse, I know. The lighthouse you insisted on buying despite that estate agent and surveyor begging you not to. The lighthouse that needs thousands and thousands spent on it to make it even vaguely habitable. The lighthouse in which we camp. The lighthouse you wouldn't dream of leaving for five minutes to come and spend time with me. The lighthouse that, by the way, has more than one room, which is more than I've got, because my life is on the farm now, and I live in a single bed in a spare room the size of a box. For you. But please, go on about it some more."

Polly had never heard Huckle so angry. It took so much to wind him up; she'd kind of taken it for granted that he would always be mellow and absorb her moods. This was new and a bit shocking.

She swallowed hard.

"Can you come home?"

"Not yet," said Huckle. "Can you come here?"

"It's the middle of the summer season."

"Well then," said Huckle, "we'll just have to carry on."

And there was a tiny little pause, in which both of them worried, just for a split second, whether or not they could.

Chapter Twenty

Huckle couldn't help being annoyed with Polly. She was at home with all her mates, her business was going well, everything was totally fine. Why did she have to be so cross with him all the time, really? Then he'd come upon Clemmie in the kitchen, bent over, sobbing her heart out over the stove. He'd run to her, petrified, thinking something was wrong with the baby. But she was scared, that was all. He had cursed and said he was absolutely emailing Dubose, and she had begged him not to, and he had wanted to kick the wall in frustration. Instead, he'd gone back to the accounts: hay, corn, feed stocks. This was a good farm. There was no reason why Dubose couldn't make a good happy living here, a good happy life. None at all.

Polly tossed and turned half the night, then finally gave up around three and got up and started kneading and twisting fresh dough, as usual the only thing that could calm her down. She wanted to call Huckle, but what would happen? Another fight?

He'd made his position very clear. She prodded, as she kneaded, at her deepest, darkest fear: that he was happier in America than he was at home with her. She couldn't help feeling this way. She knew he was working hard, but even so. Life had, she fondly imagined, to be easier there.

They didn't have any of the comforts of the modern world in Polbearne, not really. One motorbike, one tatty old falling-down lighthouse in desperate need of care and attention; no Wi-Fi or theater or culture or even half-decent television reception; one half of a career that earned pennies and finished at eleven o'clock every morning . . .

She tried not to let her tears plop into the dough. Even Rob Harrison, the very early-morning DJ, couldn't perk her up. She loved Huckle, loved him to bits, but she also loved her job, she loved Mount Polbearne, her life was here: everything she'd made herself, everything she'd built up from nothing. And she was accepted here, finally—well, more or less: this was her home.

Her heart churned as she kneaded the dough, her brain going around and around on a track. It was a great relief when Jayden, bless his heart, did indeed arrive at 5 a.m., which meant she had to dry her tears as quickly as she was able. He did a thorough scrub-down of the kitchen, which helped a lot, while also mentioning excitedly that he'd popped into the post office on the mainland and said he was available, and had spoken to the postman there who'd had the Mount Polbearne route for twenty years, even though it drove him crazy with the lack of street names and the fact that half the surnames were the same, and the many, many hours he'd spent waiting for the tide to turn so he could get his delivery in, and the heaviness of lugging his bag across on his bicycle, which was not at all designed to be ridden on slippery wet cobbles, and he hated that damn island and if it was up to him, the villagers would all have to make their way across to the mainland like normal bloody people if they wanted their mail, it was an absolute bloody scandal and had given him sciatica. Anyway, that was everything he had to say on the subject. So, the postie was coming up for retirement, and Jayden had come away with an application form, which was making him quite excited. He reckoned he could start at Polly's at five, do his rounds and be finished with his two jobs for the day by nine.

"So I'll be getting double bubble AND have my whole day to myself," he said with some satisfaction. "That'll be the life for me. And I'll save up. For the best damn car Mount Polbearne's ever seen."

"Mount Polbearne's only got four cars," Polly pointed out. It really wasn't worth bringing them over from the mainland: there was nowhere to drive to, plus the salt water and sea air ate through the metal in about six months. Plus insurance was utterly insane. So insane, in fact, that Polly was highly suspicious that anybody who had a car was actually insured at all.

"Well, mine will easily be the best car, then, won't it?" said Jayden with unavoidable logic as they carried the half-baked fresh loaves downstairs to fill Nan the Van to the rafters. By now it was pink and golden outside, the heavy clouds of yesterday dispersed; it was going to be the most beautiful day.

"So can Huckle come back now?" Jayden said.

"Oh for God's sake, can everyone stop asking me that?"

Jayden's friendly boyish face crinkled.

"Oh," he said. "That must make you sad."

"Yes, it does," Polly said weakly.

"Can't you just tell him to come back now you've got your super van? And me working for you, and that stunning model girl."

"Selina?"

"Yeah."

"Hang on, I thought Flora was the most beautiful woman you'd ever seen in your life and she'd completely broken your heart."

"Yeah," said Jayden. "But I appreciate . . . well, most ladies really."

"Really?"

"Yeah," said Jayden shyly. "I didn't meet many growing up. Only got brothers, then with the fishing . . . I think you're all lovely. You all smell so nice."

"Uh, all right," said Polly hurriedly.

"Oh, I didn't mean you. You're my boss."

"Oh. Right."

"Anyway, I hope Huckle comes back soon," said Jayden. "I really miss him."

"Thank you, Jayden," said Polly, pushing open the lighthouse door. She only locked it in the summer during the daytime, and that was only after she'd come home once to find a family of wide-eyed holidaymakers in her sitting room, with the father extemporizing, ". . . *and then one day the lighthouse keepers simply vanished without a trace,*" at which she'd had to shoo them out, which had scared the children of the party, who thought she was the lighthouse ghost. Since then she'd had a "Private Property" sign put up at the bottom of the steps, even though a) she thought it looked a bit mean and petty, given that the view really did belong to everyone, and b) it didn't stop people coming up the steps anyway, walking right around the lighthouse and patting her van.

As they reached the van, she got such a shock that she nearly dropped her tray. They both stood and stared at it together. On the closed side—the side facing the sea, away from the lighthouse—scrawled in huge, angry letters was the word 'SLAG.'

"Oh God," said Polly. "Oh my. Oh dear."

Carefully, before she dropped them, she put the loaves on the ground, and her hands flew to her mouth.

Jayden shook his head.

"Who on earth would do that?"

He turned to her.

"There was no one here when I came up. But I didn't see it, it's facing the other way, and it was dark."

"I know," said Polly. "Why would you? Oh God. Oh God, who would . . ."

There was a pause.

"Malcolm," said Polly and Jayden at the same time.

"He must have found out how well the van is doing," said Polly. She'd gone completely white.

"And that you've given me a job," said Jayden.

Polly shook her head. The word was so abrasive, so shocking and nasty.

Jayden ran back into the lighthouse and re-emerged with some cleaning products and a brush, but it was no use, they couldn't get it off. It was properly done with spray paint. The entire van would need to be resprayed.

"I'm going to kill him," said Jayden.

"What's happening to our town?" said Polly. "It was always so happy here. And now it's shouting and spray paint and graffiti and just awful things."

"Are you going to tell Huckle?"

Polly thought of everything she hadn't told Huckle—the harassment, the shouting—for fear of him getting cross and being unable to do anything from so far away and wanting her just to leave. She shook her head.

"He'll be too annoyed," she said. She sniffed heavily.

"Thank God you're here," she said to Jayden, who frowned.

"I think I might have made things worse," he said. "I think it might be because of me and the bakery thing. Tipped him over the edge."

"I'm not a slag, though," said Polly. "Not that that makes any difference."

Jayden went back toward the lighthouse again.

"Do you have any old sheets?"

"Um," said Polly. "Only one." It was the one she used to line Neil's box when it was cold in the wintertime.

"Can we use it?" said Jayden. "You need to cover this up, otherwise people will point and laugh and say things."

"Thanks, Jayden," said Polly. "Uh, yeah. It's in the cupboard to the right of the fourth stairway."

"Fourth, huh?" said Jayden. "Seriously, I don't know how you can live here."

Those words echoed in Polly's brain. Out at sea, the fishing boats were streaming in and the waves glowed pink and gold in the early-morning sun. It was as beautiful a place as could be imagined, the chill of the dawn being burnt off by the rising sun, as gently as the bread rising in its pans, waiting to be turned golden in the heat of the oven; waiting with the promise of the new day to be grabbed and relished. And yet everything inside Polly felt like it was crumbling to dust.

One of the fishing boats puttered over, fearfully close to the rocks.

"Wassat, Polly?" shouted Archie, looking concerned. He pointed at the van. "Who done that?"

Polly shrugged. "The new baker guy, I think."

Archie's face grew dark.

"Right, that's it," he said. "I've had absolutely enough of this. We're boycotting."

"We tried to boycott before," said Kendall, "but we got a bit hungry. Their stuff is horrible, but you know."

"Sssh," said Archie. "You weren't meant to say."

"That's okay," said Polly. "I don't mind, really. You can't come out across the causeway every time you need a sandwich."

"We will now," said Archie. "And we'll tell everyone else as well."

"And we'll set the bakery on fire," said Kendall.

"No, don't do that," said Polly and Archie at once.

"Still, that is a terrible thing," said Archie, shaking his head. "I'm sorry to see it in our town, I really am."

Polly nodded. "Me too."

"It feels like . . . it just feels like so much has gone wrong since last year."

Polly looked at Archie with concern. Every time she had thought he might be getting a little better, grieving a little less, carrying a little less of the weight of the world around with him on the boat, it seemed not to be so. Selina was horribly up and down, but at least she tried. And Polly herself . . . she just felt so stuck.

Jayden came down with the old sheet.

"Ahoy!" he shouted. "Did you see what that prick did to Polly?"

"We're going to burn down the bakery!" said Kendall.

"No we're not!" said Archie again.

"Oh yeah, burn it down," said Jayden. "He totally deserves it."

"Yeah!" said Kendall.

"Maybe just the sheet for now," said Polly. "Thank you. No burning down. I mean it."

Archie nodded.

"We'll come and fix the van," he said. "Just let us get the haul in, and we'll see you in a bit."

Polly and Jayden drove carefully across to the car park and set up their stall with Neil's old sheet hiding the ugly word. They began to serve the usual crowd of customers—more today, in fact, because it was so beautiful outside—and handed out buns and baguettes with alacrity.

Someone cornered Polly saying they made a local cheese and might she be interested in it for sandwiches. She tasted it—it was a gentle creamy blue, completely delicious, and she took their details and promised to consider it.

Jayden disappeared at eight, and Polly waited for Selina to come and help serve, but she didn't appear. Their arrangement was very casual, and it was entirely possible that Selina had taken the opportunity on this beautiful day to sunbathe, so Polly threw herself into serving and cleaning and getting things out of the oven before they burned and giving change and smiling at her regulars, and in general, although she was still shocked and upset by what had happened, she was busy enough to kind of take her mind off it.

Things got slightly better when, sure enough, the little taxi boat turned up with Archie and Sten and Kendall on it, plus a large tin of green paint.

"Sorry, me lover," said Archie. "Green is all we got because of the boat, see." *Trochilus II*, the fishing boat, was a fine sharp green color. "But I tell you, it's the best paint there is. Won't never shift once we put it on."

"I'm slightly worried about that," said Polly, who had a faint idea that she should really be getting it resprayed in a proper vehicle way, rather than painted with boat paint, but wasn't sure how she was going to pay for that or find the time to fit it in.

In any case, the boys looked so happy and willing to help, she had no choice really but to thank them, feed them with the lovely sugar buns that had somehow come out so light and fresh and fruity and delicious despite her sadness, and let them slap so much paint over the offending graffiti that it felt as if it was weighing down one side of the van.

"There we go," said Archie. "How's that, madam?"

"Thank you kindly," said Polly. "Well, it is a lot better."

In truth, it was very slightly better than a rude word, but quite a lot worse than her lovely original red and white van, but that didn't matter for now. What mattered was that the graffiti was gone. What on earth would happen tonight, Polly had no idea. Would she have to sit in wait for him?

"We're just off to torch the bakery," said young Kendall.

"Seriously, though," said Archie, leaning over, "why don't we come with you when you go to confront him? Or are you going to call Paul out?"

Paul was the duty PC, who was very rarely needed in Polbearne.

Polly hadn't considered doing either of these two things.

"Well, I don't know."

"Otherwise he'll just do it again," said Archie. "We don't mind coming. We're not working tonight anyway."

"Why not?" said Polly. "It's not like you to take a day off."

"Forecast is right grim for later."

"Seriously?"

There wasn't a cloud in the sky. Out on the blue water, white-sailed boats bobbed around as in a child's drawing. It was beautiful; a picture-perfect English seaside day, with the bread sales to prove it.

"Oh, aye. That storm that never broke yesterday, it ain't gone anywhere. I reckon it's just biding its time. Building up more, I would say."

Polly looked at the blue sky.

"I will never understand the weather."

"No one understands it," said Archie. "No one understands it but us fishermen, and nobody ever listens to us."

Polly thought of something and twirled around.

"Ah," she said. "Did we take a picture of the graffiti before we painted over it?"

"Why would you do that?" said Kendall.

"To show the police constable," said Polly.

"Ah," said the boys. Alas, in their excitement at helping, nobody had thought to do that.

"Not to worry," said Polly. "I just really hope this isn't going to happen again."

Archie frowned. "Hoping isn't enough," he said. "You're going to have to confront him, like. Has he been mean to you before?"

Polly nodded and, haltingly, described how Malcolm

had bullied her. The fishermen were shocked. As she served the last of her customers and put up her "Sold Out" sign, they debated among themselves and insisted that she come back to the island with them on the boat to talk to Malcolm—the tide was coming in and the causeway was under water.

"Just a chat," said Archie. "Unless you'd rather we went ourselves."

"Nooo," said Polly. She sighed. She hated confronting things head-on, and that seemed to be about all she was doing at the moment.

Her heart started beating faster as she cashed up the takings—up again, she couldn't help noticing: the tourists were flooding in in force, and she had put the article up in the window of Nan the Van so people could read it for themselves. Even better, the *Western Morning News* had picked it up and were coming to interview the "local success story" themselves, which would definitely help trade. So she should by rights be feeling happy. Instead, of course, she felt anything but. There was a snake in paradise.

It was still a perfect day as she locked up Nan the Van. She glanced worriedly around the car park but it seemed full of totally normal-looking families: tattooed dads, mums admonishing their children not to run toward the sea; people glancing at their watches and the tidal chart; a couple loitering by the van in case it suddenly burst into life again.

She was full of nerves. Normally she would always sit down in a boat, but today, slightly self-consciously, she stood up in the prow.

"What are you doing up there?" said Archie.

"Giving myself courage," said Polly, adjusting her balance. There was a slight swell, more noticeable than the beautiful day would suggest. "I'm pretending I'm Napoleon."

"Oh, right," said Archie. "Well, I thought that, obviously, but I didn't like to say."

"Who's Napoleon?" said Kendall. "Did he burn a lot of stuff?"

Polly stared straight ahead at the shadow of Mount Polbearne looming huge and forbidding against the sky. Normally she saw it as the loveliest and friendliest of places, bathed in freshness and light, but today it appeared as a rocky outcrop with a sinister shadow.

Still, she set her chin toward the horizon as the little boat puttered on, attempting to hold on to her courage, trying to rehearse what she was going to say.

"Just be calm and dignified," said Archie behind her. "Tell him you've got photographs you're turning over to the police."

"Um," said Polly. "Yeah, we should totally have taken those."

"And that you have a witness."

"A witness with a grudge," said Polly.

"I'm an upstanding member of the community," said Jayden. "Although I am a bit deranged by heartbroken grief. Just at the moment, you know."

"And that if he doesn't stop his campaign of harassment and intimidation, he's going to be in serious trouble."

"And THEN we're going to burn his shop down!" piped up Kendall.

They moored up opposite the Little Beach Street Bakery. It needed its paintwork touched up, Polly noticed sadly. Her own name, of course, had been painted out already, but the salt tides were harsh on the cornices, and the gray was streaking and fading. The windows were dirty, and a few dusty Empire biscuits were laid out here and there. To Polly's fury, "as mentioned in the *Bugle on Sunday*" was taped in the window with peeling sellotape.

She could cry to see what had happened to her once beloved little bakery. There were lots of cheery people walking up and down the winding cobbled streets, eating ice creams from Muriel's, fish and chips from Andy's—his beer garden was absolutely full to the brim of people enjoying the fabulous weather. Over the other side of the rocks, the beach was teeming with children picking hermit crabs out of rock pools with shrimping nets, and teenage girls giggling and fiddling with their signal-less phones and pulling down the sides of their fifties-style bikinis. Picnics were unpacked, including several of her own loaves; suncream was slathered on unimpressed toddlers; waves were run into with shrieks, then equally quickly reversed out of.

But the Little Beach Street Bakery was completely deserted.

Archie looked at her.

"Do you want us to come in with you?"

"No," said Polly, more bravely than she felt. "But could you hang about outside? Just in case he starts throwing rock-hard buns at me?"

The fishermen nodded.

"You've done a lot for us," said Jayden softly, behind her. "You can do this. We're here for you."

"With matches," added Kendall.

Polly nodded and stepped out of the boat. In a town absolutely thronged with people, she couldn't have felt more alone.

"Okay," she said. "Let's do this."

Chapter Twenty-one

She creaked open the door of the Little Beach Street Bakery; its hinges needed oiling, she thought. She left the door slightly open, then realized she was expecting Neil to hop in behind her. The fact that he didn't made her want to sob, but she managed to restrain herself.

Flora was slouching behind a very tired display of sliced white bread and a few hard-looking buns. There were more of the cheap and cheerful Empire biscuits—Polly had nothing against Empire biscuits per se, but these were wrapped in plastic and had clearly been bought in a batch simply because they had a long shelf life. The rest of the shelves were empty. It made her so sad to see it.

Flora stiffened awkwardly, straightening up her long body so you could see it for the model shape it was.

"Uh, hello, Miss Waterford."

Polly did her best to smile.

"Sold out already, then?"

"Not really," said Flora.

"Who's minding the old bakery?"

Flora shrugged. "Malc says it's more profitable to . . . uh . . . rashunalise," she said, going pink.

"Really," said Polly. It gave her absolutely no satisfaction at all to see the business being run into the ground, and she didn't feel in the least bit guilty either. You gave people rubbish or a good alternative; they'd hopefully go for the good alternative and it was nothing to be ashamed of.

"So is he around?" she asked, feeling her voice getting tight in her throat. "I need a word with him."

For a moment she hoped he might not be there, then she remembered seeing that loathsome BMW in the car park. Anyway, putting this off wasn't in the least bit helpful to anyone.

Flora shrugged again. "Reckon."

She leaned over and lowered her voice.

"You know, I thought he was different, but he's just the same as all the others."

Polly bit her tongue at that as Flora disappeared into the now idle kitchen.

"Malc! Miss Waterford's here to see you."

There was some muffled swearing. Flora re-emerged.

"He says you'll need to wait," she said, embarrassed. "Sorry."

"That's fine," said Polly. "I've sold all *my* stock."

As she stood waiting, she noticed that there was a musty, unpleasant smell in the air, a little sour. She wondered if they'd remembered to throw away her lovely yeast culture in the fridge before it took over everything.

She suspected not. That would be the smell. They were in for one hell of a shock next time they opened that fridge.

Eventually, making a big show of doing up his shirt buttons, as if he'd been in the kitchen completely naked—which he might have been; Polly would no longer put anything past him—Malcolm emerged looking impatiently at his watch.

Polly was completely enraged by this. If he had put some genuine time and effort into this place instead of wasting it on a campaign of ongoing harassment against her, then the bakery—her bakery, she couldn't help but feel—would still be a bustling, happy, going concern, full of customers and staff and children and puffins, rather than this yeasty morgue.

"Help you?" he asked sourly.

"Yes," said Polly. "I'm here to tell you that your little campaign stops now. NOW."

"What campaign?"

"The shouting, the bullying and the you-know-what," said Polly, her voice trembling. "Have you heard of hate speech? Apparently the police take it very seriously these days."

"Eh?" said Malcolm.

"You heard," said Polly. "Not to mention destruction of property—my property. Not to mention defacement and graffiti and general YOU BEING DISGUSTING."

She couldn't help it, she was shouting.

"Now you wait a minute," shouted Malcolm straight back, going brick red in the face. "It's a free country last time I looked and I can do whatever the hell I damn well please without asking you, you bird lover. And this is NOT your property, you fantasist, we've told you a million times."

"Well, you stay away from what's mine!" said Polly. "And if you lay a finger on her . . ."

"Her?" sneered Malcolm. "Who the hell do you mean? Flora likes it, don't you, darling?"

"Um," said Flora, staring at the floor.

"Not *her*. My van! Nan the Van!" shouted Polly at the top of her lungs. "Stay away from her!"

"What about your blooming van?"

"Stay away from it!"

"Come on, love, that's just friendly banter!"

"It fricking isn't!"

There was a clang as the door opened and in walked a very sleepy-looking Selina. She smelled of booze and she had heavy bags under her eyes.

"Sorry," she said, "but could you stop making all that ruddy noise? Some of us are trying to sleep upstairs."

"Uh, Selina, it's eleven o'clock in the morning," said Polly. "You're just not used to hearing anyone because he's lost all the bloody customers."

Selina stared at Polly as if she didn't recognize her at all. Malcolm was still shouting.

"And it's your bloody fault, you thieving minx!"

Polly backed out.

"I'm not going to get into this," she said. "You come near us again . . . anywhere near, I'm calling the police."

Malcolm shook his head in disbelief.

"Good," he said. "They can cart your old rust bucket away."

The brightness of the day made her blink as she emerged from the dingy shop. A little boy ran into her legs.

"SORRY," he bawled cheerfully.

"Hello there," Polly said sadly, looking down.

"Is that the bread shop?" he asked excitedly.

"Well, kind of," she said, standing aside to let him pass.

"Mummy said I can have cake in the cake shop! She said it's a very famous cake shop."

His mother came up behind her, a cheery-looking sort in a polka-dot skirt and white blouse.

"Well, it used to be," she said, peering at it unoptimistically. "I remember it from last year, it was just amazing."

"Things change," said Polly in a dull voice.

"Don't they."

"Also they have a BIRD in the cake shop!" confided the little boy.

"I don't think he's there any more," mumbled Polly. The boy's face fell.

"Don't worry, Josephus," said his mother, inspecting the dusty window display with a disappointed look. "Shall we just have an ice cream instead?"

"ICE CREAM! ICE CREAM!" shouted the little boy with the strange name, delighted, and skipped off past the bakery and up the hill with his mother. Polly sighed.

Polly sat out on the other side of the harbor wall, tears running down her face. Her place, the place she had defended, that she loved; her home, where she had thought she belonged: it was as if a toad had crept in, a big poisonous wart in the middle of everything.

Selina came by and looked as if she was going to walk straight past. Polly called her over.

"Hey," she said. "I need a friendly face."

Selina looked at her strangely. Polly thought she was being paranoid. Suddenly she felt like the world was against her. It wasn't helpful.

"Oh Selina," she said, sadly.

"What's up?"

Polly shook her head.

"I can't . . . Everything's gone wrong," she said. "Everything."

Selina sniffed and didn't say anything.

"Why are you so hungover?" said Polly.

Selina bit her lip and her face stiffened.

"Sometimes my coping mechanisms run out," she said. She looked at Polly. "Jayden came to the pub with me."

"He seemed all right this morning," said Polly.

"He must still have been drunk, then," said Selina.

Polly rubbed her back.

"It's okay. We've all been there. In fact, next time, call me. I know where Andy keeps the last of Kerensa's stock of drinkable wine."

Selina shrugged Polly's hand away.

"Yeah, whatever," she said, and headed off.

Even though it was only the middle of the afternoon and the sun was still warm, the clouds were massing again: the same heaviness in the air, the odd yellow tinge to everything. Polly wandered back toward the town and caught up with Jayden.

"Everyone is AWFUL today, Jayden," she said.

"Yeah," he said. "I feel sick."

He looked up at the sky.

"That's not a good color," he said. "I'm going to tell the boys not to go out."

"They aren't. Archie's gotten very cautious with the weather. Anyway, what's up with you?"

"I went drinking with Selina," he said.

"Just drinking?"

"Yes," said Jayden, although he flushed pink. "I won't do that again."

"Did you both get mortalled? She's being really weird today."

Jayden didn't say anything.

"Also, if you were drinking all night with Selina, how did you get up at five a.m.?"

"Did I?" said Jayden. "Oh yes. Cor, I didn't even remember that."

"Oh for goodness' sake," said Polly. "I am going to have a word with Andy. Selling drinks that make you forget things *on an island* is the most lunatic thing I ever heard. You could both have wandered off the causeway and killed yourselves. Right, away with you. Go to bed. Tomorrow we work."

Her face turned grim. "Malcolm has declared war. And we're going to win it."

Chapter Twenty-two

Polly made up what she reasonably could for the next day, knowing on some level that she had to tell Huckle about the bullying, but not wanting to use emotional blackmail to bring him home, especially given what Clemmie was going through. She sighed. How could someone hate her that much? It was a horrible feeling.

She sat in front of the lighthouse window. The clouds really were the oddest color, a kind of heavy mustard, with a purplish tint. It was an ugly color, like something you'd see in the picture of an alien land, and it made Polly very uneasy. The sun did still burst through the clouds though, and the pleasure boats were all still bobbing about. The fishing boats, on the other hand, were safely moored to the side. Archie would get a good night's sleep tonight.

She dozed off in the chair into an odd dream of

Tarnie swimming in the water; he kept surfacing and calling for Selina, but only Polly was there to hear him. She found herself telling him, no, it's not me you want, it's not me, but he couldn't hear her, just kept reaching out his long brown arms; his hair, longer now, entwined with seaweed; his blue eyes beseeching her, telling her he was confused between the deep and the world; begging her to hear him. She could not hear him. And then he SHOUTED!

She jumped up, startled, as the second gigantic clap of thunder rattled the lighthouse doors; the noise was extraordinary. It must be very close, the storm. Just as she was thinking this, a huge bolt of lightning shot across the sky in front of her eyes, illuminating the purple sea. The clouds were racing now, faster and faster; it was not yet nighttime, but it was as dark as night. The waves were moving in jagged, fearsome points, this way and that, the dips between them growing deeper and deeper. Somewhere in the lighthouse there was another huge bang. She jumped in alarm—she had left one of the windows open (she always did, in case Neil came home, even if it did occasionally soak her bathroom floor)—and started downstairs, slightly anxious, with the strange clammy foreboding that comes from waking from a deep sleep and a bad dream, to close it.

As she did so, there was another bolt of lightning, an extraordinary clap of thunder, and all the lights in the lighthouse went out.

Trapped in the dark of the circular stairway, Polly swore and hung close to the wall till she could feel her way down. Sure enough, it was the downstairs bathroom window that was open. She moved over carefully, shut the window and peered out.

This side of the lighthouse looked toward the town. But now there was no town to see: all the electricity had been knocked out. Thank God the lighthouse lamp had its own separate back-up generator that kept its beam rolling around the darkened rock of Mount Polbearne.

The little cottages looked as if they were huddling together, turning their eyes away from the onslaught of the storm, trying desperately to escape attention. The cracking noise in the sky was ear-splitting. From the window Polly saw the rain fling itself furiously against the rocks—then realized it was no longer rain, but great big hailstones, sweeping in and hurling themselves crazily against anything they could find.

"Oh lord," said Polly out loud, suddenly frightened. She heard, somewhere, the tinkle of glass—was it upstairs? Had a particularly large hailstone hit a window somewhere? There was another tinkle, and another. Polly suddenly found herself gulping a little, fearful. She wished more than ever that someone else were here; she desperately missed Huckle's large, comforting presence.

She found herself worrying about old Mrs. Brodie and Mrs. Carter up in those badly insulated cottages right at the very top of the town. Mind you, they and their families had been living through storms without electricity for generations, she supposed. It was unlikely that this would bother them much; they'd probably be miles better off than she was, living ludicrously exposed like this. For a start they wouldn't be crashing around trying to find the last remnants of those tea lights Huckle had lit for her the night he'd built the bath. She managed to find a long book of matches and light a couple of candles. It was reassuring to have some illumination, however feeble, until she caught sight of a terrifying witchy apparition appearing out of nowhere in the cloudy bathroom mirror, and screamed, the sound vanishing into the howling wind, crashing hail and another clap of thunder.

Bollocks, said Polly to herself. Bollocks bollocks bollocks. She realized she was shaking and tried telling herself not to be so silly. It was a storm. She lived on a rocky outcrop in the middle of the sea. Storms were in essence what happened.

She was suddenly so grateful for Archie's caution and wisdom. If the fleet had been out on the waves tonight, it would have been unbearable for everyone. Thank God they were all safe.

Sleep, though—as the lighthouse creaked, the tower pushing this way and that in the wind—would surely be impossible.

Some nights Polly could sleep through a storm if she was tired enough; she would feel warm and cozy in her bed, safe under the blankets. But tonight was nothing like that at all. This was torn from a different world, and she felt for her funny old home, worrying about the harbor wall and the old church at the top of the island losing chunks here and there, falling further into disrepair. It was a struggle to persuade the local council to come and empty the bins, never mind invest in a crumbling infrastructure that was falling into the sea slowly but surely, and the storm would only make things worse.

She took a candle and carefully inched her way up the stairs to the sitting room, where she could see more from the window and had less chance of being literally scared by her own reflection. Even so, her shadow advancing up the tall stairwell walls was like something from a children's story.

"That's it," she grumbled. "I am definitely getting a dog."

Once at the sitting room window, up high, she picked up her mobile, but of course there was nothing, and the ancient landline phone that had been left behind when they moved in, with its big old buttons, wasn't working either.

Had she not been so frightened, the sight from the windows would have been oddly thrilling. Under the ripping sky, there were tiny pinpoints of light here and there, scattered about on the island: candles in windows; one or two bobbing up against the wind, obviously people going to check on their neighbors; here and there a brighter torch. It was, bar the sweep of the lighthouse every twenty seconds, very much how it must have been a hundred years ago, thought Polly. Two hundred. More.

She gazed out, the noise still crashing in her ears even though the sitting room windows were closed, hypnotized, entranced by the sense of looking back into a dark world where the only light was fire, where you were indeed an island, reliant on everyone around you to get by: not the council, not the government, not ASOS or the Looe supermarket. That this was all there was, all of them in it together.

She glanced at the boats in the harbor; although kept apart by tires to stop them bumping into each other too aggressively, they were still jostling. The waves were shooting high above the harbor walls. She remembered how some nights the water would hit the windows of the flat. This was definitely one of those nights: the tide was as high as any she could remember. It was beyond wild: not a night to be out in, not at all.

She stared at the tiny candlelit village: occasionally a shadow passing here and there; a dark figure, moving quickly. Nobody was asleep tonight. She thought of all the people of Polbearne past, their names repeated so often in the graveyard above the town: the Brodies, the Tarnsforths, the Manses: all the lives—hard, dangerous lives, when things were tougher than they were now—that had gone on here, in unheated homes, dependent on a good wind and a good catch, or worse, bounty washed up from the sea.

It was this that made her love Mount Polbearne: the sense that its beauty was borrowed, temporary; that it had a hard edge too: the work and the pain that underpinned what it had always taken to live here. It had never been a home for the rich.

Until now, she supposed, with the weekenders and their second homes, and their nice fish restaurant and their loud, unabashed voices. But really, Mount Polbearne belonged to its people, the people who'd been raised here and had families here, and who had stayed through the bad times and the good.

Polly was lost in her reverie when she slowly began to realize something, then jumped up in horror. The town was dark, the world was dark; only the flashing of the lightning forking the sky illuminated them. The lighthouse had gone out.

Chapter Twenty-three

"What if the lighthouse goes out?" she had asked her solicitor, who was, she remembered, the absolute cheapest one they could find at the time. He had looked a bit uncomfortable and said, "Well, you ring the coastguard," and Huckle had sniggered and said, "Polly, just take a really big torch up there and whizz around and around," and Polly had said, "That's not very funny, it could be dangerous," and Lance, the young estate agent, had said he couldn't remember ever hearing of the lighthouse going out, and then he had paused and said, well, you know, except in the daytime, obviously. Huckle had giggled again and Polly had accused him of not taking this seriously and he had given her a big kiss on the cheek and said, "May I remind you, madam, that you are the one buying a four-story house with one room per floor and a big electric hat, which is just about the least serious thing I have ever heard of," and the solicitor had rather peevishly looked at his watch and said, "Is this bird normally allowed to walk over important paperwork?" and that had kind of been the end of that conversation.

There had been a storm before. A terrible storm that had rocked Mount Polbearne, that had destroyed half of its fishing fleet and taken one of its best men. They were only just recovering. That storm, Polly had slept through; had not realized what was happening, how serious and awful things could be.

This time, she did. And this time, she was right at the heart of it.

Now Polly deeply regretted her glibness and foolishness; she had to call the coastguard, but all the lines were down and all the mobile phones knocked out. This was a freak storm—it had come from nowhere—but the fact remained that she didn't have any way of getting in touch with someone who could make things better.

Surely they'd notice, she thought. Surely people would notice there was no lighthouse. They'd send someone straight away. It would be obvious.

Although how would they get here? The causeway was of course completely impassable, and how on earth you'd launch a boat in this . . . Nobody would, she thought, apart from the RNLI. Nobody would ever be out in a boat in this; it would be completely crazy.

She pulled a blanket around her shoulders, for the night was very chilly, and went back down to the bathroom.

Thank God for Ikea, Polly thought. It was . . . well, it was unutterably useless, but it was better than nothing.

Okay, better than absolutely nothing. She had eighty-five tea lights, more or less. She gathered them up in a pillowcase and took them upstairs, all the way to the very top, to the door that led to the outside of the lighthouse.

So. The mains electricity had failed, and the back-up generator too. This was the full extent of her technical knowledge on the subject. Huckle would have known what to do. He would have kick-started it like his bloody motorbike, it would be easy for him. But she didn't have a clue.

And thank God, she'd forgotten, but here it was: a vast old torch, hanging off the nail next to the key. She checked: it worked fine. She breathed a huge sigh of relief, then, with some trepidation, unlocked the door leading onto the walkway steps.

At first, she thought she hadn't managed to unlock the door at all, that it was jammed: the wind was pressed against it so hard, she couldn't open it. The storm showed absolutely no signs of subsiding. The hail had stopped, but in its place was a heavy, solid rain that drenched her as soon as she managed to finally force the door open. It banged hard against the metal stairwell, and she took a step out, carefully, onto the walkway.

The breath was stolen from her lungs; she couldn't breathe. The water poured down on her. The lightning crackled and buzzed all the way across the sky, now on this side, now the other, racking up the pounding waves. The thunder felt as if it was directly above her head, as if someone were throwing wardrobes across the sky. She clung to the metal balustrade, convinced that at any moment she would slip and tumble down down down the side of the lighthouse and land in a crumpled heap at the bottom. Perhaps, she thought, they would bury her in Nan the Van. She choked back a sob and tried to stop her hands from shaking, but she was utterly frozen with nerves. It took every ounce of grit and courage she had not to turn and step back into the shelter of the lighthouse and close the door, and nobody would have blamed her if she'd done exactly that.

But she did not. Whimpering just a little, in a voice that couldn't be heard at all above the storm, she inched forward, tiny bit by tiny bit, to put her hands on the opposite balustrade. The old iron wobbled precariously in the wind so that she thought she was going to catapult straight over the fragile guard rail. She thought, ruefully, of sunnier times, when they had run lithely up and down these stairs as if it were nothing at all. If she got out of this, she told herself, she was going to move to a bungalow. In a desert.

She set one foot on the ladder, then the other. I can do this, she told herself. I can do this. But that was before she put her head above the bulk of the building, into the little gap between the lighthouse tower and the metal scaffold of the light itself, sitting in its own cage high, high up in the air. At once, the wind smacked her in the face; it was as if it were deliberately trying to take her head off. She was utterly blinded by the rain, which fell straight into her open mouth until she was gasping. Her hair was plastered to her head; her clothes were soaked through.

Truthfully, Polly couldn't quite remember how she made it: not just the last few steps on the ladder, but the perilous, slippery walkway around to the lighthouse casing door. Grabbing the balustrades with both hands, she pushed herself on, one foot in front of the other. At one point she nearly lost her footing. Her ankle went under and she howled and swore at the pain, hopping up again, her heart in full panic mode. The torch was swinging from her mouth, her teeth clenched on the end of it, as she could not hold it and balance at the same time. It took everything she had to slowly push herself forward again one more time, and onward.

Finally she reached the plain door at the back of the lighthouse. She had to fumble for the key in the howling wind, trying with all her might not to let go of the torch, sobbing a little from the pain in her ankle, and terrified that she would drop the key through the grating and it would tumble down the lighthouse, lost.

Eventually she managed to still her trembling hands long enough to turn the key. She fell into the lamp room, her heart pounding, and forced the door shut behind her. And then, although it was still loud outside, it felt in that darkened room that everything was still. The roaring in Polly's ears abated to manageable levels. A couple of the smaller panes on the underside of the lighthouse construction had shattered, but the main casing was thick and intact.

But outside, oh lord, what a sight. There were no birds in the air, certainly no moon or stars, just a great boiling vat of clouds and angry water, hurtling through the sky, through the sea, until there was barely any difference between the two. And the noise, oh, the noise was unbearable even inside, because it spoke of fear, and the very real knowledge of what a storm could do to people who didn't live soft and comfortable lives on the mainland.

Polly let her pillowcase full of tea lights drop and turned on her torch, shining the light around the heavy machinery, noting the great bulb no longer rotating in its winch. She found a fuse box, but looking in it couldn't see anything that might help, even when she flicked the switches up and down. Anyway, the entire region's power was out, and this didn't charge the secondary generator, so it was useless anyway.

She swallowed hard and went toward the box that said "Generator" on it. She had never opened it before—legally speaking, this wasn't even her property; it belonged to Trinity House, and she had simply signed over access rights in return for owning the space. She didn't have the faintest clue what to do; she only knew that this was an incredibly rare occurrence.

Sure enough, once she'd found the Allen key that unlocked the panel, she found herself staring at a mass of electrical wiring. There was nothing here she could manage at all. She swore at the panel, which didn't help, but bending down, she did notice something against the wall: a huge, old-fashioned square fog lantern with a large battery inside it.

With trembling fingers she reached out and switched it on, and to her massive relief, it shone out: shone out so strongly, in fact, that it blinded her completely and she had to jump back.

As soon as her eyelids stopped dazzling, she moved forward again to pick it up carefully from behind. Then, pulling her damp blanket a little closer around her shoulders—it was freezing up in the big light tower without the main light on—she moved toward the window and shone the big beam out into the night.

It wasn't much; it hardly penetrated more than twenty meters into the howling dark. But it wasn't about what *she* could see, Polly reasoned. It was about, hopefully, allowing other people to see the lighthouse. Not that anyone could possibly be out there, could they? Not at sea. They *couldn't* be. She toyed with the idea of walking around the room to give the illusion of the light moving, but decided this wasn't necessarily helpful, and she had absolutely no idea how long the battery would last, and how long it would take the emergency services to get here. So instead she stood and shone it out of the window, as close as she could get to the sea. Mount Polbearne was hardly visible from up here, nothing more than ghostly wisps of light through the hazy tumbling rain. Come on, thought Polly. Come on, storm. Blow yourself out. Move on to a place where people will just lose a couple of roof tiles.

There was a sudden screeching noise behind her. Polly jumped up in the air.

"Christ," she said, as it came again: a kind of feedbacky noise. She turned her head to see what the hell had made it. Somewhere on the other side of the room a red light was blinking. She headed toward it. The noise went off again.

Frowning, Polly put the big lamp down on a stool by the window and turned toward the dark room to investigate.

She saw as she came closer that it was a walkie-talkie, and her heart leapt. The outside world! Thank God!

She picked it up and fiddled with various buttons. It had obviously been plugged in and was charged.

"Polly? Polly? Over. Polly? Polly? Over," came a distorted voice.

She pressed the answer button.

"Jayden, is that you?"

There was a long pause.

"Jayden?"

"No." The voice was recognizable now. It was Selina.

"Hey," said Polly. She had forgotten about Selina's strange behavior from earlier. "Are the boys there?"

"No," said Selina again. And indeed, there were fewer lights out in the streets. "They've all gone over to the beach. The RNLI picked them up and they launched from there. All down the coast it's ruinous, apparently. Mount Polbearne is the only place the boats stayed beached."

"Because we know," said Polly, pounding her fist on the old desk unit. "Oh God. We know."

She took a deep breath.

"Can you see me?" she said.

"Only a glimmer," said Selina. "I'm upstairs, though. If I were down at boat level . . . well, I don't know. Is that all the light you have?"

"No," said Polly patiently. "Actually the light is working, I just thought it would be funnier to leave it off."

"What was it like getting up there?" said Selina.

"Grim," said Polly.

There was a pause.

"All the men out there again," said Polly quietly, as they both thought of another storm.

"Archie said there were holidaymakers out there. People fiddling about in boats."

Polly instantly remembered how beautiful the afternoon had been: all those jolly sails bobbing their way to the horizon.

"Oh my God," she said. And she peered out, trying desperately to see through the maelstrom, tilting the light down to try and break through. The storm would pass, it would soon be over, and everything would be all right. All she had to do was keep tilting the light down.

Chapter Twenty-four

Polly felt drowsy, shining the light down and around the waves below. How could the storm be showing no signs of abating? It had roared on and on for two hours now at least. She dreaded to think what the brave boys were doing down along the coast with the RNLI. Although maybe everyone was safely gathered in now.

At least Mount Polbearne had no trees—none could grow in the onslaught of the wind on the hilltops. But on the mainland surely trees would be falling, blocking roads. Tiles would be off roofs; beach huts crushed like matchsticks, or simply lifted into the air. She felt for the beachside cafés and little surfing shacks strung along the hundreds of kilometers of coastline; she wondered about the lovely little kitchen at Reuben's old place and wondered if it could survive. Well, Cornwall had taken a pounding before, and it could take one again, she knew. The railway line would be flooded. Flights would be grounded. At least she wouldn't have to worry that Huckle might suddenly arrive without her having shaved her legs. She used to think that might happen, back before his staying away became normality, rather than a strange occurrence.

She gazed out into the endless night. It felt as if this was the world now: a howling apocalyptic void, not the gentle breezy place she considered home.

Suddenly, her eyes caught something. She blinked, not trusting them. Then she moved closer to the window. Damn this scratchy Perspex: it was fine for a light to shine out of, but not so good for seeing through properly. She stared ahead, then gasped.

Out on the causeway—or rather, where the causeway was when it wasn't buried beneath several meters of turbulent water—something white was waving in the barely discernible light. Polly cursed her underpowered lamp again, and strained her eyes to see. Something . . . something was moving out there. Was it a large piece of flotsam? She hoped so: something that had been torn off a big ship—a tarp or a lifebelt or something insignificant and unimportant.

But then it would not be swinging so wildly in the wind, not like that, to and fro, as if it were still attached—just—to a boom.

Just as she was swearing again, a purple light went off just beside it, like a firework, suddenly and quickly illuminating the area. A flare. Someone had let off a flare.

Then she saw it. It was a dinghy, a little wooden Laser, being pulled and pummeled this way and that by the waves. There were figures on it—Polly could see them now—two figures. One was very small. Oh my God. One of the figures was a child.

They were nowhere near land, certainly not near enough to swim for it, which would be impossible anyway: they would be swept straight onto the rocks, the very rocks the lighthouse was there to warn against.

But what remained of the boat was twisting and rocking from side to side and obviously taking on water more quickly than they could get rid of it. Her head was going down, deeper and deeper, as she came up and just—only just—surfaced over the crest of each new mountainous wave before jetting back down into the valley. It was as if she were trying to navigate a row of office blocks; the waves now were over two stories high.

Polly tried to shine the light toward the dinghy, then ran to the walkie-talkie, which crackled into life.

"I saw it," said Selina immediately. "I saw a light, but I didn't see where. Oh God, Polly, there's nobody here."

"It's over by the causeway."

"Oh God," said Selina again.

If the little boat was tossed onto the causeway in this storm, it would simply shatter into matchsticks. The two people on board would be thrown into the water in their lifejackets. Lifejackets designed to keep them afloat in seawater, not protect them against the pulling, sucking rage of a Force 9 gale.

"Selina," said Polly, trying to keep her voice as calm as possible. "I think I saw a child."

There was a pause before Selina swore viciously.

"I'll try the coastguard again," she said before cutting out abruptly.

Polly paced up and down, feeling helpless. Every time she saw the little dinghy disappear beneath the latest great crashing wave, she would say a silent prayer that it would re-emerge—but each time it did, it would do so a little later, a little lower in the water than before.

That must have been the last flare, for no more went up. It was hard to see the raggedy white sail at all; it was mere flutters, only to be glimpsed in the whorls if you already knew it was there. Nothing was worse, thought Polly, than standing by, desperate to do something but unable to move until you knew the best thing to do. She wanted just to reach out, scoop up the little boat, gather them in; she felt herself sobbing with frustration.

The walkie-talkie crackled at last and Polly grabbed it.

"Are they on their way? We need a helicopter," she rasped. "Get bloody Prince William down here."

"They're all out," said Selina, her voice panicky. "They're all out on calls. Half of bloody Cornwall was out sailing this afternoon apparently, even after the warnings. Well, half of bloody London more like."

"Fuck."

There was a long pause.

"Can you . . ." said Selina.

"It's very . . ." said Polly at the same time. She looked out. The sail fluttered, barely.

"Oh God," said Selina. "Well, I rowed a bit at college."

"I've . . . hmm, not really," said Polly. "But I know where they are."

There was a longer pause.

"Is there nobody there at all? Not even Jayden?"

"Not even Andy," said Selina. "Not even *Malcolm*."

Polly swallowed. Her heart was beating fast.

"We have to try," she said finally.

"I thought you were going to say that."

"I'll bring the big lantern."

"I'll write a will," said Selina.

Chapter Twenty-five

The climb back down didn't seem quite so perilous, now that Polly had something else to be worried about. The high winds still buffeted her, and she still got facefuls of rain flung at her, but at least this time she was expecting it. She was careful on the wobbly balustrades, and she put out the big lantern to conserve the batteries until they were really needed; surely she could pick her way across the rocks by instinct alone.

Even though she was in a frenzy of rushing, she did stop at the downstairs coat cupboard for two things: Huckle's huge, bright yellow oilskin with matching sou'wester that he used for fishing; and a wetsuit Reuben had bought her for her birthday when she'd mentioned wanting to learn to surf then never got around to it. He'd also bought her a top-of-the-range surfboard and various other bits and pieces, but she hadn't seen them for a long time and assumed they'd been sold off with the house. But the wetsuit was still here.

Getting into it—in a sweaty panic, tearing off her wet things and trying to squeeze into it—was torture, seconds flashing past as she writhed to pull it up, thinking all the while of the little figures out on the water. It was like being caught in a dream, but she focused on what she knew to be real: that outside it was incredibly cold, with very high winds and terrible seas, and she couldn't possibly help anyone else if she couldn't help herself.

Finally she had it on. It was incredibly uncomfortable, but she threw on the little booties too, and the oilskin. She reflected for a millisecond that she must look completely insane, then reminded herself that it didn't matter. She grabbed the second wetsuit—Huckle's—and the lantern, and tore out of the lighthouse, the door banging hard against the side then swinging back to slam into place.

Somehow down here at ground level it wasn't quite as bad, even though she was walking directly into the wind. Lightning cracked and showed her the steps leading down, and she felt her way carefully, trying to find the right balance between haste and safety. The waves were making a mockery of the harbor wall; they simply skidded over the top as if it weren't there. And beyond it, of course, was blackness. Polly turned her head to see the dim shape of the lighthouse disappear behind her. There was, it seemed to her, no eerier sight than a lighthouse marooned in the dark.

She passed the clattering fishing boats, making their own jarring cry of alarm, bouncing and hopping against each other. She checked the moorings as she ran lightly past, but they seemed fast.

Selina was waiting anxiously by the water taxi. Polly charged up and threw the spare wetsuit at her.

"We'll get the lifejackets on in the boat."

"Have you got the light?"

Polly made sure it was pointing out to sea before she turned it on. The strong beam made much more headway across the waves than it had done shining down feebly from the lighthouse. Just beyond its reach she could make out some snatches of white, and what might have been the orange of a lifebelt.

"There it is," she said.

They agreed that Selina would do most of the rowing. Polly would steer. The two women looked at one another, both pale.

"We can do this," said Polly. Her teeth were chattering. Selina nodded, her chin taut. She leaped into the boat as Polly held it.

Polly had been steeling herself for the onslaught, but even so the pressure and the low temperature of the deluge took her by surprise, and she gasped as the torrent of salt water unleashed itself on her. She started to bail immediately.

Selina was incredibly strong. The churning water would have been far too much for the little engine, and they set forth against the waves with sheer force alone, Selina grunting and pulling on the oars with all her might. Polly attempted to help, but she needed to steer to make sure the sea didn't carry them away.

"Left!" she shouted. "Bear left! I mean port! I mean . . . No. I do mean port. It has the same number of letters as left. PORT!"

"Left is fine!" screamed back Selina.

Standing up, Polly took the brunt of every smashing wave as they plowed on, and for the first time she truly understood what Tarnie had once told her: that it was possible to drown at sea without ever going beneath the surface of the water.

She shone the light ahead and around but could not get a fix. Please, please let them not be too late. Let this not be in vain. It couldn't be. It couldn't. There couldn't be nothing left of what had been there: the day trip, the family, the little boat. People didn't just disappear into the sea.

Except if there was one lesson she'd learned from living in this strange and astonishingly beautiful part of the world, it was that they could, and they did. The sea was beautiful, it was life-enhancing, but it did not belong to you. It was not there to be tamed: the ocean was wild, and she would take what was hers.

Selina was growing exhausted as they advanced slowly against the oncoming wind, and Polly was trying to shout encouraging things when she saw it.

"There!" she screamed, stretching up and nearly toppling in. "There!"

There was hardly anything: no sail left, no mast at all, nothing except a stripy cushion, of all things, bobbing up and down in the water.

"Go there!" screamed Polly as it floated away from them. "There!"

"It's just flotsam," said Selina. "Just the wreckage. It's nothing, Polly, just garbage. Let's keep looking."

"No!" said Polly, sure she'd seen something. "No, go on."

Selina sighed, thrashing hard with her oars. Polly reached out for the cushion, perilously far over—and just at the very second she did so, Selina said something.

"WHAT?" It was a struggle to hear anything above the wind.

"I know," said Selina, looking straight at her, out of breath. "Just in case . . . in case . . . I know about you and Tarnie."

Polly shook her head, spraying water around her.

"Jayden told me, last night, when we got drunk. Then I went and did that to your van. I'm sorry."

"You did what?" Polly turned back to the sea, her heart pounding. "You wrote on Nan the Van?"

Finding the cushion as it bobbed up and down in the waves was tricky, but Polly trained her light on it, and as she finally caught it in the beam, she saw underneath it a flash of orange, and a glimpse of something that could only be hair.

"THERE!"

Newly invigorated, Selina took off through the dense rain, the waves battering them again and again. Polly's throat was raw with salt water, the inside of her nose felt scoured; her eyes stung and she could hardly keep them open.

"THERE!"

They were drawing closer now and a final burst of adrenaline from Selina managed it. Polly leaned over the prow, and Selina held on to the back of her oilskin, absurdly too big, with her teeth, while continuing to row for their lives.

"Seriously, you're telling me NOW?"

Selina couldn't speak with the oilskin in her teeth, but muttered something that sounded like "Sorry about the van."

The large cushion hit the front of the boat. Underneath it, fingers clinging, white and unfeeling, to the zipped end was a man, his nose and mouth barely above the water. Hanging on around his neck, eyes closed, so that Polly was at first gripped by a terrible fear, was a small boy.

The man was so exhausted he didn't see them, didn't acknowledge their presence even when Polly shone the light full at him, then away again, not wanting to blind him.

"Get the boy first," said Selina.

Polly had to pull hard to get the semi-conscious child to untether his grip. The man didn't even notice. Together they pulled the boy into the boat, then unzipped the waterproof safety bag with the silver blankets, and wrapped the little fellow up tight. Selina checked him for vital signs.

"He's breathing," she said. "But we'd better hurry."

Polly made several attempts to prize the man from the cushion; he would not, or could not, let go. Finally she stood up and shucked off her oilskin, then put her lifejacket back on over the wetsuit.

"I promise I didn't know he was married, Selina. I promise."

Then she turned around and dived into the formidable sea.

Polly fought panic in the rise and noise of the waves, managed to cling on to herself, let her life jacket bring her up. She grabbed the man from behind, and, with a strength she had absolutely not known she possessed, heaved him up, with a wave, to break over the boat. Selina grabbed him, letting him drop gracelessly into the bottom of the boat like a sack of potatoes.

"I HATE THE SEA!" Selina was yelling. Then her

eyes widened as she saw something coming up behind them. "POLLLLLY!!!!!"

Polly scrambled into the boat just as a particularly huge wave picked it up as if it were a surfboard and sent it plunging straight toward the coastline.

"PORT! LEFT! PORT! LEFT!" screamed Selina, hand on the tiller, desperately trying to steer a course between the rocks. Polly scrambled up, drenched, and held the light up, but it was unimportant now. Selina could not control the boat, and they were being pushed along so quickly by the force of the water that everything now would be down to luck.

Polly made the mistake of glancing behind her into the dark. At first, and oddly, it was as if there were a thick black curtain appearing behind her, or a vast gaping maw; something, at any rate, so unnatural, so unspeakable, that her mouth fell open.

Then she realized what it was: a great wall of water, a huge wave rising from the deep.

Selina had dropped the oars. The two women moved together, clutching hands, trying somehow to steady themselves. They braced their feet, either side of the bodies at the bottom of the boat, trying their best to hold on to them, keep them safe.

For a second, the wall of water was like a windbreak: it protected them from the storm and the noise, and for an instant everything went eerily quiet. Then, BOOM!

It was like being shot out of a gun. An unimaginable force, huge and all-encompassing, grabbed the little boat and simply threw it toward the shore. All was chaos and Polly found a terrible scream coming out of her mouth. They were at an absurd forty-five-degree angle, falling off a wall of water, like in a cartoon, thought Polly.

Time slowed down. Everything slowed down: the

noise and the shouting; the water; the grabbing hands everywhere. Polly lost her grip on Selina. Everything seemed to fade away, leaving her feeling all alone and, oddly, quite calm.

She found herself hoping it would be quick, that her brains would be dashed out and she would know nothing about it. Then, suddenly, she was thinking about Huckle, and how happy they had been. The first time they had made love, in that golden room the color of honey; lying on the sand drinking champagne at Reuben's wedding; the time he had handed her his umbrella in the rain and they had run across the dunes; the ridiculous attempt he had made to lift her across the threshold of the light-house and all the way up its 178 stairs, which had ended in utter failure and hysterical laughter. She thought of her family, of course, her life. But what she clung to, what she thought of most vividly, was the straw-haired man with the slightly wonky nose and the golden chest and the easy laugh and the slow way of talking; and a simple drop of honey, trenchant and sweet, rolled on his strong hand, given to her to lick, from one of his hives, in a garden heavy with buzzing and flowers and the soft warmth of a beautiful early spring morning . . .

CRASH!

The noise knocked her back to reality, and she found herself thrown up and out of the water, fleeing with it; the sky, suddenly, briefly, parting above her head, one hopeful star emerging, catching her eye, as she wondered at it; then SPLASH, she was in the freezing, roiling water, completely engulfed, and the waves were sucking her out, sucking her out to sea, then CRASH, she was being thrown onto the shore again, tossed like an old shoe on the waves. She felt herself being sucked out again, a deep pull underneath her, and something in her shouted no! and she pushed frantically and scrambled and scrabbled her way back with her feet; felt shingle below them, dug in, threw her hands down onto the small stones, and pushed herself forward again and again. This time she would not let the sea take her; it would not take her, it would not take anyone close to her, not ever again, and now inside her she felt warm for the first time, as if some kind of flame had been lit; a determined flame, pushing her ahead, and on up the rocky outcrop between the harbor wall and the causeway. She scrambled up higher, out of the waves' reach, then turned around to see what the ocean had wrought.

Thank God, there was Selina, choking, coughing, but already pulling herself up; there was the man, and the small shape of the boy still in the blanket.

And now, above them, were dozens of villagers, hands coming down to help, pulling them up and wrapping them in blankets and giving them hot mugs of tea; and voices chattering and asking were they all right, were they all right? And were they all there?

Chapter Twenty-six

Polly was hauled up over the wall, her teeth still chattering. All her strength—the strength that had pulled the child into the boat, that had helped her bail, that had dragged her out of the sea's grasp when they had crashed ashore—all of it had gone, had deserted her completely, and her legs collapsed in a jelly wobble.

To her extraordinary embarrassment, they had to lift her up, as if she were a ten-ton seal that had washed ashore, and sit her down before she collapsed. Even with the wetsuit on, she was shivering from head to toe.

"You'll have to get out of that," said Muriel, ever practical. Polly nodded. The idea of actually taking off a piece of clothing seemed well beyond her physical capabilities right at this particular moment.

Muriel was the first to say it, but not the last.

"What on earth . . . what on EARTH were you thinking? You're town girls! You're absolutely crazy, you could have killed yourselves. Easily!"

"Are they . . . are they all . . ."

"Everyone's back," said someone. "It's all right, my lover. You've done great."

"But . . . BUT . . ." said Polly. "You're not listening! You're not listening."

She knew where she had seen the yellow curly hair of the little boy, had just realized it, and something snatched at her heart in a panic.

"NO!" she shouted through her chattering teeth. "You have to listen to me! You have to! There's . . . I saw that family. I saw them before. There's a mother. I saw her this morning!"

This morning seemed unimaginably long ago.

"There might be another person!"

Suddenly there were a lot of other people there. The RNLI boat had come back in—with, she gathered later, the crew of a Looe fishing trawler that had foolhardily set out to sea—and now Archie and Kendall had materialized in front of her, Archie shaking his head.

"I can't believe you went out in the taxi boat," he said furiously. "You're not trained! You could have been killed!"

"I'll get trained," said Polly. "But Archie. There were three. There were three. You have to go out again."

Archie's face—his rugged, weary face that had spent the entire year anxious, worried about his new command—his face stiffened and he looked at Polly.

"Are you sure?"

Polly's mind was foggy, but she was sure of one thing: if the mother hadn't gone to sea, she'd have been raising merry hell.

"Yes, I'm sure," she said.

Archie nodded, just once, and turned around.

"Come on, boys," he said to the tired-looking men behind him. "We're back out."

There was not a murmur of dissent; not a complaint. Kendall, Jayden, Sten and the rest fell into line without delay; obeyed their captain without question; and they were gone, back into the wild night.

Then Polly threw up all over the harbor wall.

Another figure came up to the group, gesticulating and pointing. Wearily Polly turned her head in his direction. Oh lord, it was Malcolm. What on earth could he possibly want now?

To her amazement—she hadn't been able to hear what he was saying, the roar of the wind in her ears was still so strong; in fact, she had begun to think it would never leave her—the group began to follow him, even Patrick, who had been working on the limp forms of the little boy and the man. Two strong arms, one on either side, grabbed Polly and dragged her along with them, but she was barely there.

"I have to go," she muttered. "I have to go back. I have to light the lamps. I have to show the light in the lighthouse . . ."

She looked down and was surprised to find her fingers were still holding tight to the lantern. It no longer worked—it had either been bashed or saturated, or the batteries had run out—but it was still there.

"It's okay," said Muriel's soothing voice. "The ladies are taking storm lanterns down there. Don't worry. Don't worry."

And indeed, although the wind was still high and furious, and the rain still squalled, the thunder wasn't quite so frequent and the lightning was more and more of an afterthought as what felt like the entire village traipsed along the harborside.

The Little Beach Street Bakery was lit up by candles and all the torches that could be found. It was also incredibly warm. Malcolm had opened up the unused kitchen at the back and turned on every oven. Polly realized just how freezing she'd been.

Someone scrambled off to make great big vats of tea. It was the single best cup of tea Polly had ever tasted, the single best anything, as she sat in an armchair that someone had brought in, dimly watching as people got busy. Nobody spoke to her; if they went past, they just patted her gently on the head or the arm, making sure she was all right. She was quite happy about this. There would be talking, and police, and recriminations, and explanations, and her mother to calm down, and oh lord, Huckle. But for now she had her tea, plus she was watching, anxiously, for signs of life in the rescued pair.

Nobody knew how long they'd been in the water; Polly, when asked, described how she had seen the figures on the wrecked boat from the lighthouse, and that couldn't have been more than forty minutes, maybe half an hour, earlier, which seemed astonishing to her: surely it had taken hours? Apparently not.

On the other hand, in water this wild and cold, it really didn't take long, particularly in children. Patrick looked worried and was sweating in the all-encompassing warmth of the bakery.

The little boy suddenly coughed and moved his head, then, just as Polly had done, threw up a vast amount of sea water all over the floor.

One of the women shuffled between the little boy and his dad, who was still unconscious, to stop him seeing him.

Patrick sat down at the boy's head.

"Hello," he said. "What's your name?"

"Josephus," said Polly, suddenly remembering. "His name is Josephus."

"Josephus?" said someone doubtfully.

"Yes," said Polly. "That's why I remembered it."

"Josephus?" said Patrick softly.

The little boy opened his eyes dully. He couldn't seem to focus.

"Hello there," said Patrick. The boy blinked.

"Cold," he said.

"I know," said Patrick. "That's why we're getting you nice and warm."

"Where's my mum?"

"Um," said Patrick. "Let's just get you nice and cozy."

"I want my mum."

"Sssh," said Patrick, not knowing what else to say. "We're looking for your mummy."

The boy tried to sit up and was sick again.

"Is this because I was bad?" he said. "Daddy said not to go near the side of the boat. Is it because I went near the side of the boat?"

"Absolutely not," said Patrick, "Absolutely not. Come here."

And he lifted the child, wrapped in his blanket, his limbs still blue with cold, toward the open oven.

"Ow," said Josephus as the blood started to flow back into his nerve endings and bring them back to life. "Ow, that hurts."

"We're going to get you something good to drink," promised Patrick.

"Fanta?" said Josephus.

"No," said Patrick calmly. "Not Fanta."

Muriel brought some very milky tea and handed it over. From the floor there came a groan. The man was stirring too.

"DADDY!" said the boy, seeing him. He tried to get up, but his limbs wouldn't hold him. "DADDY!"

Patrick carried the boy over to his dad. The man moved his head from side to side.

"Wake up, Daddy!" said the boy, his fingers going to the man's eyes.

"No, don't do that," said Patrick, leaning forward, but not before the man had indeed opened his eyes.

"Josephus?" he said. "Is that you, Josephus?"

"DADDY!"

The little boy flung his arms around his father's neck as the man closed his eyes; not, thankfully, lapsing into unconsciousness again, but simply with howling gratitude. He tried to lift his arms to put them around the boy, but couldn't manage.

"Right, you two," said Muriel practically. "Closer to the ovens, please. You're not the only reprobates who need to be brought back to life tonight."

Someone brought in a bottle of whisky.

"None of that," ordered Patrick. "It's not good for blood flow, cuts it down."

"Um," said Muriel. "Actually it's for Polly, Selina and everybody else."

Polly took the bottle. Selina had gone upstairs to

change and had come down looking thin and very young in a sweater that was far too big for her. She glanced at Polly anxiously. Both of them were shaking. Polly got up on wobbly legs and held Selina, then they both sat back down in the big armchair as other people fussed around Josephus and his father. Polly took a huge slug of the whisky. While she actually preferred the taste of sea water—and both made her splutter about the same amount—she enjoyed the sudden heat that spread through her to her toes, and the way her fingers started to gradually uncurl. She leaned against Selina, and they both stared into the flames of the wood-burning stove.

"I can't believe I haven't seen the bugger in a year," said Selina. "It must be a year, right?"

She turned to look at Polly.

"Was it . . . I mean, was it serious?"

Polly shook her head.

"Not at all," she said quietly. "It was just a few times. I was so lonely. I didn't know anyone, Mrs. Manse was really horrible to me, and I was just so alone . . . single for the first time in seven years, in a strange new town and a new place. He was kind to me."

Selina winced a bit at this.

"I think I wasn't being very kind to him at the time," she said. "I can see why he went for you. Nice smiley Polly, 'everyone have a lovely bun.' I bet you never pestered him about moving out of Polbearne, or getting a better job."

"I hardly knew him," said Polly. "Obviously I didn't know him at all."

Selina's face crinkled.

"But why did you make friends with me? I don't understand. Are you sick in the head?"

"No," said Polly. "I wanted to tell you, to apologize. But I didn't know how and it didn't come up and then I was worried about Neil and got a bit distracted. I was a coward. I kind of hoped it wouldn't come up. Which was a stupid thing to think."

"Well, yes," said Selina. "There's about fourteen people on this godforsaken rock."

"And one of them's Jayden," said Polly. "It was Jayden who told me Tarnie was married. I didn't know before that."

"You said," said Selina drily.

"Anyway, as soon as I found out, I stopped seeing him straightaway. So Jayden did me a favor."

"Why did you even look at Tarnie, with a gorgeous hunk like Huckle kicking about? That's what I don't understand," said Selina after a while.

"Well, Huckle wasn't at all interested to begin with," said Polly. "But it wasn't just that. Tarnie was . . . he was lovely, Selina. He was handsome and kind and had the loveliest eyes and he was funny and he looked after his crew and . . ."

Selina didn't make any noise. None at all. Polly supposed later it was like when people laughed or sneezed: some let it all out, some just couldn't.

When Selina cried, she made no sound at all. But it was the first time, the only time, Polly had known her to cry at all.

She cried and cried for what felt like hours while Polly sat there stroking her hair, letting her tears soak her jeans, and they stared into the fire, waiting, waiting for the boys to come back in: hoping against hope.

"Oh God, this woman has to come back," said Selina much later. "Because they leave . . . they leave SUCH a mess behind."

"Sssh," said Polly, looking around. "Sssh."

"He was a good guy, wasn't he?" Selina went on. "I feel like I've been hating him and blaming him all year."

"Did that make it easier?"

"It did yesterday," said Selina. "If I could think of him as some awful prick, well, then maybe I might miss him less."

"It makes perfect sense," said Polly. "But I miss him and I barely knew him. The boys on the boat still miss him so much they can't even see straight. Look at Archie. I don't think he's slept a night through yet. Even Jayden . . . It's like the solid ground beneath their feet melted away when we lost him."

"I just . . . I wanted him cut out, do you understand?" said Selina. "I wanted him cut out of my brain, or my body, like an appendix. I've tried to drink him out, move him out, screw him out. And he won't bloody go." She managed a half-smile.

"That's because you loved him," said Polly.

"You know, when Lucas went for your bird," said Selina, "I was so scared. So scared that I'd lose a friend, that no one would talk to me again, that I'd be hounded out of town. Because I really have nowhere left to go."

"Don't be daft," said Polly. "We need you here; everyone else that's moved in has been a right cock."

They both smiled a bit at this.

"But I didn't realize that I would have to share Tarnie with the whole town."

"You do," said Polly.

"I have to learn to live with his ghost."

They passed the bottle between them again.

"You were living with his ghost anyway," said Polly. "Now you're here, you just have to figure out how to cohabit in a friendly way."

"I'm sorry about your van," said Selina again.

"Oh, yeah," said Polly. She looked around for Malcolm, but when the door opened, it was Archie who stepped into the Little Beach Street Bakery.

Chapter Twenty-seven

The man, whose name was Paul, and the little boy were curled up in front of the fire, piled with blankets. The man wasn't talking, just staring into the fire. The little boy had, thankfully, fallen asleep, wrapped up and cozy, only the blue tip of his nose any indication of his ordeal.

The room fell silent. Archie stepped forward toward the man.

"Excuse me, sir, but is your wife's name Kristen?"

There was a long pause, and everyone in the room fell quiet.

"Um, yes." His voice was a rasping whisper.

The entire room held its breath. Archie nodded.

"We found her."

"Oh my God. Oh my God. Oh my God." Paul leapt

to his feet, seizing Archie's hand and pumping it up and down.

"Coastguard picked her up by helicopter. She had the rescue kit?"

Paul nodded, tears streaming down his face.

"Yes—we were trying to open it, to stay together: I got a flare out, then I was trying to light it and . . ." His voice choked up and he could barely talk. "Then she just . . . she got caught by a rip, she got pulled out farther and farther away, and she had her lifejacket on, and was clinging to the box, and . . ."

"It's got a beacon in it," said Archie. "She must have figured out a way to set it off. Which I have to say is pretty good thinking when you're being pulled out to sea by a rip tide. She was amazing, in fact."

Paul leaned forward, put his head in his hands and started sobbing.

"It was such a beautiful day."

"Did you not look at the shipping forecast?" said Archie.

Paul shook his head.

"No, I thought . . . I mean, I'm an experienced sailor, but I've never seen anything like this."

"It blew up fast," said someone, and there was general muttered agreement.

"You weren't the only ones caught tonight," said Archie. "But you were the damn luckiest, that's for sure."

Paul nodded, tears squeezing out from under his closed lids, as he hugged the little boy close to him. Selina handed him the whisky bottle.

"They don't know when they can get to us," said Archie.

Just as he said that, there was the flip-flip-flip of a

helicopter overhead, its powerful beams illuminating the window of the Little Beach Street Bakery, lighting up its dusty, empty windows.

The medics bustled and made busy with Paul and the little boy. Muriel patted Polly's shoulder, understanding how difficult it was for her, even now, to be back in her old bakery. The faces of the Polbearnites were smiling and happy, making way for the professionals, chatting to each other about the miraculous recovery of the woman who'd gone into the water.

"Do you know what?" said Muriel gently to Polly. "Tonight, everyone was saved. Thanks to you, everyone came home safely. I think Mount Polbearne is finally healing."

Polly swallowed hard. Her ribs suddenly felt sore, and a massive bone-weariness swept over her.

"Do you really think so?"

Muriel nodded. "And I think you should go and get some sleep. There'll be a lot of questions tomorrow. You should get your head down now, while you can."

Jayden stormed into the bakery, head held high, chest puffed out proudly.

"Jayden, I need a word with you," said Polly weakly, but Jayden waved her off. He marched, pink-faced and damp, straight up to Flora, who was standing by the back wall.

"Flora," he said. "I know you're too beautiful to look at. But I don't care. I am a fantastic rescuer and a good baker too, and I want to talk about baking with you and do baking with you and make amazing things with you.

And do other stuff too but we can get to that. I like you absolutely just for you. So. Um."

He slightly ran out of steam. "Would you like to go to the pub?"

"All right," said Flora shyly.

Polly thought Muriel's advice was the best she'd ever heard. Storm or no storm, she'd sleep through this. She got up carefully. Suddenly a medic was standing in front of her.

"You were in the boat?"

"I'm fine," said Polly. "Just tired."

"Well I'm going to check you over in any case. And you'll need to see your own doctor in a few days. Make sure you're not traumatized."

"Traumatized by what?" said Selina. "We're fine. It was brilliant fun actually."

And weirdly, thought Polly, Selina did look fine. Revitalized, as if her crashing experience had given her more energy, not less. There was a sparkle back in her eyes.

The medic ignored her and carried on examining Polly.

"Yup, just as I thought. Bruised ribs. Want to come with us?"

"For some bruised ribs?"

"Some people like going in helicopters."

"Well, that's nice," said Polly. "But no thanks. I'll take some paracetamol if you have it."

The medic quickly and expertly bandaged her up and handed her a packet of aspirin.

"There you go. Couple of those every two hours, you'll be right as rain."

"I know," said Polly in a resigned tone. "We get a lot of rain."

"Polly Waterford?" said a voice. A short, chubby middle-aged man was standing there, with a wide-eyed lad next to him.

"Uh, yeah?" she said, exhausted.

"Hi. We're here to fix your lighthouse. We hitched a lift with the big boys."

"I got to go on a helicopter," said the young lad. "It were amazing. In the storm and everything."

"See?" said the medic.

"Fine," said Polly. Her shoulders were dropping. "Okay, right, be right with you."

The whisky was passed around again, but Polly didn't want any more.

"Can't you just go on your own, mate?" said Jayden, full of newfound swagger. "It won't be locked. Will it, Poll?"

Polly shook her head and waved her hands.

"No, it isn't locked, but I have to come over anyway."

Suddenly the idea of having to climb all those stairs again, back in the cold lighthouse, before she even looked at the damage that must have been done to it, seemed a little overwhelming.

"Oh no you don't," said Selina. "You're staying right here. Upstairs. It's warm and cozy, and there are clean sheets on your old bed. Or there will be in about ten seconds."

"Where are you going to sleep?" said Polly in surprise. Selina smiled.

"I couldn't sleep now for any money. Also, Andy's opening up," she added. "He says nobody's getting any sleep in the storm anyway, so he might as well make some money. You want to come?"

"No," said Polly. "Oh God, I would love to sleep, though."

"Up you go," said Selina. "Don't wait up! I'll sleep on the sofa when I get in."

"Are you sure?"

Selina smiled, and the two women hugged and left, and the other villagers applauded them as they went.

It was the oddest thing, to go back to what had once been her flat, only to find it all different. It smelled different: perfume and body lotion and a whiff of cat litter, although Lucas was nowhere to be seen on such a night.

Exhausted, Polly grabbed a blanket off the sofa and went to the old chair by the window that she used to sit in. It was still very windy and wet outside, but the thunder and lightning had passed on, out to sea. The worst was very definitely over. She looked up. At the top of the lighthouse, the men had already set up torches and were clearly beginning to work. Out on the harbor, the helicopter was taking off, Paul and Josephus safely aboard. It was rather thrilling to see it rise in the air seemingly right in front of her nose. Still no light, of course, in the village, nor on the coast. Now that the helicopter had gone, they were plunged back into gloom. She could hear, though, cheerful noises coming from the pub. They were celebrating. And she should be celebrating too. They had come through the storm. They had saved that little family—goodness, she still felt shaky about that. She knew she would have to sit down and process everything. But for now, in this dark little corner of the world, she felt suddenly overwhelmed by tiredness. There would be no bread tomorrow. Just this once. Just this once . . .

The last thing she remembered as she dozed off was a sudden dazzling halo of light as the lighthouse lamp came back on and swung around to the island, bringing safety once more.

Malcolm walked with his head down slowly past the pub, the windows lit with candles, the noise and the laughter steady and cozy. Flora and Jayden were huddled together, concentrating on something. He wondered what it was. Selina was laughing in the candlelight, her face looking young and carefree. The lighthouse beam illuminated Beach Street once more. They saw him outside, and nodded, but nobody invited him in, and he trudged on.

Archie shucked off his oilskin at the outside door of the cottage. He took off his boots and crept stealthily into the little house at the top end of the town, checking first on the three little ones, pink-faced and oblivious in their bunks, little puffs of sleeping breath on the air. Then he strode over to look at the baby, whose tiny fists were clenched, whose eyes were moving under their lids, the thick lashes reflecting on to the round rosy cheeks, swaddled up cozy and tight in his crib.

At last his heavy tread went to the front bedroom, where his wife, he knew, would be lying unsleeping. He walked straight around to her side of the bed, and she sat up as he took her in his arms.

"I'm back," he said quietly, and she buried her pillow-warmed face in his shoulder and nestled into him.

"I know," she said.

"But . . . I'm really back," he said.

"My love," she said, embracing him tightly, as the lighthouse beam came around again.

Chapter Twenty-eight

Huckle had just negotiated a massively better price for feed lots when the phone in his pocket buzzed. He ignored it: it was a beautiful morning and he had just saved the farm a load of money and was feeling rather good about himself.

Then it buzzed again.

He took it out.

He froze.

"What's up, son?" The shopkeeper's face was concerned.

Huckle shook his head, and all the color drained from his face as he stared at his phone. Now it was pinging and pinging and pinging: *Chaos as huge storms batter southern Cornwall; Widespread floods and power cuts as Mount Polbearne suffers its most bruising storms in 150 years.* The headlines seemed to go on and on. Huckle couldn't scroll through them quickly enough.

"I have to leave," he said, suddenly. "Something has happened."

"Nothing bad, I hope," said the man.

"I don't know," said Huckle. "I just don't know."

Out in the street he called the farm phone before he lost the signal.

"Clemmie?"

"Uh-huh?"

"I'm telling Dubose. I have to go."

"But I don't—"

"We should have told him right away. We shouldn't have waited. I shouldn't have stayed. He needs to know, and he needs to know now, and if this can't make him change his ways, well, I'll help you find a new manager for the farm."

He paused.

"But it can't be me. Not any more."

"But . . ." Her voice sounded so sad.

"Clemmie," said Huckle. "Either he will or he won't, but he's that baby's daddy and he needs to face up to it, and you need to know. I can't stay forever."

"I know."

There was a pause.

"Do you want to email or will I?"

"I'll do it."

"Clemmie, I am so sorry, but you have to. Because I have to go."

Looking out into the hot afternoon sun of Georgia, peach fields stretching out across the flat landscape, it was almost impossible to believe in the extraordinary forces tearing everything apart halfway across the world. He turned his phone on to BBC News. They were showing footage taken on people's phones from far away of apocalyptic scenes in the dark. And this was on the mainland. He couldn't bear to think what it might be like farther out at sea, where it would be even wilder.

Why? Why had he stayed so long? Why hadn't he just let Dubose fix his own messes right from the start? Because of Clemmie, of course. But still.

Then he heard a line that stopped his heart.

"News reaches us that the storm has grown so intense it has even cut off the Mount Polbearne lighthouse. All nearby shipping has been warned to find safe harbor immediately."

Safe harbor, thought Huckle, desperately. Safe harbor.

He couldn't get a flight into the southwest of the UK: all the airports were closed. The nearest he could get was London, leaving in two hours. He took it.

Huckle was not a nervous flyer. He was not, in general, a nervous anything. But he had never known a flight like this. The flight time—eight hours—was cut down to six as they were propelled across the Atlantic by speeding winds. The turbulence threw the plane up and down, bounced it about as if it were nothing. Even the flight attendants looked concerned, and calm as he was, Huckle didn't like an anxious-looking flight attendant. Not, he thought, that he'd have slept anyway. He looked at the little piece of paper he'd taken from Candice's house, tucked away in his wallet, and put it away again frowning.

The plane bumped steadily up and down until there was no one on the flight not covered in coffee. Eventually, weaving its way from side to side, it touched down, and after a stutter, some jumping, and that invariable moment when Huckle thought, hang on, aren't we coming in too fast, finally ground to a halt.

Even here in London, heavy rain was chucking itself against the windows in the light of a very murky gray dawn. It was too early in the morning for the trains to be running, and as he soon saw, they weren't running to the west of the country anyway. Everything was canceled; all the lines were shut.

He ran to the nearest car hire place and asked for a jeep.

"Would you like our additional insurance, sir?" the pretty young girl at the desk asked him.

"Yes," he growled without thinking about it.

The car was sturdy, heavy-duty and, best of all, very high off the ground. Huckle grabbed another coffee and rubbed his eyes, which were gritty with tiredness. Then he hit the road.

Visibility was absolutely dreadful. Great lorries threw up huge piles of spray on the motorway. After such a long period of dry weather, the ground was hard, and the fields Huckle could see as he sped down the road at precisely 71 miles per hour, trying to balance his anxiety to get there with his anxiety not to be pulled over by the police—although it did occur to him that after a Force 9 storm, the police were probably a lot busier elsewhere— were flooded.

As he drew closer to his destination, he began to see the storm's true effects. Trees that had been there for hundreds of years were uprooted, bent over, simply scattered across the wayside. The rain was still constant, but there was no thunder or lightning, just a messy blasted wasteland.

After Dartmoor, he had to get on to the little roads, and here the first real difficulties appeared. Every so often he would see the twinkling yellow lights of the highway patrol, rescuing stranded vehicles or moving tree trunks out of the way. He had the radio playing, and the stern British voice was recommending all travel in the area be avoided unless absolutely necessary. Huckle didn't care. This was absolutely necessary.

He took the hard shoulder when he needed to; skirted to the other side of the road, made the jeep attempt steep and muddy angles. There were almost no other vehicles on the road; those that were were emergency vehicles or army trucks full of young men, obviously drafted to lend a hand. One tried to flag him down, presumably to ask him what the hell he was doing there, but Huckle pretended not to see them, and they carried on. He was just trying to get home.

All the way he was kicking himself for being so stupid. All this time he had thought Polly was being the stubborn one. But of course Polly was just doing what Polly did, in her own quiet, competent way. It was him: he had been the stubborn one, the one who was so absolutely sure that he knew what was best for them, the definite best way for them to work, to get money together.

He had, he thought ruefully, gotten a little caught up in the world of being helpful; of making money for the farm; of believing that they needed nice things, or fancy things. And it wasn't that nice things weren't important; Polly knew that. But they weren't as important as all the other stuff they had.

He thought of Candice and Ron, ruthlessly earning and spending, with serious expressions on their faces, filling their garage with skis and snowmobiles and pool equipment and framing their expensive holiday landmark pictures, as if this was another box ticked in some obscure life competition in which they didn't even know who they were playing against, nor really what the rules were, apart from the one they all ignored, which was that the richest people anyone knew also tended to be among the unhappiest. He thought of Dubose, unable to settle down to the most basic of decent lives: looking after his family, tending the land. Always searching for something else, the next thing, a better thing, the promise.

And, Huckle thought, maneuvering carefully around a tire that had obviously fallen off the back of someone else's jeep and wondering if this was what life would be like after the zombie apocalypse, he'd gotten caught up in it too. He'd gotten sucked back into it again, even though he'd been so pleased to break free from it in the first place; even though he knew, had always known, that that life wasn't for him; knowing that he had tasted actual, proper contentment. Oh God, was he going to lose it now?

He reached the turnoff for Mount Polbearne and tried calling Polly again. Both lines were dead, as they had been ever since his flight landed. And now his signal had gone too. He hadn't seen another car for forty minutes. He told himself to stop being ridiculous; he was being absurdly pessimistic. It would be . . .

He swallowed. He couldn't think about it. He couldn't be too late. He couldn't be. Up to now he'd managed to keep his panic under control, focusing on one thing at a time. His job. His flight. The turbulence. The drive. Compartmentalize. Compartmentalize. Get through it.

He had never ever once allowed himself to think that something might have happened to Polly. Not until this moment.

Huckle was not an introspective man. This had driven Candice crazy—she was always trying to get him to go to therapy with her, just for the experience—but Polly liked it. He was practical. He fixed things. He was careful. He rode the motorbike. If Polly was upset or cross about something, he would listen to her, hear her out, then suggest he make them Spanish omelettes and they could curl up on the sofa and watch something with zombies in it. Most problems, when it came down to it, could pretty much be cured, or at least helped, by curling up on the sofa with an omelette, watching something with zombies in it.

But now, as he put his head down on the steering wheel in front of the dark landscape ahead of him, he tried to fight his imagination, which was galloping away with him. He had an image, so strong, of Polly falling down the stairs in the dark; or going out to help someone and being swept away from the harbor wall—it happened, it did happen in terrible weather, on the news, you saw it; or being underneath a stone that falls off a house, or . . . A million horrible scenarios crossed his mind, and he felt a cold hand grip his heart at the thought of her not being there; of a life without his sweet, funny, kind, hard-working Poll, banging on about her puffin . . .

He shook his head. He couldn't think like this, he couldn't. He had to go on. He had to.

Chapter Twenty-nine

The roads got worse and worse. Just as Huckle wanted to go his fastest, just as he absolutely had to, needed to know, he had to inch along. A shed by the side of the road with its roof off. No livestock to be seen anywhere. A collapsed barn, roof tiles smashed everywhere you looked, hedges obliterated. People were indoors, hiding away, not even assessing the damage yet. Nobody would be going to work today.

Suddenly he was rounding the headland, the first glimpse of Mount Polbearne, just past the railway station. He felt utterly done in, completely exhausted.

The rain, which had been steadily getting lighter, suddenly, as he crested the hill, stopped altogether, and a tentative, weak spot of sunlight appeared from behind the clouds. He couldn't help it: he stopped the car and got out. Mount Polbearne looked as forbidding and daunting as he had ever seen it. But there was something wrong. He looked closely. It was the church at the top; something had happened. The old ruin up there that had never quite gotten fixed. Its shape had changed. Obviously a few more stones had come off in the storm. He shook his head. He couldn't see the lighthouse from this angle. Onward.

Even though it was officially low tide, water was still sloshing over the causeway. It was filthy, filled with the flotsam and jetsam of what had clearly been a very, very grim night. Huckle didn't care. This was why he had rented the goddam jeep.

He put it in a very low gear and slowly, slowly began to advance through the waves. He was so high up, it was impossible to see what he was driving through, and very hard, due to the murkiness of the water, to know where exactly the road was beneath the wheels of his jeep. He was nearly standing up on the pedals, but he could not stop, or the water would submerge him. It was already creeping through the bottom of the door. He swallowed hard. One tiny fault in either direction would see him straight into the deep water. He took his seat belt off and opened his window. Just in case. Just in case.

Slowly, incredibly slowly, he rolled on, straining for a glimpse of the pinky yellow stones beneath the vehicle. A wake opened up behind him, the water rolling here and there as he prayed for the grip of the jeep's tires and tried to gauge where exactly he was with reference to the town's walls.

He said a short prayer. At one point he came too close to the edge of the road, and felt the tires lose purchase. For a second he thought this was it, that it was all over, but his hands automatically jerked the wheel and the car righted itself. Huckle let out a massive pent-up gasp and inadvertently pushed on the accelerator too hard, causing the car to spurt a little through the water and requiring him to pull back on course equally quickly. His pulse rate was going through the roof and he had to force himself to keep to the endless slow and steady pace.

There was one lone figure out and about, he saw, as he eventually approached, very, very gingerly, like a man on a high wire, the little road next to the jetty on Mount Polbearne. It was Patrick the vet, out walking his dog and picking up rubbish, starting on what would be a huge clean-up process. He tipped his hat as Huckle, shaking slightly, his brow damp with sweat, turned into the car park, breathing heavily as he pulled on the handbrake.

"Hello there," said Patrick, as if they were just passing in the street. "Is that one of those car boats, then?"

"No," said Huckle faintly. "No, it's not one of those car boats."

"Hmm," said Patrick. "Well, you sailed it nicely, anyway. You should have been here last night, you can't imagine what it was like. I've never seen anything like it, and I've lived here fifty-eight years."

"I heard," said Huckle, wild-eyed suddenly. "Have you . . . I mean, where's Polly?"

Patrick wrinkled his forehead.

"Do you know," he said, "I can't remember where she went."

He looked around in astonishment as Huckle pushed past him and tore off along the harbor.

"I was going to say," he added, "after the amazing things she did last night. Do you know, I don't think I've had enough sleep. I wish the bakery were open to give me a cup of coffee."

"POLL!"

The door to the lighthouse was lying open, and Huckle charged up the stairs, drenched in sweat. The place was in disarray. Tools were lying about as if they'd been thrown down. He burst into the sitting room. It was a mess: cups and plates lying about. But no Polly. It was as if she'd simply disappeared. Huckle's heart was in his mouth. What had happened here?

"POLLY!"

He charged up and down, but there was no sign of her. He shook his head. Where was she? He noticed the van—it must be Nan the Van, he thought—as he ran back outside. No wonder it had been so cheap; Polly hadn't mentioned it was half painted green with bog-standard paint. He shook his head and raced on past it.

The doors of the Little Beach Street Bakery were open too, but there was no food in any of its windows. Malcolm was standing outside disconsolately. His night of popularity had been just about the best thing that had ever happened to him, and he had been very sad when they had all gone off to the pub, not even inviting him. He looked around with a sigh, only to see a huge, wild-eyed blond man bearing down on him. He had only met Huckle once and didn't remember who he was.

"YOU!" the giant roared. "YOU! Where the fuck is Polly? You took her shop, you took her job, you've made a total balls-up of it by all accounts, and you have bloody ruined her life and . . ."

He ran out of breath.

"Where the fuck is she?"

Huckle knew he shouldn't really be taking his frustration out on Malcolm, but he couldn't help himself.

"Seriously, tell me, you little fat lump!"

Malcolm quivered. Like all bullies, he was a terrific coward, always had been. Plus, Flora had disappeared last night, leaving him to turn off the ovens and tidy up all the pools of water and coats and jackets that were everywhere, which was more work, frankly, than he liked to undertake at any one time. As he had climbed the dark and lonely road to Mrs. Manse's chilly, dank old flat and her creaking bed with its dusty counterpane, he had sworn that that was it, he was done with this bloody place.

And that was before this man started shouting at him in the street.

"Where is she?"

Malcolm wanted to say, how the hell should I know, but all the fight had gone out of him. He was done. Tiredly he jerked his thumb toward the flat above the shop.

"She's up there," he said wearily, just as a great slosh of water overflowed from his clogged-up drain, which Polly had always got Jayden to do after a rainstorm, and cascaded down the back of his one suit.

Huckle stared up at the window of her old flat.

"You're sure?"

Malcolm blinked crossly and was about to say something sarcastic, but Huckle had already dashed past him as if he weren't even there. As he turned away to try and dry himself off, the sun came out.

Chapter Thirty

Polly had absolutely no idea where she was when she woke up, but the sun was dazzling through the window, the light reflecting off the water, as if the storm had been nothing more than a dream. She shook her head. Where was she? What was going on? What was that loud banging on the door?

She sat up, then groaned. Her ribs were on fire; it was agony this morning, far worse than it had been last night. And her head was full, overspilling. She had a quick panic about missing the morning bread before remembering there was no bread that morning; could not be. She jumped up. It must be Selina banging at the door. She must have locked her out last night. Oh goodness, she hadn't meant to. Well, at least she hadn't disturbed the bed.

Polly moved carefully toward the door, rubbing her

face, which was still streaked in salt. Her hair was a mass of untameable frizz, which was going to need some serious work to get it back to normal. Well, she could think about that later.

"Sorry, sorry," she shouted, her voice still cracked and hoarse. "I must have let the snub lock fall . . ."

Her voice trailed off as she opened the door. To her total and utter shock, there, shining golden in the morning light, somehow taller and broader than she remembered, was Huckle.

"Oh my God," she croaked. Then again, "Oh my God."

Huckle looked a total state. He was wearing a stained shirt. His shoes and trousers were soaking wet. His hair was sticking up, his eyes were red and puffy. He was covered in stubble. He was the most beautiful thing she'd ever seen.

Polly felt his heart beating up against hers. He was hurting her ribs, crushing her like that. She couldn't have cared less.

"Jesus," Huckle was saying, over and over again. "Jesus! I can't let you out of my sight for a second!"

He pulled away and noticed her face.

"Okay. A couple of months."

She shook her head and nestled back into him.

"I'm so sorry, I'm sorry. I know you only went for me, for us. I'm sorry I gave you such a hard time about it. I'm sorry I put you through all that."

"Are you kidding?" said Huckle. "I'm such an idiot, Polly. SUCH an idiot. I don't know what I was thinking. Nothing is worth being apart from you. Nothing."

"Not even Nan the Van?"

"Oh yes, I need to speak to you about that," said

Huckle, and Polly rolled her eyes and said all in good time, but first of all, please, could they go home?

Polly ran the big copper bath as full as she could, steam filling the little bathroom, emptying the cistern. She hurled in all the posh smellies, and they shed their clothes and got into the bath together, and gently, carefully, Huckle washed her all over, and exclaimed at her ribs, and shampooed her hair while she told him the whole story from the beginning, and he listened open-mouthed to all of it and told her how brave she'd been. And as she told it, Polly began to feel its burden, the weight of what she'd been through, lift and lessen a bit, although she did cry at the part when they brought the boy in without his mother, and Huckle shushed her and felt privileged to have heard the story for the first time, even though over the next few weeks she'd be made to repeat it absolutely everywhere as the family went to the papers about their amazing rescue. Which was, Patrick later pointed out, the second stupid thing they had done, because of course the papers totally eviscerated them for going out in weather like that, and they got named Britain's worst parents and the entire thing was a massive scandal. Anyway, the papers dug up the picture of Polly looking mad and depressed and staring out to sea and used it loads of times, which was a bit tedious until everything died down and she could stop explaining that actually it was Selina who'd done all the really hard work; she'd just been carrying the light.

Huckle carefully combed out her hair, until they were both warm and clean and comfortable again, then carried her up the stairs and, as gently as he could, showed her how pleased he was to see her, which Polly was unsurprised to find made her feel even better than she had before; as if all her fears and worries had simply been swept away.

And then they slept, both of them, through the sun of the afternoon, until a policeman appeared to write down everything that had happened. They both felt sheepish about letting everyone else clear up the detritus, so after that, they grabbed bin bags in the late-afternoon golden haze and went down to the beach to help pick up the driftwood and the general rubbish. It was impossible to even believe what conditions had been like the previous evening.

Every step they took, people came up to them asking after them both, delighted to see Huckle again, ready to tell him once more what it had been like. Only Polly knew what Huckle himself had been through; how brave he had been too, in more ways than one. As he was regaled with tales that he listened to as politely as he always did—which is to say, very—she would move in close and gently squeeze his hand, and he would squeeze hers back, and they wouldn't have to say anything at all, except every so often Huckle would check his phone and sigh, and Polly would give him a worried look.

Finally, at around 6 p.m., it came. The low ring. Huckle looked at Polly and she looked at him.

"If you have to go back," she'd said, and he'd simply shaken his head and said no, never, and she'd said what about Clemmie, and Huckle had said they'd cross that bridge when they came to it.

They held hands as he answered the phone.

"Hello?"

There was a long pause. Finally, Dubose's voice, so similar to Huckle's, spoke.

"Hey, bro."

There was another long silence. Then Dubose went on.

"I can't . . . Man, I'm going to be a dad."

There was a long chat after that, and amends made, and promises too—which Huckle didn't think would be kept, but Polly maybe did; and extreme protestations of gratitude at how Huckle had turned the farm around, which Huckle absolutely deserved.

"It was the paperwork getting me down, man," said Dubose. "I couldn't get on top of it, I just panicked."

"Mmm," said Huckle. They were on speakerphone.

"Could you . . . say goodbye to that sweet chick? Tell her I didn't mean it."

Polly nodded.

"I will," she lied. She intended never to mention Dubose to Selina ever again.

The rest of Mount Polbearne turned in early that night, but Polly, overwhelmed, and Huckle, jet-lagged, sat on the harbor wall with their fish and chips, kicking their heels, gazing out at the beautiful pink and gold sunset. It was like a different world.

"I wondered," said Huckle. "I wondered, what with the storm and everything . . . I wondered if you would be thinking . . ."

They were watching the seagulls circle overhead, the noisy pests conscious that there were chips in the area. Polly read his mind.

"If Neil would come back? Like he did before?"

She reached for another chip and shook her head.

"No," she said. "No. I've accepted it. I know you thought I never would, but I have. Puffins aren't pets. They aren't meant to live with us. It was hard, but it was the right thing to do."

"Do you really believe that, though?" said Huckle. "Truly?"

Polly nodded. Her eyes were suddenly filled with tears.

"It doesn't mean I didn't love him," she insisted.

"Oh, I know that."

"It's only *because* I loved him . . . really loved him, that I could give him up. Do the right thing."

She sighed, toying with her little wooden fork. "God, it sucks being grown-up sometimes. I'm sorry if I . . . if I took my sadness about Neil out on you. You didn't deserve that. I was just so lonely."

"That's okay," said Huckle. "I was lonely too. Incredibly lonely."

"I know," said Polly. "It's just, every time we spoke, you were . . ."

There was a pause.

"I don't know why they say love means never having to say you're sorry," said Polly suddenly. "I think it means having to say you're sorry A LOT."

Huckle nodded in agreement. Then he turned to her.

"I really love you," he said. He smiled and, suddenly, fingered his pocket.

Polly looked at him.

Suddenly, the bay, which had been completely free of boats—all shipping had been ordered to stay away from the region as a precautionary measure—was split apart by a roaring noise, and the tranquillity of the scene was shattered.

They both stared for a moment, then sat up straight.

"Is that . . ." said Polly.

"Oh my God, it's only the bloody Riva," said Huckle. Reuben's beautiful Italian motorboat had been his pride and joy.

Polly craned her eyes against the sun.

"Who is that?"

"No way."

Resplendent in too-tight red shorts, a vest top with a gold necklace and the ubiquitous bug-shaped Oakley glasses was Reuben, standing up at the front waving like mad; and next to him, wearing a fuchsia-pink dress that billowed in the wind, was Kerensa.

"NO WAY!"

Polly and Huckle jumped up, waving, as Reuben and Kerensa slooshed the boat in with some style and tied her up at the jetty, with Huckle's help.

"What on earth?" said Huckle. "Did you steal this?"

"Nope," said Reuben, grinning broadly.

"Ooh, chips," said Kerensa, helping herself to Polly's. "Hey, what's up?"

"Um, there was a huge storm."

"Oh yeah, I heard about that in the papers. We were in London. Anything happen?"

"Never mind," said Polly, who was suddenly far more interested in what they were up to. "What were you doing in London?"

"Well," said Reuben, puffing out his little chest. "It was brilliant obviously being Kerensa's sex slave . . ."

"It was nice," agreed Kerensa. "But I couldn't take that fricking micro-scooter one second longer. Man, it was a buzz kill."

"So," said Reuben, "I just invented something impossibly brilliant and sold it."

They looked at him. There was a very long pause.

"What is it?" said Polly suspiciously.

"If I could explain it to you, they wouldn't pay me all that money for it, duh," said Reuben. "And I haven't even been to Shanghai yet. You could go to jail for knowing."

"What IS it?" said Polly.

Reuben rolled his eyes.

"Okay, how deep is your understanding of the mathematics of quantum code in lithium inputs? Because I guess we'd start there."

"Okay, never mind," said Polly. "No. All I need to understand at this point is lighthouse maintenance."

"Which you don't even need," said Huckle. "Because I am home and I am staying."

He kissed her on the shoulder.

"Oh yeah, Huckle's home," said Polly, seeing as no one had mentioned it. Kerensa and Reuben just shook their heads.

"What?" said Polly, a touch of doubt in her eyes. They were both looking at him with furious expressions.

"How could it have taken you so long, man?" said Reuben. "Seriously, how could you even go without pipe for all that time?"

"Don't be vulgar," said Kerensa. "But really, Huckle, Reuben's right: how the fuck could you stay away for so long?"

Huckle held up his hands.

"I know, I know. I was an idiot."

"Unbelievable," said Kerensa. "Of course, Polly was fighting them off all over town."

"Of course I WASN'T," said Polly. "Duh."

"Sssh," said Kerensa. "I'm reminding him how

incredibly attractive you are, in case he thinks about heading off again."

"Which I only did in the first place for that bloody van, I should point out."

"Yes, that van you earned the money for two days after you got there," said Kerensa. "Anyway, it doesn't matter now," she went on. "Reuben! Buy my friend a bakery! And I'll put you in sex prison again."

"I would like that," said Reuben. "Okay."

"No!" said Polly. "We've been through this. I don't want you to buy me anything. I want to make it on my own. And I can. Nan the Van and I are doing brilliantly. Well, we're doing okay. We're doing fine."

They all turned to look at the Little Beach Street Bakery. Its facing had taken a real battering in the night, and the paint was peeling off one corner. It looked so sad. Inside, however, two people were moving about. Polly screwed her eyes up.

"Well, bloody hell," she said. "Looks like Jayden's mum is in tonight."

"What do you mean?"

She indicated the two shadowy figures.

"If Jayden's mum is in, Jayden is out . . ."

If you screwed your eyes up, you could just make out, inside the dusty windows of the bakery, Jayden and Flora embracing passionately.

"She's going to miss that tide again," predicted Polly.

"Jayden did an interview for the local news," said Huckle. "I saw them do it. They wanted you and I said I'd ask you. Then I forgot. Sorry."

"Oh God," said Polly. "I couldn't think of anything worse. Thank goodness."

Just then, a forlorn figure walked past them from out

of the back door of the bakery. He was carrying a small case and a petty cash tin. He stopped to look at Jayden and Flora, who didn't even notice him, then carried on past the front door.

It was Malcolm. His face was downcast.

"Hey, numbnuts!" shouted Reuben.

"Stop that, Reuben," said Polly. She couldn't even hate Malcolm now, not after everything that had happened. Now that she had everyone back around her. It didn't seem to matter now, how he had made her feel.

Malcolm had stopped, as if it was totally inevitable that everybody in Polbearne would call him a numbnuts.

"What?"

"How much for your bakery? That you've totally ruined."

Malcolm snuffled. "It's not my bakery," he said. "It's my mum's. She . . . she doesn't want me working there anymore."

"Why not?" said Polly, getting up, concerned. She moved forward. "It wasn't me, Malcolm, I didn't take any of your business. The people that came to me weren't even from here. And I'm sorry I thought you did that to my van. I really am."

"No," said Malcolm. "It wasn't anything to do with you. Although how could you think I would do that to your van? Don't answer that."

"Hmm," said Polly. "So what was it then?"

"I took a little bit of money," said Malcolm. He looked sullen and very much like the child he must once have been. "Just a tiny bit, to get by. Nothing really. Just a bit of petty cash."

He held up the box and his face took on a sly look.

"I'm taking what's left."

"You stole from your own mother?" said Huckle, aghast.

"Just . . ." Malcolm sighed. "I saw this really, really nice trumpet."

Reuben blinked.

"Did you get it?"

"No," said Malcolm. "I was saving up for it. Then Flora wanted me to buy her a stupid mixer, Christ knows what for, and . . . well, it got slightly out of control."

"Oh dear," said Polly. "Oh dear, Malcolm, that was stupid." She shook her head. "Such a waste. It was a lovely little business here. Lovely."

"You can probably have it back if you like," mumbled Malcolm. "All she's done is bend my ear about how much better it did under you and what an idiot I am. That's all I've had off my mum my whole life."

Reuben went up to him.

"How much is this trumpet you want?"

Malcolm sighed. "Six hundred and ninety-nine pounds. I'll never get it now."

Reuben took out his wallet and uncreased a bunch of notes.

"Reuben!" said Polly, shocked at the sight.

"What?" said Reuben. "This is all foreign money anyhow. It just looks like bumwad to me."

He peeled off seven notes and handed them over to Malcolm.

"Now, take this, buy a trumpet and FIND YOUR AWESOME," he commanded.

"Find my what?"

"FIND YOUR AWESOME."

"Awesome?"

"Say it. Be the best trumpet player in the world."

"Say I'm awesome?"

"Say you're awesome. Come on, say it."

"I'm awesome?"

"YOU'RE AWESOME."

"I'm awesome," mumbled Malcolm.

"SHOUT!"

"I'M AWESOME!"

"And again!"

Malcolm moved toward the causeway, heading for the mainland.

"I'M AWESOME!"

"YOU'RE AWESOME!"

"I'M AWESOME!"

"YOU'RE AWESOME!"

"I'm awesome," came fading across the sea.

"Numbnuts," said Reuben.

A couple of months later, Jayden was merrily cleaning behind the oven with the fervor of a man in love when he found something: it was a CD, labelled "Flora."

He went up to the old bakery, where Polly had commanded Flora to do nothing but bake all day, whatever she liked, the more experimental the better. Flora was working on cherry coconut biscuits, with Jayden writing the results down in a little book of recipes. They were an outstanding team. A lank strand of hair had fallen out of her hairnet and was swaying in front of her face. Jayden had learned better than to tell her how beautiful he found it.

Jayden asked her about the CD, and she said she didn't know what it was; Malcolm had given it to her and she'd never bothered to stick it on because she didn't like him very much, and Jayden said did she like him that much and she blushed and said he was all right, which was very much the best compliment Jayden had ever had from a woman under seventy years old, and the fact that it was from the most beautiful girl anyone in Polbearne had ever seen made him happier than he'd have thought possible.

Then they did stick it on, and discovered what it was: it was Malcolm, playing the trumpet. Great big streams of silver notes cascaded out of the speakers: jolly tunes, marching tunes, and sad, melancholy laments that tugged at the soul. It was beautiful.

Chapter Thirty-one

Polly was nowhere to be found in the sitting room when Huckle went looking for her just before bed. Tonight, several weeks on from the storm, the moon was clear, and the stars popped out above them. He had meant to tempt her up onto the gantry again, where the light was once again shining out clean and bright over the town and the rocks, keeping them safe. The workmen had repaired all the broken glass panes, put in a fresh generator that should never fail, and left a full instruction manual. And four storm lanterns.

Instead he found her, of course, in the kitchen. Her sleeves were rolled up and dusty with flour, and she was rolling out cheese croissants for the morning, equally spaced on the big wooden work surface. He watched her for a while, busy, hard at work, totally absorbed, oblivious to his presence.

"Aren't you meant to be wearing a hairnet?" he finally teased gently. She looked up and grinned at him.

"I have VERY CLEAN HAIR. In a ponytail, you will notice. Please don't call environmental health, I've had enough problems."

"Do you really think she'll let you have Nan the Van next to the shop?" asked Huckle, smiling.

"I've been saying it for years: Mount Polbearne needs coffee. Good coffee. And I'm going to do it. Well, Selina's going to do it."

"So you're expanding?"

Polly smiled. "Well, don't you think it will be good?"

"More work for you."

"I like work," said Polly. "Also, we're going to do a lot of honey teas. So you'd better get to work as well, mister."

He was not in the slightest bit worried about this. He came over and kissed Polly lightly on the back of her neck.

"Come to bed," he said.

"Eleven minutes." She smiled at him. "Quicker if you stick all these trays in the dishwasher."

"It's done," he said, helping her clean up, the two of them gently chatting, watching the setting sun through the window.

Later, in bed, just before she came up, he took the crumpled piece of paper out of his wallet one last time and stared at it. It was the advertisement for the engagement ring he had seen, flicking through Candice's expensive magazine in her front room that day; the ring that he had been saving for, had wanted to present to her triumphantly: a rock on a rock, he had planned to say, which sounded better in his head than when he'd tried it out in front of the mirror.

It could wait. They could wait. The diamonds that glinted in the ad: they looked so cold.

But here, with the heat and warmth of the rising bread, the golden evening, the perfect sky going down on a perfect summer's day, when the winding streets of Mount Polbearne had been full of happy children with sandwiches and buckets and spades and ice creams, and cheerful, relaxed parents, and Jayden, taking time after the lunchtime shift to go and fondly polish the new and improved taxi boat Reuben had bought the town, only spoiling it slightly by suggesting the town might show its gratitude by electing him mayor or making him king or something . . . here, all Huckle felt was warmth, in the room, in his heart, in the smile of the strawberry-blond girl with the dab of flour on the tip of her freckly nose, who even now was walking into the room, lighting up the room just by being there.

Epilogue

Polly stared at it. Jayden was crating up the van and didn't see it.

"Huckle!"

Huckle was awake, had gotten up when he smelled one of the many different coffee roasts Polly had been trying out in the kitchen for Nan the Coffee Van. Everyone was caffeinated all the time. He ran down the steps in twos.

"What?"

Polly held it up. It had been lying on the front doorstep.

"What is that?"

"What do you think it is?"

Huckle rubbed his eyes.

"A feather?"

"A feather. Yes."

Polly looked around.

"An oily black feather. Who do we know who has oily black feathers?"

Huckle frowned. He'd thought this was kind of over.

Polly walked down another couple of steps. There was another one.

"Oh Poll, come on, you don't think . . ."

"Who leaves a trail of black feathers?"

"A sinister Yakuza gang," said Huckle. "Come on, I have three stops today, all beauticians, and you know what they're like."

Polly wasn't listening. She'd gone around the far side of the lighthouse, past the little rockery made of shells that some bored keeper had cultivated many decades ago. She vanished from view. There was a long silence. Huckle looked at the sun coming up. It had been the most glorious summer.

"HUCKLE!!!!!!"

Huckle went around to the back of the lighthouse. There was nothing there, just rocks leading down to the other side of the headland, more lapping water.

He gasped.

"No way."

Silhouetted against the pink sky, Polly was bending down and staring, at a distance, but very, very intently, at a small, chubby bird with a yellow band around its foot.

The bird was staring back. Huckle wondered why Polly didn't move forward, then he saw it.

The bird was in a nest.

Not only that, there was another bird there.

Not only THAT . . .

"Bloody hell," he heard Polly say. "Is that an EGG?"

She put her hand out, and tentatively—glancing at the other bird, as if to check it was okay—the little puffin hopped out of the nest, then, with a highly familiar wobbly-toddler gait, marched up to Polly. Again glancing back at the nest, it carefully hopped onto her outstretched hand, then, a little more boldly, up her arm. Until, in a final swooping motion, Neil was on Polly's shoulder, leaning in under her ear, eeping with all his might.

"NEIL!!!!!!"

Huckle shook his head.

"He came back," he said in disbelief.

Polly looked up at him, eyes shining.

"Everyone came back," she said. "Oh my good lord." She rubbed Neil behind his ears. "Are you going to be a daddy? Goodness!"

Huckle couldn't help it: he let out a guffaw of laughter.

"Cor," he said. "Well. You were right."

Polly smiled. "I know," she said proudly. "Well, I had my doubts."

"No," said Huckle stoutly, coming and putting his arm around her shoulders and tickling Neil's feathers too. The other bird in the nest eyed them both, eeping crossly.

"Mrs. Neil," said Huckle. "It will be an honor to make your acquaintance. Once you look slightly less likely to peck my eye out."

"She's nesting," said Polly, her eyes wet. "Oh Huckle, Neil brought his family home."

"No," said Huckle. "You are his family too. He brought his family together."

He looked out at the rising sun and suddenly realized what he was about to do.

He glanced around desperately and saw a bunch of seaweed on the rocks. Aw, Jeez. It wasn't the four-carat diamond, but for now, it was going to have to do. He knelt down and brought Polly with him, as if they were going to take a closer look at the nest without threatening the other bird. Neil hopped off Polly and over to the nest, to show it off.

"Yes, it's amazing," Polly was saying to Neil. Huckle grabbed the seaweed.

"You're amazing," he said. His voice didn't come out right, it was all croaky. He cleared his throat and tried again.

"*You're* amazing," he said. "Polly. You."

She looked at him.

"Thanks, darling," she said. "But how incredible . . ."

Huckle's voice wouldn't stay steady.

"You have to pay me more attention than Neil just this once," he said, wobbling. "Because while we're down here . . ."

"What?" said Polly, still staring awestruck at her bird.

"Um, well, I have asked Neil's permission, and . . ."

Polly looked at him. He had coiled the seaweed into the shape of a ring.

"What's this?"

"I wanted to get you . . . I wanted to buy you the biggest diamond ring there ever was, but . . ."

Polly shook her head. "But who cares about things like that?"

Huckle shrugged.

"I just wanted the best for you . . . Anyway, it doesn't matter . . . Oh, I'm not making a very good job of this, but . . . will you marry—"

Neil grabbed the end of the seaweed and tried to eat it. Huckle stared at Polly, his eyes damp suddenly. Polly grabbed the seaweed back.

"No," she said quietly but firmly to Neil. "I love you

and it is good to see you back and have you home. But no. You are not allowed to eat the most beautiful . . . the most wonderful . . ."

She broke down.

"The most amazing engagement ring . . . Oh God, Huckle! HUCKLE!"

"Could you quickly say a handy yes or no?" said Huckle. "Before I fall into the sea?"

Polly stood up and flung her arms around him.

"YES YES YES YES!" she hollered at the top of her voice.

"You sound like Selina and that new boyfriend of hers," observed Jayden, who was still carrying rolls out to Nan the Van.

Carefully Huckle tied the seaweed around Polly's fourth finger. "We'll choose another," he said.

"I like this one," said Polly stubbornly, and kissed him, then kissed him again. "Oh my! Oh my goodness!"

"I can't believe you're surprised," said Huckle. "Everyone else in this entire town is totally going to yawn when we tell them. They've been on at me for months. I can't go into the bakery without Malcolm's mother harrumphing at me and making remarks about honest women."

"Well, I don't care about anyone else in this town," said Polly. "Except when I'm feeding them and taking their money and relying on them for friendship and emotional support."

Huckle beamed at her as she held up the ring and admired it.

"I don't want another ring," she said. "Maybe you could just make me a new one every week when it starts to smell."

"We're going to have health and safety around again."

Huckle took her in his arms.

"Do you . . . I mean . . . Do you think you could love me as much as you love Neil?"

"Shut up," said Polly. "Totally almost!"

Then he held her close again and swung her around in the bright pink dawn light as another perfect summer's day came in over Mount Polbearne, and the little village started to stir, and Mrs. Neil fluffed herself importantly on her egg, and Jayden kept on loading up the trays of bread, and Polly and Huckle kissed on and on as if nothing could ever part them again, and Neil fluttered and flittered and flew up, around and around the whole height of the lighthouse, higher and higher, his feathers catching the very first rays of the morning sun.

"And are you still dreaming about him?"

Selina's face was distant.

"Yes," she said, with a noise like a small sigh escaping her lips. "Sometimes. But now, it's just like he's there. Do you understand? Just like he's there and it's nice to see him."

"And how does that make you feel?"

"Happy. Sad. Happy and sad. Isn't that good enough?"

The therapist closed her notebook.

"Yes," she said. "Yes, it is."

Acknowledgments

Huge thanks to Rebecca Saunders, Jo Unwin, Manpreet Grewal, Hannah Green, Emma Williams, Charlie King, Jo Wickham, Victoria Gilder, David Shelley, the design team, the sales team and absolutely everyone at Little, Brown U.K.: it's a fantastic team.

Thank you to everyone who got in touch after *Little Beach Street Bakery,* particularly Neil fans (you can speak to him on Twitter at @neilthepuffin). It is really amazing to get your messages—do get in touch if you would like at www.facebook.com/thatwriterjennycolgan or @jennycolgan on Twitter.

Thank you dear friends and of course Mr. B and the wee bees, without whom a) nothing would be any fun at all, and b) there'd probably be fewer terrible drawings of puffins plastering every single wall in the house.

A special mention to the RNLI, an amazing organization that remains, whatever the AA thinks, Britain's fourth emergency service.